Ransom

Ransom

Lee Rowan

Cheyenne Publishing

Camas, Washington

www.cheyennepublishing.com

ISBN: 978-0-9797773-3-2

Cover art by Alex Beecroft

Published by Cheyenne Publishing
Camas, Washington
Mailing Address:
    P. O. Box 872412 Vancouver, WA 98687-2412
Website: www.cheyennepublishing.com

Other books by Lee Rowan from Cheyenne Publishing:

Winds of Change – The Royal Navy Series Book Two
Eye of the Storm – The Royal Navy Series Book Three
Walking Wounded

Books by other authors from Cheyenne Publishing:

The Filly by Mark R. Probst
Frost Fair by Erastes
Speak Its Name: A Trilogy
L. A. Mischief by P. A. Brown
Hidden Conflict: Tales from Lost Voices in Battle

Dedication

PS, I Love You

Prologue

It could have been a play, Archer thought as he stood in respectful silence, his midshipman's hat tucked under his arm. The scene before him was like some outdoor theatrical, David and Goliath re-enacted in modern dress. Two men also in midshipmen's uniforms, the elder burly and red-faced, the younger slim and deathly pale, stood back-to-back in a sunny glade not far from Plymouth harbor. Each held a pistol in his right hand.

The warm breeze and sylvan loveliness of the place were lost on the principals and on two of the three onlookers. Three only, not the four participants demanded by the code of duelling—but the proprieties were fulfilled nonetheless. Archer himself and Mr. Parrish, the purser of HMS *Titan*, stood as seconds. Their ship's surgeon, Dr. Dean, had agreed to also act as referee. Not only were the rules thus properly observed, knowledge of the affair could be kept within the confines of the ship.

The doctor raised his voice. "Mr. Correy, Mr. Marshall… Gentlemen, you are certain you cannot be reconciled?"

"Oh, I could be, easily," said the larger man. "Mr. Marshall knows well that I would be happy to make our acquaintance a closer one."

"No," said Marshall. He bit his lip, pushed a stray lock of black hair behind his ear. "Impossible."

"Very well," said Dean. "Gentlemen, take 10 paces."

They did.

"On the count of three, turn and fire. One. Two. Three."

Both turned quickly; the shots sounded as one. After a moment, Correy toppled slowly to one side. By the time the surgeon reached him, he had breathed his last.

"Best clear out before someone comes," said Parrish, Correy's second. His attitude seemed cold-blooded, but Archer knew that Correy had asked the purser to be his second only because Parrish had a cousin who owned a livery stable, and could rent them the necessary carriages cheaply. Why the man had agreed was anyone's guess—to help his cousin, perhaps. And Mr. Parrish was right in urging haste. Duelling might be common enough but it was still illegal and Captain Cooper disapproved of it.

Archer clapped his bicorne upon his blond head and helped the others carry the dead man to the carriage in which he had arrived. Dean got in with the body; Parrish climbed up and took the reins.

"What—what happens now?" Marshall asked. For all his earlier resolve, he seemed at a loss now, clearly anxious about the possible consequences of his victory.

The surgeon shook his head. "Lad," he said, rather kindly, "You've not been aboard *Titan* long, have you?"

"Only since last week."

"Then my guess is that Captain Cooper will not be sorry to report Mr. Correy's death in a duel with an unknown landsman. And if Correy's family is wise, they'll let it go at that. Every man aboard knew his habits, but he was too clever to leave evidence."

"You've done the ship a service," Parrish said. "Begone, now. And clean your pistol." He snapped the reins and clucked to the horse. In a moment the carriage disappeared from view.

"Come, Mr. Marshall," Archer said. "Quickly, before someone comes to see about the gunfire."

"Mr. Archer, is he serious?"

"Yes, completely. Come, sir, he was right, we must be

off." They climbed into the light trap they'd hired in town, and Archer skillfully guided the horse back onto the road-way.

Marshall was silent for a long time. "I...have never killed in cold blood before," he said at last. "Nor ever killed an Englishman." He turned and met Archer's eyes, looking for an instant like the 18-year-old boy he was rather than the correct officer and gentleman he had been while facing death. "Tell me, Mr. Archer...what else could I have done?"

"Nothing," Archer said. "In fact, what you did do—that was more than anyone could have hoped for." He had liked Marshall from the moment the quiet, serious midshipman came aboard the *Titan,* even though Marshall's time in the service gave him seniority over Archer himself. That imme-diate affinity was part of the reason he had agreed to act as Marshall's second in this affair; his new shipmate was all alone, but that hadn't stopped him from standing up to a bully. "The man was a menace, sir. He made life hell for any boy above the age of consent. Younger than 14, a boy could charge rape, so he let the children alone. Older, the victim dared not speak—he could be hanged himself, for participat-ing."

"In the first place," Marshall still seemed to be trying to convince someone, most likely himself, that he'd been in the right. "In the first place, the Articles of War specifically for-bid sodomy between men, on penalty of death."

"Indeed."

"I've never—I have served three years in His Majesty's Navy, Mr. Archer. On a sloop, to be sure, and under a strict captain. I know all men have human weaknesses, but I have never seen such a blatant disregard for common decency!"

"I believe Captain Cooper has been in an awkward posi-tion," Archer said. "He knew Correy was untrustworthy, but the man was clever and deceitful. He bribed the men under his command to act as his spies and lookouts, and Correy's family has influence enough to lose Cooper his command if he had acted without ironclad evidence. The Captain did the best he could to keep Correy from power—he never made him acting lieutenant, nor recommended him for the lieutenant's examination."

"His family must have been influential indeed, for him to flout the Articles," Marshall replied. "How could he make such a proposition, bald-faced, and even threaten me? To claim he'd had a boy flogged for refusing him—!"

"He did, more or less," Archer said. "Correy made his wishes known and the boy refused, so Correy brought him before Captain Cooper and charged that the youngster had made the proposition himself. The boy was so flustered he must have appeared guilty of something. The Captain had him caned, not flogged, for 'unclean behavior'."

"What?"

"He had to do something; Correy swore on the Bible and all the boy could do was deny he'd done anything. At least there's no death penalty for it. And refusing didn't even help the lad. Correy had his way with him eventually, poor little bastard."

"My God." Marshall let out a long breath. "Thank you for telling me that, Mr. Archer," he said. "I will not speak of this to anyone, but you have eased my conscience."

Archer smiled. "You have made the *Titan* a safer place for our youngsters, sir. It is I who should thank you."

They drove on again in silence. Marshall seemed at ease, but Archer's spirit was now in turmoil. His gratitude was far deeper than that of a concerned officer; Marshall had freed him from a demon who had made his existence a living hell.

He had not told Marshall that the boy he spoke of had been himself.

And he had not, and never could, tell Marshall that he just had fallen in love with a brave and beautiful gentleman who would likely shoot him dead if he ever gave voice to his feelings.

Chapter 1

Captain's Log, HMS Calypso, in for repair, Portsmouth. 16-7-1799

We have been forced to return to Portsmouth to repair major damage suffered during our recent encounter with a French convoy. Two small supply ships (see list) were sent ahead under the command of 2nd Lt. Watson and 3rd Lt. Barnes; 1st Lt. Drinkwater commands the captured corvette Etienne, *while the two remaining merchantmen are under the command of 4th Lt. Marshall and Midshipman (Act. Lt.) Archer. Due to the condition of the* Calypso, *we have traveled with these last three vessels in convoy.*

⚓ ⚓ ⚓

His Majesty's Frigate *Calypso* limped gamely into port on a hot July morning, half her foremast gone, the mizzen missing altogether, and other damage becoming more apparent as she neared. Two holes gaped in her hull, fortunately well above the waterline. Part of the aft quarterdeck was rigged with a canvas cover whose shape suggested that the captain's own cabin was no longer habitable, and scorch marks beneath a splintered gunport hinted at worse damage below. But despite her wounds, the *Calypso* brought a captured French corvette in her wake, much less damaged and now crewed by English sailors.

After *Etienne* came two of the smaller merchant ships she had been escorting, *Brigitte* and *Fifine*, with an oddly mixed cargo: fine silks and brandy in one ship, and small arms, from pistols to light field cannon, in the other. The unusual pairing had occasioned the expected jokes about the new French high society, but either cargo would fetch a handsome price in England. Adding to that the value of the three captured ships, as well as the two from that same convoy that had come into port earlier, it was clear that Captain Smith had annexed another rich prize to his long record.

From the tiny deck commanding *Brigitte*, Lt. William Marshall had no time to consider what his share of the prize money might be, much less what to do with it. He had his hands full watching the wind, maintaining safe distance from the other ships, and seeing to it that his skeleton crew remained alert. When he finally received Smith's signal to drop anchor, his order to let go was a tremendous shout of relief. Since earning his rank of lieutenant, he had waited months for the chance to command a prize ship—to be in sole command of a vessel sailing under the flag of England. The prize money that would come his way was fine to contemplate, as well. He would be able to buy a new uniform jacket to replace the one that had been singed in battle not long ago.

His delight was slightly dimmed by the fact that he had been in sight of the *Calypso* for the entire trip, rather than on his own. If the *Calypso* had not been so badly damaged, he would have felt like a small boy escorted by an older brother, but Captain Smith had kept the larger vessels in the convoy together for safety; at one point he had been prepared to move the entire crew to the French ships if the *Calypso* had foundered on her way into port.

Marshall glanced over to where *Fifine* was dropping anchor under the command of his friend and shipmate, David Archer, who looked up and waved a greeting. The luck had gone their way in generous measure. It was Davy's first command as an Acting Lieutenant, and with just a bit more luck he might be able to sit for and pass his lieutenant's examination during the weeks that *Calypso* would be in dock for repair. That would be a fine thing—something to cele-brate and cash to fund a feast.

But, as always, pleasure had to wait upon duty. Ar-rangements for turning the prizes over to the Crown used up all morning and most of the afternoon. By the time the two young men reported back to the *Calypso*, they had received a grueling education in port procedure.

And there was no rest for the wicked. As they climbed back aboard, Captain Smith met them at the rail. He towered over them, as he towered over nearly everyone; his gold-trimmed bicorne added half a head to his impressive six-foot-two. "Gentlemen," he said, returning their hasty salutes. "Make yourselves presentable and meet me here in ten min-utes. You will accompany me to the repair dock ... and to dinner."

"Yes sir!"

"Presentable?" David Archer asked under his breath as they hurried belowdecks. "I thought we were!"

"Look in the glass before you say that," Marshall warned. "Your hair wants combing." He felt his chin. His beard, curly and black as a gypsy's, grew annoyingly fast. "And I need a shave. I didn't bother this morning, the wind brought us in so quickly."

"Neither did I, but mine doesn't show the way yours does. I'd better tend to it, though. It would take a braver man than I to show up unshaven to dinner with Captain Smith."

They tidied up quickly, as was their habit, sharing a basin of water and a tiny shaving glass in Archer's cabin, and scrambling into full dress uniform. The Captain—or to give him his due, Sir Paul Andrew Smith, Baronet—never let his officers forget that they carried the full weight of England's dignity upon their shoulders. Marshall was simply grateful that the Captain did not require his officers to wear an itchy powdered wig or to coat their hair with the stuff. On deck or ashore, there was never a question of who commanded *Ca-lypso,* but he was not the sort of officer to require his men to do anything he would not attempt himself, and he despised wigs. Marshall had always wondered if it was impatience with the time a wig required, or the Captain's pride in his own abundant mane, still glossy brown despite his having passed 40.

"Am I fit for polite company?" David inquired, doffing his hat and making a leg. As usual, he was by far the more elegant of the pair, the sun-lightened gold of his hair an elegant contrast to the dark blue of his uniform.

"Yes, and the dockmaster's company as well. And I?"

"You'll do. Though much of the credit must go to your tailor."

"Tailor! Davy, I must see—"

Archer laughed, and propelled him out into the gangway. "You must see the Captain immediately. The tailor will wait, we're not leaving port for at least a week."

They hurried back abovedeck with all the decorum they could manage, and bade farewell to First Lieutenant Drinkwater, who was left in command of the *Calypso* while her captain went ashore. The captain's launch conveyed them to the sally port, and from there they returned to the cobbled streets of Portsmouth.

Captain Smith surveyed the busy thoroughfare and consulted his watch. "Gentlemen, it has been hours since breakfast and I expect that, like myself, in the flurry of arrival you neglected to eat." No one would ever accuse Sir Paul of being a lenient captain. But he was not a harsh one, either.

"You are correct, sir," Marshall admitted.

"We shall dine first, then. Your first meal ashore as an officer, is it not?"

Again, Marshall had to agree.

"Then it's high time you had the practice. The society of officers and gentlemen is a step up from the midshipmen's mess."

The inn to which Smith escorted them was also a step up from what a midshipman could afford. Marshall suspected the Captain was not too far from his own youth to remember what a treat it was for young men who'd been eating beef, biscuit, and salt pork for the last four months to address themselves to fresh-cooked food in an establishment much finer than any they would have chosen for themselves. Savoury soup, meat pie, fresh-baked bread so hot the butter melted on it, game hens with sage and onion stuffing, soft cheese and ripe pippin apples... Marshall was in a minor level of heaven by the time they sat contemplating glasses of ruby-colored port, though he was sufficiently earthbound to pay attention to the Captain's detailed exposition of what work had to be done on their poor battered ship. He was intimately acquainted with the damage—the last French salvo had killed two men in his gun crew when it took out part of *Calypso's* starboard rail.

"Now, then, gentlemen," Smith said as they left the inn, "I believe we are sufficiently fortified to face the master of the repair dock. He holds the life of your ship in his hands. It is his duty to make repairs, but that can be a long, slow process if he takes a dislike to a captain. Far better to encourage him, let him know how important he is to His Majesty's Navy, perhaps using some of your prize to commission non-regulation improvements; that can be a very sound investment. And the truth is, we are bringing in a very complicated piece of work. The poor girl's internal structure has been—"

"Captain! Captain Smith, sir!"

The man who came running up behind them wore the uniform of a shore-service lieutenant. He stopped, saluted smartly, and said, "Admiral Roberts' compliments, sir; he would like to see you as soon as possible."

"I had planned to attend directly after I'd seen to my ship," Smith said, frowning. "Can this not wait?"

The lieutenant's ruddy face pinched in distress. "I was told immediately, sir, if you please. He's sent a coach."

"Oh, very well." Smith glanced at Marshall and Archer. "Well, come along, gentlemen." He frowned at the stranger. "I trust this won't take long?"

"I'm sure I couldn't say, sir."

They followed him along to the waiting coach. It must be an important matter, indeed; the offices of the port authority were only 20 minutes' walk away.

Marshall climbed in and settled himself beside Archer, enjoying the novelty. He had only been in a coach a handful of times; the first had been the long, weary journey that brought him from his little village in Worcester to Spithead, six long years ago. He was fifteen then, not even old enough to shave, and had just been accepted as a midshipman in His Britannic Majesty's Navy.

And now he was Lieutenant William Marshall, officer and gentleman. Tomorrow, 17 July, he would turn 21. He had seen battle at sea, survived minor wounds, and had even seen a little of Italy. Even though he had been at sea since his middle teens, Marshall still felt as though his life was something from a book of adventure tales. The years at his father's parsonage, peaceful and monotonous, seemed like a dim, half-forgotten dream.

Now, of course, he wondered what the Port Admiral had in mind. He couldn't mean to send the crippled *Calypso* on a mission; she would go to the bottom in even a mild storm. More likely Admiral Roberts simply wanted to hear Captain Smith's report and was not inclined to wait until ship's business had been concluded.

"What the devil does he think he's doing?" Smith said suddenly, jerking Marshall from his reverie. "He's turning the wrong way. Driver!"

Marshall glanced out and saw that they had, indeed, turned off down an alleyway. And then wooden shutters flapped down over the windows, throwing them into near-total darkness as the coach picked up speed. Marshall pushed at the shutter beside him, but it held fast.

"He'll have us over if he keeps on like this," Archer said, rattling the shutter on his window. "It feels as though they've slid a bolt across."

"The hinges," Smith snapped. A ringing rasp said he'd drawn his sword. Marshall followed suit, and they slid the blades through the narrow crack at the top of the shutter, levering at the edge. The hinges squeaked protestingly as the screws came loose, but the shutter held firm.

"It's fitted into the frame," Archer reported. "These aren't just for bad weather."

The coach pitched into another abrupt turn, and they were all thrown to the right. Marshall's sword caught on something; he felt carefully, and found it had ripped a jagged hole in the leather seat-cover.

"Put your swords on the floor, easy to hand," the Captain said. "We'll just see if we can kick the door out."

That would have worked, if they'd had time. The door began to loosen under their blows, but before they could kick it free of its frame the coach turned again, slowed, and passed into a building. As it rolled to a halt, the door sagged open and swung crookedly on one hinge. All that was visible beyond was a row of empty stalls.

"Come on out," a voice called. "You're surrounded. Quick, now, an' no tricks."

"If they're on both sides of us they can't risk crossfire," Smith said, low. "I'll break right. Follow as you see fit."

He leaped out, diving out of sight, with Marshall and Archer right behind him. A scruffy figure with a stick, his face swathed in a dirty mask, dove after him. Smith struck his arm and the stick dropped, the wounded man clutching a bloody wrist. But these bandits had played this game before, and as the Captain spun to meet a swinging club, another villain, also masked, leaned over the edge of the hayloft and clipped his skull with the back of a shovel. Marshall, back to back with Archer in a circle of masked, club-wielding ruffians, saw Smith fall. He lunged, trying to break through the circle, but his sword was knocked aside. Archer was having no better luck.

"Give it up, boyos," one of their enemies said. "We have orders to take you alive, but accidents happen all the time." He drew a dirk, long and deadly in the lantern light, and laid it across Smith's throat. "You wouldn't want to lose your captain by accident, would you?"

Marshall stopped, breathing hard. He traded a glance with Archer, who looked as frustrated as he felt. But there really was nothing else to do; if these men didn't intend to kill them outright, they might have a chance to escape later. "And where are we to be taken, alive? France?"

He hardly expected the general hilarity that erupted at his question, but he didn't have time to consider another. David dropped at his feet an instant before something struck him hard from behind.

Chapter 2

M arshall felt a rocking motion before his senses returned fully. It was not the rocking of a ship, and he realized he could not smell the sea. Slitting his eyes against a throbbing headache, he found himself lying on his back with boards above him, too close—less than a foot away. Dust motes floated in the dim afternoon light filtering through cracks between the boards, behind and to one side of his head. Not a boat...a waggon of some sort?

He looked to his right and saw Captain Smith, lying apparently unconscious. Archer, eyes shut, lay to his left. He turned on one side, reaching to shake the Captain, and was brought fully awake when a chain yanked his hand back down.

A whisper of movement from behind caught his attention. "Will?"

"Davy." He twisted back to peer at Archer. "Are you all right?"

"I'm awake," Archer replied tightly. "But I'm not going to open my eyes just now. If I don't look, it's not too bad."

Archer had once been trapped between decks after a battle that stove in *Calypso*'s hull. It had taken hours to free him from a hole just about the size of a coffin, and another half-hour to revive him; he had nearly suffocated. Archer'd been uneasy about enclosed spaces ever since.

"It is reminiscent of that wretched mess you were in 'tweendecks, isn't it? I'd never really appreciated what that must have been like."

"Too damned reminiscent." Archer's voice was brittle. "Will, I don't know how much of this I can stand—"

Marshall stretched, managing to reach Archer's hand. It was icy, but his grip was like steel. "Hold fast, Davy. They can't mean to go very far like this. Take deep breaths."

"Why?"

"I don't know, it's something my father used to tell his parishioners when they were worried. Said the Lord breathed life into Adam and since then we've ignored the gift. He said it's calming. It does help, when I remember to do it."

"It's always hardest remembering what to do, isn't it?" Marshall heard him take a couple of breaths, experimentally. "I think your father was right. At least it occupies the mind."

The edge was out of his voice, now, and his hand relaxed a bit. "See if you can't get some sleep, Davy. I'll stand watch until the Captain wakes."

"Is he hurt?"

"Don't know, I can't reach him. Captain? Captain Smith?"

Smith moved his head and made a noise between a groan and a growl. "Mr. Marshall. Mr. Archer, are you over there?"

"Yes, sir."

"How long have we been in this damned box, Mr. Marshall?"

"I'm not sure, sir. We were all knocked unconscious during the fight. The light has changed since I woke, about fifteen minutes ago; I think it's nearly sunset."

"Mm."

"I asked them if they were French, sir. They seemed to find that most amusing."

"That's good to know." Marshall could see his captain making the same visual survey he had done. "At least an hour, perhaps longer. It lacked two hours until sunset when we were taken."

"Yes, sir. And it's much darker—" As he spoke, the last glimmers of light faded. Marshall had the wretched notion that this was what it would feel like to be buried alive. He knew air was coming in; he had seen the light through cracks in the waggon. But the dark felt smothering, and Archer's hand tightened on his once more.

"Doesn't sound as though there's much traffic," Smith mused aloud. "We can try shouting if we hear anything approach, but I suspect if shouting would help we would have been gagged." His chains clanked. "It seems I am secured. Mr. Archer, any luck with your bonds?"

"None, sir."

"Damn. Well, gentlemen, I intended this as a training excursion; it seems we all have a lesson to learn about vigilance. Although we may be overheard, even now, I am going to give you your orders for the time being. If you see an opportunity for escape, take it. Use your own judgment. Do not endanger yourselves unnecessarily. I believe I know what is happening here."

Marshall blinked. "Sir?"

"In a recent dispatch, ranking military officers were warned of a rash of abductions by a gang of masked men. The object has been ransom. I saw to it that my family was discreetly guarded, but it never occurred to me that these brigands would be mad enough to kidnap a party of naval officers. They'll find they have made a serious mistake."

"Yes, sir." It did seem a stupid thing to do. On the other hand, they were now prisoners, and the arrangements for keeping them so seemed quite thorough.

"Mr. Archer," Smith went on, "your father the Earl will not be pleased to hear you have come to this strait."

"No, sir, but I expect he'll buy me back." David's tone was ironic. "They can't ask much for a fourth son, at any rate."

"Do not assess your value solely by the order of your birth, Mr. Archer. Mr. Marshall..." He lowered his voice. "Until further notice, you are my dead cousin's son, raised by her husband, the Reverend Mr. Marshall."

"Sir?"

"Apparently, if this gang receives their ransom, their

well-heeled prisoners are returned alive, sometimes weeks later, rowed ashore miles from where they were picked up. They have no idea where they've been, except that they were on a ship of some sort. Unfortunately, when others—those unable to pay—are taken prisoner with the target, they have been found dead or not found at all. You will be less expendable if you have a social connection, and, in the event we cannot arrange our own escape, I will of course see to it that you are both ransomed."

Marshall swallowed, enormously touched. "Sir, I-I could never repay—"

"I would take it as a very great insult if you try, Lieutenant," Smith growled. "If it was my position which has put you in this danger, it is my responsibility to get you out."

"Yes, sir."

"Good. For the moment, since there seems to be little we can do, we shall rest and stand watches. I shall wake you, Mr. Marshall, and you wake Mr. Archer, in turn. Two hours to a watch, as nearly as you can estimate."

"Yes, sir. Thank you, sir." Marshall made himself as comfortable as possible on the unyielding wooden floor. He listened to Archer's careful breathing, waiting until the grasp on his hand loosened before seeking refuge in sleep. He hardly hoped he'd be able to relax, but between the long day, the persistent headache, and the monotony of the cart's motion, his body overrode his mental activity and let him drift off.

Marshall started awake with Smith shouting in his ear. He had no time to catch the exact words; a trapdoor flew up just above their faces, and a sharp blade pressed against his throat. He swallowed and held very still.

"We'll have ye quiet," a voice muttered, "'Or you'll get your throats cut, starting with this pup. D'ye understand?"

"Very well," Smith said. The door slammed shut, dust spattering them. "I heard a horseman approach," he continued. "A confederate, I'm afraid."

"Shall I take watch now, sir?" Marshall offered.

"No need, Mr. Marshall. I feel no inclination to slumber. We have been traveling regularly for quite some time, now. We could be as far as 15 or 20 miles away, though whether up or down the coast, I cannot say. If they mean to put us aboard a ship, there is no shortage of beaches suitable for clandestine landing."

"Do you think they are in league with smugglers, sir?" Marshall asked.

"It seems likely. This waggon is obviously designed for contraband cargo, human or otherwise."

"Aye, sir, it is."

"Mr. Archer?"

"Sir?"

"It seems we are to be allowed moderate conversation until we arrive at our destination. I therefore intend to drill you in the sort of questions that may be asked on your examination for the rank of Lieutenant. Mr. Marshall, you are welcome to exercise your wits, but please do not contribute your answers. Mr. Archer, a sail is sighted. What is the first thing you would look for to determine whether this ship is friend or foe?"

"If by 'foe' you mean French, sir?"

"I do."

"The first sign would be whether all three masts were the same height; that would be a French ship. I would also see if the sail were very clean, as their ships spend most of their time in port. Either way, I would be prepared for an enemy, since the French use captured English ships as we use theirs."

"Very good. What are the best and worst points of sailing of your current ship? How would you utilize the good points and compensate for the bad?"

As the practice drill went on, Marshall began to wonder if Smith had feigned unconsciousness earlier. He seemed to realize that Archer needed some kind of distraction, and focusing his attention on his upcoming examination was an effective strategy. Not only did it give Archer chance to prepare for the ordeal—and however difficult the conditions of examination, they could hardly be worse than these—it held out the prospect of hope, the tacit assurance that the Captain would not waste Archer's time or his own if he never expected him to live to take the examination.

But then, Marshall wondered morosely, might he not do that very thing to bolster the morale of his junior lieutenants? Any kind of activity was better than lying helpless and worrying.

Be that as it might, the distraction proved effective for Marshall, letting him move about mentally even though his body was confined, and he was delighted to discover that Archer was, as far as he could tell, eminently ready to be tested. Smith's questions ranged from the ridiculously simple—definition of a halyard, for instance—to very complex.

And then there was one question that sounded familiar: "You are close-hauled on the port tack, beating up-channel with a nor'easterly wind blowing hard, with Dover bearing north two miles. The wind veers four points and takes you flat aback."

It was the very question that had caused Marshall to fail his first examination, though he'd passed on his second try. Apparently the problem was giving David some trouble, too, since he had no ready answer.

"You are now dismasted, Mr. Archer," Smith droned, "with Dover cliffs under your lee. What are you going to do?"

Drown, thought Marshall. There had to be an answer—and although he had some ideas, he had always been too self-conscious to bring up the subject with anyone, much less the Captain or Mr. Drinkwater, who might have known what the examination board was looking for. Thank God the board at his second examination had asked him questions he knew how to answer, or he'd still be in the middies' berth.

"Mr. Archer?"

"May I ask something, sir?" David asked cautiously.

"In an examination, that would be ill-advised. Do you not

understand the question?"

"No, sir, the question is clear enough. But—sir, why would anyone bring a ship that close in to Dover? The wind there is so unreliable, and the way the shore angles out..."

Exactly. That was one of the things that had tied Marshall's tongue at his own examination. What sort of imbecile would risk his vessel to the flukey wind, near that rocky, sloping trap of a coastline?

"Very true, Mr. Archer. Since you know better, let us assume your commander made this perhaps unwise decision, and was knocked unconscious when the masts came down. You did not put your ship in this position, but you are the senior officer responsible for saving your ship and crew. What are your orders, sir?"

"I—I would bear to starboard and maintain the port tack, jury rig a sail, if there were time...and run downwind, as far as possible, to clear the lee shore."

Good, Davy! Marshall cheered silently. *That might do it—*

"And if the wind changes another two points, driving you in to shore?"

David paused for a long breath. "I would get an anchor down, sir, two if possible—"

"One of your anchors was lost when a Frenchman attempted a cutting-out during the middle watch. You had no replacement. The other anchor fouls halfway down and reduces your maneuverability, but does slow your progress toward the cliffs. What will you do now?"

Was there no answer to the damned question? Marshall shared Archer's frustration. After a moment, David said, "I'm sorry, sir, but—I should send a boat to shore with a hawser, and give the order to prepare to abandon ship. I realize that cannot be the correct answer—"

"But it is, Mr. Archer," Smith said.

"Sir?"

"Much as we all hate to admit it," the Captain said, "there are sometimes circumstances that put us entirely at

their mercy. And sometimes there is no mercy to be had."
His words hung in the darkness. "But how we bear ourselves
under such conditions may mean the difference between ig-
nominious defeat and final victory. This situation actually
occurred, and the question has been in use in examinations
for some years, now. Its purpose is to remind our confident
young officers of human limitation. You see, Mr. Marshall,
your difficulty with this problem was not such a black mark
after all."

"It never occurred to me that there might be no answer,
sir," Marshall admitted. "Congratulations, Mr. Archer."

Smith cleared his throat. "Now, then, this question does
have an answer. You have run aground on a mud shoal at the
mouth of a harbor occupied by hostile forces. What is the
standard method for freeing your ship, and how will you defend yourself while doing so?"

The questions went on for another hour or so, but finally
the Captain's deep voice grew weary. "One last question,
gentlemen, and bear this one in your minds until we are free:
You have been abducted by persons unknown, with the pre-
sumed goal of extracting ransom. How can you free yourself
and your shipmates, with the best possible outcome including capture of your abductors?"

Supplemental Log, HMS Calypso, in for repair, Portsmouth.
Lt. Anthony Drinkwater, in temporary command. 16-7-1799

At 4 pm, Captain Smith, Lt. Marshall, and M'man Archer left
the ship with the intention of establishing a schedule with the
shipwright for repair of Calypso. Although they were sched-
uled to return by 8 pm, I had by that time received no word
from the Captain. This being entirely uncharacteristic, in-
deed, the first time in my memory that Captain Smith has not
been where he said he would be at the appointed time, I sent
Ship's Master Korthals to ascertain his whereabouts. He re-
ported back at 9:15, to wit, the Captain's party had never

reached the shipwright. I have sent Mr. Korthals out again with three ratings (Barrow, O'Reilly, and Klingler) to see if they can determine what has become of our officers.

⚓ ⚓ ⚓

Marshall took the first watch. He let the others sleep past watch change, taking the time to review their capture. There must have been something he could have done; if only he could figure out what it was, he might have some idea of what to do next. Finally, he decided that the only thing that might have helped would have been a pistol, even though it was not a normal part of his uniform. Too late now.

He began to wonder if he'd been in this compartment too long. The smell of the sea was back. Why now, when he'd not noticed it before? Had the kidnappers perhaps gone inland at first to avoid suspicion?

He was still wondering whether he should wake Smith when the matter was decided for him. The rumble of the wheels changed; they were on a paved road again, and that shift in rhythm brought the Captain awake. "All quiet, Mr. Marshall?"

"So far, sir."

Smith sniffed. "And we are back at the coast. It won't be long now. Well, Mr. Marshall, any solutions to our dilemma?"

"Only hindsight, sir. Pistols would have been helpful."

"In future, they will be. Damn! I cannot comprehend the short-sighted stupidity of a criminal who would abduct Naval officers! Does the fool not realize England is an island and the Navy is what keeps her safe?"

Marshall was surprised by his vehemence; the way he spoke almost made England sound like a flesh-and-blood woman. But, of course, it was Smith's own personality, his force of will, that shaped his crew into a single-minded fighting force. "I suppose not, sir. Or he just doesn't care."

"No, I expect not. Get some rest, Mr. Marshall."

But this time, sleep wouldn't come. After a long journey

along bumpy roads, the sounds outside changed. They stopped; harness jingled, horses stamped. They moved again, then stopped once more, and the trapdoor opened to reveal the roof of another barn, dimly lit by a couple of lanterns.

Someone held a light above them. "End of the ride, boyos," said the spokesman of the masked men who'd captured them. "One at a time now. Just behave, and you'll all get back to your ship safe and sound." He put the knife back at Marshall's throat. "You first, Captain."

"Where are we?" Archer asked quietly as two other bandits unloaded Smith.

"I don't know." Marshall spoke carefully, hoping the knife-man wasn't too excitable. "The next step on our little journey, apparently."

"Exactly right," his captor said. "Just a little more shaking around, and you'll be back at sea. Ah, now you." He turned the knife on Archer as Marshall was released from the irons.

When he straightened his aching back, his heart sank. He could see at least eight enemies, mostly armed with clubs. Captain Smith, his hands tied, was being lifted into one of the barrels used to store food aboard ship. "Now, don't get the idea this is what happens every time," the talkative bandit said. "I thought biscuit barrels were just the thing for sailors, but we do it different each time. Climb down, now."

"Barrels?" Archer said.

"You heard me. There's holes for air, you won't smother. Just remember, if a barrel gets noisy, we drop it over the side."

As he was pushed into the container, Smith shot Marshall a look that almost made him feel sorry for these pirates. But as the Captain's glare vanished beneath the lid, Marshall was suddenly worried. How would Davy take this confinement? But he would have to. There was no chance these ruffians would have any pity for his fear, even if Marshall tried to explain, and he couldn't humiliate his friend that way.

He climbed off the waggon under the bandits' watchful

eyes, let them tie his hands and load him into a barrel. The one with Smith in it was already being hoisted onto a cart that held several identical barrels, no doubt filled with perfectly ordinary biscuit.

"Keep 'im uncorked 'til we get this one trussed." They pulled Archer out of storage. He glanced around, saw the last empty barrel, and met Marshall's eyes.

Marshall saw the panic there, and forced himself to speak lightly. "Well, Davy, this will be a story for our grandchildren someday, won't it?"

Archer swallowed, but managed a sickly grin as they tied him. "I-I suppose next they'll stuff us through a keyhole." The joke would have been more convincing if his voice hadn't cracked.

A hand grabbed Marshall's shoulder. "Inside, now."

He resisted for a moment. "Dover cliffs, Davy. Keep breathing." Then the hand pushed him down and the lid shut off the dim light. As it was hammered into place, he closed his eyes. David was right, it was a little easier this way. And he could still hear, as his tiny prison swayed and wobbled up until it settled on the cart. Then something banged against his barrel. Archer's, probably. The cart shook as the rest of the cargo was loaded on, then jolted as they got underway.

Breathe, you fool. He deliberately loosened his muscles, tried to take the advice he'd given Archer. He wanted to hammer at the lid until they let him back out. He didn't dare. They'd probably kill him, and even if they did not, he'd wish they had. And if he felt like this, how was Davy faring?

He let his head drop back against the staves. If he were up in the maintop, on lookout, he'd be sitting on a perch not much bigger than this, enjoying the cool solitude. On a cloudy, moonless night it would be just as dark as this, but there would be a breeze, and even at anchor the *Calypso* would be moving. The four hours' middle watch, dark to dawn, would fly past. And he was not alone here, not really. Archer was right beside him, Captain Smith only a few feet away.

He relaxed a little with the familiar images, and wished he could share the relief with Davy. That brought the worry back. No. Davy would be all right. He was stronger than he knew; he would get through this. They all would.

And they would find the answer to the Captain's final question. He did not know how, but when they met this as yet unknown enemy—whom he was already beginning to hate—they would find a way to stop him.

Supplemental Log, HMS Calypso, in for repair, Portsmouth.
Lt. Anthony Drinkwater, in temporary command. 16-7-1799

Our search party has returned. Captain Smith and his party dined at the Anchor and left at approximately 6:30 pm, and shortly thereafter were seen entering a coach in company with a shore-service Lieutenant, whom we have been unable to locate or identify. The search party has requested permission to return to their task, and I am granting it, as these seamen are part of the gunnery crews commanded by Mr. Marshall and Mr. Archer, and have demonstrated great personal loyalty to these fine young officers. I believe they present no risk of desertion, and moreover have access to a level of society that would be closed to most officers. We all hope for the uneventful return of our Captain and his party, but I have already informed the Port Authority of their disappearance, whereupon Admiral Roberts ordered a thorough search of all ships that have been in port since 3:30 this past evening. His office reports employing no officer answering the description of the man seen with our shipmates. The Admiral has expressed his concern that this unexplained disappearance may be connected with a recent series of abductions. It hardly seems likely that such knaves would be foolhardy enough to seize our Captain, but of course no abductor could know Captain Smith as we do. However, one extremely successful merchant captain was abducted from this very port 18 months ago, so the villains are familiar with this territory. I have issued pistols for our search party, and so great is the loyalty of this crew that many other men have volunteered to join the search. I have authorized leave for those I believe trustworthy. (See list, attached).

The trip was much shorter than Marshall had expected. After only a few minutes ride on the cart, he was unloaded onto a dock, then into a boat—a fairly small one, and, judging by the exaggerated rocking motion, not a well-balanced craft. The last bit, out to the ship, was worst, but it was also the shortest. That probably meant they had gone through an actual port, since a smugglers' rendezvous would mean a long haul from a quiet beach to an anchored ship. Portsmouth was the only major Navy port in the area; villages would have launched from a beach or estuary. This had to be Portsmouth again. A clever scheme, to return them to the port from which they'd been taken. Every ship in the harbor would have been searched by now.

After an unpleasant couple of minutes while the barrels were swayed aboard, he felt the familiar solidity of a deck again. The muffled voices he heard through the oak sounded much the same as any crew bringing aboard any cargo.

Then another voice rose above the muttering. "Good evening, gentlemen." Something thumped on his barrel; two more thumps said the others were close by. "Welcome to the good ship *Elusive,* though that is of course not the name on her prow. I am her Captain; you may address me as Captain Adrian, or 'sir'. My men will be escorting you to your quarters. Captain Smith, if all goes well, you will not see your men again until our visit has ended. I have found my guests much less prone to attempt escape if they are separated. You note I say 'attempt' because that is as far as it ever gets. I will be down to see you when you are settled in."

It was no surprise that Smith would be jailed separately, but Marshall had hoped otherwise. He had little time to worry about it as his barrel was hoisted and joggled down a flight of steps. They were clever, these brigands, leaving no chance of anyone ashore or aboard a nearby ship seeing prisoners being taken out of barrels. And no chance of their getting a look at this ship, either.

Finally the jostling stopped, and some metal implement scraped at the barrel lid. As that came away, the whole thing tilted again, and he was dragged out and dropped on a deck. Just beside him, a couple of masked sailors with crowbars were at work on the other barrel.

"Good morning," said the voice he'd heard above. "Is it Marshall or Archer?"

"Marshall." He scrambled up awkwardly, straightening to face his captor. All he could really see was a silhouette; there was only one lantern in the narrow passage, and it was behind the man, but he gave the impression of relative youth—a year or two either side of 30—and physical vigor. "Captain...Adrian?"

The man's head inclined slightly, and Marshall could see that he, too, was wearing a mask over his eyes, as well as a reddish beard that hid the rest of his face. "At your service."

"Please forgive me if I doubt that."

"Doubt anything you like. Has he been searched?"

"Twice, sir," one of the men said. "Sword, clasp-knife, flint and tinder, one pound, two shillings, and fourpence."

"You are wise not to carry much on shore leave, Lieutenant. One never knows what sort of footpad may be lurking. What's wrong there? He is breathing, isn't he?"

They had pried the lid off David's barrel; he wasn't moving. Marshall craned his neck to see within, trying to keep his fear out of his face.

"Yes, sir, just out cold."

Adrian nodded and they dumped Archer out on the floor, face down. "Midshipman?" Adrian asked, prodding him with a toe.

"Acting Lieutenant," Marshall corrected. He couldn't see any blood. What the devil had they done to him?

"Well, see if you can't persuade him to act conscious; he

may need to write a letter." He nodded toward a door that stood open. "Free their hands and lock them up." As two of the men untied Archer and tossed him through the doorway, he turned to Marshall. "And do you have family or friends who might be willing to stand ransom for, say, £5,000?"

The sum was staggering. His pay had jumped from a midshipman's annual £22 to £100, but there was no hope of ever repaying £5,000, even if his career did last another 50 years. It would take every bit of prize money he might ever earn, and more. Captain Smith could not have expected anything of this sort when he made his generous offer. "You had better speak to my Captain on that subject." Smith could reconsider, make the decision. With luck, they might be able to escape before it came to the test.

"Be assured I shall. Have a pleasant rest, Lieutenant."

The cell was less than eight feet square, with a ceiling a little lower than Marshall's six feet of height. He noticed that only because the rough boards scraped his head as he stepped inside; his attention was focused on Davy, lying face-down in the straw that covered the floor.

"Davy?" Marshall found a couple of scraps of sailcloth in the corner, unfolded one, and rolled Archer over onto the makeshift cot. It was difficult to see much, since the only light came from a lantern hung just outside the barred window set in the door, but there was no sign of a wound on the white waistcoat of his dress uniform. A smear of blood on his mouth, though; it looked like he'd bitten through his lip. What on earth... Archer had never shown any sign of apoplexy—could it be his heart? Had they knocked him unconscious first? "Davy, for God's sake, say something!"

"Mm?"

Marshall let out the breath he didn't realize he'd been holding. Archer stirred, blinked, and rolled up on one elbow. "Will. Where are we?"

He glanced around. Three buckets stood near the door, and one had a wooden cup beside it. He checked first, taking nothing for granted, but it did hold fresh water. He scooped some into the cup and offered it to Archer. "We're on board a ship. The *Elusive,* he called her, though that's apparently not actually her name. And the captain and crew are all masked."

"Sounds too clever for words. Are you sure it isn't just a fancy-dress ball?"

"Davy, what happened? You were unconscious. Are you all right?"

"Well enough." Archer put the cup back. "It was what you said about breathing. I was trying to distract myself, seeing how long I could hold a breath, and all of a sudden I blacked out. So I just did that every time I woke up." He shrugged. "Not very heroic."

"Ingenious was probably better than heroic; there was nothing to be done but wait it out."

"Where's the Captain?"

Marshall briefly outlined what had happened on their arrival. "It felt like we came down seven or eight steps. I think this ship's a bit smaller than the *Calypso,* but it was hard to tell from inside a barrel."

"I suppose this is an improvement." Archer stood, cautious until he was sure he'd clear the ceiling, then frowned. "Damn. You can't stand up in here, can you?"

"No, but I can lie down without kicking the slop-bucket. It could be worse."

"The door is locked, of course?"

"Bolt on the outside." Marshall thumped at it, noting there was no handle on their side.

He heard footsteps, then a masked face peered in. "Leave the door alone, or you'll be sorry."

"...and a guard," Marshall continued, ignoring him. "Friendly bastard." The face disappeared, followed by footsteps that stopped five steps away, not close enough for a prisoner to reach.

Archer continued circling the little cell, running his hands along the walls. Marshall hoped he'd settle down soon; he was restless enough himself. "Will, look!"

"What?" He got up to see, and found that they had a window of sorts—a small square port about 18 inches on a side, bisected by a single upright metal bar, with a board outside hinged at the bottom and tilting away at an angle. He could reach up far enough to feel the top edge of the board, and two metal rings bolted to its corners. It moved slightly when he pulled at it. "I think it's some kind of shutter, Davy, like a gunport in reverse. We can't see out, and they can pull it shut if another vessel comes close enough to hear us."

"At least it's fresh air."

"Yes. And when it's light we can see if we might be able to throw something out."

"A message in a bottle?" Archer asked facetiously.

"If we had one. Like as not they'd see it themselves, from above. I don't see what we can do until morning, though that should be soon; dawn's around 5:30." As if in confirmation, a ship's bell rang once, echoing through the ventilator. "An hour's sleep, then. If nothing else, we can use the time to practice navigation problems for your examination." Mathematics, he knew, was Archer's least favorite aspect of seamanship, though he was competent enough at it.

"That certainly gives me something to look forward to." Archer shoved the straw around. "Looks like they were expecting livestock, not human beings. You'd think they could at least give us a couple of hammocks."

"We won't be here long enough to be bothered." Marshall tried to sound confident.

Archer's look said he knew they were both already bothered, but he nodded. "Do you think we should stand watches?"

"Not at this point, no. Get some rest, Davy. It's been a rotten day."

"It's already tomorrow." Archer gave him an apologetic smile. "Happy birthday, Will."

Chapter 3

Supplemental Log, HMS Calypso, in for repair, Portsmouth.
Lt. Anthony Drinkwater, in temporary command. 17-7-1799

We are now fairly convinced that Captain Smith, Lt. Marshall, and M'man Archer were taken by the gang mentioned in the previous entry. Our gunnery crew located a retired cooper who, despite considerable inebriation, related being nearly run down by a closed coach matching the description of the one our men were seen entering, being driven at unreasonable speed, from whence issued shouts and sounds of a struggle. As this is the same method used to abduct the previous victim, only one conclusion is possible. Our marines are now conducting a search of all waterfront buildings, hoping to locate the coach and hence the driver. We are also awaiting contact from the abductors, as ransom seems the most likely aim of this heinous act. I am, in the meantime, attending to the repair and refitting of the Calypso. When she will sail again, and whether it will be under the command of her rightful Captain, God only knows.

"**A**re you satisfied with your new quarters, Captain?"

Smith had to duck to enter the cramped berth, and its ceiling was too damned low. But in the course of his career he'd slept in worse places, and this did have basic furnishings: a cot stowed on a hook, a straight-backed chair, and a small table that held a candle-lantern, paper, and writing implements.

Gesturing at the table, he scowled at the figure standing outside his cell. "For producing a ransom note, I presume?"

"Not just yet. The presence of your traveling companions means that I must reconsider my requirements. For the moment, it will suffice if you pen a brief message that you and your officers are alive and well, and further communiqués will be forthcoming."

"Decided to raise the price, have you?" With the lantern hanging on the wall behind the man who called himself captain of this ship, Smith couldn't read his face. Not that he needed to. He'd seen more than enough posturing popinjays who let a little power go to their heads.

"Captain, you have no idea what a pleasure it is to converse with a ready wit. You do anticipate me. Since we had no idea that you would be in company…"

"No doubt. However, I dislike the principle of paying extortion. It encourages bad habits. Since you appear to be a gentleman, I propose that we arm ourselves and settle this on the field of honor."

"I had heard that you have been a rather vocal opponent of duelling, sir. Why this sudden change?"

"It will save His Majesty's courts the trouble and expense of a trial," Smith said shortly. "You might also consider that the penalty for high treason is far more unpleasant than a bullet at dawn."

"I suppose I should be flattered at your offer, but I regret to admit that I'm only a simple merchant, and I've no intention of risking damage to rare and valuable merchandise. I do not claim to be a gentleman, sir."

"But you could claim to be a coward. As might be deduced from the nature of your 'merchandise'."

Adrian ignored the blatant insult. "I do understand your reluctance to write such a letter, and the embarrassment you may suffer over your capture, but I must insist. You have in your party a young man of no commercial value, and I would be perfectly happy to have him shot as a demonstration of my sincerity."

Smith had to be grateful for the man's absolute predictability. If he had singled Marshall out himself, it would have looked suspicious. But he must guard against overconfidence on his own part; if this villain were the dimwitted fop he appeared to be, he would already have been apprehended. "Indeed, my men are not expendable, sir. I am as concerned for their safety as for my own. If you had captured the lowliest landsman who cleans the bilges, you would still be interfering with your country's defense."

"Are you concerned enough to pay for his safety, Captain? I am quite willing to charge full freight for this otherwise worthless lieutenant."

Perhaps he was as stupid as he seemed. He was no judge of character. But Smith was content to let Adrian go on underestimating the resourceful young man. "Mr. Marshall is in fact the son of one of my cousins," he said. "His father is sensitive to accusations of nepotism, so we have agreed to let young William prove himself on his own merits."

"I see. Well, then, if you are so concerned for his health, and presumably for Mr. Archer's, I suggest you apply quill to paper."

"And what will you do with this letter?"

"Forward it to your man of business, of course. This is a business transaction, after all."

Smith held up a restraining hand. "I gather you have not tried this experiment with Navy men before?"

"Why do you ask?"

"You would do better to have it delivered to the *Calypso*, in care of my First Lieutenant, Mr. Anthony Drinkwater."

"This is not a Navy affair."

"I have been endeavoring to make something clear to you: as a Captain in His Majesty's Navy, virtually every aspect of my life is, in fact, a Navy affair. Should you write to my man of business, he would be required to forward the correspondence to the Admiralty. Once that occurs, your enterprise will be mired in a morass of official procedure that could see us both greybeards before you see a penny of ransom. Is that your intention?"

The silhouette at the barred door hesitated. "Is this some kind of trick?"

"I prefer to make our acquaintance as brief as possible, sir," Smith said with unfeigned annoyance. "Mr. Drinkwater will have the authority to contact both my man of business and the Admiralty. What is more, he can expedite the liquidation of the prizes we brought in yesterday afternoon—I presume by now it is yesterday—thereby obtaining funds to purchase our release. Is such alacrity not also in your interests?"

"Of course," Adrian admitted reluctantly. "I confess to reservations, Captain; you seem far too ready with your suggestions. I must be wary of such helpfulness."

"Your activities are notorious by now, and those who might be your targets have been warned. Once we had ruled out the possibility of capture by agents of the French, our extended tour of the countryside provided me with ample time to consider various courses of action. I have spent the last several years commanding a frigate in wartime service, sir. If I were not accustomed to quick decisions, my ship would no longer be afloat."

His captor laughed. "I see. Well, then, Captain, I suggest you produce a suitable letter. Quickly."

Smith held the quill close to the lantern. The point looked fresh and usable. "Do you wish to dictate its contents?"

"I will leave that to your discretion, though of course I shall read it first. Simply give it to the guard who will be outside this door."

Smith nodded. "And what of my men?"

"As long as you all behave yourselves, they will not be harmed. They are in similar accommodations—slightly less comfortable, I'm afraid, as their cabin is where I usually put any servants traveling with my guests. They will have fresh water to drink and seawater for washing—as you have—"

Smith glanced down. Three buckets stood near the door; two held water and one of them had a lid. "And they will eat the same food as my crew. I suspect it will be a trifle better than what they get from His Majesty. Does that meet with your approval?"

"Nothing about this idiocy meets with my approval," Smith snapped. "You may still wish to reconsider your course of action. Once this reaches the Admiralty, every Navy ship in every harbor will be alerted to what has occurred. Do you realize, sir, that there are over 100,000 men sailing in His Majesty's service? Do you truly believe you can evade them all?"

"I have thus far, Captain. Please attend to that letter. I will have some refreshment sent as soon as you are finished."

Smith waited until his footsteps had died away, then went to the door and peered out. The guard Adrian had mentioned was standing against the wall opposite the door, a few feet away, well out of arm's reach. Excellent.

He moved the chair so that his back would be to the door, sat, and extracted a small stoppered medicine vial from an inside pocket of his waistcoat. Whether they'd missed it or were simply not so depraved as to deny him a medication he might require did not matter. With luck, they would regret the oversight.

Supplemental Log, HMS Calypso, in for repair, Portsmouth.
Lt. Anthony Drinkwater, in temporary command. 17-7-1799

The coach has been located. It was found in a warehouse at the far end of a row of such buildings, but it was empty and untended, therefore no one has been found who could provide an account of what might have taken place there. After much inquiry, the owner of the vehicle was also located, and proved to be a reputable liveryman who had hired the coach out to a man claiming to need it for a month-long trip, who had left such a generous deposit as to allay suspicion. The liveryman's description of the man who rented the coach tal-

lies closely with that of our nonexistent shore-service lieu-
tenant, who, to the best of the liveryman's knowledge, was no
one he had ever seen before or since. My suspicion is that we
will find him only when we find our missing officers. The
liveryman was much annoyed at the alteration to his vehicle
(shutters had been added that made of it a prison) and the
damage to the door. It appears our officers put up a valiant
struggle and must have been overcome by a vastly superior
force. However, no blood was found, which at least gives us
some cause for hope.

"Guard!" Smith stood at the barred window, holding the
letters just inside until the guard, a short, wiry man with a
balding forehead and skinny pigtail, moved close enough to
be spoken to in a normal tone. "Take these to that brigand
who calls himself your captain. The first is what he asked
for; the second is to Mr. Archer's father. As Archer's commanding officer, it is my duty to inform him what has be-
fallen his son. Both letters should be sent via my first lieutenant."

The guard nodded, reaching for the papers. "A moment,"
Smith said. "Do you know who I am?"

He saw a moment's hesitation, then the fellow nodded,
reluctantly. "Yessir."

"Then you know I can and will make good on my promises. Whatever Adrian is paying you, I can match it—double
it. A year's wages—and a new position, far out of his
reach—if you'll help me and my men escape."

"Well, bless you, sir, that's a handsome offer," the man
replied. "Hear that?"

"Best we've had all year, I reckon." A second, bulkier
guard stepped into sight. "Real prompt with it, 'e was, too.
You want to tell Cap'n, or shall I?"

"Go on along, I guess you'll want to collect that bet from
Cook. Bet five pound, he did, that you'd try it before you
slept or et," he elaborated to Smith as the other man clumped

off down the companionway. "Ever'body tries it, some sooner'n others."

"You're a sailor," Smith said, recognizing the man as a type he might find on his own foredeck. "You know what the sea would be like for English ships without His Majesty's Navy. How can you involve yourself in this?"

The man shifted uneasily, scratching at the edge of his mask. "Well, sir, most of us 'as to make a living. And the pay an' grub's better, and not much getting shot at." He darted a glance off toward the door. "Seein's who you are, I'll give you a warnin', like. Bert's the Cap'n's man, he'd as soon stick a knife in you as not. Cap'n always has two guards, usually one of 'em's his. And he sees makin' an offer as an escape attempt. Don't do it. You'll pay for it—or your lads will—one way or another."

"Then help me," Smith urged. He was surprised at finding so receptive an audience, and more than a little suspicious, but willing to take a chance. "You don't sound like you belong here."

The man shook his head. "It's as much as my life's worth to say what I've said already, an' I hope you'll be a gentleman an' keep it to yourself. 'Sides, I can't do much. You won't have the same guards two nights runnin'. Just sit tight, let 'im collect the ransom, and you'll be out of 'ere, slick as a weasel."

"Damn it, man, there's a war on!"

"An' your ship's in dock for a month, at least. I saw 'er meself, that's no tenpenny job. You'll be out before then, Cap'n. Unless your agent's run off with your money."

Smith snorted, and returned to his chair. They had taken his money and watch—with a promise to return the watch, a gift from his wife, and engraved—but left a sheaf of notes on the damage to the *Calypso* and the repairs that would be needed. He spread them out on the table and turned his attention to the matters he should be dealing with.

Mr. Drinkwater would have his hands full. Not only were the repairs to the ship extensive, he would need to find space in a hulk to quarter those crewmen who would not be staying aboard to help with repairs—mostly the artificers—or trusted to return from shore leave—which was to say, at least half of the rest of them. The *Calypso's* reputation for capturing prizes gave her an advantage over less fortunate ships in attracting enlistments, but no few of her crew would have eaten, drunk, gambled, or whored away that money in a week's time.

But Drinkwater could handle that; he had a keen sense of how to deal with the men. He had not had experience in handling such an extensive repair, nor the problem of a missing captain and two officers and the uproar that would cause further up the chain of command. However, this might prove a good means of evaluating whether Mr. Drinkwater was ready for promotion to Commander. He very likely was. Whether or not he had the ambition for an independent command, Smith was not certain, but he had to assume it was so. One of the drawbacks of command: it meant training one's officers up until they could be trusted with one's life—and more importantly, one's ship—and as soon as they reached that point, in all fairness one had to nominate them for promotion to independent command.

Well, the practice improved the Service, and in the long run that benefited England, and so every Englishman, including himself. And it was tremendously gratifying to see some honor posted in the Gazette and recognize the name of a protégé who had gone on to distinguish himself.

Smith had already begun to see that happening with his two youngest officers. Marshall never lost an opportunity to exercise his leadership, but he had a cool head and the chances he took were sometimes hair-raising but never stupid. He was respectful to senior officers, as well—none of the overconfidence that could lead to disgrace. There was no doubt in his mind that Marshall was going to leave his mark on the world, if he could avoid getting himself killed in the process.

Archer seemed to be shaping up, as well. Smith had been

less sure of that young man; the scuttlebutt that reached him in its roundabout way suggested Archer had indulged in an unacceptable liaison with a fellow midshipman on his previous posting. But Smith had seen such things happen, too often, when a captain was careless and junior officers inclined to bully. He'd seen nothing to Archer's discredit since that young man joined his crew.

To his credit, Archer had risked his own life to save Marshall, throwing himself into a powder room to get his shipmate out before a spreading fire blew the cabin to splinters. Archer's promotion to Acting Lieutenant had been based on that as much as his ability, and he had fulfilled his new responsibilies to a degree that erased any doubts. Archer might not have Marshall's talent in a crisis—few did—but the Navy had constant need of good, steady officers who could do their duty; they were the backbone of the Service.

Then the thought he had been steadfastly putting out of his mind came echoing back. *"You'll pay for it—or your lads will."* He needed to know what the fellow meant by that. It was not pleasant to realize that he would almost certainly find out.

Chapter 4

"Oatmeal," Archer said mournfully, the morning of their first full day aboard ship. "I wonder how much of our careers will be spent eating oatmeal. It seems to be the universal solvent." But he dutifully spooned up the last bit of the uninteresting mass.

Marshall had finished his and was working on a biscuit. "If you only count oatmeal in prison, I think the percentage would be rather low. If you include ordinary shipboard meals, it may be the better part of our lives. It could be worse, Davy," he said philosophically. "It could be garbanzos."

Archer had to smile at that. During a blockade of supply ships, the *Calypso* had subsisted for nearly a month on a captured cargo of Spanish chickpeas. "I suppose you like oatmeal."

Marshall shrugged. "It's fuel. I've no quarrel with oats. Although, I admit, I had hoped to squander a few shillings, while we were in port, on eggs-and-bacon."

"And real tea, with cream," Archer said. "And scones."

"Well, at least the biscuit is fresh. It seems only yesterday we made the acquaintance of these biscuits. Reliable traveling companions, wouldn't you say?"

"And we know exactly where they've been."

Marshall grimaced. "I wish we knew exactly where we are."

They were at sea, rather than in port; that much was obvious from the motion of the ship, which had weighed anchor almost immediately after they had been brought on board. Marshall had been constructing elaborate patterns of straw, basing his calculations on where they might be if they had left Portsmouth, if the wind was what it had been when they were last in the open air, if, if... Finally, having too little data, he scattered the straws in disgust and they worked on navigation problems for a while.

Thus far, the routine in their little cell had been much like the routine on the *Calypso,* except for the matter of being confined. An early, simple breakfast: oatmeal and biscuit. Then dinner: biscuit, and a piece of cheese. Supper was biscuit, dried beef, and halfway decent tea. Three guards came to remove the slop bucket and pour water into the other two; they had to put the containers next to the door and stand well back, which seemed a fair enough trade for fresh water and hygiene.

The ventilator had proved a great disappointment. If they'd had a crowbar or hammer and chisel, they could have removed the heavy bar and, very likely, squeezed out...which would have left them sticking out of the side of the ship like a cannon. And it was possible that this little room had originally been a gunport; the wood around the port was newer than the rest of the hull, as though extra space had been filled in. But, again, it would take more than their fingernails to get through it, and there was nothing but the sea outside.

The guards came again late in the afternoon of the second day. By that point they were playing chess on a board they'd drawn with a bit of chalk Archer had found in his pocket. The men were fashioned from straw. Pawns, single stalks, were no trouble, but the other chessmen tended to fall to pieces. This element of unpredictability made the game more interesting.

One man knocked on the door and pressed his masked face to the grate. "Which of you's Archer?"

Archer met Marshall's look, then rose warily to his feet. "I am."

The face vanished and a pan of water slid under the flap

at the door's base. "You're 'aving supper with the Captain. We're giving you a razor, but you 'ave to put it back out before we opens the door." The statement was followed by the item named, resting on a bit of silvered glass.

"They're afraid we'll leap out and shave them," Marshall said scornfully, but in truth the caution was reasonable. A razor could be a vicious weapon, and neither of them would hesitate to use it as such.

"What about Lt. Marshall?" Archer asked.

"'E stays 'ere. Only one o' you out at a time."

"Then why don't you give the Captain my regrets. I prefer to stay here."

"Then you both misses supper."

"Go on, Davy," Marshall said, too quietly for the guards to hear. "You might learn something about our position."

He really didn't want to go. "Is that an order?"

Marshall looked exasperated. "Davy... Go. At least you'll get out of here for a bit."

Of course, it was William himself who was chafing at the confinement. It was typical of his generous spirit that he would want to give what he couldn't have himself. Archer nodded. "All right," he told the guard. "It may take a little while."

"Sing out when you're done." Footsteps clumped away.

The water was warmish, the bit of soap in it nearly dissolved. Marshall held the pan for him, angling the mirror to catch the uncertain light from the air vent. "This Adrian must be a fastidious bastard," he said as Archer scraped at three days' worth of beard. "At least regarding his guests. He looks like he's not shaved in years."

"I wonder if Captain Smith will be there." It would be heartening to see him.

"I doubt it. If he won't face the two of us together, I doubt he'd risk the Captain. Be careful, Davy. He may try to get information that he can sell to the French."

Archer glanced up in alarm. "You think so?"

"I don't know. Come to think of it, I don't suppose we

really know much that isn't public knowledge. But a man who'll interfere with naval officers in wartime could do anything."

"I'll remind him that this is treason, if you think it'll help—"

"No." Marshall frowned as if worrying a toothache. "Just...be careful."

"It will be my watchword." Archer rinsed the razor. "Damned if I'm going to be thorough. D'you want to use this?"

Marshall rubbed his chin. "I may as well." They traded places and he made a quick job of it, gazing thoughtfully at the razor when he finished. "Too bad we have to give this back, it could be useful."

"The edge would be gone long before we could cut our way out," Archer said pragmatically. The timbers of the hull were at least a foot thick; even the walls of their compartment would be an inch or better.

"I know." He handed it back, and Archer dumped the razor in the basin, slid it back out, and pounded on the door.

Boots thumped in the companionway. "Stand away from the door." A guard looked in to see that they had obeyed; a bolt was drawn back outside, and the door swung open to show three pistols aimed inside. "Aw'right, you come out, you stay back."

As soon as Archer was outside, the door was shut again, the bolt thrown home. His hope of seeing anything helpful was dashed immediately; one of the guards tied his hands in front of him while another shook out the folds of a huge, hooded grey cloak. He had one glimpse of Marshall looking out the barred window, frowning in chagrin, before the heavy wool fell over his face. The free end of the rope that bound his hands was wrapped around the outside of the cloak, and he was pushed forward.

Someone warned him of steps going up, but neglected to say how many, and he staggered onto a deck, was turned and taken 14 paces, then back down a shorter set of steps. Fourteen somewhat hampered paces from the hatchway to the quarterdeck. Not much, but a start.

A door creaked. "Please be seated, Mr. Archer," a cultured voice invited. "I believe you will appreciate the change of scenery."

The guards who'd brought him here pulled the enveloping cloak away and loosed Archer's wrists as they pushed him into the captain's cabin. It was furnished as grandly as any fine home he had ever visited: a small but elegant dining table, china dishes, crystal goblets. The meal looked sumptuous. Besides the wine and bread, there were roast fowl, green beans, a pie, and two covered dishes. The only concession to shipboard life was a plate of the ubiquitous biscuit.

And at the head of the table sat Captain Adrian, in a suit of unrelieved black, cut in a parody of a Royal Navy uniform. A strange costume, made stranger by the black silk mask concealing his upper face. David understood what Will had meant about Adrian's not shaving—between the mask and a short reddish beard and moustache, very little of him was visible.

If he were to remove the mask and shave, he would be unidentifiable...if not for his eyes. They were an icy, nearly colorless blue, with such peculiar intensity that they made the mask useless. Archer would know those eyes again even if he saw them staring out of a block of wood. He wondered if Adrian knew how ineffective his disguise really was, or if he simply enjoyed the drama of it all. Archer had seen enough theatre to recognize the trappings.

He nodded politely. "Captain," he said, and sat at the indicated chair. But the eating utensils beside his plate were at odds with the refinement of the table. They appeared to be carved from some sort of soft, spongy wood, and the knife had no point.

"You are not my first dinner guest, Mr. Archer," Adrian said, observing his expression, "and I have had one or two who were quite inventive. I have found it simpler to remove the temptation to pilfer tableware. If any meat needs cutting, my cook attends to it in the galley."

"I see." This prison might have the trappings of elegance, but it was a prison nonetheless.

Adrian seemed to feel a need to elaborate. "Not that it would do you any good, but one of my men was once stabbed with a fork, and I was forced to have his assailant beaten. One of the rules aboard this ship is that any attempt to escape, however unsuccessful, is punished swiftly and severely. It would save us both a great deal of trouble if you would simply give me your parole."

"I'm afraid I can't do that." Archer was mildly surprised that Adrian would make the suggestion. Not only would it be counter to Captain Smith's very clear orders, the prospect of giving his word to this kidnapper was out of the question. He offered no further explanation, remembering his promise to be as noncommittal and uninformative as possible.

Silence proved easier than he had expected, so easy that it became unsettling. Adrian watched him closely with those blank-mirror eyes, saying little as they ate. Archer, for his part, felt no obligation to shoulder the burden of polite conversation with someone who'd kidnapped him.

Eventually, though, Adrian pushed his plate away. "You are no doubt wondering why I invited you to join me," he said.

Archer was tempted to point out that he'd received an order, not an invitation. *No. Be careful.* "Of course."

"Curiosity, Mr. Archer. In my line of business it is essential to research my subjects, but the bare facts really tell so little. I know of your captain, of course; what Englishman doesn't? But I was surprised to learn he had a nephew—or cousin, isn't it? Were you aware of his relationship with Mr. Marshall?"

"I believe the Captain mentioned it, once," Archer hedged. Never mind when he'd mentioned it, or under what circumstances. "But I understand they both prefer that Mr. Marshall succeed on his own merits, rather than through connections."

"How very noble. Most gentlemen would think it strange not to make full use of such an advantage."

This certainly didn't seem to be a fishing expedition for military information. "I do not believe that Captain Smith would keep any officer on board who was not prepared to earn his way," he said honestly, "relative or not. Nor do I believe that Mr. Marshall wishes or requires an unfair advantage."

"He has moved up more quickly than you have," Adrian interjected with an unpleasant smile.

"He has seen several years' more active duty than I." Archer began to see the direction this conversation was headed. Would it be useful to let Adrian think there was a rivalry between him and William? Possibly, but not until they had discussed it between themselves, and even then it was an unpleasant prospect.

Archer recognized that he was not as ambitious as Marshall was. At first he had been a little envious of his friend's success, but it was impossible to hold ill feelings toward Will. In the years they'd sailed together, he had grown fonder of the serious minister's son than he was of his own brothers. Now, for the most part, he enjoyed being nearly neck-and-neck with Will, like runners pacing one another in a long-distance race.

And it wasn't as though Will would ever do anything to hold him back; as soon as Captain Smith told Archer to prepare himself for the examination, Will had done everything he could to help him. And being one step behind Will nourished Archer's secret dream: when Will was Captain of his own ship he might take Archer with him as his lieutenant.

But he dared not daydream now, under Adrian's watchful eyes, and the man clearly expected a more elaborate answer. "I am satisfied with my progress, sir. From what I have seen aboard *Calypso*, there is no shortage of opportunity to prove one's ability."

"Ah, yes. Service on a frigate, the intrepid huntinghawks of the Fleet. Such an exciting life, while my own merchant's lot is so routine. Have you any tales you might share?"

"Only what you might read in the *Naval Gazette*." Archer shook his head. "I doubt I can tell you much about our latest catch; your men captured us before we could unload the French ships, and I know nothing of the papers they carried."

"I understand the *Calypso* was damaged. Will she be in long for repairs?"

There it was, a question of military significance. "I really couldn't say," Archer said. "Had your men waited an hour or two, I could have told you. Of course, if you were to put us back ashore so we might continue on our business, I would be happy to answer your question by letter."

The masked captain smiled. "No, I think not. Mere idle curiosity." He rose and went to the sideboard to pour a glass of brandy for himself—odd, that he had no one waiting table—and David hastily rolled a piece of chicken into his napkin and tucked it into his pocket, unbuttoning the jacket to make his prize less visible. Unless they searched his clothes, Will would get a share of this bounty. And if they did catch him, it was unlikely even Adrian could consider poultry a dangerous weapon.

"Would you care for some brandy, Mr. Archer?" Adrian asked politely. "Claret? Port?"

Archer weighed the possibility of alcohol dulling his wits against the tightly-wound state of his nerves. "A little port, thank you." How strange to be carrying on such a bland drawing-room conversation with a pirate. A biscuit slid neatly into the other pocket as Adrian turned back to the sideboard.

The port was poured, the bottle returned to the bracket that secured it against the ship's rolling. Adrian brought the glasses back and raised his own. "A toast?"

"My Captain's good health," Archer suggested. "And a speedy conclusion to our visit."

"And a profitable one," Adrian added. "Mr. Archer, I believe your presence with your captain, while unexpected, will prove fortuitous."

"How so?" Another trifle of information to store away. As Smith had surmised, he had been the target.

"I had expected only the Captain, or perhaps your first lieutenant, Mr. Drinkwater. His family would no doubt have come well up to the mark as regards ransom. But Mr. Drinkwater, however worthy and well-funded, is rather stout. I do not believe that excess weight is becoming to an officer, do you?"

"Mr. Drinkwater is a fine officer," Archer said, puzzled by the irrelevancy. "He is competent, intelligent, and has excellent rapport with the men. I have learned much from him."

"And a loyal, well-spoken lad you are," Adrian responded smoothly. "As well as a most attractive young man."

If Archer had been a dog, his hackles would have stood on end. He reached for his glass, took a sip of the port, and said nothing. It could be simple, clumsy flattery, but Adrian hardly seemed the clumsy type.

"As I was saying, your presence here promises to make my evenings more interesting. Haven't you served as a cabin boy, Mr. Archer? My instinct for such matters is unerring."

The way he asked the question set off alarms. "I joined His Majesty's Navy as a midshipman," Archer said carefully. He stared into the wineglass, wishing he were back with Marshall in the dark, cramped safety of the cell.

"Lad, you know perfectly well what I'm talking about; there is no point in being so deliberately obtuse. I refer, of course, to a function that would require you be at least partly out of uniform."

Archer wondered wildly if there were some sort of target painted on his back, but he forced his voice to coldness. "I take your meaning, sir. I also take offense."

Adrian laughed. "And next I suppose you'll ask for satisfaction. Well, laddie, that's all I want, myself...but I expect to get it from your pretty little arse."

Archer's fingers spasmed, snapping the crystal cup from its delicate stem. Tawny port soaked into the crisp linen cloth. "If you are soliciting my cooperation, the answer is no."

He laughed again. "I don't require your cooperation, Mr. Archer. But I would prefer it. It's so tedious when a poor fellow's all trussed up, it dulls the enjoyment."

An odd sense of detachment numbed Archer's mind, as though this were some weirdly civilized dream that split appearance from reality. The tone of Adrian's words was calm, even cheerful; the content was a threat. His heart was thumping; he wanted to run. But there was nowhere to run. Even if he made it through the door, at least three guards waited outside. Archer could not guess what this bastard would do to Will or Captain Smith if he failed to follow the undefined rules of this game.

Formal speech seemed to be one of them, though it was difficult speaking politely through clenched teeth. "I think it unlikely that I would enjoy such an experience under any circumstances, so I must again decline." *No thank you, I'd rather not be violated today, if you don't mind.*

"Ah." Adrian tilted his head to one side, a professor examining a curiosity. "Perhaps I was hasty. I thought you were a connoisseur, like myself."

Archer frowned, not quite following.

"Of male beauty. I had thought perhaps that you and Mr. Marshall—?"

Ice touched his heart, started to seep down through his body. "No." *No. Leave him out of this, damn you!*

"Are you certain? He seemed quite...solicitous...of your welfare, when you first arrived."

"Mr. Marshall is a—a conscientious officer. He would be equally concerned for any of his men."

"Oh, of course." A knowing smile.

No, no, no! He had to divert the bastard from Will. "There was another officer aboard our former ship who...labored under a similar misconception. Mr. Marshall called him out."

"Oh, really? And—?"

"He shot him dead." *As he would you.*

Adrian patted his lips with his napkin. "My word. Well, so much for Mr. Marshall, I suppose. But I notice you have said nothing of yourself. Poor lad, I expect all you've known is a brutal bit of buggery below decks—that 'other officer', no doubt. We'll have to do something to remedy that."

Numbness began to give way to anger. Archer clutched at it, willing it to warm the frozen knot of fear in his chest. "Captain, this is preposterous. You are making an assumption about me—a very personal and offensive assumption—based on no evidence whatsoever. On that baseless assumption, you further assume my acquiescence to a proposal that I find repellent. This, in addition to the fact that I was violently abducted and am here entirely against my will." He saw Adrian start to respond, and finished quickly. "I am sure you have force of arms sufficient to impose your will, but you deceive yourself if you mistake coercion for cooperation."

The cold eyes bored into him. "You have not denied the assumption."

Terror and outrage balanced on a sword's point. He knew Adrian could tell he was frightened. He didn't care. He was a man now, not a boy. "I deny your right to make the assumption."

Adrian smiled thinly. "Sooner or later, laddie, you'll find you want to cooperate. But for now, if my suggestion does not appeal, you can return to your cell. Perhaps things will look differently in the morning." He rang a small handbell and stood, gesturing toward the door. Weak with relief, hardly believing the ordeal was over even for the moment, Archer rose hastily and followed.

Then Adrian stopped, his hand on the knob. "Remember, Mr. Archer, any violence on your part will bring severe retribution upon your shipmates." With that, he moved up close behind, pulling Archer against him and running his hands down the front of his body. Trapped between the trespassing hands and the hot breath against his ear, Archer froze, closed his eyes, and waited for what he knew must happen next.

But ... it did not. Adrian's fingers roamed across him for a horrible eternity, stroking, probing—and then he abruptly pushed the door open and thrust Archer out into the arms of the guards who'd brought him there. "Tell Mr. Brown to inform me when we are out of sight."

"Aye, sir."

Archer stood trembling with shock while they replaced the loop on his wrists, draped the cloak about him, wound the line around. He managed to make it back to the cell, but his legs gave out as he stumbled inside. He dropped onto the straw and fell back against the bulkhead.

Marshall, who'd been lying out of the angle of light, rolled over and sat up beside him, putting a hand on his shoulder. "Davy, what's wrong? You look as though you've seen a ghost."

True enough. The ghost of George Correy. He shrugged away, afraid of accepting the comfort, afraid he'd go to pieces. "I'm all right." *Stay calm. Deep breaths.*

He could not break down in front of Will. He had to hold himself together until the guards took away the lantern outside their door. Once it was dark he could let himself feel. "I-I shouldn't have had spirits, it went straight to my head when I stood up."

Marshall frowned, but did not press him. "I'd have thought a drink would do you good. How did it go—did you learn anything?"

Although William's presence was a tonic, if he didn't change the subject he was going to start shaking again. "Good food, disgusting company. Did they ever feed you?"

"No," Marshall said lightly. "I seem to be forgotten this evening. They did refill the water. Some kind of cat-and-mouse game, I suppose, though I can't see what purpose it serves. Does he expect to start us fighting over a missed meal?"

Genuine happiness unfroze Archer's face as he remembered his subterfuge. "If that's his intention, he'd better watch the larder more closely." He carefully extracted the fragrant, greasy napkin from one pocket and a reliably unsquashable biscuit from the other. "Adrian struck me as the sort to play divide-and-conquer. He tried to suggest I should be jealous that you outrank me. Here's one for our side."

Will's expression said more about how hungry he was than his diffident words had. Archer's warm satisfaction at watching his friend eat helped, for a few minutes, to push away the fear that was beginning to gnaw at him. Adrian was not especially subtle, but he did not need to be. Treat him well and starve Marshall, then remind him how easily he could help his friend...Adrian might well have known he'd taken the food.

"Davy," Will said, polishing off the last of the biscuit, "if I were an admiral, you'd be promoted on the spot. But what are we going to do with the bones?" They both stared around the tiny, bare cell.

"Not in the straw, we don't want rats for company."

"No, there are too many outside as it is. Out the port, then... Ah." Will lifted the lid of the slop bucket and popped them in. "I doubt they'll inspect this too closely."

Archer shrugged. "If they do, we'll tell them I have terrible digestion."

For some reason, that sent Marshall into a fit of stifled giggles. Then, just as he was settling down, the notion of pirates reading the entrails of a slop bucket struck Archer as hilarious, and that set Marshall off again. Every time their eyes met, control went out the window. It was nervous laughter, of course, and they both knew it; but it celebrated the one small triumph over their captors, and it shook the numbing fear loose from Archer's throat.

"I think we had better get some sleep," Marshall said finally, looking carefully away.

"Wait." Archer lowered his voice, although they had both quickly gotten into the habit of speaking in undertones.

"Before I forget, I do have a few things to report. The man at the helm right now is called Brown, though I suspect that name is as genuine as Adrian."

"It could be, that's a common enough name."

"True, but why would any of them use their real names and wear masks? There are 14 steps to the quarterdeck, from the hatch we came down. It's a fair-sized ship, as you guessed, I think somewhat larger than the prizes we brought in, but it doesn't have the sound or feel of something as big as the *Calypso*. Also, Adrian mentioned that you and I were caught by mistake, just as the Captain thought. They were actually after the Captain or Mr. Drinkwater."

"He mentioned the lieutenant by name?"

"Yes. And he knew Drinkwater's family is well off. I wonder how long they knew we were coming into port. It was not a scheduled return."

"The first two ships we captured arrived the day before we did," Marshall said. "They couldn't have learned anything more than that we were on the way, 18 or 20 hours notice, at best. Of course, the officers' list is easy to get. I wonder if he was waiting for our captain, specifically, or any officer worth a good ransom?"

"I don't know. Adrian seems scornful when he mentions officers and gentlemen, but his manners suggest that he is one, or was. His cabin makes our captain's look Spartan." Smith's quarters had a fleet-wide reputation for their simple elegance; the Captain exercised his rank's prerogative of a private stock of wine and other small comforts, but his indulgence was hardly on the same scale. "Most of the food was perishable stuff, everything but the biscuit. He must have a flock of hens aboard somewhere, and a wine cellar. I would guess this ship probably never travels very far from land."

"Careful, Mr. Archer," Marshall warned. "You're showing a definite talent for intrigue. We don't want to lose you to the spy service."

"No danger of that," Archer assured him. "If they ever

tried to send me into France in disguise, the Frogs would know me in an instant—from my knees knocking together."

Marshall smiled and cuffed him on the shoulder, and they arranged themselves for the night. It didn't take long: shoes in one corner, jackets rolled as pillows, and shirts airing out at the port. The bits of sailcloth were just large enough to keep the sharp stalks from being a nuisance. It was too warm in the stuffy cell to need any cover.

They had guessed the time within minutes; before they were completely settled, a crewman came and took the lantern away. Without it, night was dark enough to escape into sleep. Archer prayed it would be too dark to dream.

Chapter 5

Supplemental Log, HMS Calypso, in for repair, Portsmouth. Lt. Anthony Drinkwater, in temporary command. 18-7-1799

No further news.

Exhausted by the nerve-wracking dinner engagement, Archer slept like the dead, but a mob of masked sailors thumping into the cell brought him abruptly awake. The lantern light showed Marshall struggling in the grip of two burly seamen; a third gave him a single hard punch in the stomach that doubled him over while another shoved his hands forward to be bound.

Archer was too startled and groggy to put up a fight; by the time he could, someone had a knee in his back and an arm around his throat. Shirtless and barefoot, they were tied, blindfolded and dragged out of the room, up the stairs, and outside to the edge of the quarterdeck. Someone spun him around, pushed him a few steps further. His wrists, still bound, were pulled up and secured above his head.

As he stood trying to get his bearings, he heard Adrian's voice just beside him. "You'll hardly benefit from the lesson if you can't see it, will you?" The blindfold was pulled away.

He was at the gratings—well, that was no surprise. He had offended the bastard; aboard any ship, flogging was the most likely punishment for a variety of offenses. He'd taken a couple of beatings aboard *Titan,* when Correy had contrived to shift the blame for his own transgressions. But there was something peculiar about this arrangement.

He frowned through the metal latticework, and realized that he was wrong-way on, facing the maindeck...and suddenly Marshall was thrown against the other side, so their faces were only inches apart. In the light of a bright three-quarters moon, Archer saw that they were lashing Will to the grating spreadeagled, so he couldn't move at all. Looking past his friend's shoulder, he saw two more sailors bring Captain Smith on deck, also blindfolded, stopping some 20 feet away.

Archer had been half-expecting reprisal, but he had never imagined this. Twisting to look over his own shoulder, he saw Adrian watching him greedily, waiting. His gut tightened. Well, with 40 or 50 men to one, it had always been a foregone conclusion, hadn't it? "All right," he breathed, his mouth dry. "You've made your point. I'll do it."

"Of course you will." Adrian's smile was ripe with self-confidence. "I never had any doubt. But this is a consequence, not a threat." He raised his voice. "Let these gentlemen see what's going on so they understand how very serious I am."

He strode onto the main deck, and Archer reflected that a stage career might have saved them all a lot of grief. "Men," Adrian announced, "We have had an escape attempt this evening. It was not Lt. Marshall himself who essayed it, of course, but he will have to bear the burden for it, this time."

Marshall blinked at Archer in surprise as his blindfold came off. "So that's why you were so winded when you came back. Why didn't you say something?"

"I'm sorry," Archer whispered. "But I didn't—" Someone hit him from behind. He'd have to explain later. No. He'd have to come up with some plausible lie, later. He couldn't possibly explain.

"I don't want to disfigure such a splendid young specimen," Adrian continued. Hearing the undertone, Archer went cold. "So we'll use the cane this time. Next time, it will be the cat. Bosun—oh, before you begin, give Mr. Archer a small sample."

The flexible rattan cane whistled shrilly as it slashed

down across Archer's back. The shock of it caught him un-
prepared and it was all he could do not to yelp. He caught his
breath and tensed, waiting for the next. He'd just about decided that was all when the bosun, craftily watching for his
guard to go down, gave him two more in quick succession.

"That's enough," Adrian said. "It is Mr. Marshall's turn,
after all. A dozen, if you please."

"Predictable," Will muttered. His face twisted as the first
blow landed, but his mobile mouth compressed, and no
sound escaped but a faint gasp of impact. The grate rattled
each time his body jerked in reaction.

It was too close; Archer couldn't bear to watch. Not that
the punishment was especially severe—they'd each had this
sort of thing a time or two as midshipmen, on *Titan*—but
knowing that he was responsible made it almost unbearable.
His own back stinging in sympathy, he stared out past Will,
past their captors, to where Captain Smith stood, hands tied
behind him and surrounded by half a dozen guards. His face
was granite, eyes hooded by the angle of moonlight, but
something about his posture made Archer think of a loaded
cannon awaiting the match.

Adrian's voice pulled his attention back. "That's 12."
Will let out a breath and sagged against the iron. "And one
for good measure." After it had landed, too fast for him to
brace against it, Adrian caught Marshall's hair and yanked
his head back. "And have you any words for the shipmate
who brought this upon you, Lieutenant?"

Will bared his teeth in a wild, dangerous smile. "I certainly do." His eyes challenged Archer to share the joke, and
his voice was strong and clear. "Well done, Mr. Archer. Better luck next time."

The cane came down hard. No set number, and the bosun
put his full strength into every blow. Archer only felt it sec-
ondhand, and that was bad enough. It went on and on; he lost
count around 30. He could see that the punishment was
breaking through Marshall's resolve; his gasps were very
nearly sobs by the time it finally stopped. "Will," he hissed,

"for God's sake don't antagonize him. How will we escape if you can't move?"

Thank God, Captain Smith must have had the same notion. In the quiet after the last stroke fell, his voice cut like a sword across Marshall's labored breathing. "Hold your tongue, Mr. Marshall." Smith turned to Adrian. "I do not usually take pleasure in seeing a man hang, sir. But in your case I shall make an exception."

"The sentiment is hardly original, sir," Adrian said mockingly. He strolled over to inspect his handiwork. "No lasting harm, I'm sure. We don't want to damage valuable merchandise, after all." His eyes met Archer's through the grating. "You will see to it this does not happen again?"

Not trusting his voice, Archer gave a tight nod.

"Very good." Adrian gestured, and his men hurried to release them from the gratings. Will moved unsteadily, his face and posture rigid; Archer tried to stay close enough to give him something to lean against. His skin was clammy where they touched, and he was already shivering. When they were standing on the maindeck, near Smith, Adrian surveyed them all with satisfaction. "I trust you gentlemen now realize who is captain aboard this ship?"

In unconscious unison, they both looked to Smith, and Archer seized the chance to communicate. "We made no escape attempt, sir."

"Thank you, Mr. Archer," Smith said, his answer nearly drowned by Adrian's furious, "Get them below!"

"Silence!" Smith roared. It was an order that would quell the deck of the *Calypso* in mid-battle, and he seized the moment of quiet that followed. "You have been playing at pirates far too long. You men—all of you—are no longer simple criminals, you are traitors so long as you follow this man, and no port in the land will be haven to you. England is at war, you fools—and you are interfering with officers in His Majesty's Navy!" His glare raked the deck. "I am prepared to offer amnesty to any man who renounces this treasonous swine and accepts his duty to his country!"

Even Archer found himself swayed by the force of the Captain's personality; he was ready to renounce the treasonous swine on the spot even though he bore him no allegiance, and he guessed that half the men present felt the same. If the three of them had not been bound, Smith might actually have carried the day. But the precarious moment passed as Adrian stormed over, caught Smith by one arm, and threw him bodily to the deck. Then he grabbed two of the sailors who had been standing openmouthed and pushed them toward Smith. "Take him below and lock him up and report to the bosun for a flogging!"

As they took the Captain away, Adrian whirled on his men, half of whom were still staring at the little drama, and pointed to Marshall and Archer. "Get them below, *now!* If I see any more disobedience, I'll have you all shot!"

"By whom?" Will murmured, too quietly for anyone but Archer to hear.

If he had not been so battered already, Archer would have elbowed him in the ribs. He scowled instead, and Marshall managed to restrain his irony until they were back in their cell. They weren't blindfolded this time, possibly because there was nothing much to be seen: no other cell door along this companionway. The Captain must be imprisoned elsewhere.

Once inside, Will's brave mask dropped. He caught at the bulkhead with both hands, his body shaking, while Archer swiftly leveled the straw that had been kicked around, straightened the sailcloth, and found his purloined table linen. He couldn't do much, but anything to keep down the welts would help.

"Come on, Will," he said, supporting him under the elbows, careful not to touch his back. "Lie down and keep still. We need to get some sea water on those stripes. You probably aren't feeling it all yet, but they're going to hurt like blazes."

"I...was beginning to notice." Moving very carefully,

Will stretched out face-down while Archer soaked the cloth in the wash-bucket. "It was worth it, though. Did you see that bastard's face when Captain Smith shouted? He had no idea what to do. If the Captain had had one minute more the crew would've been singing 'God Save the King'."

"But he didn't have that minute." Archer hated to sound a sour note, but he couldn't imagine what Adrian was going to do to salve his wounded pride, and he was quite sure that, whatever it might be, he wouldn't like it. He lifted up the dripping cloth, reluctant to put salt water on the stripes where the skin had split. Had to be done, though; it would slow the bleeding. "Brace yourself, Will. I'm sorry."

William's whole body jerked at the touch. "Thank you. He didn't have it this time, but, Davy, what he did has changed everything."

"It's made Adrian madder than a hornet, I could see that."

"No, think about it. The Captain said he had his own family guarded. This crew has probably been kidnapping wives, children, maybe older folk—landsmen, if all they knew was that they were on a ship. We could tell much more, just from the way she moves. And we know we've been out of port most of this time. They've probably never dealt with sailors at all, and when they went for Captain Smith, they overreached themselves." His grin was a faint echo of what it had been above. "Now they've got a tiger by the tail. I don't know if the Captain can actually grant amnesty, but I'd wager he could wangle a pardon for any sailor who helps us."

"They're criminals," Archer objected. "What do they care?"

"They may be rogues, Davy, but they're English rogues; at least some will have families in England. And they're sailors. Every man on that deck who heard our Captain now knows what a real captain looks like, and they know that what they've got is no match for him. And Adrian will know

that, too, so he'll have to set his crew to watching one another, and he can't be sure a few of them won't conspire
against him."

"I hope you're right." What Will said was making sense,
and it seemed to be distracting him from the pain, though
how he could think at all, the way his back looked, was beyond Archer. The cloth was already warm from the heat rising off the welts; he'd have a rainbow of bruises by daybreak. "It's best to keep this cool. Would you rather I take it
off or pour water on?"

"Whatever's easier, Davy. Thank you." He set his teeth
as Archer rinsed and replaced the cloth, then rattled on. "We
must be ready to take advantage of any disaffection in the
crew. All we need is information on this ship's position, and,
if we're near land—"

"We may be," Archer interrupted. "When they brought
me back, Adrian told the guard to tell Brown to let him know
when they were out of sight. He could have meant out of
sight of land, so there was no chance of anyone with a spy-
glass seeing us on deck."

"Or out of sight of other ships. If that's so, and we could
get a few minutes on a clear deck—"

He broke off with a strangled cry. Archer caught his
shoulders and steadied him. "The worst starts a little while
after you think it's over, Will. It passes."

"How—long?"

"I don't know, the most I ever got was a dozen. Moving
makes it worse, though. Try to keep still." Will muttered
something. "What?"

"Still...worth it. To watch that arrogant bastard realize
he's caught a man who's stronger than he is."

Archer noticed pale dawn light beginning to seep through
the ventilator. "Try to rest, Will. See if you can sleep."

"You must be joking."

"You're one to talk. God in Heaven, Will, whatever possessed you to goad him like that?"

"I hate bullies." His voice was rough with pain. "Reminds me of that bastard Correy."

That hit Archer like a blow. Did William have second sight? Then he realized it took no clairvoyance to see the similarity. "Well, there's no shortage of bullies in the world, and we've certainly met our share..."

He checked the cloth again, rinsed it mechanically. *And I'm no better at facing them now than then.* There was no need for Will to be lying here suffering. He'd taken the beating as though he'd won a prize, thinking it meant Archer had been following Smith's orders, when all he'd been trying to do was protect his own cowardly self from something he had no hope of escaping. *It's not as though he means to kill me, not if he wants the ransom.* And besides, he had already capitulated. Adrian could send for him at any time, have him delivered to his cabin, and he was powerless to prevent it.

Better not to think about that just now. "Will, would you like some water? To drink, I mean."

"I would." It took a few moments, getting Will up on his side, letting him drink, getting him settled again. "Thank you. Davy—"

"Yes?"

"When all this started, you said something—to Adrian— it sounded like you were agreeing to something. What was all that?"

Archer had turned to rinse the cloth; Will couldn't see him cringe as he scrambled to avoid an outright lie. "You were right, when you thought he wanted—information. It slipped my mind last night, but he did ask about what the *Calypso*'s been up to. He wanted a list of the ships we captured. And he wanted to know how long the old girl would be in for repairs. I told him we'd been captured before we learned about the repairs, and I couldn't discuss military information until I'd spoken to the Captain."

"Oh. Good, Davy. Exactly right."

"I thought I should talk to you first, in the morning, and we could decide upon some useless information to feed him." He knelt to replace the cloth and bowed his head. "I—I had no idea he'd do this, Will, can you forgive me?" The last, at least, was entirely the truth.

"There's nothing to forgive, Davy," Will said wearily. "You were doing your duty. Besides, he almost had to make a show of force at some point, just to discourage us trying to get away. We don't even know that this wasn't all for Captain Smith's benefit. It may have been to threaten the Captain—my 'uncle'—into cooperating. Since they haven't just killed me out of hand, he must have given them that story." He rested his chin on his fists. "We know the Captain is challenging Adrian's authority. Aboard his own ship there is no greater threat. If he loses control of his crew, Smith will step in and take it."

"But it was clear he wanted something from me—" Archer despised himself for the half-truth, but the whole truth would have been worse.

"He may simply be trying to break you—I'm sorry, I don't mean that as it sounded—to force you to give him information—to prove that he has the power to do it, not because the information is of any use."

"You may be right." Archer pulled out his handkerchief, moistened it, and wiped Will's face. That he did not protest the attention was an indication of his pain. He was precisely right, too, even if he had not guessed Adrian's aim. *And the bastard does have the power, Will, because he can hurt you, and I cannot bear that. Damn him to hell, how did he know?*

"I'm sure he's getting fat with ransom, but watching that performance of his, above...he's doing it for power, Davy. For control." Will's speech was slower, now, and his dark eyes looked dull. The pain was wearing him out. "He must have had spies in Portsmouth when we came in. He knows what we brought home. Unless there were some secret dispatches on one of those ships—things we really don't know about—it just doesn't matter. All that information will be in the *Naval Gazette*. Don't torture yourself, Davy. Let him think he's won. Play for time."

"I thought I might tell him about prize captures that have

already been published. You're right; no acting lieutenant is going to be privy to secret documents, anyway."

"I think the Captain will be the key to our getting out. We must be ready when he makes his move. God, if I can ever be half what he is..." His voice trailed off as his eyelids slid shut.

"You already are," Archer said quietly. "Half, at least."

When he was sure William was asleep, he covered his friend with the second bit of sailcloth so he wouldn't take a chill, then spread out both their jackets to lie on himself. He rolled up their shirts as a pillow and settled on his side, shifting until he found a position that didn't pull at the welts on his own back—nothing compared to Will's, but damnably uncomfortable. His mind drifted as he watched the narrow bars of light from the ventilator creep slowly across the wall. Inevitably, the prospect of what lay ahead, probably by the time the sun went down, began to loom.

Archer suspected his friend had guessed what Correy had done to him, years back, but he was grateful they had never spoken of it. He couldn't bring himself to tell William what was really at stake here, either.

Am I that obvious? Can anyone tell, just looking at me? He hoped not. He had never intentionally done anything to try to attract another man—he certainly had not invited Correy's attentions—but there had been a few invitations, from friends in the theatre, invitations he had never accepted, and no hard feelings. He had been in the throes of a much more conventional romance, back then, with the lovely understudy to the celebrated Mrs. Sarah Siddons.

But the invitations had been there, nonetheless. And now this. Will might wonder, as he was beginning to, himself, whether Archer wasn't sending some sort of signal that suggested he would welcome such attentions.

And if William wondered that, he might also wonder if he wanted to keep a friend who was sending such signals. That sort of association would sound the death knell for a young officer's ambitions, and Will was highly ambitious.

All to the good, because he was going to be a captain who would take his place beside Jervis, Nelson, and Pellew in the pages of history. Men like that were rare, and England needed them.

It was almost funny that Will could look at such men and not recognize himself—as when he'd said that Adrian had caught a man stronger than he was. He'd caught two at once, and it probably frightened the hell out of him.

Maybe that's why he went after me. A corvette won't take on two frigates if there's a lightly-armed sloop handy. I'm an easy target. And he knows he can use us against each other. He enjoys that, it gives him power.

He should have taken advantage of Adrian's expectation that he would be jealous of William. There would have been no point in having him beaten if he thought Archer would be pleased to see it happen. That probably wouldn't have worked, though. He could wear the mask of manners society expected; he couldn't pretend to hate the best friend he'd ever had... a man he loved.

But he could provide a diversion. Those two frigates would find it easier to defeat the corvette if the corvette was preoccupied with trying to sink the sloop. If Adrian's vigilance was lulled by a victory on one front, he might neglect the more important battle. It was not the sort of diversionary tactic that would ever be taught, pray God, but it might serve the purpose. Let him think he'd won, as Will had said. Play for time. *Somehow I don't think he would have said that if I'd told him the whole truth. Even so...he's right.*

But all the old terror, Correy's legacy, was still dragging at Archer like an anchor, and he didn't know if he could slip that cable. He had to do that. He had to. If he held onto it, bottled it up as he'd been forced to before, he'd probably start having noisy nightmares again. Will would know for certain that something was wrong.

He had survived worse. He truly had. Adrian was a lecherous swine, but he didn't seem to be interested in beating his prey to a pulp, as Correy had done. It wasn't likely to be as bad as being wounded, which Archer had also survived. Or even that horrible infestation of bedbugs some of the men brought aboard from a whorehouse in Verona—it took a month to get rid of them, and every man in the crew had been covered in bites.

And with regard to vermin of various species...however threatening he was, Adrian was not Correy. Dangerous, yes, and smoothly vicious, but he had no chance to blackmail his victim, no power to ruin Archer's career and wreck the rest of his life. *He can't put me in more of a prison than I'm in now, or throw me overboard, or do anything much worse than kill me. Which he won't do if he can help it, because he wants the ransom.*

His duty was to do what he could to get them out of this. He was grown, now, no longer a frightened 16-year-old. It was not a task he would have chosen, but what he wanted was not the issue. This wasn't about what he wanted, it was about doing his duty.

More important still, it would keep the son of a bitch away from William. The way Adrian had looked at him, stretched half-naked on the gratings, twisted Archer up inside. *Leave him alone, you bastard. Keep your filthy hands off him!*

It was not just protectiveness. Archer had realized almost immediately that what he felt for William was far more than the love of a friend. His feelings went much further than the Articles of War permitted. The strength of the attraction shocked him; after Correy, desire for another man was the last thing he had ever thought to feel. But there it was, however futile. Still, if he wanted to keep Will's friendship, he knew he had to keep any other feelings entirely to himself.

He studied Will's sleeping face, so close in this tiny cell. The curly black hair was matted down with sweat, his mouth softened in sleep, the lines of pain eased by unconsciousness. William had been protecting him almost since they'd met, one way or another. He'd removed the towering threat of George Correy and set a standard of achievement that Archer found he had to live up to. His love for Will brought out a courage he didn't know he had on that French ship. William was always there—he had helped Archer master his panic in that damned waggon only a few days ago. It was not just life that Archer owed him, but the self-respect without which life was insupportable.

High time he paid back a little of that debt. And if he had to whore himself to do it...

Well, it wasn't as if that were anything that had not happened before. Last time, he'd sold himself for mere survival. Now, at least, he'd be doing his duty, helping his Captain, protecting his friend. That was worth the price. He would never be able to give himself *to* William, but he could give himself *for* him, shield him, and perhaps atone for the shameful, unnatural desire. If he were very lucky, this might even break him of it, as a horrible hangover might cure a first-time drunkard.

Not likely. When he considered William in that light, he felt only eagerness. He wanted to know how it would feel to hold him as a lover would, to kiss that soft sensuous mouth, to learn what he might do to give pleasure. But the thought of Adrian—the arrogance, the hands claiming his body, the ugliness of soul that would take pleasure in causing such pain to force service to his appetites... There was nothing in common between the two.

Except me.

And it was nothing new. He knew he could survive this. More to the point, Will might not. And to see his bright soul tarnished, beaten down... *No. Never. Not if I can prevent it.*

I don't think Adrian can possibly be any worse than Correy.

Oh, God...

Breathe.

Chapter 6

Captain Smith had just time enough for the ink to dry before he heard the footsteps outside his door. He looked over the missive once more; it appeared to be in order.

Adrian had come for it himself, this time. "Have you finished the letter, Captain?"

"Yes." He wondered if Drinkwater had been able to make any sense of his veiled reference to espionage. It was a long chance; the man would be knee-deep in the thousand important details that were by rights a captain's responsibility, and the reference would probably slip past him.

Even so, there was one small consolation: if Adrian had detected anything wrong with that first letter, he would not be standing there waiting for this one. "Twenty thousand for me and five each for my men," he said, passing the paper out through the bars. "That first seems a bit high, surely?"

"The three of you have already been more troublesome than any of my previous guests."

"I'm delighted to hear it."

Adrian took the page closer to the lantern outside—not, fortunately, close enough to warm the paper. "This appears satisfactory. I will send it on its way later this morning." He turned, then stopped as if remembering something. "By the way, Captain, I've decided how I'm going to punish one of your men for your little outburst earlier." When Smith merely frowned, he said, "Aren't you curious?"

"I'm not about to beg for clues; no doubt I'll find out eventually.

"No doubt. Well, then, if you have no questions..."

"I do have one. You appeared to be implying to Mr. Marshall that Mr. Archer had been the one who tried to escape. Was there a reason, or were you merely being...whimsical?"

"What an interesting way to put it, Captain. But yes, there is a reason. I find it useful to remind my guests they have only one another to blame for their misfortunes. For instance, this next time I will make it clear to...your young officer...that your noble and patriotic display is the cause of his discomfort. You will get full credit this time, Captain. Never fear."

"Piracy," Smith said, in the same conversational tone, "is something for which I may summarily hang a man, when I catch him, without the bother of a trial."

"But I have caught you, Captain, not the reverse. You seem to have an unhealthy preoccupation with hanging."

"I intend you will find it permanently unhealthy." Smith turned on his heel and extinguished the lantern. After a moment Adrian realized he would get no more amusement here. He left, slamming the door in a display of ill temper.

Alone, Smith sat heavily in the chair. It had been a risk to let the blackguard know he valued Marshall. It made a target of him. But not doing so might have meant his death. Of course, the best men were always the first to be risked, the ones sent into danger to get the job done because they stood the best chance of accomplishing it. Calculated risk, the daily lot of a ship's captain. And it never got easier.

He sighed. Damn that young man's impudence! A dozen would have been unpleasant; what he got for baiting the bastard would leave him barely able to move for at least a day or two. His defiance had been splendid to see, but hardly worth the cost.

Well, he was young, strong, and resilient, and, one could hope, intelligent enough not to make the same mistake twice. Archer had shown a fine spirit, too, snatching the opportunity to communicate even though he knew the risk. They had both demonstrated, in a way no argument could, that even the prospect of severe punishment was not enough to command their allegiance to anyone but their own captain. That one priceless moment gave him the chance to start undermining Adrian's hold on his crew.

Smith wished he'd had time to explain to them that the escape attempt had been his own, but those two would not need explanations. They would manage. They would recognize Adrian's games as clearly as Smith did.

He only hoped they would survive them.

Supplemental Log, HMS Calypso, in for repair, Portsmouth. Lt. Anthony Drinkwater, in temporary command. 19-7-1799

No further news. However, Ad. Roberts informs me that his recommendation to keep Captain Smith on the books of the Calypso has been approved, with the proviso that if he has not been returned to us by the time she is restored to seaworthiness, another captain will be assigned. The shipwrights have given me an estimate of six to eight weeks, and examination of the records of other abductions reveals that all abductees were returned within six weeks. It looks to be a near thing. We hope daily for contact.

"Wake up, Will."

Marshall was just conscious enough to find the tapping on his arm an intolerable nuisance. Then he realized he was lying on his face. Why in blazes had he tried to sleep this way? He pushed up on one arm, and a wave of pain knocked him down. And he remembered.

"Will?"

"Just—just a moment, Davy. I'm trying to decide if I want to wake up, or die now and get it over with."

"You must move."

He squinted at Archer. The sun must be just over their little port; it was almost bright in the cell. "Last night you said I had to hold still." He didn't mean to sound like a petulant child, but he was becoming acutely aware of how much the act of breathing shifted the muscles in one's back. It felt as though someone had poured molten lead from his neck to his waist and it had cooled just enough to immobilize him.

"Yes, but now you have to move about, otherwise you'll be too stiff to move at all. Wait."

Cool wetness eased the sullen heat, and he relaxed under the dripping cloth. "Bless you, Davy. Give me a moment."

He was just becoming halfway comfortable and dozing off again when Archer was back at it. "Get up, Will. Breakfast."

"Oh, for heaven's sake—" He gathered himself, started to push up, and decided it really wasn't worth the effort. "Why don't you eat it, Davy, I'm really not—"

"No." Archer put the plate down an inch from his nose. Two white objects rolled around beside a biscuit. "Look. Those hens I hypothesized must have outdone themselves, we've got boiled eggs this morning. Weren't you just wishing for eggs awhile back? Get. Up."

"This is insubordination," Marshall grumbled.

"This is my chance at revenge for all that gruel you shoveled into me when we had that fever aboard ship. Come on, William."

He gritted his teeth and tried to do it all at once, lurching to his hands and knees. "Damn it to *hell,* I'll have that bastard's guts for garters—"

"Swear all you like, but keep moving." Archer shifted the plate away and helped Will get vertical close enough to the bulkhead to lean against it sideways, leaning back being clearly out of the question for the moment.

"Thank you, Davy," he said when he got his breath back. "I do appreciate—"

"It's no more than you've done for me. Much less." Even though he'd accomplished his objective, Archer looked like he was on his way to a funeral. "I know I once said this would never happen," he said hollowly. "I wish I'd not been so damnably wrong." He pushed the plate over, and retrieved mugs of tea from just inside the door. "I should have ..." He shook his head.

Marshall had no notion why his friend was indulging in self-recrimination. "You weren't holding the stick, Davy. You weren't giving the orders. And unless you're some kind of twisted Machiavel who thrives on discomfort, you certainly didn't have us abducted."

Archer smiled, though it appeared to take some effort. "If I had, I would've hired someone else to do the job."

"I believe I can guess why he wants that list of prizes," Marshall said. He bit into one of his eggs and realized he was starving. "I don't know why I didn't think of this last night, but I'll wager he's trying to decide how high to set the Captain's ransom. Which really makes me wonder if this wasn't a very sudden decision—a change of plan."

"Do you think he intended to abduct someone else?"

"It would make more sense, Davy. This abduction ran as smoothly as a military exercise—it must have taken days to plan and prepare. He would've needed more time than he had notice we were coming. Put yourself in his place."

Archer grimaced. "No thank you."

"I'm serious. Suppose he was preparing to abduct someone—all kinds of people go through Portsmouth—and then he learned that the Navy's hunters had caught a fat prize and were bringing in three more ships. Even if he only asked for Captain Smith's share of the five ships we captured this time, he could probably retire."

"That does make sense," Archer said. "If we had tackled the door of that carriage just a minute sooner, the attempt would have failed. But if he'd only been expecting one person, and that one not used to battle—"

"Exactly."

"But how does that help us?"

"I don't know," Marshall admitted. "Not yet." He shifted his shoulders a bit, finding the limits of movement and forcing himself past them. "We can't know what information will be useful in the long run, but the more we know or can guess about our enemy, the better chance we have of beating him." Archer had cleaned his plate, which reminded him of something else. "Davy, is there anything more you remember from yesterday?"

Archer put the dish down, frowning. "What do you mean?"

"Any details, no matter how small. For instance, what does the bolt on the outside of this door look like? It was wide open last night, and when they first brought us in; I didn't see the design. If there were no one on guard to stop us, do you think we could get it open?"

"Oh." Archer closed his eyes briefly. "There are two. Well, one is just an iron hook-and-eye, level with the corner of the window. The sort of thing you'd find on a storeroom door, which I suppose this was. I think we might reach that one. The other is a plain wooden bar about a foot and a half below the window. It must weigh several pounds, but I think if we had a hook and line we might eventually open it. Anything else?"

"What's the arrangement in Adrian's cabin? Did the guards stay with you?"

"No." Archer gulped the last of his tea, picked up the plates and took them to the door flap. "There was no guard. But I was reminded that you and the Captain would pay if I...misbehaved." He looked around restlessly and went to the port, gripping the bar with both hands and peering up at the sky. "He had two guards just outside, in easy call, and signalled them before letting me out. I don't know if he changes the signal—he'd be a fool if he didn't—or what they might do if he didn't signal by a certain time. I was locked in there with him, Will—even if I'd somehow managed to kill him, they could've thrown you both overboard before they came in to settle with me."

What had him so jittery, all of a sudden? "Davy, I didn't mean to suggest you should've attacked him. That would have been dangerously premature. We need to at least know where the Captain is before we get to tactics. Though it's an idea, if you think you could take him."

"I wouldn't want to bet your lives on it," Archer said grimly, "or I'd have tried last night. Believe me, the thought did occur. I think he'd anticipated that I might try an attack of some sort; I was given nothing sharp enough to use as a weapon, and he watched me like a hawk."

"Was he armed?" Marshall finished his own tea and made the painful discovery that he couldn't stretch far enough to reach the door. "Damn!"

"Here." Archer added his cup to the dishes and pushed them through the flap, then checked outside the door and sat close enough to speak very quietly. "I never saw his back; he might have had a pistol behind him, in his belt. Wouldn't you?"

"Perhaps not. If he had guards close at hand, it might be safer to be unarmed; he could fend you off until they came to his aid. If he did have a gun, and you got it away from him, then he'd be the prisoner."

"And if I couldn't, he might blow a hole in his profits. Probably not worth the risk, either way."

"Do you think he's going to call you back soon?"

The color drained from Archer's face. He looked away and swallowed before answering. "I'm sure of it."

"Davy, what's wrong?"

He shook himself. "Nothing. Just—After last night, I don't—" He stopped, took a deep breath. "One wrong word, and you could be back at the gratings. Or worse. I'm sorry I'm such a coward."

He was working himself into a state, and Marshall couldn't see why. "That's enough of that!" He said it more sharply than he'd intended, but it did get Archer's attention. "Davy, when I was cornered in that powder room on the *Impulsive*, you got me out. I'd have been blown all over the Atlantic if you hadn't. I don't want to hear you calling yourself a coward ever again."

"That wasn't courage," Archer said.

"Oh, for—what was it, plum duff?"

"No. I—I was scared witless, Will. It looked certain we were going to be taken prisoner anyway. And I was going to have to watch you die first. I had to do something. I thought there was a chance and if I couldn't save you, at least it would be quick."

Marshall sighed in exasperation. "Well, Barrow said it was the bravest thing he'd ever seen, and I'm inclined to agree. If that happens to be how you define cowardice, you have my full permission to go on being cowardly. Just call it something else, if you please!"

He had meant to make a joke of it, but Archer only nodded glumly.

"Very well. Now, what about the deck? I thought I saw four small guns, maybe six- or eight-pounders."

"I saw the same. There might have been a little stern-chaser, as well. I couldn't be sure, what with the moonlight and other distractions. And if there's a stern-chaser—"

"— probably a bow-chaser, too. Six small guns. A merchant vessel, then. She almost has to be. Just enough armament for protection from minor piracy. There must be a perfectly legitimate cargo to cover what's really going on."

"And it's likely a cargo necessary to the war, or he'd have lost crew to the press gangs by now," Archer suggested. "He couldn't afford to keep losing sailors who know what he's up to. Sooner or later, someone would be bound to talk."

"That's true...Davy, that's brilliant! Even if we can't escape on our own, we've got him, now. All we need to do, once we're free, is get hold of the harbormaster's list of ships present on the 16th and 17th, and check their cargos. Busy as Portsmouth is, the list for two days can't be very long."

He really couldn't understand why Archer didn't share his enthusiasm.

Chapter 7

Supplemental Log, HMS Calypso, in for repair, Portsmouth.
Lt. Anthony Drinkwater, in temporary command. 20-7-1799

They are alive! Barrow has just brought in a letter from
Captain Smith, addressed to Port Admiral Roberts and my-
self. As the letter must be carried to Ad. Roberts directly, I
reproduce it here:

> *Sirs: I regret to inform you that Mr. Marshall, Mr.*
> *Archer, and I have been detained by a group of brigands*
> *who, as you are aware, have been conducting a series of ab-*
> *ductions for the purpose of ransom. They seem unconcerned*
> *with the damage this may do their country. At present we are*
> *at an unknown location and will apparently remain so until*
> *ransom is paid. Unfortunately, our abductors have not yet*
> *set their price on us, so we must waste yet more time await-*
> *ing their decision. Please contact my business agent immedi-*
> *ately and ask him to see to it that funds are available com-*
> *mensurate with what has been previously demanded by these*
> *criminals. I would prefer to have my agent deal with the ran-*
> *som for all three of us; the fewer details involved, the less*
> *delay. I enclose a letter to Mr. Archer's father, the Earl of*
> *Grenbrook; please see that he receives it with all due haste.*
> *As I would have likely taken a brief shore leave while re-*
> *pairs were effected on* Calypso, *I hope the Admiralty will*
> *consider this excursion as that leave. Mr. Drinkwater, I have*
> *every confidence in your ability to manage the situation; it is*

no more complex than the one we faced off France last summer. Please assure the men that we shall return as soon as possible; I have every expectation that this should be well before Calypso *is ready to return to service. If for some reason our hopes are not realized, please enter into the record that Mr. Marshall and Mr. Archer have conducted themselves with fortitude and valor as shining examples of England's finest; and tell my wife and family that my thoughts were with them, as they are with you all.*

I have the honour to be (Etc.)
Captain Sir Paul Andrew Smith, (Etc.)

Mr. Korthals is continuing to direct the search for the man who paid a boy to carry this letter to our crewmen. We do not hold much hope, as the child (age 6) is quite incoherent with excitement due to the effect his errand had on O'Reilly. (Mr. Bowles has succeeded in extricating O'Reilly from the constable's clutches; O'Reilly' vehemence in detaining a passerby who resembled the child's description, who, as it transpired, was not the right man, had caused him to be taken into custody.)

"Stand away from the door."

The order came almost as a relief to Archer, who had spent the past day and a half in continual anxiety. After yesterday morning's dithering, he had done his best to hide his nervousness from Marshall, who of course had no way of knowing what the problem really was.

It helped that William had his own body's distractions to contend with. He had slept a long time but seemed to be mending rapidly—so much so that he had already resumed wearing his uniform shirt and waistcoat, though he was not yet ready to button the latter. Only someone who knew him well would notice the slight delay and stiffness in his movements as he got to his feet.

The routine was a repeat of the one two days previous,

with one startling difference: the guards, different ones this time, ordered Archer to stand back, and Marshall to come forward. He blinked, started to reach down for his jacket—and Archer scooped it up to conceal the fact that Will couldn't move that quickly. He helped his friend into it, and brushed off clinging bits of straw. What was going on? They'd got it wrong, they shouldn't be taking Will—
"To what do I owe the honor?" Marshall asked.

On cue—the allusion was unavoidable—Adrian stepped into the doorway. "You can thank your captain for this, Lieutenant. That stirring speech of his cannot go unrewarded."

Even having to stand slightly stooped, Marshall, his face blank, somehow managed to look down at Adrian. "I'm not in proper dress for the occasion; if you'll give me a moment—"

"Oh, I'm not letting you back on deck; we've had quite enough attempted rabblerousing, I don't care to see if it's a family trait. I also doubt you're ready for another session with the bosun. Unless you insist."

Apparently Marshall considered Smith's order to restrain himself as ongoing. Without a flicker of expression, he said, "Not at all."

"And your manners are improving. Excellent."

Giving Archer a smile over his shoulder, Will stepped outside. "Until later, Mr. Archer." The routine with the cloak was repeated on him, the only difference being that the door was not closed. Archer kept an encouraging smile pasted on his face until the hood blocked Will's view, then he let numbness steal all expression. He had dreaded this moment for himself; he had not realized how much worse it would be to anticipate it happening to his friend. But why was Adrian doing this?

Three guards took Marshall away; Adrian had brought two more with him, who remained in the hall. "Well, Mr. Archer, are you ready to dine?"

What? Oh, thank God. So that wasn't where he was taking Will. Archer let himself breathe again, but his stomach still felt like a lump of ice. "Unless you find it stimulating to watch a meal retrace its passage, I would rather not bother with food."

"Such eagerness. I'm flattered."

A dozen cutting replies crossed Archer's mind; he bit them back. Despairing of an answer, he asked, "What are you going to do to him?"

"A rather ingenuous question, don't you think?" Adrian ran a finger along Archer's jaw, tsk'd at the stubble.

"Not at all." Ingenuous? That he'd worry about William? What was the bastard playing at? "I—I was under the impression that we had a bargain—"

"A gentlemen's agreement?" Adrian seemed about to laugh.

"If you like." Gentlemen? Hardly. "At any rate, an agreement that Mr. Marshall would come to no harm if I were to..." He swallowed, the bitterness rising like gall. Bad enough to contemplate, how to put it into words without sounding like a dockside whore? "...to...attend you in your cabin..."

"Willingly?"

He was smiling now, damn him. "No. That is not possible. But...without contention."

"Do you really think you could contend against all my men?"

Archer quelled a flare of anger. "I have lived on His Majesty's warships since I was 16," he said carefully. "I have survived battles where men were slipping in the blood that ran along the deck. Surprising as it may seem to you, I do know how to fight."

With a little shock he realized that was the truth, and it gave him strength enough to say the rest. "If you did not hold hostages, yes, I would fight you." *You condescending bastard.* "I expect you'd kill me, but I would do my best to take at least some of you with me."

His captor laughed aloud. "Ah, so there's steel in the sheath. Even better." He stroked Archer's hair. "So much more rewarding to master a spirited creature. I don't doubt you will do your best, laddie. In time."

Was there anything he did not turn into a double entendre? Standing rigid, ignoring the touch, Archer tried to sound reasonable. "You see my point, I'm sure. I am only trying to determine whether I have an accurate understanding of our—agreement—and whether you intend to honor it."

"Yes, I see." Adrian's hand closed around the tail of hair at the base of David's neck, and Archer held very still, barely breathing. "But surely you realize that our agreement is not the only element in play here. I could scarcely overlook Captain Smith's behavior and expect to maintain discipline, you know. I thought I was extremely generous in giving your friend a day's respite."

He let go, but leaned closer. "Allow me to ease your mind. At the moment, Mr. Marshall is facing only a spell of close confinement." He patted Archer's shoulder in false reassurance. "Don't worry, laddie, you'll get him back, safe and sound—when you've fulfilled your part of the bargain."

Archer could think of no response, but it seemed none was expected. Adrian was speaking to hear himself speak.

"Think of it as an incentive. As to his situation in future... I am a gourmet, not a glutton. I appreciate Mr. Marshall's considerable charms, but I shan't concern myself with them until I have had my fill of yours. So his welfare rather depends upon you, don't you think?"

So William would be, if not safe, at least a little removed from danger. For the moment. "I think...." Archer swallowed. "I think my actions really matter very little. You might prefer me to believe his safety rests in my hands, to hold me responsible should you decide to torment him further."

Adrian laughed. "You are perceptive, laddie, but you underestimate your own appeal. I intend to enjoy you slowly and thoroughly. But since you mentioned fighting, let me warn you—your friend will indeed be punished for your transgressions. I insist upon your full cooperation. If you think to refuse me anything—*anything,* mind—he will be back at the gratings. Three strokes for every 'no' you utter. Do you understand?"

Archer nodded once, not really surprised.

"Good. I may as well inform you now, regarding other offenses, so you will not waste time considering them. If you kill any of my men, Mr. Marshall will lose a finger for each death or serious injury. An eye for an eye, so to speak."

"You care so much for your men?" It seemed inconceivable.

"I do not wish my tools destroyed," Adrian said with a shrug. "If you merely injure anyone, I shall turn your friend over to the crew for a space of time determined by the severity of your offense. There are no few who would enjoy him, and none of them are as considerate as I. If you raise a hand to me—pay attention, now," he said, lifting Archer's chin with one finger "— he's for the gratings, then the crew, and then the gelding knife. I have a man who lived with the Turks for a year or two; he can do it so fast your head would spin. Do you understand *that?*"

"Yes," Archer whispered. His head was already spinning. Christ. What kind of madman had they fallen in with?

"Yes, what?"

"Yes—" His voice squeaked a bit; he cleared his throat and met the icy stare. *No. I will not call you 'sir' unless you order it.* "Yes, I understand."

Adrian smiled, apparently choosing not to acknowledge his minor rebellion. "I'm so glad. If you should happen to kill me, the crew has permission to do what they like with all of you. I have naturally left instructions for your friend to be killed as well, but they may choose to have him ransomed, or sold into slavery in North Africa. That, by the way, is what will happen if for any reason we are unable to ransom you. A good merchant knows many ways to turn a profit."

He caught one of Archer's wrists and held it up, observing a slight tremor in his hand. "Fairly quivering with anticipation. Perhaps I should send my barber down to help you shave."

Archer closed his fingers into a fist and twisted it away. "I'll manage."

"In the finest naval tradition, I'm sure. The shaving gear will be here shortly."

He left and swung the door shut, then looked in through the window. "Please don't think about cutting your throat, Mr. Archer. I'd have to send your friend back to clean up the mess."

"I wouldn't give you the satisfaction." Archer was amazed at how steady his voice was, and pleased to see Adrian at a momentary loss.

But he had to have the last word. "That would hardly be my first choice. Don't dawdle."

Archer kept his composure until the man had gone. Then he sank down against the wall, wrapping his arms around himself. *How will I ever—Never mind how. Just take one moment at a time. Don't think. Just breathe.*

The shaving things appeared. Archer looked at the razor for a long moment. No. Somehow, even when things were at their worst with Correy, suicide had never seemed a possibility. And in this situation, it really would be the coward's way out.

He shaved by touch, not carefully; there was no way to prop up the mirror where he could see it, and he really did not give a damn. Halfway through, it struck him that he had been genuinely relieved to find that Adrian had not arbitrarily decided that Marshall would be a more entertaining dinner guest. William's safety truly meant more to him than his own. The thought was somehow heartening.

I wonder how Will would deal with this.

To his very great surprise, he realized that the answer was, probably, not very well. That notion was startling. But when Correy first started pushing, testing the newcomer, Will had fought. Never mind that he had been alone, that he had no way of knowing that Correy was a bully who only attacked when he was sure of winning; Will simply stood up for himself, even though his life had been on the line.

In this situation, though, he'd dare not fight. William would risk his own life, but not theirs. He would ultimately be forced to submit, and Archer had no doubt that his determination would hold...but it would damage him, take some last bit of innocence he probably didn't even know he had.

And that's not a problem for me, is it? Not anymore.

At any rate, this was not Marshall's demon. It was his own, and no one else could face it for him.

A fatalistic calm settled over Archer as he wiped his face, put on his jacket, was muffled and escorted above. His hands felt like cold stone, his mouth so dry he might have been chewing cotton. What was it Captain Smith had said, a thousand years ago, in the waggon? *"There are some circumstances that put us entirely at their mercy. And sometimes there is no mercy to be had."*

"Let him think he's won. Play for time." I hope to God the Captain's plan is working. I hope he really has one.

Fourteen steps from the hatch to the quarterdeck. Down three steps. And the cloak came off and one guard knocked at the door and Adrian waited within with that smug, self-satisfied smile.

No mercy to be had.

I'll just have to manage without it.

Chapter 8

When we get back to the Calypso, I am never going belowdecks again. Marshall didn't really mean it, but he was almost ready to volunteer for another beating if it meant he would be able to stand up straight for a little while.

Adrian apparently had a strange sense of humor. He'd simply had Marshall moved from one small space to another space that was the same overall capacity, but instead of a room six by six by eight, this was a storage locker four feet high, six feet deep, and nearly a dozen long. Mathematically, in fact, it was exactly the same size as the room he'd been in for the last five days, but this was one case where mathematics did not tell the whole story. The thing was half-full of scraps of old sails, and Marshall was fairly certain he was not entirely alone in here; to be sure, all ships had rats, but from the squeaks and rustling he knew that he was tremendously outnumbered. He had never had any great fondness for rats, and being in such close quarters was giving him a sincere aversion to their company.

He slipped and scrambled to the far end of the locker, where a louvered vent let in a little light and sea air. Propped open to one side was a shutter that could be slid into place to close it against bad weather. He was glad they'd left it open; he never would have found it otherwise.

Marshall pressed his face against it, and saw the late afternoon sun dancing on the water. It was not until then that he realized how much he had missed the sight. Being shut up in that cell had been wearing at him without his even knowing it.

A deep breath of daylight helped. Very well, he was in a long narrow box, with rats. He wasn't going to get much sleep between now and whenever they let him out. What could he do in the meantime?

Get the place in order, for a start. If he'd been in charge of the men responsible for this mess, their ears would be singed. He took off his jacket and waistcoat and laboriously began folding and shifting the bundles of canvas until he had cleared the four feet of decking below the vent, then made a stack of larger scraps that would serve as a seat of sorts.

It took time, and he found himself having to rest more often than he expected; his back was taking its time healing. Perhaps the exercise would help speed things along. Having something active to do gave an unexpected boost to his spirits, at any rate.

As he worked, he discovered that many of the sails had been torn or cut raggedly, and the threads could be unraveled. What was it David had said—that with a line, they might get their door unbarred? If he were here long enough, he might be able to braid one out of this stuff, or at least unravel a supply they could work on in the cell. He didn't think he'd be searched when they took him back, and rope was always useful.

He sat on his little divan, leaned back—and arched forward with a curse. Better not try that, yet. He got up and shifted the canvas so he could lean sideways. That would do, and he had a couple of feet clear in front of him; nothing would be able to creep up without his seeing it.

Until it got dark. Dear God. They could come at him in the dark.

Well, all this canvas had to be good for something. A smaller piece, rolled up, would serve as a kind of bat to fend off anything he might see or hear. That took only a moment, and he felt slightly better with the flimsy weapon in hand. Rats weren't completely stupid; he had nothing for them to eat. Even if—oh, Lord, he mustn't think about it—even if the half-healed stripes on his back smelled attractive, he was too large to be easy prey, and if he made enough of a fuss, the vermin would learn to leave him alone. They got in here, there must be a way for them to get out.

While he had light, he decided to clear a little more room. He toyed briefly with the notion of heaping the old sails in front of the door, blocking it, so they'd have to dig him out.

But that would be a waste of time. Antagonizing the guards would not make them more amenable to Captain Smith's offer. And, after all, he wanted out as soon as possible. He wanted out of here right now.

Not likely.

He returned to folding and stacking the sails. The rat-noises seemed to have diminished; maybe they'd decided to go somewhere quieter. *Yes, go away! Go bother your damned captain.*

I wonder if he's taken Davy off to dinner again. That would make sense. If Adrian did not realize that any information Archer gave him was already cleared by Marshall, he might think it would be clever to hold the interrogation while Marshall was out of the way. Or he might threaten to separate them until Archer gave him the list. In which case, with luck, he might not be here too long.

He hoped Archer had been able to settle down a bit. David had no reason to feel responsible for that beating. Neither of them had any control over Adrian's whims, and Marshall strongly suspected the whole business was just a game, anyway. Somehow, as painful as the experience had been— and still was—it had not been as bad as he'd expected. The helplessness had been the worst. And it wouldn't matter much, in the long run, if Adrian decided to knock him around a bit more. Davy shouldn't let it bother him, it wasn't worth agonizing over...though he would have felt terrible, himself, if their positions had been reversed.

He had another couple of feet clear. That should do nicely. *The rats can have the first six feet, I'll take the second.* Marshall picked up one last scrap, shook it out and something dropped from the canvas, hit the deck, and rolled. Something metallic.

Supplemental Log, HMS Calypso, in for repair, Portsmouth. Lt. Anthony Drinkwater, in temporary command. 20-7-1799

More news! Upon rereading Captain Smith's letter, preparatory to sending it to Ad. Roberts, I was struck by his reference to a previous expedition to France which was required to be carried out in considerable secrecy. After that adventure, Capt. Smith discussed with me the desirability of documenting the conduct of activities that must be done in secret but may later be subject to official scrutiny. To that end, he has been investigating various substances that may write invisibly and yet be revealed when the paper is subjected to proper treatment, usually heat. Hoping that my surmise would prove correct, I conducted an experiment upon his letters with our cook's flatiron. The letter to the Earl is only that, but the other is a treasure trove! Again, I reproduce the captain's words so that we may retain a record:

Well done, Mr. Drinkwater! Abducted in carriage by sham Lt. who has left the area. Waste no time on him. Driven through countryside in freight waggon, then, I believe, returned to P'mouth & brought on board between 3-4 am, in biscuit barrels; find ship that took on provisions at that hour. Ship's captain calls himself "Adrian." My height, age appx. 30, red hair, beard, athletic build. Well-spoken, well-organized, arrogant. All crew aboard masked in our presence, & seem to be a mix of ratings & landsmen. I am held separate from the others; if you find this ship, a surprise attack in force holds the best chance of extricating us alive. Any approach <u>must</u> be clandestine; these blackguards have spies in Portsmouth, quite possibly even on HM's ships. I will, of course, try constantly to effect our escape independent of your efforts, & I am certain Mr. Marshall & Mr.

Archer will be doing the same. Good hunting!

Smith

The wind had shifted. The cell was cooler tonight. And empty. They had not brought William back, after all. Was that really such a surprise?

He hasn't gotten everything he wants, yet. Christ, how long is this going to take? Archer gave up trying to catch sight of the moon, and dropped back down to the straw. He didn't want to sleep. There was no escape in dreams, anymore; Adrian followed him even there.

Whatever he had expected after that string of vicious threats, it had not been a bizarre parody of seduction. After seeing Will beaten, he'd expected something like Correy's treatment; being thrown over a barrel and raped was painful and humiliating, but soon over. Instead, he had been treated as though he were actually there of his own volition. Apparently Adrian had decided that he would eventually induce cooperation if he drew the process out long enough.

Does the son of a bitch think he could ever do anything that would make me want him? Does he think I'm going to forget what Will's back looks like?

Or maybe it was just clever strategy. Archer recognized the effect this treatment was having on him, even as he observed it. His own reaction last night, before they took Marshall away, had been relief at an end to the waiting. And now... Rationally, he was relieved that he had experienced nothing worse than being stripped, fondled, and forced to bring that bastard to release with his hands. The memory made his skin crawl.

Still, he was relieved that Adrian had, so far, not actually caused him any real pain. So far...so far it had not been too bad. Reason said he should be thankful.

But stronger than reason was an overriding desire to just get it over with; at one point he had caught himself about to say as much.

That would have been a mistake. In the first place, there was no reason to expect that anything would be over. This would probably go on until they were released, or found a chance to escape. And anything that might be interpreted as carnal desire—which was surely how Adrian would interpret it—should be avoided.

Besides, his real task was buying time. Adrian seemed to have his own timetable for this procedure, likely something he had worked out on previous "guests," if his bragging was to be believed, and accelerating the pace would be worse than useless.

Could that son of a bitch's claims be true? Out of nine abductions, could four women and two boys in their teens have simply gone back to their lives and said nothing about having been mistreated in such a fashion?

And what are you planning to say about it, Archer? Whom would you want to tell? Your captain? Your family? Perhaps your dearest friend?

Of course the others kept quiet. The boys, certainly. And the women... Unless Adrian got some poor unmarried girl with child, his victims would have no reason to make the shameful truth known. They would bury it deep, and try to forget. No doubt Adrian would claim their silence was because they had enjoyed his attentions; he was so damned full of himself he probably even believed it.

Archer drew his knees up, rested his arms and head upon them. What he wouldn't give for a pistol. If he could only kill Adrian somehow, surely the Captain could convince at least some of the crew to help.

Unless one of the crew, acting on orders, killed Smith before he could open negotiations. An attack was too dangerous to try at this point. Will could make that decision; Archer wouldn't dare. He could not be objective.

Besides, he had no weapon, and he knew, now, that he would need one. A gun, for preference; a sword, perhaps... a knife would put the odds well in Adrian's favor. For all his affectations, he was quick, and surprisingly powerful, strong enough to pin both Archer's hands with one of his own, holding him helpless, bending him backwards and off-balance while the other hand moved down—

No! Archer jerked upright, shaking off sleep. He leaned over to the washbucket and splashed water on his face. This was not going to work. Sooner or later, sleep would overcome him. He had hoped Will would be back when he returned, with some plan or idea that would at least be a distraction. And, however false the sense of security might be, the cell felt safe when William was here.

Perhaps it was better that he was not, at least not until Archer could collect himself and decide what to tell him. But where was he? What if Adrian had William up in his cabin now? *No. He was yawning when he let me go. The bastard has to sleep sometime. I don't think he'd be fool enough to tackle Will when he was tired.*

Not yet, anyway. Thus far, his attitude toward Marshall carried none of the smug assurance he displayed toward Archer. And he would not have asked, slyly, "Do you plan to tell Mr. Marshall how you spent the evening?"

When hell freezes over.

Another thing Archer needed to do was determine whether he was going to start having screaming nightmares again. So far, he had not. For all its similarities, this situation was different from the one with Correy, though he was not sure exactly what the difference was. Back then, he had just tried to ignore what was happening, block it out. He had spent whole days on the *Titan* when he could not have said, from one minute to the next, exactly what he'd been doing. It had felt like being mildly drunk, just enough to numb his feelings. And then he'd climb into his hammock and wake up with someone telling him to be quiet, and he'd be all right for awhile, until Correy started in on him again.

Now... At some point this past evening, the numbness had evaporated. He was still afraid, still revolted...but at the same time he had a sense of standing just a step back from it all, in some safe vantage point, and knowing that whatever Adrian might do to his body, there was a part of him the bastard couldn't touch.

It felt oddly like what had happened when he'd run into that powder room after William. Part of him was terrified, but that other self had a broader view and knew that either way, live or die, he would be satisfied with the outcome. He knew that the pain of seeing William hurt or killed would be worse than death. Perhaps that was it—the consolation of knowing that he was shielding the one he loved.

He wondered if this might be some odd kind of courage, but that hardly seemed likely. If it were courage, he would not keep wondering where Will was, and fearing that Adrian had decided to separate them permanently. Courage should feel stronger; it should banish uncertainty. And courage ought at least to be of some use against this damnable loneliness.

Supplemental Log, HMS Calypso, in for repair, Portsmouth. Lt. Anthony Drinkwater, in temporary command. 21-7-1799

No further news.

Chapter 9

A t the sound of footsteps outside the door to his odd little
prison, Marshall shook himself out of an exhausted
doze. As he straightened, every muscle in his body protested.
He turned just enough to see outside, and realized that the
sun was in almost the same position as when he'd been put
in here the evening before.

If he'd realized he would be in here this long without
food or water, he would have wasted less energy on tidying
the place and might not have been so dizzy and lightheaded.
But maybe the effort was not wasted; he now had the whole
room cleared, and the rats had not bothered him, even in the
dark. Unfortunately, he'd had to stay awake to be sure of
that, and he felt as though his brain were stuffed with oakum.

He might try to overpower the guard...no. Not from ten
feet away. By the time he'd levered himself off his stack of
scraps and covered half the distance, the door had opened, a
bucket was pushed inside, and the door was pulled shut. A
cup floated in what smelled like water; he checked first, then
poured it down his parched throat. "Thank you," he called.

"Stand away from the door," someone ordered. Marshall
moved back a couple of feet, but the door opened only a few
inches. He could see nothing but a hand on the latch. "You in
there. Marshall."

"Yes?"

"Cap'n asks you, don't mention the water. Our orders
was to put you in here, that's all. We've got no orders about
takin' you out or feedin' you. But you're supposed to stay

alive an' healthy, so, somebody comes to get you, just pour out that water, understand? Hide the bucket."

"Yes. I understand. Thank you." The door started to swing shut. "Wait!"

"No tricks!"

"No, no." He wished desperately that he weren't so stupid with weariness. "You heard our Captain—Captain Smith—the other night?"

"I heard 'im. Talked pretty big for somebody's locked up."

"It's not just talk. He wouldn't say anything unless he meant it. Talk to him yourself. If you help us escape, you can come, too, he can see you get protection—"

The door shut abruptly, and the sound of footsteps died away. Stooping, Marshall took his prize back to the vent and built a stack of cloth to keep it up off the floor, then rewarded himself with another drink, savoring it this time. It was amazing how wonderful a cup of stale, lukewarm water could taste after a day without.

So what did this mean? If his thoughts weren't whirling so, they might make more sense. Did they have an ally among the crew now, or was it simply some sailor who was slightly more compassionate than his fellows and willing to take a small risk? Or was this some convoluted game of Adrian's? If so, there seemed little purpose to it, unless he thought it would be worthwhile to tie up his prisoners' time and attention in attempting to bribe guards who were trying to elicit such attempts?

Marshall shook his head and tried vainly to retrace the logic of that thought. It made far more sense to act on the simplest explanation: somebody realized that a dehydrated prisoner was more likely to fall ill, which would mean more work for everyone, and "anticipated" that the reasonable order would be to provide water. That did, of course, require an assumption that Adrian was giving reasonable orders, which in Marshall's mind was no small leap of faith.

But, assuming the simpler cause, he now had two pieces

of information that suggested Adrian's hold over his crew was not absolute. First the water—but also the disarray of this storage area. A captain who was paying proper attention to the condition of his ship would not have tolerated this mess. It would, at least nominally, be an officer or bosun's responsibility...and that was another odd thing: Adrian seemed to have no second-in-command, no one who would oversee the details that a captain shouldn't be bothered with. Granted, it was a smaller crew than would normally be found on a ship of war, and fewer officers were necessary. But none at all? And was this how he always ran things, or a recent development?

And the item Marshall had found last night—part of a carpenter's tool, possibly an adze—had been tangled with wood splinters and a couple of feet of footropes in a piece of torn topgallant. Somebody had obviously broken the tool while ripping the rigging from a spar, then bundled the whole mess up and stuffed it in here. Even if the tool had broken in an emergency—a storm, perhaps—on an orderly ship it would have been removed from the cloth scraps and taken back to the ship's carpenter.

Suspicious as he was of Adrian and his games, Marshall refused to believe that the tool had been deliberately left for him to find. The man was devious, not stupid; the metal fragment was four or five inches long and tapered to a sharp edge. He could use it as a weapon—a poor one, but enough to do considerable damage.

What he was beginning to suspect, though, was that Adrian might have decided to put him down here for the duration of their stay. *God, I hope not.* He looked outside again, recognizing that the sparkle of light on the water was beginning to fade. It would be dark soon, and he wasn't going to be able to stay awake indefinitely. And the rats were still there.

⚓ ⚓ ⚓

Supplemental Log, HMS Calypso, in for repair, Portsmouth.
Lt. Anthony Drinkwater, in temporary command. 22-7-1799

No further news.

Archer pushed a fragment of beef across his plate and trapped it with his rounded butter knife. He was now allowed silver utensils, though not a sharp knife. *I wonder how long it will be before he stops waiting for me to ask about William.*

But he would not ask. He would not do anything that might bring William under Adrian's scrutiny. He probably would not see either his friend or his Captain until this ordeal was over, one way or another; he was trying to resign himself to that, and was determined not to let on how much the isolation wore away at him. There were worse things than being alone. If it came to a choice between solitude and present company...

Adrian had been insistent that he sit down to a meal before whatever else was planned for the evening, and Archer had seen nothing to be gained by resisting. He hadn't felt like bothering with the food that had been brought to the cell for breakfast or dinner, though he had left the biscuits tucked into the port vent in case they brought William back while he was gone. They wouldn't, of course. Better not to hope. Still, his stomach was letting him know it had noticed the omission, so he ate. It was fuel. If the food had flavor, he was not aware of it.

"How was your day?" Adrian inquired, as though this were a perfectly normal social occasion, rather than a slow circling of prey by predator.

"Tedious." The sense of detachment was very strong. What exactly would happen, if he refused to follow the script? There seemed so little to lose that he gave in to the temptation. "Now I'm supposed to say, 'and yours?' and exchange meaningless pleasantries." He glanced up. "Is this charade serving any useful purpose?"

"Other than amusing me, not really." Adrian took a sip of wine. "But your question is equally amusing. I had not anticipated it. I find that refreshing."

"Even a mouse will occasionally bite," Archer said.

The cold eyes narrowed. "Not literally, I hope. Or your friend will find himself singing soprano."

"I meant it metaphorically, of course," Archer said quickly. He decided it would be prudent to omit the remarks about food poisoning that leapt to mind. "Would you like me to review the rules?"

"That's not necessary." Adrian had taken far too much pleasure in his first recitation of his 'rules,' and there was no hope of forgetting them. "I am to do exactly as you tell me, without resistance, or my shipmates will suffer, isn't that correct?"

Adrian relaxed a trifle. "Essentially, yes."

Archer bent his head over his plate and made his face a studied blank. Was this weird feeling the sort of thing that had compelled Marshall to defy Adrian at the gratings? It was not courage; he was sure of that, now. Perhaps it was some bastard offspring of fear. He felt as though he had been so frightened for so long that the emotion had burned out like a carbonized lampwick.

It left him feeling curiously free, and the sensation was most unsettling, since the situation really was dangerous. Even if he no longer cared what happened to himself, the others were depending on him. He had to tread carefully; Adrian seemed to sense that something in the balance of power between them had undergone a subtle shift.

"The question is," Adrian said abruptly, "can I trust you?"

Trust? Detachment deserted him as sudden rage fought to answer. *How dare you ask me that!* Archer was grateful for the past years' practice in disciplining his emotions. If he showed anger, or even laughed, there would be hell to pay. But to play the craven...

He took a breath instead, and met the colorless eyes.

"Not even for an instant," he said levelly. "But my shipmates can."

Supplemental Log, HMS Calypso, in for repair, Portsmouth.
Lt. Anthony Drinkwater, in temporary command. 23-7-1799

No further news.

Night and day, and now night again. The North Star vanished into the same clouds that had swallowed the moon. Before long, there was nothing to be seen through the little port but darkness as deep as that inside the room. Marshall let his head droop against the louvers and wondered how much risk he would really be running if he let himself sleep for a few minutes.

Except it wouldn't be a few minutes. If he fell asleep now, he would not wake before morning. Unless his four-legged messmates woke him. They were livelier at night, it seemed; from the sound of it, they were holding a party in the far corner.

They can't keep me in here forever.

Oh, no? Why not?

I wonder if it's true that talking to oneself is a sign of madness. Or is that only true when one starts to answer?

"I'm just tired, that's all," he said aloud. The party in the corner fell suddenly silent at the sound. "If you don't take your festivities elsewhere," he warned, "I'll sing to you." There, that ought to frighten them. He enjoyed singing, but his more musical shipmates had complained that he could never hit the same note twice, so he generally restrained himself.

I wonder if making idle threats to rodents is a sign of anything. Frustration, for certain.

He wondered whether he would have any chance of getting to Davy or the Captain if he used the metal scrap he'd found to pry loose the door of this locker. If he could do it. Far more likely he'd just attract the attention of whoever was guarding the door; he had no doubt someone was out there. And they'd just take the tool away. Better to wait until he was back in the cell—unless, God forbid, it began to look like he'd be here indefinitely.

At least he had water, now. He celebrated the fact by raising a half-cup. He was trying to ration it out, not knowing how long it would have to last, and had only drunk about a third of the bucket's contents. For the time being, his stomach had stopped expecting anything else; he didn't feel hungry anymore, just listless. Not a serious problem. Yet. There had been days in the Horse Latitudes, when the ship was becalmed, when the whole crew had lasted five days with nothing but rainwater, and it had been hotter during the day there, and colder at night. *And I have no duties to keep me busy; I can rest.*

He'd had his fill of resting.

He tried stretching, just to remind himself how it felt, and discovered his back really couldn't move comfortably just yet. When it was light he might lie down on the floor full-length for a little while, rats be damned.

But the pain was worth it. For all he knew, Smith might already have an insurrection organized. Well, no, probably not; not this soon. At best, a crewman or two might be considering whether their luck was coming to an end, and weighing the Captain's reputation against what they knew of their current commander. Most would probably stick with what they knew rather than take a chance; that was true of people in general.

He had exaggerated—though not by much—when he told Archer that Smith would take control of the ship. All they really needed was to get a boat over the side. They wouldn't need many confederates. Someone to unlock the cell doors in the wee hours might be all that would be required—a handful of men on watch, who could escape with them and help row the boat.

Escape.

For some reason, he kept thinking of Archer, remembering the stricken look on Davy's face as the guards had taken him away. What was worrying him so? Yes, being separated was unpleasant, but hardly the end of the world. Of course, Davy didn't know that all they'd done was lock him up here; he might be imagining the worst. For all Marshall knew, Adrian might have said he was going to put him on the rack, or some other outlandish threat.

Or was it that outlandish? Yes, of course; he was tired, he was not thinking clearly. If anything really hideous had been done to the other folk who'd been abducted, Captain Smith would surely have said something, or at least would have seemed more concerned. He had sounded more angry than worried.

But that was before they were brought aboard, before Adrian started his power games. The whole situation had changed very suddenly, from nearly unbelievable to painfully grim. This business of the "escape attempt" that apparently never happened—was it because they were Royal Navy? Had Adrian realized the stakes had been raised, and responded with a preemptive attack? Too many questions, and no answers, and Marshall knew his mind was too foggy to make sense of any of them. There were only two questions that mattered, really: what was happening to David and Captain Smith...*and when in God's name are they going to let me out of here?*

Chapter 10

Smith opened his eyes in the darkness. Had there been a sound? The lantern outside the door was so dim it barely gave any light, but he saw a faint silhouette at the bars. "Cap'n?"

"Yes." Not one of his own men; pity. But not that snake of a pirate, either. Smith climbed out of the cot and approached the door warily. "What is it? And where's your watchdog?"

"Gone to the 'ead with a bellyache. 'E'll be awhile. I wanted to ask you about what you said the other night."

Smith recognized the man; it was the one who had reported his initial offer to Adrian. Bert, the other guard had called him. Bert, who apparently was Adrian's right-hand man. Or was he? "What of it? I do not propose to see my men mistreated again because your captain is bored."

"At's what I wanted to talk to you about, sir. The Cap'n's got us all in deeper'n I ever signed on for."

"What did you sign on for?" Adrian could hardly punish Marshall or Archer if one of his own men were loquacious. No, belay that; he could and would do anything he thought he could get away with, regardless of what any of them said or did. "Abduction seems a risky line of work."

"I signed on because nobody else'd take on a man on the run from a charge o' thievery. We had a hangin' captain, an' I've got a wife an' two kids."

"What did you steal?"

"Not a damn thing, Cap'n. But the goddamn crooked

purser said different, an' him bein' a warrant officer an' me a
gunner's mate, who'd you think they listened to? Cap'n
Adrian, 'e's got a whole crew o' men with black marks on
'em, and most earned 'em fair."

"Why?"

"This damn' ransom business. 'E wanted men as
wouldn't care about stickin' it to the nobs. It was funny, at
first—'e kidnapped 'imself to make sure it'd work."

"He what?" Smith could hardly believe his ears. "Are
you telling me that the first abduction was a test?"

"Yessir. An' it worked. But the cargo's honest, mostly."

"What is it?"

"Gunpowder. The pay's good."

"Because it's a risky cargo." And vital to the war, so his
crew would have protection from impressment. Shrewd. And
it spoke of influence, that he could get a contract for ship-
ping powder. Everything he'd just heard confirmed Smith's
original estimate of Adrian. "And you want out. Why now?"

The man chewed his lip. "Cap'n, I've wanted out since
the first time somebody got killed. A coachman, 'e was,
tryin' to protect 'is lady. Takin' money from them's got
more'n they need, that's one thing. Like Robin Hood, and
the crew gets shares, same as with a prize ship. But this ..."
He shook his head. "Even Cap'n Adrian's partner left a couple months back. Least, Cap'n said 'e left. Disappeared one
night when we were in port. 'E might've left on 'is own."

But, his expression said, he might have gone over the
side in the dead of night, with a weight at his feet. "So the
situation is deteriorating—I mean, it's getting worse," he explained, when the man frowned.

"A lot worse. And I think you've got 'im worried, too."

"Good." It was no more than a fair exchange. Smith was
inclined to believe this man; his years of command had de-
veloped a certain intuition regarding crewmen, and this one
felt more honest than his helpful, pigtailed shipmate. Besides, there was no need for such an elaborate story, and it

made sense, which was a first on this mad ship. "What about my men?"

"Well, the tall one with the mouth on 'im—" Smith had to suppress a smile at the description, "— Cap'n's put 'im in the sail locker night before last, no food or water, that's for you talkin' on deck. I dunno when 'e's gettin' out, I think the Cap'n's forgotten 'e's in there. But I took 'im some water yesterday, an' you wouldn't believe it, 'e'd cleaned the place up."

That definitely had the ring of truth to it. Good to know that Marshall was fit enough to engage in such activity. "And Archer?"

"Cap'n's 'ad 'im up for dinner, two, three times now. Supposed to make the other lad jealous..." He frowned, seeming about to say something more.

It was no news that Adrian was the sort to engage in stupid games. "I doubt it will matter to either of them."

"No, sir. But it's a bad business..." He looked down the companionway nervously. "I'll hear 'im comin' but it won't be long now. You meant what you said about amnesty?"

"I'll sign you on my own ship, if you do your part, and no questions asked. But I need to know more. Where the devil are we? How far—"

Footsteps interrupted him. "Not now!" hissed Bert. He took two long steps away from the door and slouched against the bulkhead. By the time the door creaked open, he was deep in the process of stoking a stinking clay pipe—not a smart habit on a powder barge, but he didn't seem to be having any luck in lighting it.

Smith heard the other guard enter with some comment about things being quiet, and made certain his return to the cot was noiseless.

⚓ ⚓ ⚓

"Hey! Wake up, in there! Time to go."

Marshall shook his head, trying to loosen the fog. What

time of day or night—? The moon was up outside, so high he could only see its reflection in the water. Late, then. Seven bells, maybe eight. Well, it didn't matter what time it was, if they were ready to let him out. "Just a moment," he called.

"Hurry it up."

He checked to be sure the shard of broken adze was still rolled in an edge of his shirt, tucked tightly beneath waist-coat and breeches, and took a last drink from the nearly-empty water bucket before tipping it over behind a stack of sailcloth. Then, a bit wobbly, he made his way to the hatch.

Not knowing whether either of the masked guards was his unseen benefactor, he greeted them pleasantly, where-upon they went through the routine of tying and muffling him. They didn't say where they were going; they didn't say anything. But when the cloak came off, he was outside the familiar cell, and he was able to confirm Archer's observa-tion of the door latches. If he had not been at least half-awake for the past 60 hours or so, he might have felt more satisfaction in the fact; right now, he was so exhausted he could barely feel his fingers.

Archer was curled up in the corner, his back to the door. He looked to be sound asleep, and Marshall managed to ar-range his own sleeping-mat without waking him. The straw smelled fresh; sometime in the last day or so, it must have been swept out and replaced. Top marks to the innkeeper. Marshall rolled his jacket into a pillow and had a long, luxu-rious stretch before sliding into blessed oblivion.

⚓ ⚓ ⚓

"No, laddie, that wasn't what you were expecting, was it?" The weight rolled off his back, the hardness that had been pressing against him was gone. "We'll get to that, no need to hurry. The Frenchie who showed me this called it frottage. Pleasant, don't you think?" One hand gripped his shoulder as he buried his head between his arms, trying to disappear into the cushions piled on the floor; another rubbed oil between his thighs. "But I'm not finished yet. Roll

over now, I want to watch your face..."

"No!" Archer rolled and pushed away in a panic, banging into a wall in the dark. His own shout woke him. He sat up, the wall at his back, and tried to slow his breath enough to stop his heart hammering. Not Adrian's cabin, back in the cell, it was all right, just a dream, he was alone, safe for now...

Something stirred nearby. He was not alone.

"Davy? Are you—"

"Will?" *When did he come back? This isn't real, is it? Oh, God, am I awake or dreaming?* He really couldn't tell.

"Keep quiet in there, damn you." Footsteps clumped up and somebody held a lantern up to the door's window. "I got a starter out here, if we have to come in you'll both feel it."

"Bad dream," Marshall said shortly, scowling in the dim light. "We're awake now, thank you."

The ill-tempered guard apparently decided it was not worth the trouble to open the door. "Keep it quiet, then."

Darkness again. But that glimpse was enough. William was back, alive and whole and apparently quite cross. Archer swallowed, half-afraid to test his perceptions.

"Will. Are you all right?"

"Yes. You?"

"Well enough. Where were you? When—"

"Davy." A warm hand settled on his arm. "It's good to be back, I've things to tell you, but right now I'm so tired I can't even think. Can it wait a few hours?"

"I'm sorry. Of course it can."

"Good." Marshall gave his arm a little shake. "We'll talk later."

William lay back, took one deep breath, and seemed to be asleep almost immediately. Archer settled down himself, his mind whirling. When had they brought him back? Was this real? In the dark, it was hard to tell what was real and what was wishful thinking, but the slow, steady breathing beside him sounded exactly as it should.

He reached out carefully, not touching William but letting his hand get near enough to feel the heat of his body...and then he drew back, feeling foolish. He would know in the morning. Not long, now. It had to be very late, or very early; he hadn't been brought back himself until two bells, and it had been a very long time before he'd slept.

Sleep was dragging at him now. It was almost as if relief were making him tired...or letting him feel how weary he really was. Archer rubbed at his eyes and was startled to find they were wet. The sense of detachment he'd felt earlier was gone; in its place was a mix of joy and fear. His dear William was back. He wasn't alone any more.

And once again, he had something to lose.

Chapter 11

Supplemental Log, HMS Calypso, in for repair, Portsmouth. Lt. Anthony Drinkwater, in temporary command. 24-7-1799

No further news. Acting upon Captain Smith's instruction to identify the ship that took on supplies the night of the abduction, we have been checking records. Unfortunately, many of the ships that sailed with the tide the morning of 17-7-99 had taken on provisions the night before. Even eliminating naval vessels, at least for the time being (a ship in active service sails under orders, and the presence of three captive officers on board could hardly be overlooked!), we are obliged to consider some 20 ships of varying size, as there is no way to be certain exactly when they took supplies on board. I am awaiting the ransom demand with the hope that the Captain will be able to provide some small details that will narrow our search.

Archer opened his eyes and took a deep breath. He felt good. Rested. Almost his usual self. How very strange.

"Good morning, Davy."

"Will!" He sat up to find Marshall sitting tailor-fashion beside the door, smiling, his hands busy with a ragged piece of string. "You're back. It wasn't a dream."

"Things do seem a bit unreal in the small hours, but I appear to have served my sentence. Wait." He stood and checked at the door, then lifted the flap at the bottom and peered out at floor level. All clear, apparently; he turned back. "Davy, look what I found."

He held out a piece of metal. Archer examined it. Something like a chisel, but curved, and rough at one end. "Part of some kind of tool, isn't it?"

"It's part of a way out." Marshall nodded at the port vent. "We'll have to work at night, and very quietly, but I think we can get that bar loose. Have you been here all the time? Were you here when they changed the straw?"

"No. Adrian's been having me up for dinner the nights you've been gone." *And for dessert afterwards.* He bit his lip and put the thought out of mind. "I've been gone an hour or more each time. I think they cleaned it last night."

"Then they don't examine the port hatch carefully. I found this—" He pulled a bundle from behind him, the wrapped biscuits Archer had wedged in the hatch. "I ate one of them. Sorry."

"That's why I left them there, Will."

"Oh. Thank you. Now, from what I remember of that other night—" William arranged straws on the floor, "The hatch was here, the masts about here and here." He glanced up, and went on, at Archer's nod, "I don't think our port can be too far from the base of the mizzen rigging. If we can get out, we might be able to go right up the side."

"Where did you get this?" Archer gave the tool back; Marshall wrapped it in his shirttail and tucked it into his waistband.

"They put me in a sail locker that looked as though it hadn't been cleaned in months. It was a shambles. Adrian may flail about threatening to shoot his crew, but there's a lack of practical discipline on this ship. And I got this from unravelling sail." He pulled wads of thread out of his pockets. "We should be able to twist it into twine, I remembered what you said about getting the door open. We don't have a hook, yet, but—" He frowned. "What's so funny?"

Archer could not keep himself from laughing. "They lock you up to punish you and you come back ready to scale the battlements. I'm not laughing at you, Will, I'm thinking of that bastard's face when they come down here and find us gone."

"What I'm hoping to do first is go out very late and scout around the deck. If he had the whole crew on deck to watch him put us in our place, they don't number more than 50— less than half the crew of a fighting ship. With half of them asleep, and at least four outside the cells guarding us and the Captain, there should not be many on deck in the late watches. I want to see if we're in sight of land and find out where the Captain is. Davy, the other night, did you see which direction they brought him from?"

"Larboard, I think." He closed his eyes and tried to picture the scene. "Yes. They brought him across the deck, even though they took him below starboard."

"Then he's most likely opposite where we are. I doubt they'd have more than one or two cells, you can't kidnap large numbers of people quietly and they'd be too much bother."

"Two cells," Archer said. "That's one thing Adrian let slip; it seems bragging is a hobby of his. He's mainly confirmed what the Captain said: he's done this nine times before, usually taking one person, sometimes with a servant. I think this is the first time he's caught three at once. You guessed right, too; it's mainly been wives and older children, the youngest a boy of 14." Another mental path he was not going to follow just now. "Splitting parties up and using them as hostages against one another is part of the drill. I gather we've drawn the servants' quarters."

"It's better than the midshipman's berth on *Titan*," Marshall said. "Except for that bar on the door."

"And the guards outside."

"Yes, but we may be seeing results of the Captain's efforts there, soon. One of the guards brought me water one night, Davy, and asked me not to tell that he'd done it. I didn't see who it was, but I repeated the Captain's offer and told the guard to talk to him if he could. We'll see what may come of that."

He seemed pleased; Archer grimly realized that Adrian had meant William to go two and a half days without water, in high summer. And longer without food, counting from dinner three days ago. "Why don't you eat that other biscuit, Will?"

"If we're getting breakfast, it should be here soon. Otherwise, we'll share. Apart from supper, have you been fed?"

"Better than you."

"Davy, stop that," Marshall said patiently, returning to the threads he'd been twisting into string. "It's what he wants. I'm supposed to be jealous of you, and you're supposed to feel guilty. Don't let him do that."

"Doesn't it bother you at all?"

"It bothers me that we're here. The rest of it..." William shrugged. "This is war; he's the enemy. He may not think in those terms, but that's what it amounts to. We can't afford to waste our energy on his little diversions. Remember, a prisoner's duties are survival, escape, and sabotage. Remember that examination question the Captain gave us: how do we escape and turn the tables on Adrian?"

Archer nodded.

"Anyway, I think you should dine like a king, considering what you're having to put up with."

Oh, my God—how—? Confused panic froze him for a moment; he felt stripped naked. "What—what do you mean?"

"Having to spend all that time with his Royal Arrogance. That sneaking pirate carries on like he's heir to the throne." Marshall looked up and frowned. "You know, Davy, the other night you said you thought he was a gentleman. I think you're right. Maybe even more than that; he acts like he's very well-born. Raised with privilege, but no respect for others."

"Yes," Archer said, smothering his relief. "There's something about his attitude that reminds me of my brother Ronald."

"I'm sorry to hear it. Is he your father's heir?"

"No. Mark is all right. He's 12 years older than I. We've never been especially close, but he'll be a good Earl. Very steady, down-to-earth, cares about the land. Ronald was born second—well, third, really, my eldest sister was second—but he acts like the lord of creation. And he has that nasty streak, too. I don't think he's ever forgiven my mother for producing Mark first."

"It must be nice, though, having a big family." Apart from a couple of cousins somewhere, Archer remembered, Marshall was alone now; his father had died about a year ago. "How many of you are there?"

"Seven living. Mark, Mary, Ronald, Anne, Amelia, me, and Eugenie. The four eldest are married, now, and it gets a bit chaotic at holidays, with the nieces and nephews. At least, it used to, but I don't expect that's changed much; I've not been home for a holiday since the war began, and Anne had twins last year. You know, Will, if we ever have shore leave in London, you should come home and meet my family. Some of them are always in Town, even in summer."

"I'm sure your father would be delighted," Marshall said skeptically.

"Why not? You're a perfectly respectable officer in His Majesty's Navy, you're my friend, you don't have family of your own in England to visit..." Marshall looked so serious he could not resist teasing. "...and my father still has two daughters to marry off."

Marshall's eyebrows flew up, and Archer laughed again. "Honestly, Will, after some of the characters I dragged in from my undesirable haunts, I'm sure he would be delighted." And the girls would be delighted, too, he realized with a melancholy twinge. What an ironic twist that would be, if William were to marry one of them. But it would be a blood tie, a kind of closeness to bind their friendship...the most he could ever hope for.

Will had the strangest expression on his face, as though the idea of anyone being pleased to meet him was beyond the realm of possibility. "You should start thinking ahead, you know," Archer told him in all seriousness. "Nelson wasn't born an Admiral—and he was a minister's son just as you are. Before too long you'll be Sir William, I'm sure of it. You need to start meeting people."

"The Captain joined at 12 and it was 23 years before he had his own ship." Marshall shook his head. "If it took him that long... I'll be happy if I make Captain by 40."

"It won't take that long," Archer said. "Not if the war lasts, and peace doesn't look to be breaking out anytime soon."

"We should think about your promotion first," Marshall said. "When is the examination scheduled?"

"Yesterday, I think," Archer said with mild regret. "It was supposed to be on the 24th, wasn't it?"

"Damn! Well, whenever you take it, as long as you pass, all this time as acting lieutenant will count."

Right now, rank seemed quite insignificant. "I just want to get out of here, Will. There will be other examinations. I can wait." If a sorcerer were to offer a trade—all future promotions in exchange for Adrian falling overboard immediately—he'd happily spend the rest of his life as a midshipman.

"You will have to, I suppose. But you're right. We need to concentrate on escape. We should start getting some exercise, to be sure we can manage that port—"

Archer held up a hand. "Someone's coming."

Marshall stowed his string and shifted over to where he was visible when the guard looked in. They must have looked innocuous; he ducked out of sight and breakfast slid under the door. Oatmeal, biscuit, a couple of apples, and tea. A feast.

"I thought so," Marshall said. "When we're together, the food games stop. He's becoming predictable."

The day went by too quickly. They sorted out Marshall's hoard of thread and twisted it into ten feet of twine that could be doubled or tripled into a cord heavy enough to pull the door bolt, if they got the chance and something to hook onto it. They worked out a tentative escape plan: if they could get out the porthole and see land, they would immediately try for the Captain. If they were out of sight of land, or if the odds seemed overwhelming, they would wait and see whether Smith could manage anything with the crew, and try to reach his porthole from the outside.

After they ate, William calculated that he had spent 65 of the previous 72 hours trying to stay awake. He was determined to spend as much of the night as possible working on the wood that supported the top of the porthole bar, hoping to loosen it in a way that would allow the bar to stay in place unless pushed out. The practical thing to do would be to sleep away the daylight hours, so he settled down and was dead to the world almost immediately.

Archer tried to follow his example, but found himself unwilling to spend the time unconscious. They had come for him at eight bells the night before; assuming tonight would be the same, he had another four or five hours of peace, and he wanted to enjoy them. Without Marshall's energetic optimism, though, he soon found himself going round and round the same thoughts, like an ox propelling a millstone. Sooner or later, they'd be back. Sooner or later, he would have to face Adrian once more.

But now there was hope. There would be an end to it; Captain Smith might recruit help, and William was going to get that port clear by sheer determination, if necessary. Well, they'd both be doing that: one to work, one to keep watch. And even if none of that got them out, the ostensible point of this exercise was to exchange them for ransom, so one way or another there would be an end to it.

That could not come soon enough.

He could not reach the porthole without disturbing Will, so he closed his eyes and tried to imagine himself as far away as possible. Back home at Christmas, or on the streets of London, or sitting in the theatre waiting for that little stage to be magically transformed into another time and place...

But those memories seemed too far away now, part of a

world that was no longer his. The one image that he could call up clearly was of the time he had first climbed to the main topgallant yard to find out whether he could really see all the way across the Channel. The sun was so bright, the sea a blanket of diamonds, the wind singing, and the heady sensation of freedom stronger than any drink.

He had tried to explain that in a letter to his worried sister, when Amelia had expressed dismay at the size of the living quarters aboard *Calypso*. What difference did it make if you slept in a berth two feet by six? Cramped quarters didn't matter if you were only in them when you slept. Up on deck you had the whole world, farther than the eye could see. And 100 feet above that, up in the rigging, the only one with a better view was God Himself. There was nothing like it in the world...

"Davy." He opened his eyes to find Marshall kneeling beside him, his expression sober. "They've brought dinner for me and the shaving things for you. Your presence is 'requested and required...'"

Chapter 12

There was not enough room to pace in Smith's quarters. He paced regardless, diagonally, having set the chair and table in a corner. By now, Drinkwater should have at least received the first letter, and perhaps the second as well. How long the second took would depend in part on how it was sent; if Adrian put a courier aboard some ship that took it by sea, it should be there already; if overland, it could take much longer. Smith suspected some connection with smugglers, another effect of having a crew drawn entirely from the wrong side of the law; they would have contact with all manner of clandestine activities.

That guess depended, of course, on whether Bert had been telling the truth, but no honest crew would participate in a string of kidnappings and murders. Adding to the man's credibility was the fact that the better part of a day had passed with no untoward effects of their conversation; apparently he had not reported it. If Adrian was becoming unstable, it was quite likely before too long Smith would hear from others who wanted a way out when their intrigue fell apart.

He hoped that Drinkwater would find the hidden messages and use the information to good purpose. He had considerable faith in Drinkwater's intelligence, but he could make no plans based on assistance from that quarter. If he got it, well and good; all he and the others would have to do would be to stay alive until this ship was secured. Otherwise, he would have to make do with two sound men, one agent, and whatever other assistance he could lure away from this crew.

But even one secret ally might be enough, if he could manage to be in the right place at the right time. Although the rotating watch schedule for guards would complicate that in one way, it helped in another. Any unauthorized contact with Marshall and Archer might be more dangerous than helpful, but since the guards did change, sooner or later he should be able to pass a message to his men so they could coordinate their efforts.

He needed more information, first. Without knowledge of the ship's location and course, Smith could only guess at the various possibilities. Assuming the worst, they might be well out from shore, if this ship was making deliveries to ships of war on patrol in the Channel. The only time they would have a decent chance at escape would be when another ship was near, though that would actually give them a good opportunity: three naval officers in dress uniform fleeing a merchant ship would certainly seize the attention of anyone aboard one of His Majesty's vessels. Unfortunately, he had heard nothing so far to suggest that was happening. The shutter over his port would undoubtedly be closed if another ship were near.

The way they'd been sailing, deliveries to shore batteries were more likely; those could be accomplished by anchoring and sending the powder ashore in boats. That would also fit with the odd timetable Adrian had set for the ransom note; it made no sense that he would send that first letter, then follow up with his demands the next day, unless he had some means of transporting the note from wherever they were. Having the second letter arrive from an entirely unexpected direction would also make tracking them more difficult.

Escaping to shore, if the shore was close enough, seemed the easier plan so long as the weather held fair and Adrian did not have confederates ashore. That was unlikely. Having a conspirator in every port would mean too many men to pay off and guarantee that sooner or later, the secret would out.

If the sea was calm they would not even need a boat to escape; with small barrels to keep them afloat, they could slip over the side and reach the shore inconspicuously. Even those along England's coast who turned a blind eye to smugglers knew His Majesty's Navy kept them safe from invasion; most of them could be relied upon for assistance. It was not unreasonable pride to expect seafaring folk to recognize the name of Captain Smith of the *Calypso*.

Smith hoped that Adrian was too overconfident to realize that once they left the ship—assuming they left it alive—this would be his final abduction. He might mask himself and his crew, but in his eagerness to demonstrate his power over his prisoners, he had let them see far too much of his ship, which in its own way was at least as individual as one of her crew. Any of them would recognize the configuration of sails, railings, and guns the next time he saw them.

Once they were back on board *Calypso,* all the Admiralty had to do was assign them to a few weeks of channel patrol. There were not so many merchant brigs carrying powder that this one could disappear among them. Really, it should not even require a patrol. The harbormaster's lists ought to give them Adrian's real identity, as captain and probably owner. But Smith would greatly prefer catching him with a fully-armed frigate, not a clerk's dusty papers.

Of course, Adrian could avoid the risk by tipping them all overboard once he had the ransom. As he might, if he intended this to be his last venture into such a high-risk enterprise. If that were the case, though, they should by rights be dead already. From what Smith remembered, the exchange in earlier cases had not been direct; the money had been delivered, the prisoners returned later, at another location.

He had been instructed to order a particular signal flown from the *Calypso* when the ransom was ready; presumably Drinkwater would be contacted once more, with instructions for delivery. Smith wished he knew more about the procedure; another question to ask his informant, although in all likelihood an ordinary sailor wouldn't know much. Somehow, Drinkwater would have to find a way to watch the ransom and follow it—Drinkwater, or whoever was assigned to make the delivery. Smith hoped that Admiral Roberts would make use of the *Calypso's* dry-docked but highly motivated crew to retrieve her missing officers.

Still, he did not want it to come to that. Considering the opposition, if he could not find a way to extract them from this situation himself, he hardly deserved to be ransomed.

⚓ ⚓ ⚓

Dinner in the captain's cabin was excellent. Again. Except, of course, for the presence of the captain. Archer dealt with the food automatically, always aware of Adrian's eyes on him. Oddly, there was very little conversation; this change in the routine worried him.

"Well, Mr. Archer," Adrian said, at last, lounging back in his chair when the meal ended. "Tell me, have you been enjoying Mr. Marshall's company?"

Archer didn't look up. "Yes. Thank you." Adrian certainly had the knack of attacking at the point of greatest weakness. But, of course, he had been studying his prey for some time now, and this was probably his chief source of amusement.

"I'm so glad. It seemed that you were a little...dull, yesterday evening. Of course, I could spend more time with you myself, but I do have other duties."

"Please don't trouble yourself on my account."

"Oh, it's no trouble, I assure you. But it is more efficient to have you both in one place. Has Mr. Marshall recovered from his unpleasant experience of the other evening?"

Was this another threat? Safest to assume so. A reminder, at any rate. "I believe he is better," Archer said cautiously, staring at a glint of deep red reflected in his wine. William was in fact doing very well, now that he'd finally had some sleep. Just about now he was probably considering exactly how to address the issue of escape with that metal thing he'd found. "I have no intention of doing anything that might result in another 'unpleasant experience' for him, if that's what you're suggesting."

"Of course not. I was merely wondering if you had decided you preferred separate quarters. And do try that wine. The Spanish call it sangria. I find it's a painless way to absorb a ration of lemon juice. See what you think."

The Borgias' own recipe, no doubt. Archer raised the glass. The flavor was sharper and sweeter than he'd expected, an interesting contrast to the spicy stew that had been the main dish. Better still, he didn't have to respond immediately if he were drinking, and a little alcohol would dull the edge. "It's very good. As to the accommodations..." If he let Adrian see how much Marshall's company meant to him, Will would be thrown back into that filthy cubbyhole on the slightest pretext. But if he pretended he wanted to be alone, Adrian might call his bluff. There was no winning; it was Adrian's game. Archer shrugged. "The fact that we are still your 'guests' makes it clear that what I prefer is completely irrelevant."

Adrian laughed. "You are stubborn, aren't you, laddie? I don't quite own you yet, do I?"

You never will. "If you'd rather I kept silent?" Archer offered, sipping at the wine. That would be so much easier than this fencing.

"Oh, no, this is far more amusing. The contrast of physical compliance and verbal rebellion is quite piquant. I keep anticipating that moment of surrender. It reminds me of another recent guest—a charming lass, an Irish girl."

Archer said nothing.

Adrian rattled on. "Stunning little thing. Porcelain skin, jet black hair. She was just a maidservant; her mistress was so pleased with my company that we had to keep them on an extra week before I could persuade her to go back to her stodgy husband. But that maid! Screamed like a banshee, but after a period of training and adjustment she became very...fond...of some of the crew."

There was a certain fascination in listening to the man talk; it was amazing how he could make something so ugly sound so innocuous. "What became of her?" Archer asked, playing the game, wondering if the girl had actually existed at all. He hoped not.

"She was a troublesome wench. I passed her along to the crew; I think they finally threw her overboard." Archer's stomach twisted. "Or the cook spirited her away. She may still be down in the galley, for all I know. Of course her mistress didn't ransom her, the girl knew far too much about what she'd been up to, not that anyone was likely to believe her."

He seemed to be speaking from a great distance. Archer blinked, rubbed his eyes. Something was—not exactly wrong with him—but not quite right. His eyelids seemed heavy, though he had certainly had plenty of sleep. And, oddly, his breeches felt uncomfortably confining.

Then he saw Adrian grinning like a red fox and his mind intuitively made the jump. "What—" His mouth was not working properly; he had to concentrate. "What did you put in the wine?"

"Just a drop of laudanum, laddie. I'm going to be busy tomorrow night, so I wanted to make this evening memorable. I want you nice and relaxed."

"Very well." Quite deliberately, Archer picked up the cup and drained it.

Adrian only laughed. "Oh, excellent! There's not enough to put you to sleep, if that's what you were hoping." He laughed again at Archer's expression. "It was, wasn't it. I am sorry to disappoint you. Come along, now."

Archer had to concentrate again, to remember where he'd put his feet, but he managed to stand unaided. Then he focused on Adrian, saw that he was holding a length of rope, and found that the thought of being tied down and completely helpless woke the fear he thought had been burned out. He tried to make his voice matter-of-fact. "That—that really won't be necessary."

"I should hope not. But do you know, I find I sometimes enjoy it, after all. I think you might fight this time, even though you know better. Did you really think I couldn't tell you've been resisting all along?" He doubled up the rope and tucked it into his pocket, reached for Archer's neckcloth and began working the knot apart. "But this evening I decided to expedite matters. The laudanum, to relax you...and a bit of Spanish fly in the stew, as encouragement. You've been curbing your instincts long enough, I think. Tonight I am determined to see some response to all my efforts."

Pulling the neckcloth free, he slid his hand down inquisitively, and Archer was horrified to feel his body react to the touch. Adrian smiled broadly, steering him toward the bed. "Yes, indeed, it's time to get you out of uniform. I can see I'm going to enjoy the evening's amusements, laddie...and so will you."

No, I will not. And Laddie is what my father's sheepman calls his colley dog. Archer knew what was coming this time; why Adrian expected him to enjoy it, Spanish fly notwithstanding, he could not imagine. But the laudanum was beginning to give him a sense of being wrapped in cotton wool; that ought to help. He could...perhaps he could ignore the other sensations. And in an odd way, he was pleased that Adrian felt uneasy enough to take precautions. He was not considered an entirely safe target, after all. *You don't own me, you bastard. And I will kill you if I can.*

Chapter 13

Supplemental Log, HMS Calypso, in for repair, Portsmouth. Lt. Anthony Drinkwater, in temporary command. 25-7-1799

We have received a second letter from Captain Smith. I do not reproduce it, as it states simply that they were all alive as of 19-7-99; the fact that he does not add "and well," and a comment in his secret communication, give me some cause for concern. Ransom is set at £20,000 for the Captain and an additional £5,000 each for Mr. Marshall and Mr. Archer. When the ransom is ready we are to fly "enemy sighted," which I must assume is this pirate's idea of a joke, from Calypso's sole remaining mast, and will expect to hear shortly thereafter regarding delivery. This letter contained a second secret note, including a sketch of the ship's deck with mast and gun placement. We will know it when we see it! I here reproduce the letter and the sketch:

Mr. Dr: Ship is merchant brig. See sketch/masts. Light arms, at least 4 sm. cannon, prob. bow/stern chasers. Commendations to Marshall & Archer for courage under extreme difficulty. One crewman claims to have seen damage to Calypso: short, wiry, balding, thin pigtail, moves like sailor. Possible ally or spy for captain. Ask Admiralty to investigate deserters/cashiered officers fitting Adrian's description who left service shortly before abductions began, correlate with ships in port 17/7/99.

A Drinkwater—Private entry, personal journal:

I have not included in my report to Ad. Roberts a private postscript, writ small, that Captain Smith appended to the bottom of his last letter. We are sailing in deep waters, and it appears that our adversary may have powerful allies. If, God forbid, we lose our officers, I shall be forced to make this document public, but for now I am keeping it secret in the hopes of avoiding a scandal.

Mr. Drinkwater, cut this postscript from the letter. ***This is a direct order and I take full responsibility.*** *I regret burdening you with this knowledge, but I fear you may receive less than wholehearted cooperation from high places. "Adrian" may be difficult to trace, as there will likely be rank and political influence involved. We are dealing with a rogue, a man of rank who has turned. Although not as clever as he believes himself to be, he is unstable &, I believe, much more dangerous than a simple pirate. If you succeed in boarding, make him your primary target; the body of the crew may be reasoned with if the head is removed. Shoot him on sight. If he is captured, and I am dead, hang him immediately for piracy; he must not leave this ship alive.*

⚓ ⚓ ⚓

The morning of their tenth day as prisoners looked bright and clear; a sliver of sunlight came through the barred port. Marshall scratched another line beside the tally he and Archer had been keeping on the wall, and returned to his mat. He was weary, and knew that this was the sensible time to rest, but sleep would not come.

He was disappointed at how little they'd been able to accomplish the night before. He was now certain that they could get out this way, and he had pulled on the ropes supporting the shutter hard enough to be sure they would take his weight. But it was slow work. The frame of the port, an eight-inch oak beam, had been set into timbers that filled in what must have originally been a gunport; Marshall's guess was that this was a former warship that was still seaworthy but no longer structurally sound enough to support cannon recoil. Holes had been bored into the frame, and the bar set into them. Which meant that if he could dig an angled groove into the top beam and cut out a notch above the bar, the bar could be slipped out and replaced, held perfectly upright in its track in the lower beam.

So far, though, he had dug out barely an inch. They had worked for a couple of hours, but dawn came early this time of year, the adze blade was none too sharp, and they had to do the work as noiselessly as possible. Marshall's back was not ready for an all-night stint of work in such a contorted position, either; his shoulders had seized up long before he had wanted to quit.

David had taken a turn at woodcarving, but his arms weren't quite long enough to reach out, around, and above the bar at the necessary angle, and he was very tired when he returned, almost dead on his feet; Marshall finally had to tell him to stop trying. They would be at it for at least another two nights. Longer, if Davy was going to be kept out past midnight and come back groggy and out-of-sorts the way he had last night.

Marshall had tried to find out what went on at dinner, but Archer's answer was vague: "Very little. He talks, endlessly, about all the people he's held prisoner and how amazingly clever he is. Or he drags out that list of prize ships, and tries to find inconsistencies in what I've told him. Or he does something completely irrational. Last night, for some reason, he kept me tied to—to a chair—for a couple of hours, while he sat and read a book. Not aloud, mind you. Just reading to himself."

The contrast in David's mood had been so marked from earlier in the day that Marshall was worried. Perhaps the irritability had mainly been lack of sleep. Or was Adrian doing something else—waging a war of nerves? The notion of him puttering around his cabin with Davy sitting there tied up certainly did not sound rational. Granted, the man was amoral, and Marshall knew firsthand that he enjoyed demonstrating his power, but what was the point? Was he actually mad—or slipping into madness? There was something dangerous going on, and Archer seemed to be the focus of it; his nightmares said as much.

As if he'd heard the thought, David started to mutter and shift restlessly, as he'd been doing off and on since they'd settled down, just before dawn. Marshall reached over and rested a hand on his arm, trying to keep the worry out of his voice. "It's all right, Davy, everything's all right, go back to sleep."

That calmed him for the moment, even if it were not completely true. Damn that bastard. Why Archer?

Well, he answered himself, however irrational Adrian might be, he had enough sense not to play such games with Captain Smith. If he had even tried, he would not have gotten far. And he might have decided that the Captain's supposed "cousin" might be an equally tough nut to crack. But Davy...Davy had been unconscious when they arrived; Adrian had probably thought he'd fainted from fright, and like any bully, he went for the first sign of vulnerability like flies to a wound.

The bastard would not have been so sure of himself if he'd ever seen David Archer in battle; he'd been given command of the prize ship *Fifine* because he'd led the boarding party and captured her captain. But this was nothing like a fair fight. Archer was bound by the knowledge that anything he did or said might trigger a reprisal against the others. A nasty little trap from a nasty little mind. Would it be worth another beating to see Davy sink a fist into that supercilious smirk? Oh, yes.

But, however satisfying, that would take a day or more off their escape time while he recovered. If they used a cat-o'-nine-tails, as Adrian had threatened, maybe longer. Or they might just put him back in the sail locker, with its four-foot ceiling and a port too small to climb through. They might do both...or even separate him and Archer permanently. Not only would that wreck their best chance for escape, it might endanger Davy, too, if the nightmares grew too noisy and out of control.

No. Marshall rubbed his eyes, which were now refusing to stay open. They would have to play out this hand as it was dealt. If the sessions with Adrian got too much for David, surely he would say something?

No, probably not. He was too worried—needlessly—about proving his courage. *I'll just have to keep an eye on him, see if there's anything I can do.* Which, realistically, would probably not be much.

Archer made a small unhappy sound; Marshall patted his arm again and shushed him. *I'm sorry, Davy, you're going to have to bear with it a little longer. We'll get out of this as soon as we can, I promise.*

⚓ ⚓ ⚓

Supplemental Log, HMS Calypso, in for repair, Portsmouth. Lt. Anthony Drinkwater, in temporary command. 26-7-1799

No further news.

⚓ ⚓ ⚓

Captain Smith noted the arrival of dinner with little interest. He had seen no sign of his potential ally since that first encounter three days earlier. He realized that an irregular rotation of guards would mean long intervals where no contact was possible; that made the delay no more tolerable. The information he needed could be obtained in a minute or less: where was the ship, how far from shore, what was her course; where were his men; where were the weapons kept? With those questions answered, he would have the basis for strategy.

In the meantime, however, all he could do was eat what would probably be a reasonably palatable meal. Tea, biscuit, some sort of stew, an apple: quite normal shipboard food. He hoped Marshall and Archer were faring as well, and wondered whether they had been considering that last examination question. There had to be a way out of this, and he fully expected that the two of them would eventually come up with something. They had, after all, been under his command for more than a year and had been reading from his own library of naval and military history. They were bright young men with keen minds, and Marshall was particularly creative.

But he ought to be doing more himself; it was hardly fitting for the captain of a frigate to sit about waiting for a junior lieutenant, even a remarkably inventive one, to initiate a rescue, and it went against the grain to let someone else take the initiative.

His spoon clinked against something in the stew. It felt like quite a large object—a chunk of bone, perhaps, or even a rock; peculiar objects occasionally found their way into ships' supplies, since they were usually opened far from the place of purchase. It had been years since he'd had to watch out for such oddities, though; the *Calypso's* cook was conscientious about what went to her captain's table. Ah, well, a sharp, good-sized piece of bone might be useful as a tool.

He tilted the bowl and scooped, and stared at the object for a moment before recognizing it: a large, well-worn clasp knife, garnished with a couple of split peas, and a slice of carrot stuck in the hinge.

⚓ ⚓ ⚓

Dinner for the *Calypso's* most junior officers—both of them—arrived an hour or so before sunset. Archer looked at the second plate as though he expected it to explode. Marshall could see nothing alarming in the hash of beef and potatoes, nor the biscuit beside it. The mug of strong tea was even better. "What's wrong, Davy?"

"Nothing," Archer said, with a cautious smile. "Nothing at all. Something may be right for once." At Marshall's look he explained, "Adrian said he had business tonight, that he wouldn't be expecting me. Of course I didn't believe him."

"Honesty would be the last thing to expect from him. Do you have any idea what the business is?"

"Not a hint. He said only that he would be occupied with business this evening."

Marshall nodded and addressed himself to the meal. "If it's legitimate, he's either making a delivery ashore, or to another ship. Otherwise, it might be news of the ransom."

David's eyes widened hopefully. "You think it could be that? This soon?"

"Not likely, but possible. I'm sure he had the Captain's letter by the time we sailed, and he must have left someone back in Portsmouth to deliver it and wait for a response. A fast cutter might catch up to us by now, or he might have a rendezvous arranged with a courier ashore. We'd have a better idea of whether that's likely if we had any idea where we are."

"If we can get outside, the stars should tell us something."

"As long as it's clear. And if you're here for the whole night, we can get to work at lights-out. Are you feeling rested?"

"I'm ready to start right now." The prospect of getting something done, or perhaps of a night away from Adrian's poisonous company, seemed to make a great difference in Archer's mood. "Will, I was thinking. We don't have a whetstone, but do you think we could sharpen that thing on a shoe buckle?"

"Like a carving steel?" Marshall grinned. For once, there might be an advantage to having economized by getting his shoes made with pinchbeck—cut steel—instead of the more expensive but softer silver. "We can try. I don't think it's possible to make the edge any duller."

He finished eating quickly and shifted to sit against the wall beside the door, so he'd have a moment to hide what he was doing if a guard approached; Archer moved to keep an eye on the door. The adze blade made hardly any noise. After a couple of minutes, he could see a small but definite improvement in the edge. "Good thinking, Davy. This will save us hours, in the long run." He worked for another few minutes, then hid the tool again; the guards never waited long to collect the dishes. "And they brought us tea to help stay awake," he said, emptying his cup. "Very thoughtful."

"Do you think we can finish tonight?" Archer asked, pushing the dishes back under the door flap.

"We can try. It's three inches of oak, though, and we don't know how deeply the bar is set." They both heard the footsteps outside, and stopped talking until the guard glanced in, took the dishes, and went away. "If we do get through tonight, it will probably be near dawn by the time we finish."

Archer nodded. "I suppose it would be too risky to go out tonight anyway, if Adrian's expecting company. You wouldn't want to be hanging on the rigging when another ship appears, or have one of the boats spot you on the way back from shore."

"If they are dealing with Navy vessels, being seen might not be a bad thing...No. With another ship nearby, the crew would be on the alert; I'd be hauled back in before I could signal. But it just occurred to me: once we have the bar out, do you think you could use this adze as a weapon? You might have a chance at Adrian—"

"No." Archer bit his lip. "I couldn't hide it, I—he—he has them search me when I go in. And coming out; anything I took in would be confiscated and he'd want to know where I got it. Besides, Will, I think I'd need something a little more...emphatic...than a carpenter's discard. If you should happen to find a pistol lying around..."

"You'll be the first to know." Archer's reaction, that immediate tension and choppy speech, worried Marshall. Then again, to be fair, if he were contemplating an action that risked causing harm to Davy or the Captain, he would probably be tense, too. Better to switch to something concrete. "What's the physical layout in his cabin, Davy? Are there windows?" He pushed a handful of straw at Archer and swept a space clear on the floor.

"Yes, all across the rear, same as in *Calypso.* Big enough to climb through, too, but they're shuttered. From the inside. Possibly the outside, too, I couldn't tell."

Archer laid straws out in a rough rectangle. "The cabin is all one room, not separate cabins like *Calypso's* arrangement. It's smaller, of course. No gunports. The table is to the right when you enter. It's large enough that it might seat six, but there are only four chairs." He placed smaller bits of straw as he spoke. "Sideboard here by the table, desk and chart table back at the aft windows, a wardrobe and two large chests along the larboard wall, and the sleeping area along the other." More straws. Clearly, David had kept his mind on his duty and paid attention to his surroundings. "It's curtained off, but he—left it open, and there's a chest of drawers and a settle just inside the curtains, here, forming a partial wall for the sleeping cabin. Storage drawers under the berth, as well."

"That's a fair amount of storage space. I'd wager he lives aboard year-round. And with the business he's in, there have to be weapons somewhere in that room."

"There probably are," Archer agreed. "But I don't anticipate having the chance to look. You were right about him not being armed, though. I haven't seen a weapon on him. As far as I can tell, he does rely on the guards for that."

"There must be a weak point. Some way..." Marshall rubbed his chin, frowning at the straws. "What I'm thinking of, Davy, is that if you had the chance to kill Adrian, or even knock him unconscious, you might arm yourself and get out through the window. If we could coordinate our movements so that I was on deck creating a diversion at the same time, I could hold the crew's attention and you could get below and free the Captain."

Archer's brows drew together. "I hear too many 'ifs,' my friend. This sounds like a good plan for getting you killed."

"I'm sure they'd try to recapture me first. Remember, to them we're merchandise. I can't believe he'll get his money without having to prove somehow that we're still alive. Besides, unless I can capture a weapon myself, I'll be unarmed. They'd have no reason to kill me."

"I suppose not..."

He could see that Archer was less than enthusiastic. "It's just speculation at this point, Davy, and I'm supposing that land will be close enough to make an escape feasible. I don't propose running us all out on a yardarm if we're in the middle of the sea with no help at hand."

"Oh." Archer looked relieved. "You sounded as though you planned to begin any minute."

"I would like to." He smiled, patted the pocket where the adze bit was hidden. "But we do have that port to deal with first."

"As soon as they take that damned lantern away." Archer frowned suddenly. "Will?"

Marshall felt it, too. The deck beneath them shivered slightly, as the ship lost momentum. She was slowing, heaving to, her sails slackened to let the wind pass them by. "So early," Marshall said. "This must be ordinary, legitimate business. It's not even dark yet."

"Nearly sundown." Archer glanced at the evening light that angled through the port. "Oh, no..."

Somewhere above them, someone was pulling on a pair of ropes. The shutter over their window creaked, then tilted up until the flow of light and air stopped altogether.

Marshall got up to check. The shutter fit inside the frame, concealing the notch that he'd dug out. But there wasn't room to work on it, not even space to manipulate the blade.

He turned away and slumped to the floor. When he met Archer's eyes he saw that words were unnecessary. He said them anyway, in the vain hope that shared disappointment might be less bitter. "We can't, Davy. They'll be watching for any attempt. We don't dare work on it at all, tonight."

Chapter 14

Supplemental Log, HMS Calypso, in for repair, Portsmouth.
Lt. Anthony Drinkwater, in temporary command. 27-7-1799

I have been informed that the ransom for Captain Smith and our two officers is being assembled and should be ready within two or three days' time. Ad. Roberts will assign a special squad of marines to guard the chest that contains it, and has given me temporary command of the captured merchant vessel Fifine *to make the delivery. We will be carrying seventy-five crewmen from* Calypso, *as well as our usual marine contingent; we will follow whatever instructions we may receive for delivery of the ransom, but I am being given considerable latitude in judgement with regard to possible rescue and capture of the abductors. The information from Capt. Smith has been forwarded to the Admiralty by post chaise; their reply, if any, should reach us at approximately the same time as the strongbox.*

Dark. Close, cramped air. Straw prickling through the sailcloth spread beneath him, and the endless rocking of the ocean. Marshall blinked, suddenly awake in the shipboard cell, and wondered what had wakened him. Then Archer blurted incoherently in his sleep and flung an arm out, hitting him across the face.

He was up in the rigging, naked and cold, helpless as a fly in a spider's web, with the whole crew watching. Will was down there, and the Captain, staring as if they couldn't believe he would be up here like this. "There, laddie," *Adrian whispered from behind him,* "You liked that, didn't you? You did. Say it."

He wanted to push the bastard off, wanted to let go himself and fall to the deck, or into the sea. He couldn't get his hands free, couldn't move at all. "I'd sooner lie with a rotting corpse," *he spat.*

The shrouds shook as someone else climbed up. He barely recognized the face, half-gone and eaten by fishes, but he knew who it was as it came closer, the gaping hole in the center of a ragged shirt, seaweed in the hair.

"Hello, boy."

Correy. How—?

"That's a good little whore, come to Georgie..." *A skeletal hand reached for him, bones poking out through disintegrating flesh. On the deck below, William turned away in disgust.*

"Davy," Marshall whispered. "Davy!" He caught his friend by the shoulders. "Wake up!" But Archer, trapped in his nightmare, only fought harder. Worse, he started shouting. Marshall had to clap a hand over his mouth and roll on top of him to stop his thrashing. Damn these nightmares! He didn't want Archer whipped for creating a disturbance, and his own back would not welcome another beating. "Davy!" he hissed.

The struggling body stilled under his hand. "Wha—Will?"

"Yes. Davy, please, you must be quiet—"

His words were cut off as David's arms snaked round his bare shoulders, pulling him down. Not an embrace; it was like a drowning man clutching at a straw. Marshall turned his face to get Archer's hair out of his mouth, and his lips brushed against David's. They parted, and he was lost. A surge of wild pleasure engulfed him; he found himself holding Davy just as tightly, just as close. It wasn't exactly passion—more some strange mix of protectiveness and a need he'd never realized, a craving for something tangible in this fearful dark place where all the rules that shaped their world were suspended. For an instant he teetered between sensation and control, then the riptide of feeling yanked him under.

Some small part of his mind worried over the problem while his body hurled itself eagerly into the maelstrom. Wildfire blazed from his mouth all the way to his toes, kindling a flame in his groin as he felt himself harden. His lips tingled, the sweet hot touch of Davy's mouth drawing his tongue deep inside—like kissing a girl but nothing like it, no courtesy, no caution, just a blinding urgency, almost the bloodlust of battle.

But he didn't want to kill Davy or hurt him—God, no, he just wanted to get closer, somehow. He could feel his own blood racing, could sense another pulse through the thin barrier of cloth between them. He had never in his whole lonely life felt so close to another human being, but there was a familiarity about this, as though he knew exactly what to do. It was incredible, glorious, and hovering just out of reach was the tantalizing promise of one tiny bit more, and he wanted it desperately.

Archer was writhing against him now, one hand tangled in his hair, the other arm locked around his waist. He abandoned himself to the rhythm, hands sliding down with a will of their own to catch Archer's hips. Davy whimpered, and suddenly they were fumbling with fly buttons—their own, each other's, it hardly mattered. Trousers slid away and they were twined together in the straw, rolling around like a couple of young animals, slippery with the sweat of their furious struggle, frantic but silent.

It was like being on deck in a hurricane: no control, no chance of mastery, just holding on for dear life and hoping to survive the cataclysm. Davy's shirt was an obstacle, bunching up between them, and they wrestled that off, lips separating only long enough to get the thing over his head and out of their way.

The wave broke almost immediately as their naked bodies touched full length, small cries drowning in each others' throats. The tidal surge seemed to go on forever, then slowly ebbed until they were two separate beings again, two gasping, spent bodies, two very shocked and bewildered young men. But Davy held his face for a moment longer, time enough for a gentle, piercingly tender kiss. "Thank you," he breathed.

Released, Marshall rolled away, dazed, his body still humming like rigging in a gale. As the feelings calmed and his brain cleared, he realized that what had felt like an age could have lasted barely a minute or two. Had they been overheard? The only sounds he could detect were Archer's ragged breathing, the rustle of the straw, the creaking of the ship. No alarm outside.

Hardly necessary. Alarm was shrieking within him, and he tried to still it with mundanity. "We—we had better wash up." He groped for the water bucket, shivering as the cold wetness splashed against his belly, rinsing himself, passing the refilled cup to Archer.

His breeches had wrapped themselves around one ankle, and the small problem of untangling them and pulling them back on gave him a moment to try to think. It was like swimming in glue. The enormity of what he had just done nearly paralyzed him. What in the world had possessed him? And Davy had *thanked* him. For stopping, of course. If he could voluntarily drop dead, this very moment, he would. But of course it couldn't be that easy.

He couldn't see David in the darkness, didn't have to look him in the face; that was a small comfort, since it meant Davy couldn't see him, either. He couldn't hear Davy's breathing anymore, but sensed that he was waiting. Speechless with fury, most likely.

Oh, God, now what? He sagged against the bulkhead, face in his hands, and struggled for words. Finally, he took refuge in formality, pushing the phrases out through a throat almost too tight to breathe. "Mr. Archer, I—I most humbly beg your pardon. That was inexcusable, I don't know what came over me—"

Archer had curled into a tight ball, choking on pain, curs-
ing his own stupidity. He could have just released William,
apologized, pretended to be asleep, something. If only he
hadn't said anything! Well, he wouldn't have to worry anymore about being a pawn in the hostage game; now Will
could simply find the Captain and leave. *Or I can just attack
Adrian, if I can't kill him I'll just go on fighting until he has
to kill me.* He heard Will say something about washing, took
the cup that was thrust into his hand, used it to rinse away
the stickiness on his belly. For all the good it would do. *This
won't wash off.*

Then he heard Will's voice, and his mind finally made
sense of the words. Except that the words didn't make sense.
Why in God's name should William be apologizing to him?
But he sounded terribly upset, as why shouldn't he, and he
seemed to be standing there waiting for an answer. What
came over *him?* That was too absurd. Archer swallowed. "I
seem to recall having something to do with it." His voice
sounded almost calm, strange in his own ears. Well, he had
just destroyed the last bit of anything that made his life worth
living. What was there left to fear? Poor Will was breathing
heavily, as though he'd run a mile. "Will, for God's sake,
please sit down before you fall over."

Marshall slid to the deck with a thud, knotting his hands
together to keep them from shaking. "If you wish," he said
woodenly, "When we return to *Calypso* I shall place myself
under arrest for—for indecently assaulting an officer under
my command, I shall resign my commission—"

"Are you mad?" Panic flooded out any other feeling,
though Archer had just enough control to keep his voice low.
"Will, that's a hanging offense. Have you ever seen a hanging? I have." Terror made him babble. "I was eight. My father thought it would be an eye-opening experience. He was
right. I didn't sleep for three days." He took a deep breath
and continued, trying to sound more reasonable. "Even if
you had...done anything to harm me, do you think I would
say one word to send you to the gallows?"

Gallows. Maybe he could get hold of that cord they'd woven, hang himself while William slept. It would be a coward's apology, though, and Will would only blame himself. "It would make as much sense for me to place myself under arrest for seducing my commanding officer." But, no, that would ruin Will, too. "They probably would hang us both, for idiocy, if we were fools enough to confess to such a thing."

He was at a loss for what to say, but the words kept pouring out, regardless. "Or I could report that our genial host has been indecently assaulting both of us and you chose to take responsibility for it all. That's at least closer to the truth, isn't it?" He stopped in horror, aware of what he'd just revealed.

"What—no, the beating was unreasonable, but hardly—" Marshall suddenly realized what David wasn't quite saying. "Oh my God. Davy. No..."

Archer said nothing. *That's torn it.*

Marshall had a sudden awful insight. "That's what you were talking about at the gratings, wasn't it? That's what all of it was about—the beating, and the maneuvers with food. He's like Correy. He wanted you, and you refused him."

"Yes," Archer said distantly. *Goodbye, my friend.*

"And the next night—after they'd taken me away?" No response. It was as if Archer were a thousand miles away, not right beside him. Marshall wanted to touch him but was almost afraid to. "Davy, for God's sake, you should know I'd rather be beaten bloody than to have you—abused—on my behalf!"

"I know you would," Archer said, very quietly. "And that helped. So very much. But it wouldn't have made any difference. He made it quite clear that my consent was not required." Nothing would have made any difference, and the stakes were too high. "He wasn't just threatening to beat you, Will, he was talking about—about mutilation. And I believe him." He felt tears spilling from his eyes. He couldn't stop them. *I wanted to protect you. I didn't mean to drag you into it.* "I'm sorry."

Marshall had never felt so furious—or so helpless. "Is there anything I can do?"

"You already have. You're still speaking to me." *For now, at least.* "Really, it's...not even as bad as Correy. Not as physically brutal. And at least this way I've been...able to keep some small illusion of dignity, and distract him from—from whatever the Captain may be up to. It's not your fault, Will, and I don't think there's anything you can do to stop him."

Remorse tore at Marshall. "I didn't have to make it worse. I'm no better than Correy—"

Archer seized his arms in the darkness, and shook him. He hadn't meant to touch William at all, contaminate him, but he couldn't let him go on like that. "You are *nothing* like Correy," he whispered fiercely. "His only pleasure lay in hurting. Were you trying to hurt me?" Stupid question.

"No!"

"Did—did you feel that I was trying to hurt you?" *Oh, please...*

"Of course not, Davy, but—"

Thank God. Archer let go. "All right. There's your difference. You were trying to help me, and it...got out of hand." He was silent for a long moment. He'd been lying, keeping quiet, trying to hide, all for nothing. Best to make a clean breast of it and let Marshall make up his own mind. It was utterly unfair to let him blame himself for any of this. Archer took a deep breath and said briskly, "Would you like me to tell you what happened a few minutes ago?"

"I know—"

"No, you don't. Not all of it. What happened was, I was dreaming I was back with Adrian, and he was..." He faltered, his nerve failing. "...amusing himself. Then all of a sudden the dream changed and it was you. I realize now you must have been trying to get away, but I—I thought you were trying to kiss me and that meant I was still dreaming, because of course that couldn't really be happening, and I was so...relieved..." *Liar. The word is 'happy'.* "That—that by the time I realized it wasn't a dream anymore, I couldn't stop."

"And I took advantage of you."

"No." *How plainly do I have to say it?* "Quite the opposite, Will. You didn't do anything wrong to me. I made a stupid mistake. I won't blame you for a moment if you hate me for it. I'm quite sure that you never..."

He stopped, trying to gather the courage to finish.

"Davy? Are you all right?"

"No." *I will never be all right again.* He forced himself to speak, stumbling over the words. "But it is *not* you, Will. It's me." *Get it all out, give him the truth, let him decide.* "Will, Correy wasn't the first. I'd had similar... difficulties...with an older boy at school. And now this bastard. I swear I don't know why it happens, I didn't choose it, but I've learned to survive it." *Stop stalling, you snivelling coward. Give him the truth.* "What you did—or, to be precise, how you responded to what I did—I think it was the kindest thing anyone's ever done for me. I have never before—under such circumstances—cared about the other fellow. Or not been hurt, or afraid. Or felt—loved. Will, you were—*not*—forcing me."

Marshall felt the blood rush to his face, felt a little sick. The naked expression of emotion was all the more excruciating because it was true. He did love Davy. He'd thought it was as a brother. But he'd never had a brother, how would he know? Davy certainly hadn't been forcing him, either. On the contrary, it had felt good, so very good—God, what did this mean? Was he some kind of ill-born monster? "Davy, we can't—"

No, we can't. Never again. "Of course not." But Archer couldn't lie and say he was sorry it had happened, just this once, a tiny bright moment of joy amidst all the pain and fear. "Of course not," he repeated. "Even if we wanted to—and I don't expect you do—Captain Smith would drop us over the side in a sack. We'd never have done it on the *Calypso*. It would never have happened at all if not for this bizarre situation."

"It shouldn't have happened at all."

"But it did." He had to remind himself that, in this matter at least, William was really quite an innocent. "It does, you know. Lieutenant Hampton...you probably didn't realize it, but he wasn't interested in women. He told me once that some captains turn a blind eye, if the parties involved are of age and discreet. And when that's not the case... if your quarrel with Correy had been over anything else, you'd never have had the chance to duel him."

"What?"

"No captain wants a sodomy trial aboard his ship, Will, you know that—except the hellfire disciplinarians. It taints everyone—and when it's rape, they often hang the victim as well. Old Captain Cooper didn't want that. Hampton told me that Cooper had been hoping someone would challenge George—I never realized that or I'd have tried it myself."

"I look back on that, Davy, and wonder where I ever found the nerve to challenge him. It was sheer luck it turned out as it did."

"Sheer arrogance on Correy's part, and overconfidence. He didn't think a vicar's son would know how to shoot!" Archer smiled at the memory. "At any rate, Will, we aren't the first. And since it did happen, I'm grateful it was with you. I trust you with my life, and you must know I'd rather die than cause you harm. If we can agree between ourselves that we both became—emotional—and acted rashly—then that's an end to it, it need never go beyond these walls."

There, that sounded reasonable. Of course, once they were back on the *Calypso,* and off this cursed ship, after Marshall had a chance to think the matter through, he would doubtless find himself more suitable friends. *I will become an embarrassment. He will remember this night every time he looks at me—and how could he ever trust me again?* But for now, since William apparently still felt responsible, they had to put this aside long enough to concentrate on escape.

Marshall could hardly believe how simple it sounded—or how calmly Archer had presented his conclusions. But then, Davy had been facing the problem for some time—and it had been Davy who'd run headlong into a burning powder room to save his shipmate. Whatever his fears, in some ways he had more courage than Marshall would ever have, himself. "You've given this some thought, then?"

"All my life, it seems. How could I avoid it?"

True enough. "How—Davy, how did Lieutenant Hampton come into it?" Marshall was still having trouble with the idea that someone he'd known as a friend could be anything like George Correy.

"I think Correy found out about him and used it to blackmail him—keep him from stopping his filthy games. But—" Archer caught his meaning. "Oh, Christ, no, Hampton wasn't after me, Will. I think he had a lover aboard ship." He had; it had been Captain Cooper himself, and that was the other piece of the blackmail chain that gave Correy such power over them all. "Lieutenant Hampton saw what Correy was up to and tried to help me." How to explain the odd relationship he'd had with their former lieutenant? Better not to try. "We weren't lovers, but he...he taught me some ways to make it easier...to keep from getting hurt. He was a good man, Will, you know that, he just had...unusual inclinations. Correy, on the other hand, was a beast. He could never even get a woman in Spithead because he was so vile. The dockside whores wouldn't have him after he beat one of them half to death. I'm not even sure he liked boys as much as he liked bullying. I wouldn't have left him alone with a sheep."

Marshall grimaced. There was an idea not worth contemplating. But never mind dead villains; it didn't seem possible that something as shatteringly intense as what had passed between them could ever work itself back into the fabric of ordinary life. "So... can we just...go on?"

"Will, what else can we do—or say? Whom would we tell? Do you want to go to the Captain and tell him? 'Excuse me, sir, Mr. Archer mistook me for a mermaid the other night, but it's all right, we shook hands and agreed to be gentlemen about it.'"

Marshall's appalled silence was answer enough.

"The only way to survive is to act as though nothing

happened. We weren't the first, I'm damned sure we won't be the last." He sighed. "But I promise you, Will, there is one thing I'm going to do if they ever change the dress code about being clean-shaven."

"What's that?"

"I'm going to grow a moustache—and maybe some stupendously ugly side-whiskers—and cover this damned pretty face."

Marshall relaxed, dizzy with relief that there might be such an easy way out of this muddle, one that would preserve this rare friendship. Half-joking, he suggested, "You could sneer."

"What?"

"Remember that look Captain Cooper used to give midshipmen who got their navigation problems wrong, when he looked as though he smelled rotten fish? You could practice that. It should repel anything."

"Oh." Silence. "There. I'm sneering. Think it's repulsive enough?"

"Davy, it's pitch-black in here."

"Well, I can't sneer any louder."

He had to smile at his friend's irrepressible humor. "You'll have to try again in the daylight."

He bit his tongue. Another day. Another day of captivity, of helplessness. Another night of Davy being taken away for "supper with the Captain." His hands curled into fists.

"It won't help," Archer said quietly, catching his mood.

"Damn it, Davy—"

"Will, there's nothing we can do. Not yet."

"No."

"We'd better get some sleep."

"Yes."

Chapter 15

They were still lying quietly, eyes open, when the window creaked and let in the dawn. Marshall sighed, realizing he was too keyed up to sleep. Just as well; he wanted to make sure the cell showed no trace of their earlier activity.

His searching glance fell on Archer's body. "Oh, my God, Davy—" An angry patchwork of bruises marred the fair skin, mostly blotches around the ribs and waist that fit the pattern of finger marks. And his wrists—

Archer flushed scarlet and grabbed for his shirt, dragging it on inside-out. He realized his mistake when he tried to do up the buttons, and put his hands over his face, almost as a child would, as though pretending he wasn't there.

Marshall reached to touch him, only for comfort, but stopped himself. "I'm sorry, Davy." He stood up and went to the port, giving his friend the pretense of privacy. He heard the rustle of cloth as David adjusted the shirt, but it was really too late; what he had already seen was burned into his mind's eye. David's whole body had been mauled; the tops of his shoulders were splotched with purple. And at the edge of one bruise, Marshall had discerned, with brutal clarity, the marks of human teeth.

"Thank you," Archer said in a small voice. Marshall glanced down, saw that he was covered, and sat against the opposite wall, staring at his own hands, wondering. Finally he could stand it no longer. "Davy. Forgive me, but—I—I have to know. Did—did I do any of that?"

"No! God, no, Will, I didn't mean for you to see, it was only—"

"You'd said this bastard wasn't as bad as Correy, but—" He touched Archer's wrist, looked at him for permission, then pushed the sleeve back. His wrists were encircled with bruises and chafe-marks. "What the hell did he tie you for?"

"Amusement," Archer said bitterly. "He didn't need the ropes, he had you. The rest of it, I earned by being insufficiently..." He grimaced. "Appreciative. After he'd gone to what he considered great lengths to make the procedure...agreeable...I told him, pretty bluntly, that I wasn't impressed. He was...extremely annoyed." He folded his arms, hunching slightly. "After he'd thrown me around for a bit he decided it would be more entertaining to continue trying to...seduce me...Will, please, can we speak of something else?"

"Of course," Marshall said, enormously relieved to change the subject. "But there is one thing you must decide."

"What's that?"

"Would you rather see this putrefied whoreson hang—or help me cut him into very small pieces?"

David's blue eyes held no humor at the grim jest. "Yes. That's the only way to stop him, you know—he'll never go to trial for this."

"He should."

"No doubt—and I'd never be able to show my face in public again. I can get through this...but I could not stand up in a court and testify to it, Will. I could not."

Archer was undoubtedly correct. What he was going through was horrible enough; making it public would be excruciating. "Of course not. I'm a damned fool. It would destroy your career."

"Oh, yes—if I have one left, after this. And you would be tarred by the same brush, Will. Everyone would assume that since we were both prisoners..."

Marshall had not thought of that. He must have looked as queasy as he felt, because Archer continued, "It's all a piece of the same cloth, my friend. Nothing has happened. Nothing at all."

He watched as William struggled with the problem—and reached the inevitable conclusion. But... "What do you mean, if you have a career left?"

Archer took a deep breath and stared off into a corner. Finally he said, "What do you suppose will happen when the Captain finds out?"

"A funeral. Adrian's. But why should he find out? I would never—"

"Think about it, Will," Archer said with weary patience. "There are no secrets on this ship. By Adrian's own admission—he likes to brag—the bastard's been doing this to every prisoner, male or female, who strikes his fancy. I'll wager he's already told Captain Smith about me—his version, of course. He's probably claimed I seduced him. The Captain won't want me anywhere near his ship."

"This isn't your doing! The Captain's a fair man—"

"Perhaps you're right." Archer's eyes looked older than his years, and the lifeless tone of his voice belied his words. "But, Will, he's a post-captain. His first concern must be the good of the Service. And I'm—tainted—now. I doubt he'll consider me worth the risk. The best I can do—if he'll let me—is leave quietly when asked and hope you don't get drawn into it." He sank down into himself for a moment, as if coming to a decision. "Will, when we get the bar out, and you go above, if you can find the Captain—just get him away. And yourself. If you're both gone, Adrian won't do anything more to me, there'd be no point—"

"Don't be ridiculous, Davy, I couldn't do that."

"After what I did to you—"

"What you did?" Marshall wanted to shake David. He wanted to hold him, comfort him, kiss his sweet beautiful face—no, he could not do that! "Smuggling food to me? Taking care of me after that beating? —Oh, you must mean protecting me by letting that bastard use you—" He couldn't go on, it was too unbelievable that David could be blaming himself. "Davy, if you are referring to some...rash, overly-emotional behavior that I thought was settled ..."

Archer tried to turn away; Marshall caught his arms, carefully, where there were no bruises. "Try holding me down against my will, Davy. From underneath. Just try. You couldn't do it."

Archer closed his eyes.

"You could not." Marshall released him. "And you did not. So if you think you did something I would be angry with you for, or ever hold against you—you must have been dreaming. I seem to recall you weren't even sure if I'd come back, one night, until I was still there in the morning."

"Will—"

"Davy, everyone has dreams where they do impossible things. You can't blame a man for what he does in a dream."

"Or a nightmare."

"No. If anyone were to ask if I remembered you...*attacking* me, I would have to say no, you must have dreamt it."

Archer finally met his eyes, and Marshall saw that he, too, wanted more than their world would allow. "It's impossible."

"Yes, I know. But I'm not suggesting we ask the Captain to marry us! As you pointed out, there was no harm intended and no harm done...unless you keep flogging yourself. If you somehow think you have to make amends to me, then just forgive yourself and I'll consider it settled."

"Will, for God's sake, my career is over. Can't you at least let me be of some use in this?"

"Davy!" Marshall caught himself and lowered his voice. "You've been under that devil's influence too long, you're starting to believe him. Whatever he might do to you, whatever he might force you to do, he couldn't turn you into a Correy if he had a century to do it."

"I don't think he could, either, Will," Archer said bleakly. "I know too well how it feels to be on the receiving end. I'm very grateful that you agree...but the decision's not yours to make."

"Or yours, either." Thank God. "Davy, if Adrian has any sense at all, he will keep this from the Captain at all costs...to use your own argument, it would suggest he's been—" It was hard to get his mind around the idea, much less find the words. "— been doing the same to both of us. Don't forget, he believes I'm Captain Smith's nephew. Can you imagine how the Captain would deal with someone who did that to his own flesh and blood?"

Marshall expected it would, in fact, be exactly the same way that Smith would deal with anyone abusing one of his midshipmen, but Archer had been made to feel too worthless to accept that anyone else might value him. "Adrian is not fool enough to risk a blood feud with anyone as forceful and well-connected as Captain Smith."

"I hadn't thought of that," Archer admitted. "But if the Captain were to come right out and ask me what Adrian did—"

"—which will most probably not happen—"

"True—but I couldn't deny it. And, Will—" David met his look and held it. "I do not want you to compromise yourself by trying to cover up for me. If you were to lose the Captain's trust, you'd never get it back."

"We have much to do before we need worry about that," Marshall said. "But what if everything goes right? Suppose we escape, and come back in force and capture this ship. Or better—suppose we get the Captain free and the three of us take Adrian prisoner. What would the best outcome be?"

Archer looked skeptical, but he made a fair effort. "All right. What he's done is piracy, that's a capital offense that doesn't require a trial. The Captain said as much up on deck. If he has the chance, he'll hang Adrian. In the best possible outcome, enough of the crew will come over for us to get the ship to port, or we'll be able to signal a passing ship for help. As for the rest—Will, this is foolish."

"What else have we to do right now? The Captain always says to go into battle intending to win. Go on, Davy. We've won our freedom, hanged this pirate who's been kidnapping and murdering people, taken over his ship—what's to become of us?"

"We'll leave the Navy, sail away in our own little sloop, and live happily ever after."

"Davy—"

"This is—oh, very well. Assuming we get out of this, we'll continue our careers, perhaps marry and raise families, and do what we can to keep predators like Correy and this bastard out of the service because we'll know them when we see them. Will that do?"

"I think it sounds like something worth living for. Isn't it better than doom, disgrace, and ruin?"

Archer sighed, obviously unconvinced. "Of course."

"Davy—just as a favor to me—would you please let yourself believe things might be all right? Not that they will, I don't ask that—but allow that there just might be hope?"

"Why?"

"Because I know how it feels to live without hope. It makes death look too easy. Without hope, Davy, you're going to get yourself killed. And without you, we'll all die. It's only the three of us against the whole crew. The Captain wouldn't leave you—"

"That's what Adrian assumes. He would never expect you to go. And if it meant you could get help and put an end to this—"

"—and even if he did, I damned well wouldn't! After what you've been through for us, how can you even think—" He closed his eyes against the pain, and against the fierce temptation to take his dear friend into his arms once more. "It's one thing if I lose you in battle. That's out of my hands. But as long as we're both breathing, I will never leave you behind, do you understand?"

Archer settled back against the bulkhead, not meeting Marshall's eyes. "It's been a week, Will. One of the guards who took me up last night told me not to worry, Adrian would get bored soon, and then he'd...look elsewhere. I doubt he meant the Captain." He held Marshall's gaze then, until he seemed sure his meaning was clear and went on, his voice nearly devoid of expression. "I shall distract him as long as I can. I don't think he'll lose interest as long as I'm resisting. It really is a matter of playing for time. Perhaps the ransom will come through—"

"No. We'll wait no longer. You can't imagine I want you to shield me—like this—" He touched Davy's shoulder, very lightly. He meant what he said, but the fear of having to undergo what his friend had endured nearly paralyzed him. He'd always known David had courage; he had never guessed how much.

A door creaked, somewhere outside, and the morning guards took up their posts. They'd have to be sure to keep their voices low. "I wish you had told me sooner, Davy," he said. As Archer opened his mouth to argue he added quickly. "No, it's all right, I understand—but I wouldn't have kept waiting for the Captain to make the first move. Not with what you're going through. We'll just have to find him when we get out."

"If we aren't working with him, an escape attempt will be a bigger risk—"

"Not an attempt," Marshall said firmly. "An escape."

Chapter 16

S mith woke to fresh air moving through his cell, and a little daylight. He had expected, when the ship hove to, that he would not have much chance to signal. He had not expected to have a guard posted directly outside his door, or to be told that any attempt would result in one of his men being killed—but when he heard the sounds outside the porthole, another ship so close he could hear her crew shouting, he understood. He could have made himself heard, if he'd been willing to pay the price.

"Cap'n?"

He hadn't moved so quickly in some time. "You're alone?"

"My mate's gone for your breakfast. Sorry it took so long to get back t'you—"

Smith wasn't waiting for conversation; the questions spilled out: "Where is this ship? When is her next delivery?"

"Lizard Point's about eight miles larboard, Cap'n. We're beatin' back toward Tor Bay, direct as we can. Out o' sight o' the coast, mostly. Nobody knows the next delivery but maybe Ship's Master Brown an' the Cap'n."

"Where are my men?"

"Just opposite you, starboard side. They're all right, so far, mostly. I wanted to tell you, sir, I talked to a friend of mine, and we're agreed to 'elp you, if you get us pardons."

"Your friend doesn't happen to be the cook, does he?"

"'Ow'd you—ah, sent you a present, did 'e? Said 'e might."

"Yes, he did. Give him my thanks...but can you be certain of him?"

"Certain's can be, sir. 'E's already 'ad 'is fill of Cap'n Adrian. I was plannin' to cut out next time we got shore leave, an' 'Enry decided to, too, after what 'e done to 'is wife."

The conversation seemed to be getting a bit far afield. "The cook's wife? What's she got to do with this?"

"Well, she wasn't 'is wife at the time, she was maid to a Milady the Cap'n kidnapped. Pretty little thing, the Cap'n...well, he brought 'er along for fun. Then it turned out this fine lady thought it'd be a lark to 'ave a flourish with this pirate, you know he carries on like cock o' the walk—"

Smith had the feeling he'd fallen into a very strange novel. "The lady who was kidnapped had an affair with Adrian? He'd...molest...his prisoners?"

Bert nodded. "Aye, 'e would. 'E does. Most of 'em. It's a bad business, sir. If I'd known what 'e was like, I'd'a taken my chances ashore. She was the first one as wanted it, though. Everyone figured it's 'is just deserts, 'e 'ad the devil's own time gettin' shed of 'er. That's when the Cap'n's partner got 'is back up. 'e didn't mind 'avin 'is bit o' fun with the prisoners, but that 'lady' wanted to stay aboard an' play pirate 'erself. Loony bitch, beggin' your pardon, sir. I 'ope 'er 'usband took a stick to 'er when 'e got 'er back. Anyway, that left 'er maid ready for the chop, she wasn't about to ransom the poor girl and let 'er gossip to the other servants. So 'Enry, that's the cook, sir, he took 'er ashore when he went for supplies, married 'er quietlike, and sent 'er back to his ma in Scotland, she's gettin' on in years."

Smith discarded the irrelevancies and cut to the point. "Ask your friend if he can put something in the food that will affect the crew—slow them down, perhaps, or send them running for the head. Is there any way you can get a message to my men? And can you get them any sort of weapons?"

"I might see 'em. Couldn't say when, though. Might be a few days. Weapons, maybe a blade, prob'ly not guns 'til you're ready to go. Anybody can't account for his pistol, 'e's in bad trouble."

"I see. I noticed guns on deck. Are they kept loaded?" That would be a foolish waste of powder on most ships, since an enemy could be seen so far off, but for Adrian it could mean a chance at escape if he were caught unawares. And he had no shortage of powder.

Bert nodded. "Just the bow-stern chasers, though. We freshens the powder reg'lar, load the rest when we need to."

"What charge?"

"Canister, mostly. We only 'ave light metal, six-pounders, so we goes for scattered shot."

"Sensible," Smith agreed. "All right. I need to know when we'll be approaching another ship, or if we get within a mile or two of land, especially if we're near landfall at night. At some point, I'm going to have to ask you to unbar this door."

"Point o' no return, I reckon."

"Exactly. And how many are in the crew?"

"Thirty-eight, plus the Cap'n an' ship's master. Smaller crew, bigger prize shares."

Thirty-eight to three—or five. Not the best odds, but adding in the element of surprise and timing their move to when most of those men would be asleep... Yes. It was feasible. "Now, you say my men are opposite here—how many guards?"

"Two, sir, same as you, and they're both there most o' the time. They have lights-out same time as you, the guards go out by the stairs so they can stay awake. Isn't any other way in to that cell. But there's probably 'alf a dozen men on deck most o' the night, two or three even in the late dog-watch."

Smith nodded. He needed to give Bert a message for Marshall—but he was reluctant. If this were some kind of elaborate trap—and however he might pride himself on his ability to judge character, it could well be—he might be setting his men up for more of Adrian's games.

But would Adrian arm him just to gain his confidence? Not likely. "If you get the chance—tell Mr. Marshall that the order to escape will come at night, with the last password we gave on sighting Spithead."

"Password?"

"Ship's code; he is one of my signal officers, and that will assure him that the message is truly from me. And— with all respect to yourself—it will assure me that you have indeed spoken to him."

"Password, Spithead..." Bert grinned. "You like things complicated, Cap'n."

"In truth, I do not. This situation—"

"'Old on." Bert darted off; Smith heard him open a door and greet the other guard. "Looks like 'e's awake already. You bring me that tea?"

Well, that was probably an end to any further information, for now—not that what he'd gotten wasn't more than he'd expected. He had not asked where weapons were kept, but the odds were they'd be stowed in the usual places, and with any luck he'd be able to glean a pistol or two from the crew.

Ideally, he could get out late and send Bert to release Marshall and Archer, then rendezvous with them on deck and—take whatever action seemed most appropriate. He was inclined to head for the quarterdeck and Adrian's cabin, to deal with the most serious threat. The navigator Brown was an unknown quantity—Smith wasn't surprised Adrian would have someone to handle the details of navigation, but as he'd told Drinkwater, stopping Adrian was the critical matter. With any luck, one would lead to the other, but putting a stop to this operation was more important than their own escape.

And they had to put a stop to it. The notion that Adrian had been assaulting his prisoners was as repellent a bit of news as Smith had encountered in any war. "Most of" his prisoners...as best he could recall, there had been nine abductions before this one. He did not know their names, but discounting the first, Adrian's test run, that meant eight: one was an elderly gentleman, one a middle-aged banker; those two were probably not bothered; three wives—one of whom had a maid who obviously had not returned with her—one young woman, and a couple of boys.

And two of my men. Not boys anymore, true, but young enough to be in danger from that sort of predator. The question wasn't whether Adrian was twisted, it was how twisted he was and how much damage he was likely to do. For the moment, Smith decided to ignore the fact that four women could not constitute "most" of eight; he would assume that Adrian confined his offenses to women. That was enough to hang him for. *Unless I have a chance to shoot him first.*

Supplemental Log, HMS Calypso, in for repair, Portsmouth. Temporarily assigned HMS Artemis, Lt. Anthony Drinkwater, commanding. 28-7-1799

Our orders have changed! After comparing notes with the harbormaster's office, we have tentatively concluded that the ship most likely to have been used to abduct our officers is the Morven, a merchant brig converted from a gunboat to noncombatant after serious structural damage. Her captain was the first victim of the series of abductions, and although his description does not closely match the one Capt. Smith provided (the colour of his hair is unknown as Capt. Black was clean-shaven and wore a powdered wig), the coincidence is too great to ignore. Ad. Roberts has released me and part of our crew to take the Fifine—temporarily renamed Artemis—and discreetly search the area between the Isle of Wight and Lizard Point, where this ship is supposed to be conducting resupply of gunpowder for ships on Channel patrol. We will also contact any other Navy ships we encounter, and enlist their aid in finding the Morven. Needless to say, we must board her by stealth or guile; even had we the metal to attack, we could not fire on what might be an innocent ship; we must first determine whether our officers are on board, and where they are being held. Additionally, the Morven is carrying a cargo of gunpowder; we would hardly do our men any service by blowing them out of the water! Capt. Smith's orders were for an attack in force, by stealth, and that is what he shall have. A cutting-out expedition is nothing new for our men, and, judging from the size of the Morven, *our forces should outnumber her crew quite handily. The delivery of the ransom will be handled by Ad. Roberts' office; I am pleased to have Capt. Smith's funds in such capable hands, as rescue by direct means is much more to my liking and ability. Those members of the* Calypso's *crew not aboard* Artemis *are berthed on a hulk under the command of 2nd Lieutenant Watson. We sail just before dawn, God and a fair wind willing.*

The guards had come with the shaving things at the usual time. Nothing was outwardly different from the previous days; Marshall would not have bothered with the ritual, but David offered, and he felt it was better to give whatever support he could. As Archer shaved, he became very quiet, distant. That had happened every time, but Marshall had not understood why. Knowing only made it worse. "Davy, there must be something I can do—"

"It's all right, Will." Their eyes met, but the distance was there, too; Archer had retreated to some kind of inner fortification. He smiled faintly, nodding at the window. "It won't be for much longer." He took the pan and razor, slid them under the door. When it opened he set his jaw, squared his shoulders, and left the cell without looking back.

The dinner they left behind for Marshall was like ashes in his mouth. He ate it mechanically, for duty's sake; his body would need it for strength to fight. He somehow managed to sleep for a while, determined that they would get to work as soon as David came back. He woke, restless and unrefreshed, not long before lights-out. They usually brought Archer back some time after two bells, one in the morning; that shouldn't be more than an hour or so.

They did not bring him back.

For an hour or more past one Marshall waited, listening
to the ship's bell, expecting to hear the squeaky hinges of the
door down the companionway. The time crawled by. He occupied himself with trying to remember as much as he could
of the deck. He had not been paying close attention when
he'd been up there, and moonlight could be deceptive. But
the moon had been just past full then; now it would be in its
last quarter. For a few days, the deck would be relatively
dark, and he could button up his uniform jacket to conceal
the white revers. Nothing much he could do about his white
breeches, though. He would just have to be very quiet and
careful about where he put his feet.

Eventually his nerves got the better of his caution. He got
out the adze blade and put the restless energy to work on the
wood. But that didn't stop him thinking, and he half-wished
for a return to his former state of ignorance.

In retrospect, he could hardly believe how oblivious he
had been. Davy's anxiety, his mood sliding down each evening as the dinner hour approached, even his speech—he had
not been stammering from nerves, he'd been editing his ac-
counts to remove any hint of what had been done to him.
And the nightmares...small wonder. *That son of a bitch—*

Marshall ran the edge of the blade into his own thumb
and stifled a curse. It was the very devil working in the dark,
and letting anger make him clumsy wasn't going to help his
friend.

*I sent him up there in the first place. He didn't want to
go.* No, that probably didn't matter. Even if Archer had refused to leave the cell, and Marshall had backed him, Adrian
was more than capable of sending men in to haul him out by
force. It would not have changed anything. He had done, and
was doing, the only thing he could do, just as David was—

His mind threw up a vivid picture.

Stop it. Think about something else. Something neutral. If
he had two and one-half inches to cut through, and he was
removing 1/64 of an inch with each dig—though the wood
was so tough that might be an overestimate—five half-inches

at 32 passes each, 160, plus however far above the bar he'd have to excavate to raise it enough to pull it free of the lower edge of the frame...How far in was it set?

He became curious about that, and worked for a while at the inner side of the wood, digging up alongside the bar. After going up an inch or so with no end in sight, he went back to patiently grubbing out the rest of it, working mechanically, trying to keep his mind a blank.

"...*the bastard's been doing this to every prisoner, male or female, who strikes his fancy...*" How in God's name could he have gotten away with it for so long? Wouldn't someone have mentioned something? If nothing else, wouldn't anyone have at least reported what Adrian looked like? Even if he kept his damned mask on... Or was he normally clean-shaven? Did he do something to his hair, a wig, perhaps? Those who had not 'struck his fancy' probably saw nothing more than a masked figure silhouetted against a lantern. But the others...

The others were likely so utterly humiliated, as Davy had been, that they'd kept silent. It was blackmail; if Adrian were caught and tried, his victims would suffer. And 'how' didn't really matter; he *had* been getting away with it. He was getting away with it right now. Davy had been gone for at least five hours, what in God's name could that fucking bastard be doing to him?

His body tingled with the flush of memory: Davy warm and naked beneath him, pulling him close, the sweet intensity. But it wouldn't be like that for David, not now—not with Adrian; that must have been horrible, judging by the way he'd come out of his nightmare. To take something so joyful, so wondrous, and twist it into torment... How had Davy borne it? "*... he didn't need the ropes, he had you ...*"

I should have gone. Damn my cowardice, I should have gone in his place.

He rested his forehead against the cold metal bar. *Stop it. Stop thinking. Keep working.*

He worked mindlessly, pausing when his hands started to

go numb, putting the tool carefully into his pocket, shaking and rubbing his arms until the feeling returned. At one point he got so lightheaded he had to lie down for awhile, and woke with a start, certain the guards had brought Archer back and found him out.

They had not. He had been dreaming. He was still alone. It must be five or six bells by now, only an hour or two until dawn. Time enough to get a little more done. Back to work.

He had run out of gruesome possibilities to explain Archer's continuing absence. All but the worst. *"It's all right, Will. It won't be for much longer."* What if David had done something desperate and—deliberately or not—gotten himself killed?

If that were the case—and Adrian made the mistake of letting Marshall within arm's reach—there was a trick he had learned from Barrow, one slow Sunday afternoon some time back, when a few of the older hands had been reminiscing about past battles and barroom brawls. Barrow had picked it up from a new hand, a Lascar, who had a formidable reputation for unarmed mayhem.

Marshall had a slight advantage in height over Adrian, though they probably weighed about the same, and the bastard looked strong. David had clearly considered himself no match without a weapon, but the trick didn't require great strength as much as speed, timing, and stubbornness. In fact, it was something that Archer could use.

It was something that Archer could use.

If he were still alive.

The adze blade clinked against metal, and Marshall frowned bemusedly in the dim dawn light. He had dug through to the bar. It moved when he twisted it. And it was getting light. And his brain was full of fog.

And Davy was still gone.

Chapter 17

"Stand away from the door."

Smith was used to this bit of shipboard routine: the buckets beside the door were exchanged for another set, one empty and two containing water. The only thing exceptional about this time was that his new recruit, Bert, was bringing in the buckets. And he glanced at Smith as he set down the one furthest from the door, then looked quite deliberately at the bit of paper sticking out from beneath it.

Smith nodded; Bert winked, and made his exit. The fellow was turning out to be quite a competent conspirator. As soon as he was sure the guards outside were nowhere near the door, the Captain slipped the paper out from under the bucket.

Bert's spelling and grammar were problematic, but his message was clear enough. A few hands had been ordered to get 40 barrels of powder ready to unload in two days. The cook was going to add a little something to the soup at dinner the day after tomorrow, since deliveries were usually made in the afternoon; Smith should avoid eating that soup if he wanted to "be at his best" the rest of the day.

Bert had not been able to get to Marshall at all; Archer was not in the cell and might be in the sail locker. He (Bert) was going to wait until they were both in one place before making contact unless he got a lucky chance. He was reluctant to give them weapons because their cell was checked from time to time and they might not be able to hide anything on their persons. The cook would not send them any of the hazardous soup. If he (Smith) wanted to take advantage of the situation, he should bend the handle of his spoon when he sent the dishes back after dinner. If he didn't, the soup would be left alone so as not to ruin the trick, "and for God's sake destroy this note."

Bert and Henry were quite a pair, Smith reflected as he got out flint and tinder to light his candle. It was disconcerting to consider how much power a ship's cook held over the health and well-being of the crew. He wondered what "little something" would be added to the soup, but he was not curious enough to risk a taste when the time came.

The slip of paper flamed and curled into ash; he crumbled it and blew the powder out the window. Was the situation one that would give them a decent chance at freedom? Even if the entire crew were indisposed, they would all be awake; surely some of them would rally enough to get in the way. And, as his confederates surmised, doctoring the soup was a trick that would certainly work once but would be risky to repeat. But he had at least a couple of hours before he had to make that decision; it couldn't be more than one or two bells, now.

His preference, if he had the choice, would be a clandestine escape late at night, close to shore. That would be the safest and held the best chance of success. Even if they weren't very near shore, they'd be in the dark of the moon in a day or two; if they could get a small boat away without being seen, they would reach shore long before morning and it would be nearly impossible for Adrian to mount a search. The question was whether that opportunity would arise any time soon.

Arise be damned. If the cook was willing to doctor the soup, that condition was not dependent on contact with other ships. They could make the opportunity when the time was right. As vehemently as Smith wanted to escape, as strongly as he abhorred the notion of having to buy his freedom from that arrogant brigand, he was not willing to get his men killed merely to save himself embarrassment. With what they knew, now, it was only a matter of time before Adrian was captured and his "business" ended. They might even, if they were very lucky, be picked up by a ship with enough speed and firepower that they could be in at the capture.

Besides, if Archer had gone missing this was not the time to engage the enemy. Thirty-eight against five was just less than eight-to-one odds; losing one man made it ten-to-one, and if Archer was not with them it meant Adrian had a hostage.

But how could anyone misplace a man on a little brig like this? It wasn't possible. Perhaps Bert had simply not been present when Archer was moved.

And why would he be moved? Surely it made more sense to keep them together. Perhaps sense was not the main concern, though; had Adrian, fearing that what was happening among his disaffected crewmen might occur, decided to make escape more difficult by hiding one of his prisoners from all but a trusted few? Or, if Archer was in the sail locker—presumably a spot less comfortable than the cells— was it some kind of punishment, as it had been for Marshall? If so, for what offense?

Or was he even on board at all? If Marshall and Archer had come up with some way for one of them to escape—no. Not unless he had been able to get to the ship that had been nearby the night before last, and Bert would certainly have heard if there'd been an escape. If Archer were not on board...

That was extremely unlikely. Adrian would not purposely throw away £5000. Which meant that if Archer were not on board, he had probably gone over the side in the night—and he was almost certainly dead.

⚓ ⚓ ⚓

In a day and a half, David had not been returned to the cell. By midday, Marshall was ready to climb out the window, daylight or no. He spent the afternoon honing the adze blade until he'd scraped a groove in his shoe buckle. By nightfall, he was nearly frantic. But the guards said nothing, ignoring his questions. The fellow who switched buckets frowned at him, brows knitted; Marshall stared back impassively. Unless Adrian was playing yet another game—a very real possibility—something was seriously wrong.

Supper, the only meal they'd brought that day, came and went, and night dragged on. Marshall had just sufficient willpower to wait until lights-out before he was back at work, scraping at the last inches of wood that kept the bar in place. Somewhere around two bells, the adze-blade bit through wood above the bar. By four bells, an hour later, he was able to slide it up and out, and it was not until he held almost two feet of iron bar in his hand that he realized he had a weapon as well as an escape route.

At least in theory. If he wanted to conceal his absence, he could not take the bar along, and in any case he was planning a reconnaissance, not an assault. His intention had been to have David replace the bar and deflect any attention.

Captain Smith had said something once, sounding like he was quoting—"No plan survives the initial encounter with the enemy." Their plan had included Archer, but the enemy had managed to scuttle it. *I'll be damned if I'll wait any longer.*

Rather than leave the cell obviously empty, he shoved some straw into a body-shaped heap and arranged the sailcloth over it. With only a hint of reflected moonlight, he could not tell if it would fool anyone, but unless they brought David back, no one was likely to see his handiwork.

He stretched up and out through the opening, reaching for the edge of the hatch, and realized his body wouldn't bend that way; he slid back inside, shucked off the confining jacket and shirt, and gave his straw twin a pillow and arms. He took his shoes and stockings off as an afterthought; most of the deckhands went barefooted, and some had light-colored sailcloth breeches. If anyone caught a brief glimpse, he might be mistaken for someone who had a legitimate reason to be on deck.

He could not go out forwards, so he tucked the bar into his waistband and tried again, backwards. It was damned awkward, but he was just able to catch the iron rings where the ropes were fastened. For one painful instant the sill of the port dug into his back, then he shoved off with his feet, hauled up with his arms, and dragged himself clear of the cell. The ropes tightened along the hull, but they held, and no head appeared at the rail above him.

For a moment he just sat there, legs dangling inside, and looked up at the stars, drunk on the wide openness and clean sea air blowing around him. He was just a few feet above the waterline; it was return from exile. But it was a little too cold to hold still for long, and he had a job to do.

The waning moonlight was enough to see that his guess about the rigging was fairly good; the closest chains looked to be about five feet away, a bit of a stretch, and he'd have to be sure he made no mistakes. The ship was moving slowly but steadily through the water, and if he were to slip off now that would be the end of it, and of him.

With great care, he fitted the bar back into position and stood, balancing on the sill and holding both hatch ropes. It was glorious to stand up straight, too—amazing how such small things could make such a difference.

He couldn't hear anything from the deck, nor did he see any hatches that resembled theirs on this side of the hull; no surprise, though he'd still had a faint hope that the Captain's cell would be accessible. The sail locker was on the opposite side, too; he'd known that from the angle of light.

Marshall slid to the edge of the sill and reached for the cable, leaning against the slight outward curve of the sea-sprayed hull. It leached the warmth out of him, bringing out gooseflesh all over his body. As if in reaction, his mind gave him a clear picture of the insane position he was in, splayed out against the hull, hanging on to the dubious security of a line meant only to hold a shutter closed, standing a few feet above the moving sea with no safety-rope around him, his fingers just barely grasping the first vertical cable.

Sheer physical fear did focus the attention wonderfully well. He could not stay here; if he didn't go back inside, he had to move. He tried to reach the chains with his right foot, but he'd had to angle too sharply for his handhold.

Nothing for it, then. With a small wordless prayer, he gathered himself and leapt, his left hand locking on to the cable just above his right. His toes scrabbled at the side of the hull for a moment, then caught in the pegs anchoring the very bottom of the chains.

Heart pounding, he hung there long enough to collect himself, then began to climb, hand-over-hand until he reached the lowest ratlines, still below the deck along the side of the hull. Even though he had done his best to take exercise, the week's confinement and short rations had worn the edge off his strength, and he rested there until his breathing steadied.

As carefully as if he were boarding an enemy ship— which he was, really—Marshall crept up the shrouds until he could see over the rail. He was a little aft of amidships, nearly even with the quarterdeck. He couldn't see much of it, but could hear two voices up there, without making out the words. Neither sounded like Adrian; he was probably asleep.

For a mad instant he wondered what would happen if he were to vault the railing, charge into Adrian's cabin, and attack him with whatever came to hand. Before he could decide whether that would be brave or stupid, he made out the forms of two guards standing before the cabin door. As it was on the opposite side of the deck, his chances of getting there without them seeing him were slight. In fact, his chances of getting on deck at all, unseen, in this light, were terrible. Not with those guards there. Were they permanent fixtures, or was Adrian up to something at this hour?

As he crouched there wondering, the guards shifted and the door to Adrian's cabin swung open. Marshall ducked back down, straining to hear. He caught what might have been, "...back to his cell.." and risked a quick look above. Sure enough, someone was muffled in that cloak—but he couldn't tell who it was. Davy? If so, thank God, but that meant they'd be putting him in the cell. And Marshall knew there was no way in the world he could get back in there quickly enough to avoid discovery.

⚓ ⚓ ⚓

Archer felt like a sleepwalker as the guards bundled him back to the cell. It had been less than a day and a half since he'd been taken out, but it felt like forever. He had a quick glimpse of Marshall lying in the corner before the lantern was taken away. "Will?" he whispered.

No response. Archer shrugged away his disappointment and moved quietly to the porthole. The bar turned easily, and, on experimenting, he found that it was ready to be removed. No wonder Will was sleeping so soundly; he must have spent every moment after lights-out working on it. The moon would be closer to dark tomorrow night, and dark the night after. One night to scout, one to make their move. The timing could not be better.

He found his folded sleeping-mat by touch and the faint reflection of moonlight that came in the hatch, and arranged it on the straw. Odd that William would be lying under his; it wasn't all that chilly tonight, at least not in here.

He lay back and tried to sleep; he knew he should. But every time he closed his eyes he was back in Adrian's cabin the night before, trying to regain control of himself after his body had emphatically rejected Adrian's attentions, along with the dinner he'd just eaten. He had never been troubled in the least by seasickness, but sometimes nerves had that same effect on his interior. Nerves, and Adrian's increasingly imaginative demands.

He rubbed the back of his hand against his mouth, reflexively. Well, there was no question that his reaction had put the bastard off, at least temporarily. It must be difficult to maintain the role of irresistibility when one's imagined paramour couldn't keep his dinner down. *He couldn't say I didn't warn him.*

That had not sweetened Adrian's temper, of course. He'd made Archer clean up the mess and then sent him off to what must have been the storage locker where Marshall had found the adze blade. One of the guards had been thoughtful enough to leave water, and Archer'd found the raised seat Will had built. A few more folded sails, and he was able to lie on it and escape into sleep, his jacket over his face to discourage rats.

Except for the isolation, it had not been bad; if he sat up he could see moonlight on the water outside, and once a mist of spray from an unusually high wave had blown against his face. His only worry had been that Adrian would turn his attention to William, but he hadn't really expected that, not yet, and his surmise was borne out when a different set of guards appeared the next evening to take him back up.

Some of his earlier detachment had returned by then; he was only a little dismayed when Adrian announced that they would repeat the previous evening's activities before dinner. But the bastard had not pushed things quite as far as he had the night before, and Archer felt he could count that as a minor victory.

Besides that, Adrian had lost the worst of his weapons without even knowing it. Whatever he might do, he could no longer threaten to tell Will—or, rather, he could threaten, or even tell him, but that no longer mattered. Archer still found it incredible that Marshall had embraced and absolved him, but it was enormously comforting, even if it were to turn out that Captain Smith and the rest of the world saw the situation differently.

He wished, selfishly, that William would wake for even a little while. His relentless optimism somehow neutralized much of Adrian's poison. But it would be unfair to waken him; it was not as if they had any more to do on the porthole, and—

Something thumped against the port, and Archer nearly jumped out of his skin. "Will!" He grabbed for his sleeping friend's arm—and his hand clutched an empty shirtsleeve. It was only his throat freezing with fright that kept him silent. Then the pieces slipped into place and he leapt up to move the bar out of the way as a bare foot landed on the hatch. Archer peered out. "Will?"

"Thank God—Davy, stand clear!" Marshall ordered in a whisper. A second foot joined the first, then he shot through the porthole like a dolphin cleaving the water. He landed off-balance; Archer caught and steadied him. Damp and shivering, Marshall seized his shoulders. "Are you all right?" he asked through chattering teeth.

"More or less." Archer handed him the bar. "I see you've had a busy night."

"Mainly the last half-hour," Marshall said in an undertone, setting the porthole to rights. "Your timing was perfect, Davy. I could hear someone on deck coming over to the rail and I'd never have got this out in time. The chains are just barely within reach, and it's much easier going than getting back." He sat on the sailcloth and pulled on his shirt. "Chilly out there. I take it my dumb twin passed muster with the guards?"

Archer sat, too, his spirits lifting. "Never mind the guards, I've been lying here for the past 15 minutes wondering when it was going to wake up. Was your excursion a success?"

"Less than I'd hoped. I don't know if Adrian posts a guard on his door all night, or only when you're up there, but if he does, it will make things more difficult. He certainly keeps strange hours."

"I know. I remember reading somewhere that the Red Indians in the colonies always attack in the small hours because men are at their lowest ebb. Perhaps that's why he moves us around at that hour."

"It makes as much sense as anything, but we're used to having the watch change every four hours. Why would he expect it to matter? Oh, to hell with his peccadillos; you're back. Are you really all right? Where have you been all this time?"

"Where you were, that sail locker. It was a bit close, but you'd already cleaned it up; anything's better than being in his quarters. I annoyed him again—don't ask," Archer added hastily. "All he did this time was banish me, and the view was pleasant."

"I enjoyed the sunsets," Marshall agreed.

"Sunrise, Will. The heading is now east-northeast."

"Out along the Channel, then back?" Marshall speculated. "The moon's position would fit that course."

"Do you think he might be returning to rendezvous with whoever picked up the ransom?"

"That seems likely. I don't think he would risk traveling far offshore unless he had to; the closer to home he stays, the safer he is from the French."

Archer nodded. "Well, what next? Do you think you can get on deck and down to the Captain?"

Even though the moon was directly above the window, giving them a bit of light, he could not see William's face. "It will be more difficult than I first thought," Marshall admitted. "That was why I wondered about the guards, above. It may be possible, if it's very dark, or I might be able to go all the way up the shrouds and down the other side. But I could not get the Captain out through the port."

"You could give him that tool, though, and he could work on it himself."

"No, I mean I'm not sure—he would fit—" Marshall made a strange sputtering noise, then lost his composure. It was just as well that Smith's cell was not too nearby, Archer reflected; the sight or sound of two junior officers smothering laughter, with himself as its object, would hardly win his approval.

"So what is the plan?" Archer asked, once they got over the idea of Captain Smith stuck halfway through the port-hole. "Go back to waiting?"

"No." No humor in that terse syllable. "No, Davy, but it must be your decision. I've an idea, but it would mean you taking most of the risk."

"Fine. What is it?"

"Remember I asked if you thought you could kill Adrian, or knock him unconscious?"

"Yes, and—unarmed—I don't believe I could. I'm sorry."

"While you were gone I remembered a trick Barrow showed me. He picked it up from Bannerjee, that little Lascar. Did you know Bannerjee once put O'Reilly to sleep in 15 seconds?"

"No, did he?" Bannerjee probably weighed 85 pounds, soaking wet. O'Reilly was about twice that. "How?"

"O'Reilly was trying to bring him back from shore leave and he was not ready to go. He got an arm round O'Reilly's neck and squeezed, and O'Reilly went down in less than a minute. It's some kind of foreign wrestling, and if done carefully it does no harm. Barrow isn't all that big; he thought it would be a useful thing to know, so he did a bit of trading."

A useful thing to know. Yes. Most of the fighting they saw was done with weapons, but a pistol had only one shot, and a sword or axe could be dropped. "And he taught it to you?"

"Yes. I traded him my spirit ration for a couple of days, and he showed me how it's done. I've never had to use it, though; I can't be certain it will work. But if it does, size and brute strength won't matter. If you could catch him unaware, if you were close enough—" He stopped awkwardly.

Archer felt himself flush. "Yes. Well, the...proximity shouldn't be difficult. And there's not much doubt he would be completely surprised, I—I haven't exactly been battling for my virtue—" Shame closed his throat.

"You have been battling for my life," Marshall said quietly. "And the Captain's. It must be far more difficult, Davy, don't you think I understand that? Please don't let him diminish you."

I had better not, I might vanish altogether. No, he had no time for self-pity. Archer almost wished Marshall had not discovered his secret. He could block out Adrian, for the most part, but there was no way to defend against William's sympathy; he was afraid if he let his guard down too far there'd be a repeat of that embarrassing display of the night before last...and he didn't dare let himself think about that, or he would drown in his own longing. He needed distraction. "Tell me, then, Professor, how does this trick work?"

"I think it must cut off the blood and vital humours to the brain. I'll show you, without using any pressure. You'd have to get behind him for a moment—" Marshall shifted, getting to his knees. "Are you ready?"

Archer nodded, shoving the past day's memories into a dark cupboard and closing the door tight. This was Will behind him, not Adrian. The love of his life. The one man in the world he was certain he could trust. It was all right. He couldn't be safer.

His body didn't quite believe him; he could only just keep from shivering. And then Archer felt something dreadful happen as Marshall leaned closer. He was suffused with a wave of desire.

"You must move very fast. The right arm goes round like this—" Warmth and safety enveloped him. *Oh, God—*

He touched Marshall's sleeve, fighting the impulse to turn and bury his face against his friend's chest. "Just a moment, Will. This is—difficult." *This is impossible. I cannot be this close to him.*

Marshall sat back. "Davy, are you all right?"

"Yes. Yes, sorry." He tightened his body as though bracing against a blow. "Go on."

"This is harder than I thought it would be," Marshall said, then laughed harshly. His hand brushed the back of Archer's collar. "Poor choice of words. Perhaps—perhaps I should be the one to go visit that bastard. I seem to have acquired some of his—characteristics—oh, God. I'm sorry, Davy."

Archer turned. William had lost weight, these past weeks. His face, always lean, was now all angles and planes. And Archer saw a hunger on that face that resonated in his own heart. "You, too?"

"We can't." Marshall said, his eyes shadowed. "Davy, we *can't*. It could be fatal. I won't risk getting us both disgraced and hanged for a few moments' pleasure."

Put that way, there was no arguing. "I wish I hadn't been half-asleep before," Archer said wistfully. "If that was all we can have. It went too fast."

"There'd be no point." Will didn't sound convinced. "We couldn't continue once we're back on the *Calypso*."

"So this would be our last chance. Perhaps our only chance."

"We'd regret it."

Archer wanted to take the too-thin face between his hands and kiss William until he stopped arguing. "And if we don't? We'll never have this chance again, Will. If we were to do...everything we want to, everything we can think of, then we'd at least have memories. I'd like some good ones to balance out the bad, but not if you don't want to—"

"It's not that, Davy. I do." The faint light in the cell faded as he spoke, clouds closing over the sliver of moon. "I—I want you so much it frightens me. What if we couldn't stop?"

Archer put his fingers over the warm lips. "Can you see either of us swooning about like a spurned maiden when we're back aboard the *Calypso*? I can't."

Marshall closed his eyes, the struggle clear on his face. But he didn't seem to want this quite as much as he feared it. And fear would poison any other feeling.

Archer hastily pulled his hand away. "Oh, God, Will. I'm sorry. It wouldn't be any good if you weren't sure."

He swallowed hard and sat down again, facing away, feeling as if his whole being were dissolving into tears. *Discipline. Don't let it show. It really is too dangerous, haven't you caused him trouble enough?* What in God's name was he thinking, anyway? Trying to turn his friend into— "I'm sorry. You're right, of course. I'm sorry. Where were we? Come, Will, show me this maneuver. Arm around the throat, then ...?" *If he strangles me by accident, this will all be over.* The thought had a certain appeal.

He sat for a long time, waiting, unable to say anything more or even to think above the turmoil within. At last he felt Marshall's arm encircle him, but around the shoulders, not the throat. Then the other arm. Then William's head bent over his, surrounding him in that warm arc of protection. It was wonderful. He sighed and relaxed into the embrace. If this was all he could have, he would take it and be grateful.

"I'll go, Davy," Marshall mumbled into his hair. "The next time that bastard sends someone down for you, we'll tell him you're sick, and I'll go instead, pretend I'm...curious. I'm sure he would be interested."

No. Oh, no. "Of course he would, but he would also be suspicious. You would have no chance, Will. He's afraid of you. He would take you, certainly, but he would have the guards tie you first."

The arms around him tightened, and William's voice was rough with emotion. "The thought of him—*using*—you..."

Archer put his hands over his friend's. "Will, I have come to a point where I put him out of my mind the moment I leave that cabin." That was not quite true, but what they had shared the other night had given him a perspective that made Adrian's imposition less significant. He would always have the comfort of that memory; it couldn't be undone. "It doesn't matter. *He* doesn't matter. Letting him hurt you in my stead would be much worse than putting up with him one more time."

"I should be able to do something—"

"I don't think you can, Will. Not this time. The best way to take him by surprise will be to keep everything just as he expects it." Regretfully, he eased away. "Come. Show me how to fight that bastard."

This was how it had to be. Control. Discipline. It wasn't just the Navy; there was no place in England, no place in the world, where they could even hold one another like this, unless one of them were dying. The feelings had to be mastered, subdued, silenced. Like not flinching when the cannon fired, or sleeping in a hammock instead of a real bed; eventually it would be easy.

No. It would never be easy. But it could be done. Had to be done.

Marshall groaned, then took a long, deep breath. "All right, Davy. You bring your arm around and jerk the elbow up under the chin, bringing the head back." This with a movement so careful it felt like a caress. "Catch your right arm with the left, then lean close so he can't move his neck back, close your arm so it presses the big vessels in the throat—" He did all that very slowly, very gently, and Archer suddenly wanted to scream. "Then squeeze as hard as you can and hold fast, no matter what." The lightest hint of pressure touched the sides of Archer's throat. His mind went blank.

The next thing he knew, he had William pinned against the bulkhead, hands at his throat, and Marshall was gripping his wrists tightly, just barely holding him off. They were both shaking with strain. "Davy—" Marshall whispered hoarsely.

He let go immediately, horrified. "Oh, my God—did I go mad?"

"No," Marshall croaked, holding his throat. "You—you just—exploded."

Archer hovered, rubbing his friend's back, feeling like a murderer. "Holy Jesus, Will, I'm sorry."

Marshall coughed, then laughed. "I'm not," he said, in a more normal voice. "If I had any doubts as to whether you were fast enough—wherever that came from, I hope you've got more."

"I don't know..." But he did; the sickening memory sprang back full-blown. "It—it was Correy—he'd choke me, sometimes. Once I almost...did not wake up." He wiped cold sweat from his face. "Christ, I'd not thought of that in years.

Will, I could have killed you!"

"Perhaps you'd better practice on me this time," Marshall suggested.

"I had better not. What if I—"

"You must be sure you can do this, Davy. You'll only get one chance, and we don't know from one day to the next if we'll be together to practice." His grin flashed in the darkness. "And I really don't want to try it on you again. You're dangerous."

Even if he was just saying that as encouragement, it made Archer feel less a victim. "All right. How long—?"

"Barrow said three minutes can kill, once a man's unconscious. Half a minute should be safe enough. I'd rather you keep it less than that."

"Twenty seconds, then. And you'd better try to get away, Will. Really fight me. I'm sure he would."

"No doubt. See if you can tell how long I stay out; that will be important. You won't have to worry about too long a hold with him, though, there'll be no tears shed if you break his damned neck." Marshall sat cross-legged on the straw. "All right, Davy. Fire as you bear."

It took four tries; the first time, Will brought his chin down, blocking the choke; the second, Archer didn't get his hands locked properly, and the third he did, but was afraid to follow through; they wrestled around ineffectually for a bit. But the fourth time he was just frustrated enough at his failures to stop being too careful: placement, lock, and pressure were all exactly right, and Marshall's struggles ceased with terrifying suddenness.

Chapter 18

"Oh, my God. Will?"

He let go, and the limp body slid bonelessly from his grasp. Marshall wasn't pretending. Archer sat back on his heels, gathering his friend into his arms, turning his face up. "Will, please—" Thank God, he was still breathing.

He'd forgotten to maintain the hold for 20 seconds. To hell with that. But he started counting the seconds to recovery; that was practically second nature, from timing his men during firing practice. Archer smoothed the hair back from William's forehead. His lips, relaxed and slightly parted, were so close, only inches away—

—And he was unconscious, and helpless, and how much difference was there, really, between taking the first slight liberty and outright rape? Archer damned himself for the impulse and shifted so their faces weren't so close. "Wake up, Will, this is not funny. Will, *please—*"

He was senseless for nearly three minutes after Archer remembered to count the seconds, then he drew a quick, deep breath and blinked. His eyes were blank and unfocused in the thin moonlight.

"Will—?"

"I'm all right," he said unconvincingly. "Dizzy. Head hurts." He blinked again, and looked more himself. "Hello, Davy." Another blink, and a smile. "Davy, you did it!"

Archer counted to 35 before Marshall even tried to move. But he seemed ridiculously pleased for someone who'd just been choked unconscious by a friend. "This will be perfect,

Davy. You can just hit him with something if he starts to come round—"

Still shocked at what he had done, Archer gave him a shake. "Are you all right? Can you move?"

"Never better. Of course I can move." He rolled his head from side to side. "The headache is almost gone now. Amazing." Then, without warning, his hand slipped behind Archer's head and pulled his face down.

The kiss was warm and tentative, unbearably sweet, and Archer had no strength to resist. But at last he came up for air. "Will, no—we mustn't—you said—"

William smiled and put his lips close to Archer's ear. "The part of me that knows better is still asleep," he said softly. "Let us be very quiet, so as not to wake it."

"It's too dangerous," Archer said without conviction.

"Probably." Another kiss, just below the ear, nearly drove coherent thought from Archer's mind. "Davy, when I left home, there was a girl…she wanted me…and I ran away. I told her I didn't want to compromise her, but the truth was, I was too afraid—I thought perhaps I'd come back after I was successful. And then I lost her; she died of a fever the winter after I left. I've regretted it ever since."

He shifted and took his weight off Archer's knees, but didn't release him. "When they didn't bring you back last night, Davy…I thought you were dead, too." One hand clenched in Archer's shirt-front, and his voice shook. "I've given the Service every minute of my life, never grudged it. And it can have the rest, gladly—save for the next couple of hours. You're right, this may be the only chance we'll ever have. If one of us were to die, tomorrow…I want the other to have those memories you spoke of."

"It's not what might happen if we die that worries me," Archer began. A thought occurred to him. "Will, do you mean to say you've never—I'm sorry, stupid question—"

"Not until two nights ago, no. I never. The vicar's son, remember? A model of propriety, Mother's *good* boy, a perfect bloodless little officer and gentleman." He rested his forehead against Archer's temple. "So when you suggested doing everything we can think of... I'm afraid you'll have to think of most of it. All I would want is what we did the other night. But slowly..."

His hand caressed Archer's face, turning it gently until their lips met. Archer leaned into the kiss, noting absently that for someone with no experience, William was running a hand along his back with exquisite care, leaving shivers in its wake. "If you still want to."

"Want" was much too mild a word. But even as his arms went around Marshall, drawing him close, his mind threw out a notion of just what it was he wanted to do.

Everything Adrian had done to him. Well, everything that didn't hurt.

To William.

He wanted to turn his beloved friend into a sodomite. An outcast. Threatened with disgrace and death at every turn.

No, I just want to love him—

It was one and the same.

And Will had been a virgin, for God's sake. *I may have already ruined him.* Archer groaned and pulled away, his whole body screaming protest. "We can't. Will, we can't, I—I never should have said anything, that bastard's made me just like him—"

"Impossible. Davy, you were right. Lieutenant Hampton was not evil. Neither are you. Neither am I. I can understand why this is forbidden." His palm cupped Archer's cheek, thumb brushing over his lips. "Nobody would ever bother getting married, there'd be no children, and how could you ever get anyone to fight? You couldn't have this on a warship, it would be worse than having women aboard."

Archer wanted to be convinced, but he could not allow it. "You can't have it *off* a warship, either. And what about the Bible—"

"The Bible says thou shalt not kill, Davy. Remember what it is we do for a living? The Bible says a lot of things that are ignored when inconvenient. There may be a God, but

I stopped believing in religion long ago, except as it's useful for discipline, and that's why I never thought of following in my father's footsteps." His laugh held no humor. "Forgive my blasphemy, but if you look at the way Christian countries like France and England go at one another, it's clear Whoever's up there has a foul sense of humor."

In his wildest dreams, Archer could not have imagined such an unlikely theological discussion, but he might have expected that once Marshall turned his excellent mind to an objective he would find a rationale for achieving it. If he weren't so close, if his hands weren't so warm, it would be easier to argue to the contrary.

But his own uncomfortable silence got William's attention. "Davy? This—this is what you want, isn't it? Just this once, and nothing that happens here goes beyond these walls..."

Half-convinced his own career was at an end, anyway, Archer wanted to say yes. But he'd already done so much damage—

Marshall shifted, an infinitesimal degree, and his hands dropped away. "I'm sorry, Davy. This must be hell for you. I don't mean to make it worse. It's your decision." He shifted again, taking the warmth with him. The loss was so great Archer nearly cried out. "But you must decide now. We've only an hour or two till dawn, and by this time tomorrow we may be off this damned tub."

Archer sat locked in an agony of indecision. "I don't want to be like him," he whispered. "I don't want to hurt you."

"You aren't. You couldn't. What he's done was against your will—nothing you wanted. If this is what you want, yes, so do I. There's your difference," Marshall gave him his own words back. "But not unless you choose it. I don't want to hurt you, either, Davy. I'll—" He seemed to be having trouble with a word. "I'll love you either way. You must know our friendship will hold, whatever you choose."

Archer could no more stop himself than he could fly. He

was drawn forward like iron to a magnet, and they melded together as though they were parts of one being. It was too dark to see anything at all, anymore, and it was easier so. He rose to his knees to help Will pull off his shirt, found his own sliding up, too, and Will's lips skimming across his collarbone, fingertips running lightly up his back. After the ordeal of unwanted attention forced upon him, of trying not to feel, the sensations were overwhelming. "Wait—"

"What's wrong?"

"Nothing. Nothing. Only—slow down, Will. Let me show you?" He felt strange asking, even stranger being the one with more experience. First time for that. Even the girl he'd been briefly and disastrously involved with, before he joined the Navy, had known more than he.

"All right." William lay back, letting him take the lead, responding enthusiastically to his kiss. Archer moved down to kiss his throat, then back up to catch the gasp of pleasure with his own mouth. Throat, collarbone... "There's salt spray all over you, Will. You taste like the sea."

"Davy..." His whisper was unsteady. "Would you mind if I touch you, too?"

How amazing and wonderful to be asked. Would he mind? He smiled against Will's lips. "Please—" a kiss, "do." He caught his breath as those warm hands slid down the sides of his chest, thumbs brushing the nipples.

"Does this feel good?"

In answer, Archer kissed down Will's throat, moving off to one side, finding a nipple with his tongue. Will's fingers dug into his hair. Archer moved to the other, easing his weight down, feeling William straining upward. Then he moved aside, skimming a hand up his hip, across his belly, covering the parted lips with his own. "Did that feel good?" he teased.

"Oh, God—"

He let his hand rest on Will's fly buttons, feeling movement beneath. "You're my senior officer," he whispered. "There's no need to salute."

Will giggled, that silly sound so uncharacteristic of his usual serious demeanor. "You ass." He caught Archer in a fierce hug and nipped his earlobe. "D'you realize I'll never see a salute again without thinking—"

Archer would have thought humor would dispel passion. It worked the other way; a flurry of quick kisses and quiet, guarded laughter left him ravenous. For some time there was no question of who was leading or following. Lying side by side, their hands were all over each other, and at some point their breeches came off. Instead of feeling vulnerable, he felt incredibly safe.

Such a strange contrast from what he'd been doing earlier, and all a matter of volition. No fear, no pain, no humiliation. It was as though William's touch were cleansing away the others, like St. Elmo's fire flickering over his body, passing back and forth between them, growing so intense he could stand it no longer. "Will, are you—?"

"—oh, yes."

A brief, frustrating tussle while Marshall tried to pull him on top, and he discovered to his surprise he didn't want to be there. There was something comforting about being held snug and safe, shielded from the world. "Will, please—"

"Davy—are you sure?"

"Yes—oh, damn it, come here!" He pulled William down onto him, their bodies not-quite matching but the difference didn't matter, the long legs wrapped around his quite well, and they found the rhythm again and shortly, apart from remembering he must keep quiet, Archer could not think at all.

Chapter 19

When his breathing steadied, he brushed a wisp of hair out of Will's ear and whispered, "Was that what you had in mind?"

"Oh, God." He rolled to one side, one arm still pillowing Archer's head. "Oh, my God. I shall never have the strength to climb out that window. How can anyone—do this—on a regular basis?"

Archer stretched, luxuriating in the sense of wellbeing. Will's warmth upon him seemed to have melted all the ice out of his soul. "Quite cheerfully, I expect." He kissed the edge of shoulder nearest his lips, breathing in the unique, tantalizing scent. They had been in close quarters before, but he didn't remember William smelling quite like this. Silly notion. They'd never been so close before, and certainly not like this.

"That's probably another reason the crew's always kept busy," Marshall said thoughtfully. "Sex requires energy."

Whatever he'd said about claiming this time for themselves, there was just some part of William's mind that was perpetually on duty. Archer suppressed a laugh and disentangled himself long enough to find their now completely bedraggled table napkin. He dipped it in the wash bucket and wiped himself off, then rinsed it again. "Brace yourself, Will, this is cold.—No, let me."

He washed a good deal more than was strictly necessary, and much more carefully, backing away from places that seemed ticklish and lingering on others. By the time he was finished he'd somehow wound up lying against Will again, and he was beginning to notice some response in the nether regions.

"I didn't think it would come back to life so quickly," Marshall said. His hands drifted down Archer's stomach, settled a little lower, fingers exploring so carefully it almost tickled. Almost. "Is this something else you were thinking of?"

Archer nearly couldn't answer; it was a struggle to think coherently over the pleasure. "Yes. Do you think we have time?"

"They rang eight bells not long ago. A little time. What shall I do?" His fingers circled, closed gently.

Thank God William had been paying attention. Archer belatedly realized that a troop of Marines could have marched past the door and he would not have noticed. Would not notice now. "Nothing. Or...whatever you want. Tell me if you don't like it."

He moved Will's hand away, reluctantly, and began a trail of kisses down his body, starting at his throat, letting his hands move in long, slow strokes. Will would like it. Archer had never encountered anything so completely overwhelming, ever before. Even from someone as hateful and contemptible as Adrian, it had shattered his control, broken him. He had been able to block out everything else. But when that bastard had tried to compel him to return it in kind, his body had revolted.

So why was he doing it now—and to someone he cared about?

This is different. He did care. He wasn't frightened, or numb, or drugged. He was reveling in a gift freely given, in the sharp, fluttering breaths as Will struggled to keep his voice in check. His flat belly quivered as Archer dipped his tongue into his navel, and brushed his fingers up one thigh, cupping the soft weight of cock and balls in his palm as he reached the top.

"Davy, what—" A shuddering indrawn breath as Archer

took him into his mouth, the body beneath him rising like a
deep ocean swell. "No, that's too...ohmigod." The hands that
were pushing him away suddenly pulled him closer, then
fingers wove through his hair, holding but not confining,
moving down to rest against the base of his neck, stroking
lightly along his shoulders.

He rode the swell until it crested, absorbed in the sensations, the heat and smoothness and warm musky scent, de-
lighting in William's response, so that he never thought of
pulling away even when his friend stiffened, thrusting up,
then relaxed with a long, deep sigh. David relaxed too, letting his cheek rest against the warm, smooth skin.

Suddenly Will was sliding around beneath him, hands
seeking, lips against his thigh. Fingers capturing him, a few
tentative, galvanizing licks—*Oh, no, he mustn't, I can't let
him*—"Will, no, you don't have to—"

He caught Archer's hands. "Davy, when you did this, it
felt...wonderful. Don't you like it?"

"It's not that—" He felt vaguely that he didn't deserve it,
that he shouldn't ask...but he hadn't asked, had he? And if he
had enjoyed the giving... "I—I didn't mean that you
should—"

"Shhh." The cool breath made him tremble, and he let
William gently put his hands aside. Then he was being
drawn down into pleasure so overwhelming he could do
nothing but feel. No need for resistance, or denial...it was
almost unbearable to be fully present in the face of such intense feeling, but worse to think of losing one instant of it.
He reached out blindly, rubbing his face against the tight
thigh muscles, nuzzling, kissing whatever he touched, blowing a thin stream of air that chilled the wet skin. He was a
little surprised to find Will rising to the occasion once more.

One last time. This would be the last time. With sudden
urgency, he reached down to Will's hair, urging him up face-
to-face despite his body's insistent demand.

"Davy, what—?"

"Please." He kissed William, tasted himself on his lips.

"We've so little time left—I want you like this." He wanted to save every detail, engrave it on his very soul. Will wrapped his arms around him and sank back onto the sailcloth, pulling Archer against him.

Last time. Was there anything else—anything William might not ask for? He was being so kind, so undemanding, he probably would not ask. "Will—"

"Mmm?" Marshall recaptured his mouth, running his tongue lightly between Archer's lips. It was most distracting, and he lost track of his thoughts for a few glorious minutes.

Their lips brushed softly as Archer pulled back. He wanted to give William everything, but—what if the offer repelled him? He'd need to weigh his words. "Would— would you like to—be inside me?"

The hands halted in their smooth slide down his back. "Do you want that?"

He'd already had everything he wanted, and more. "Do you?"

Will kissed the side of his neck, down where it was still black-and-blue, and worked his way slowly back up to murmur in his ear. "Not really, Davy." His hands resumed their slow descent, pulling their bodies closer together. "I'll try, if you're sure you want me to, but—" One hand moved from his back to cradle his cheek; he could almost feel William studying him in the darkness. "Doesn't that hurt? I should think it would."

Archer blinked back sudden tears, undone by his caring. "It—it has. Before. I think it would not, if you...went slowly."

"Davy, no..." Will's fingers found the tears, brushed them away.

"It—it's all right, Will. I wouldn't mind. It doesn't matter. I've never—been with—anyone who cared whether it hurt or not."

"You are now. And it does matter." He found Archer's lips once again, kissed him slowly and thoroughly, then started down his throat. "How can you think I'd enjoy something that hurt you? This is so good I don't think I could stand any more. Thank you for asking..." He smoothed his hands across Archer's chest, fingers making teasing circles around the nipples, starting waves of sensation that surged through the rest of his body. "...but there is something I would like, if you don't mind?"

"Anything," Archer said breathlessly.

"We do still have a bit of time. Let me—" He seemed at a loss for words. "Do a little of what you've done for me? Unless it reminds you of—"

Archer seized William's hair and stopped his mouth with his own, then said quickly, "Nothing you're doing reminds me of anyone else. Don't even name him. Just—just do anything you like." A twinge of apprehension shot through him as he said that, but it was eclipsed immediately by anticipation and overwhelmed by more light, careful touches as William's hands and lips brushed across him. He wondered dazedly if his lover had somehow mapped the bruises on his body and decided to kiss them all away. Kiss it and make it better. He chuckled.

Will stopped immediately. "Ticklish?"

"No. Only happy. That feels so good." He ran his fingers through William's hair. It was in complete disarray, stiffened from the salt spray outside and twisted into elf-locks. Probably neither of them looked like officers or gentlemen, but in the dark like this it didn't matter. There was a kind of freedom in the darkness. No sight; just scent, and taste, and hearing, and most of all touch, flowing over his body until it was almost more than he could bear. And then it was too much, and Will slid back up so they could hold each other one last time. Their lips met like the first time, only better—no fear of what the other might do or say, no uncertainty, only shared delight.

They moved together less urgently this time, a slow sweet union that was already almost a parting, like the last days of summer before cold rain began to fall. Archer let all his barriers down, allowed himself to ride the sensations like the *Calypso* on a following sea. It was different, different even than the carefree lovemaking with Mary Belle so long ago, as though the pain he'd endured at other hands had cracked open a shell. With every fiber of his body he felt William moving against him, and when the climax came for both of them it was as if his whole being flushed with a bright glow, leaving him shivering with pleasure.

He opened his eyes, half-expecting the cell to be lit with some lingering brightness, but it was still dark. Not for much longer, though.

Will held him tightly for a moment, then sighed. "We really can't risk any more, Davy." He kissed him as a lover one final time. Archer held on, drawing it out as long as he possibly could, realizing with a pang that this was going to have to last him the rest of his life. But finally they had to separate, and Will kissed him once again, chastely, on the forehead. "We'd better get dressed."

"I know." Archer breathed deeply, wondering if he could hold fast to the memory of the scent. "Will—thank you."

"I hope I can't say the pleasure was all mine—"

"Oh, no." Reluctantly, Archer moved away, and found himself so utterly weary he could barely sit up. He located the washing cloth, tidied himself up, and dragged his clothing back on. "We ought to sleep the day away, with so much to do tonight." The last word ended in a prodigious yawn.

"Yes. You sleep now, Davy. I'll wait until it's light and make certain nothing looks out of place."

"Thank you. I don't know why I'm so tired." And chilly. He found his jacket and used it as a cover, bunching extra straw up as a pillow. "G'night, Will. Or good morning ..."

"Good night, Davy."

Archer closed his eyes and slipped off into sleep, a deep velvet sleep with no need at all for dreams.

Marshall sat back, trying to sort out his thoughts. He had never imagined his body was capable of such intense pleasure, or that he could have done such things and, even now, feel no guilt at all. The rightness of it went all the way through him. It had been risky and dangerous, they could never admit having done it, or dare take the risk again—but it had not been wrong. Whatever society might say, anything so joyful was no sin. The only worry he had was that somehow they might be found out, and he didn't think that likely.

He was still astonished that he had let himself do what he had done—what they had done. What Davy had said the other night was true, though—if it had not been for these peculiar circumstances, it would probably never have happened. These circumstances...and one moment of clairvoyant certainty, just as he was losing consciousness in the choke hold. For just an instant, he had seen what had to be the future—or at least a possible future: Davy lying on the quarterdeck of this ship, motionless, eyes closed. Dead? Perhaps.

It was not imagination; he had such flashes rarely, but they were always true sight. His Irish grandmother had had the gift, and warned him that it had been passed down to him.

He wasn't grateful; he would not have called it a gift. The first time he'd 'seen' was when his mother had taken ill after giving birth to a baby sister; they'd both died within the week. Most recently, it had been his two gunners, in the last battle. When he'd seen them in his dream, their faces had been blank. He hadn't remembered that, or realized what it meant, until the French missile took out the rail and blasted his men to eternity.

And what about Davy? Were things different enough now? Had this given Davy the will to live, countered his hopelessness about the future? Or had he made it worse, waking a wish for the impossible? Try as he might, he could not force the vision. Gift or curse, it came at its own whim.

Well, he had done what he could. And it was no sacrifice; if he had given Davy any happiness, the gift had been returned a hundredfold. If they both survived the morrow, this would be a strange but wonderful dream, to be put aside when they went back to the *Calypso*. If they both died, it would matter not at all. If only one survived...

If Archer were to die, if that was what the vision had meant, it would be a grief worse than anything he'd ever known—but nothing like the guilt and regret he'd have been burdened with if he had let Davy go down into the dark without sending the love he felt with him. *And if I die, I suppose I'll find out if there really is a hell.* That seemed to cover all eventualities.

He heard the faint echo of two strikes on the ship's bell. Five a.m. The sun would be up soon, and with any luck they'd be getting breakfast in an hour or so.

Gradually the sky outside brightened and enough daylight trickled in to show that they'd left no visible evidence. He found the washrag, rinsed and concealed it in the straw. Anything else—any scent? The decks of the *Titan* had taken on a strange odor when temporary "wives" were visiting... He couldn't tell, but took the lid off the slop bucket for a minute. By the time that smell cleared out, anything else should go with it.

He was relaxed enough to feel sleepy, but he was wary of lying down beside Archer just now. The cell was only six feet wide; their mats were too near one another. It would be so easy to roll over and take Davy into his arms, warm and sleepy and trusting, and simply hold him close. It would feel so good, and he dared not risk the chance he might do it in his sleep. From now on, he'd have to find some excuse not to sleep next to Archer, at least not until these feelings subsided. Some pretext...keeping watch should sound reasonable. Would be reasonable, actually, at this point. He settled down in the corner beside the door, next to the water buckets, let his head rest against the wall, and closed his eyes for just a moment.

Chapter 20

Captain's Log, HMS Artemis (Supplemental Log, Detached duty, HMS Calypso, in for repair, Portsmouth.) Lt. Anthony Drinkwater, commanding 29-7-1799

*Tor Bay, fair weather and a good wind. Met two ships since departure (*HMS Sophia, HMS Polychrest*), and informed them as to the situation. No sign of the* Morven *thus far.*

⚓ ⚓ ⚓

"**H**ey! You! Where's the other one?"

Archer's eyes flew open at the question. A guard, peering through the barred door, was frowning at him.

"Who—Oh." William was sitting against the wall, slumped over and sleeping like the dead. Archer pointed. "Over there."

The guard scowled through at an angle. "Sick?"

"No, I don't think so. Will?"

By this time Marshall was shaking his head muzzily. He saw the guard, recognized the problem, and moved over to where he was visible. "I must have dozed off," he said. "Sorry."

"Stay where I can see you," the guard said shortly, and slid a tray under the door: Oatmeal again, biscuit, and apples.

Marshall nodded. "Yes. Thank you."

They shared out the food, and ate silently for a while. Archer glanced over occasionally, and once caught Marshall watching him with an odd, quizzical half-smile that vanished immediately. Something about the daylight turned William into a different person from the ardent lover of a few hours past—cooler, more remote. "It is strange, isn't it?" Archer voiced his thought. "Like a dream—or the memory of a dream."

"Yes," Marshall said soberly, spooning up the last of his porridge. "That's probably the best way to think of it."

Archer didn't really want to ask. "Are you sorry?"

"No. Never that." Their eyes met, and Archer caught a brief glimpse of something gentler. "But...it needs some distance, Davy. Not the best thing to have in the front of our minds."

"No, I suppose not." He cleaned his own bowl and put the dishes outside, and they were taken away.

"What we need to do is consider the next step," Marshall said under his breath, then started speaking in a normal voice about the best way to rig the *Calypso* for getting through a narrow strait during a thunderstorm with variable winds. Under that discussion they sketched out a plan of action for the night's attack; by the time they were finished, Archer was beginning to believe they might actually have a chance to get out of this.

"What a gift you have for cheering a body up, Will. You'd have been a marvelous physician."

William shook his head with a smile, but said nothing; he was clearly giving the matter some thought. "No, I don't believe I would. Our local doctor was a good man, and I respected him, but I could never have studied with him. It would be too hard to be around sick people all the time—don't laugh! I hate to see children ill, and then there was the matter of money—you seldom see a doctor who has any, no more than a minister. Not that I expect to become wealthy, but it would be pleasant to walk into an inn, as we did with the Captain, and be able to order what you like without counting pennies. And now I've made lieutenant, I'll draw half-pay even if I'm not on active duty—though I hope it never comes to that."

Archer had never needed to think about such things. His

own childhood had been comfortable, his material needs met; even now, his father sent £50 a year for his expenses, and had promised to continue until he was made lieutenant. He had to make his own way, of course; what else was a man to do? But if he fell on hard times he would never need worry about his next meal. "Well, most Navy men don't get rich, either—Captain Smith and a few others excepted, of course. I suppose we all hope to be as lucky."

"We've been lucky enough to still be alive. What about you, Davy? How did you come to choose the Navy? Family tradition?"

A year ago, if someone had asked him that, he would have simply said he'd wanted adventure, and changed the subject. But that old wound no longer smarted; it was almost funny, in retrospect. "Evasive action."

"How? From whom?"

"Do you remember I once said Drury Lane was like my second home?" Marshall nodded. "Well, there was a girl, an actress." Mary Belle Blossom. Or Maribel, or sometimes Mariabella, depending on the play. She changed it from one day to the next, along with her costumes and characters. "She understudied Mrs. Siddons once, when she played Cleopatra. Her role was only a handmaiden, but she would have been ready to play the lead. We would—" He almost said 'lie there for hours'. Not something a gentleman should reveal. "Spend hours going over Cleopatra's lines. I could probably recite the whole play, even now. I was all of fifteen, she was two or three years older."

She was pretty, bright and lively; he had been fascinated, smitten, and wholly overwhelmed. "We had...I realize now it was a simple little affair, but, Lord, I was convinced the sun rose and set on her. After a few weeks, I proposed marriage. She told me not to be silly. Then I went home and told my father." He sighed, remembering.

"I take it he was not pleased?"

"It was something like being on the *Titan's* lower gun-deck in the middle of a broadside. He called her names I'd never even heard, threatened to disown me...it was not a happy time. The next day, he informed me he'd written to the commanding officer of my brother's regiment, and he was sure I would be accepted."

"This was the dreadful brother?" Marshall interjected.

"Of course. And I would almost rather serve on this barge than enlist in Ronald's regiment. So I hied myself over to my uncle Jack, who'd served with Captain Cooper years ago, and told him I had my heart set on the Navy—which was true, as of about noon that day—and he got me aboard the *Titan*."

"Was your father upset?"

Archer laughed. "No, he surprised me. He was delighted I'd 'shown some initiative'. Actually, I think it was because I'd be even less likely to ever see the girl again. He said the Navy would 'make a man of me'." Ah, life's little ironies. "The less said about that the better, I suppose. But I did see her once more."

"Another broadside?" Marshall asked sympathetically.

"No, nothing like that. Though my pride took a thrashing. I told her I'd volunteered, and we'd have to be married immediately because I had to go join my ship. And she turned me down."

"What?"

"I couldn't believe it, either, especially after all my father'd said about fortune-hunting actresses. But she knew her own mind, that girl. She said my family would never accept her or let her stay on the stage, and she wanted a husband who'd keep her warm at night, not 'some ruddy sailor who'd come home to make babies then go off and get drowned once a year'."

It hadn't been that brusque, really; she had been very sweet, and assured him that he was so pretty and so dear he would have to beat the girls off when he came home on shore leave. At the time, it had not been much consolation.

"Did you explain you can't get drowned every year?" Marshall inquired.

"Her grammar was not the crux of the problem. And truly, it was generous of her. I had proposed, after all; it could have been messy. Lord, I was incredibly..."

"Young?" William suggested.

"Yes. And even more naive." He had done what he could to return her kindness, telling his father she had agreed not to sue for breach of promise in return for a small annuity. He'd considered telling his father what she'd really said, but His Lordship would not have believed it, and she had been living in such grinding poverty she didn't have a shift without holes in it. "She was right, in the end. If I'd married her she'd have been all alone the whole time we've been at sea. My family would have shunned her. 'Not our sort'."

"What a tale of romance. I doubt the girls in my village even noticed I was gone."

"I'm sure they did." *Unless they were all blind.* It was strange, their having this conversation now. Why had they never spoken of these things before? "You've never said why you went to sea, though, instead of apprenticing to some rich merchant. I can't see you doing something you hated for hope of a lieutenant's half-pay."

"Lord, I hope not. It was much more than security. I always wanted to see the world. My mother would read to me, when I was young, from her father's old journals. He sailed with Captain Cook, and on ships taking settlers to the colonies. He saw wonderful things."

"Did you know him?"

"No, he went down in a storm off the West Indies. I don't know what became of the journals; they may be with some things of my father's that the new vicar is holding for me. I hope so—I'd like to read them again, I would understand more of what he was saying. But it was more than that, Davy—I wanted to do something that matters, something that makes a difference. Do you remember what the Captain said about the Navy keeping England safe? We really do. If we weren't here—all of us, I mean, not just you and I—the world would be different, and England would be the worse for it. And this job is something I'm capable of doing—the maths for navigation, strategy, tactics, the fighting itself. I couldn't be a minister, it's too serious. Life and death."

"But—in battle, we kill—or at least wound—the enemy. I don't understand—"

"That's different, Davy. In battle, when the enemy is doing his best to kill you, it is different. I could never tell someone who trusted me that there was everlasting life. I don't know what happens beyond—I simply do not know, and I never had the gift of faith my father did. I learned my prayers, but I never could call myself a believer. I believe in what I can prove to be true. You don't need faith to know that a good wind fills the sails."

"That doesn't stop us praying for a good wind when we're becalmed." Archer was a little surprised at William's self-revelation. "You chose your course well," he said. "I don't imagine your father would have been able to climb up a ship's hull in the dead of night with nothing but a couple of ropes to hold on to."

"No." Marshall chuckled. "He would have advised Adrian to see a doctor for his mental aberration, and said prayers for his soul. I may be lacking in charity, but if the bastard even has a soul, I say he deserves whatever Hell may await him."

Chapter 21

Captain's Log, HMS Artemis (Supplemental Log, Detached duty, HMS Calypso, in for repair, Portsmouth.) Lt. Anthony Drinkwater, commanding 29-7-1799

Still searching. Morven *nowhere to be seen. If we have had no success in the next hour, we will beat back and search the area again.*

⚓ ⚓ ⚓

Captain Smith read the printed note that had been folded under his soup bowl. It let him know that Archer was back in his cell, and Josiah, the cook's mate—presumably the scrawny youth who brought the meal—was 'coming aboard'. As good a way as any to put it, and it shifted their numbers to six against 37. Almost down to six to one. The odds were improving all the time. Also, someone—presumably Bert—was on duty tonight and would speak to the others, then see Smith the day after tomorrow.

He disposed of the note as he had the other. Two days would suit perfectly—one day past dark of the moon, with only five or six men on deck late at night. The guards at their doors would have supper during the evening watch, with something in the food to send them off to sleep; with three confederates in the crew, they could all be freed simultaneously.

If he and his men could get on deck before the alarm was given, they might be able to dog the hatches and seal the rest of the crew below. They might, by God, be able to take this ship!

Of course, whether or not they could hold the ship was another matter. But if they got that far, it would not matter. No matter how fractious the crew, they should at least have time to lower a boat and get away. That would be the prudent course, no doubt. But what a reversal if he could sail back in command of the ship that had hauled them away in biscuit barrels!

And what presumption, to let his expectations run that far ahead. If he had learned anything in all his years at sea, it was that the course of a battle could veer faster than a friendly wind. But it was a promise of action at last, after too long a wait, with a good chance of winning their freedom. That would do, for now.

⚓ ⚓ ⚓

"There. That should do it." Marshall stepped back from the porthole so Archer could leave off watching the door and inspect his handiwork. Morning light had revealed a noticeable notch in the porthole frame, viewed from certain angles, and Marshall had tried to mask it with a mash of crumbled biscuit mixed with oatmeal, wood shavings, bits of thread, and dust.

Archer squinted up, then nodded. "I can see it because I know where to look, but I doubt anyone else would. I just hope it doesn't set so hard we have to dig it out again." He glanced at the door, then sat at an angle from the porthole, so that a guard looking in at him would have to look away from the port.

Marshall tried to see if it was visible from the door. No. Very good. He joined Archer. "As long as it holds for another 16 hours..." The prospect of action was beginning to wind him tight with anticipation. He wished there were some way to communicate with Captain Smith. Had that sailor he'd spoken to ever gone to see him?

It wouldn't matter. Smith would have observed everything they had, about the ship; he'd probably been able to draw more conclusions, from his greater experience. And it was only the interim Marshall need be concerned with. Once they got the Captain out, he would take command.

The ship's bell rang once. 8:30 a.m. Five more rounds of the bells, and it would be midnight. If Adrian kept to form, he would keep Archer up in his cabin for an hour or so past that. "You can hear the bell clearly enough above, can't you, Davy?"

"That's the third time you've asked, and the answer is still yes, of course. The bell is right above on the quarter-deck. And unless he's sent me back, you'll start up at two bells. I will be ready."

"I wish it were winter, it would be dark earlier—"

"And you would freeze to death on the damned rigging if you had to wait. Don't worry, Will, if he hasn't killed me by now—" He shrugged. "I've just been waiting for this to be over. The idea that I can do something to end it—"

"I wish there were more I could do."

"No." Archer's face settled into a harder, more determined expression than Marshall had ever seen on him. "No, I want to do this alone, Will. I need to. I think it may be the only way I can be free of him."

It was almost an echo of Marshall's own feelings, back across the years, when he'd challenged Correy. He'd known instinctively that such a predator would never quit until someone stopped him, permanently. "I understand."

"The only thing I fear," Archer went on, "is that I might not be quite strong or fast enough. If I fail—" He looked away. "He'll take it out on you, not the Captain."

"I'm not worried, Davy. You won't fail. I really was doing my best to get away from you."

"I know. But however hard you tried, you knew I—I would never have hurt you. There was no real danger. That bastard will know he's fighting for his life."

"And you'll be fighting for all of us," Marshall said. "Three against—"

The feel of the ship shifted and began to slow, as it had a few nights earlier, and the port hatch was pulled shut.

"Another ship?" Archer asked.

"It must be." With a bit of luck, they might be able to pry that hatch open long enough for at least one of them to get out and attract the attention of that other ship. If their guess as to the nature of *Elusive's* cargo was correct, it was most probably a Navy vessel, or a private ship on hire to the Navy. Word of their capture ought to be spreading by now. There would be boats coming alongside to collect the cargo; if one approached on this side, and Archer were to drop into the water and be picked up, he would be out of Adrian's reach, and safe, and he could get help. That bastard wouldn't dare fire on a Navy ship, not with those little popguns.

He could order Archer to go first...*and he will, if he thinks I'm right behind him.* Just to get David to safety would be a victory. He would not follow, of course, not with Captain Smith still a prisoner. But caught red-handed, Adrian would be a fool to do anything to either of them. "Davy, listen—"

A clatter in the companionway cut short his hasty plan. Three guards, one with a pistol and two with clubs, called them both out of the cell.

"What'll you have, boys?" the one with the pistol gestured toward the deck. "Lie down quiet 'til we've finished our business, or be trussed up and gagged so you don't attract attention?"

"You might as well put that gun away," Marshall said. "It would make more noise than both of us shouting together, as you well know."

"No more'n some clumsy hand droppin' a box," the man replied. "What'll it be?"

Marshall exchanged looks with Archer; they both lay down on the deck. Their uniforms had reached the hopelessly grimy stage days ago; this would make no difference. With luck, they were nearing the end of Adrian's capricious games.

The cargo transfer took the better part of two hours. They could hear much of what went on outside, though Marshall could not catch the name of the ship. She was Navy, though, damn it; there was no mistaking the orders shouted and bosun's whistle for sounds of a merchant vessel.

He caught Archer's eye. "I'm surprised she hasn't sent a search party aboard looking for us," he said to their guards. "It's only a matter of time. You really should consider Captain Smith's offer—"

Adrian's spokesman responded to his considerate suggestion with a boot in the ribs. "One more word from you, and you'll get a tap from my mate, here. Same goes for you," he told Archer, who was giving Marshall an exasperated look. Marshall smiled at them both; only David smiled back, with a shake of his head.

Eventually the loading was finished, and when the port in their cell was opened, they were allowed to return. The extra guards departed, the regulars returned to their posts away from the cell door, and Marshall nearly stopped breathing when he saw the wad of breadcrumb hash sitting on the sill of the porthole.

Archer followed his horrified stare and laughed. "I think we can take it as a good sign, Will." He scooped up the repellent mass and dropped it in the slop bucket. "If they didn't see that, they're not likely to see anything else."

Marshall swallowed his heart. "I hope they're on duty later tonight. Well, we should have an hour or so until lunch. What would you prefer, Davy—chess, navigation problems, or a nap?"

"Why don't you sleep?" Archer suggested. "You didn't look very comfortable this morning, and I know for certain you didn't get much rest last night."

Marshall smiled at that. "Neither did you, as I recall. And you're right, we should both be as rested as possible."

David looked away. "Well, with time this short, it might be better if we didn't sleep togeth— um, at the same time—I can stand watch."

He shrugged helplessly, and Marshall realized that David had come to the same conclusion he had about lying too close to one another. "Thanks, I think I will. We can trade watches after lunch."

His weary body seized its chance as soon as he got horizontal. With no more than a passing regret that they'd missed the chance with that Navy ship, he slipped into a deep, comfortable sleep.

⚓ ⚓ ⚓

Captain's Log, HMS Artemis (Supplemental Log, Detached duty, HMS Calypso, in for repair, Portsmouth.) Lt. Anthony Drinkwater, commanding 29-7-1799

Encountered HM Sloop Speedy, *six miles off Bolt Head, where we had good news from Cmdr. Thomas Cochrane. He received powder this very morning from the* Morven, *heading N-NE. We had passed her out of sight at some time during the night. After hearing our purpose, Captain Cochrane kindly offered to join us and assist with the capture, but I declined with thanks. We do not wish to alert our quarry, and I believe that the return of the* Speedy *might alert the pirates that something is amiss. From his description, I am convinced we have sufficient arms and crew to effect a capture. By this time tomorrow, if all goes well, we will have recovered our officers and captured a shipload of brigands!*

⚓ ⚓ ⚓

"Try to look less ferocious, Davy," Marshall advised. "You're holding that razor as if you're ready to swing over to a Frog ship and raise hell."

Archer frowned at his reflection in the little shaving mirror. William was right; he looked far too keen. He took a deep breath and tried to relax. This was no time to tighten himself up for battle; it was only eight bells, and with four hours until midnight, he had a long way to go. All in Adrian's company.

Marshall had suggested that he might put Adrian out as quickly as he could, then tie him—but the pirate had, on other occasions, left off his diversions to give orders or receive information. They couldn't risk alerting the crew too soon. It would have to be a last-minute attack, timed to clear the guards so Marshall could get on deck.

It was going to be a long night.

"That's better," Will said. "Much more wretched."

"Yes, the thought of passing time with that bastard does have a dampening effect on the spirits."

Marshall hesitated, then offered, "There's still time to try it the other way. If you'd like me to go—"

"No." Archer shook his head. "Your reach is much longer than mine, Will. I probably couldn't even get to the chains outside. We have a good plan; this is no time to tamper with it."

"You're right." Marshall's mouth tightened. "I wish to God there were another way, Davy. But at least it will be the last time."

"Yes." One way or another, this would be the end. Archer had made that decision—not quite the way William meant it—in the hour before lunch, when his friend had finally given in to his exhaustion and dozed off. It wasn't a matter of not having hope; he would keep faith with Will in that respect, make himself believe that this might all work out. It might. But he didn't expect it would. And things would be much simpler for William, really, if he did not survive.

He put the shaving things down by the door, on their side of the hatch, and peered outside. The guards were out of sight.

"Right, then," Marshall said in a low voice. "You begin at two bells, I'll be ready to come on deck at three, or as soon as you get the guards away. Are you ready?"

"As I'll ever be."

"I'll see you on deck."

Marshall held out his hand; Archer took it. He had a sudden sharp conviction that this was goodbye, and took two quick steps, pulling his friend back beside the door, out of sight. "Will, if this...goes bad...please, visit my family some-day? Tell them—" He couldn't go on; he didn't know what to say.

Marshall closed his eyes briefly. "I'll tell them they raised a hero. But—but I won't need to, Davy—"

"It will be fine, I'm sure." Time to go. "Will, I promise you, I will never do this again." He reached up, swiftly, be-fore his nerve failed, and found William's lips—and was as-tonished to find the kiss returned fiercely, Will's arms tight around him for one brief moment that brought back the in-credible unity of the previous night.

But that was over, now. Forever. Time to go. "I'm sorry," he said, stepping back. "I shouldn't have..." He went back to the door, bent to push the basin outside.

"Davy—" He glanced up; Marshall was regarding him with that odd little smile. "Don't apologize. I wanted to do that, too. I was afraid of breaking your concentration."

"Not at all." He touched his mouth, smiled. "It feels like a shield. I expect I'll need it." One more time, back into the bear pit. "Wish me luck?"

Marshall's eyes held no doubt at all. "Of course. But it's not just luck, Mr. Archer. You can do it."

Archer forced a nod. "Of course," he echoed, then pushed the basin and razor out for the guards to collect. A moment later, the door swung open to reveal his escort.

"Boarding party away," William said, too low for the guards to hear. The boarding party had no difficulty assum-ing a suitably glum and apprehensive demeanor before the cloak masked the need for artifice.

⚓ ⚓ ⚓

Captain's Log, HMS Artemis (Supplemental Log, Detached duty, HMS Calypso, in for repair, Portsmouth.) Lt. Anthony Drinkwater, commanding 30-7-1799

Despite having sailed a course that should have enabled us to intercept the Morven, *we have missed her. She must have changed course at some point since her encounter with the* Speedy, *which of course Capt. Cochrane could not have anticipated. We shall begin a sweep covering as wide an area as possible, and hope for the best.*

Adrian was in rare form at dinner, extremely pleased with himself, and by the time the meal ended Archer knew how Damocles must have felt. Every question, every innuendo made him feel that he had "escape" written across his forehead. Until tonight he had drunk anything Adrian offered, grateful for the numbing, but tonight he sipped at the wine only so as not to do anything out of the ordinary. He could not risk the chance that Adrian might have decided to drug him again.

He had no awareness of what he ate, but, though oblivious to the food, he was very aware of cutlery. When observed as a source of improvised weapons for an all-or-nothing attack, the table had much to choose from, all fairly unpleasant when applied with ill intent: the edge of a broken plate, a blunt knife, a wine-bottle from the sideboard, even the table itself. He thought that with the element of surprise he could kill Adrian, as long as he did not mind being killed himself. But that was not the plan; that was his own secondary strategy, in case all else failed.

"You seem quiet this evening, Mr. Archer," Adrian remarked toward the end of the meal. "Are you unwell?"

"No. Not at all." *Sick to death of your company, thank you.* "I was only...wondering...if you have had any word, as yet, on our ransom."

"It's not two weeks since you joined us. Early days. Are you really in such a hurry to get back to a ship unfit to sail?"

"To rejoin my ship's company, yes."

"And you'd not miss...any of this?" Adrian's gesture was aimed at the table, but obviously included the rest of the cabin, the carpets, the absurdly luxurious sleeping quarters.

And himself. Was the man entirely out of touch with reality?

"I hardly think so," Archer said, but an inner voice told him that this was an opportunity, and he had better consider his words. Adrian's weak point was his conceit; play up to it, and he might be lulled. "I am—accustomed—to Navy accommodations."

"But let us suppose you were not ransomed with your shipmates. You could accustom yourself to something more agreeable than His Majesty's meager comforts, I'm sure."

Not ransomed? Stay here permanently—was that really what he was hinting at? Did he imagine this docility would continue, without Will and the Captain as hostages? Archer decided to pretend he had missed the suggestion. "Shipboard life has taught me to adapt to a variety of circumstances." That was true enough; Adrian would supply his own interpretation. Strange, after 12 days of being denied physical integrity, that he was so reluctant to utter convenient lies. Perhaps it was that he had nothing left but his word.

"Only 'adapt'? I would have thought there was a time...or two...when you appeared to be rather enjoying yourself."

Archer's face burned. *When I was down on the floor, heaving my guts out? Oh, yes, that was delightful.* He looked down, quickly, before Adrian could see that it was anger, and not some other emotion. His hands were tight fists in his lap, but he said nothing.

Predictably—William was right, the villain was so very predictable—Adrian laughed. "Ah, the truth will out. I thought so. It was when we used the ropes, wasn't it? Not having to worry about keeping you in check allows me to be so much more creative."

Oh, please, no... The one thing they had not considered in their strategy, a detail Archer had put out of his mind. And trying to dissuade Adrian would only fix his intention more securely. How long had it been, last time? Hours. Even after he'd exhausted himself, Adrian had seemed to enjoy leaving him tied and helpless; although Archer had altered details in what he told William, that part of it was true.

But Will would not leave the cell for three long hours. And Adrian bored easily. In time it should be possible to divert him to some other activity. *It's really not as though I have any choice.* And he could escape, now, in a way. He could close his eyes, and his mind, and he could remember.

"Well, laddie, what do you say? Are you ready for dessert?"

He reached back to the night before, to William, to that incredible invisible fire that had flowed between them...and found it was still there, swirling just within his skin like some magical shield. It did not matter what Adrian might do, or make him do. His body could endure the insult; his soul was wrapped in an embrace that Adrian could never penetrate or even understand.

Archer stood, half in a trance. In a strange way, he almost pitied his captor. Adrian would never get what he wanted. Let the bastard convince himself he was irresistible. Let him deceive himself. Let him think whatever he liked...and, just for one moment, let him lower his guard.

Chapter 22

The ship's bell rang once. Marshall put the last touches on his sleeping straw figure, barely visible in the near-total dark, and sat down beside the door to wait. He had to give David time; it would be a waste of energy to spend an extra half-hour hanging on the shrouds in the chill night air.

If what he'd seen on deck the night before was the usual arrangement, there would be three men on duty; he had seen two on the quarter-deck, one in the forecastle—plus a pair of guards outside Adrian's door. Archer would get those two into the cabin; with luck, he might draw in the foc'sleman, as well. Someone would stay at the wheel no matter what, but with any luck their attention would be on the captain's cabin. To get down to the Captain's cell, he would have to cover the 10 or 15 feet to the nearest ladder below, and deal with whatever guards might be there. And then...

Then, God willing, Captain Smith would take command and they could get back above and seal the hatches and lower a boat. Adrian must have something in his cabin that would show their position; he was not likely to keep false charts just in case his unarmed prisoners overpowered his crew.

The attack would be completely unexpected; it might even be easy, unless the Captain intended to take the ship. In that case, things could get very exciting. But it would all depend on whether Archer could put Adrian out of commission, lure the guards into the cabin, and keep them all quiet for a crucial few minutes.

Could he do it? If asked, Marshall would have responded, "of course," but he had to admit just a hint of doubt. If Adrian had not spent nearly two weeks overpowering Archer, beating him down mentally and physically, he would have felt more sure.

As to exactly how that had been done—and what was being done now—he dared not let himself think about it. If Davy felt shielded in any way, well and good, but Marshall felt more vulnerable than he ever had before, as though part of himself were up there. Whether it was true knowing, or just the memory of last night, of the enormous, terrifying trust Davy had given him—whatever it was, he had to find some way to block that connection. What they'd shared had been temporary, and for just that once. It could not continue. Eventually, probably fairly soon, he and Archer would go their separate ways, be posted to different ships. The nature of life in the Navy was essentially solitary. Careers were unpredictable. Friends moved on. Sometimes, friends died.

Marshall closed his eyes, and felt a phantom touch still lingering on his lips. He shouldn't have allowed Davy to do that. He should have stopped him. He should have—but it had taken all his strength just to keep from locking his arms around Davy, so tightly they couldn't take him away.

But that was just a dangerous illusion. Circumstances had already taken him away. They had no future together as anything but friends, shipmates. That wasn't so bad, was it? It had been enough until last night; it would have to be enough in the future.

And it's time to get Davy out of there and stop that bastard, once and for all. Get on with it. Get moving.

He rose in the dark and worked the iron bar out of its track. He would take it with him this time, secured with that useful twine. It was a poor weapon, but he needed every advantage he could get. If Archer appeared to be having trouble, perhaps he could—

No. He had to get the Captain free as quickly as possible so he would not be a hostage if the below-decks crew were alerted. No need to worry about David's ability. If that incredible burst of murderous rage that exploded out of him last night was a sample of what he'd been bottling up, Marshall would not want to be standing anywhere near Adrian when David unleashed it. As long as it wasn't blind fury, which could get him killed.

He stilled the inner debate. Davy knew what was at stake; he had chosen to go this course. He knew what he was doing, and he would be all right.

Pray God he would be all right.

⚓ ⚓ ⚓

Archer wiggled his fingers slightly, then rubbed them together, and was rewarded when the tingling in the fingertips diminished. Good. As long as he kept moving his hands, they didn't go to sleep. And his arms were all right. If only the rope were just a bit longer, he might be able to untie it. But it was a single length, run through a couple of eyelets screwed into the bulkhead—moving a hand in one direction pulled the other hand out of reach.

Eight bells had sounded at least 20 minutes ago. Midnight. In just a little over half an hour, William was going to be out on that rigging, expecting that Archer would have done his part.

He had done nothing; Adrian was lying draped half across him, deep asleep. Too much brandy. The bastard had an unerring ability to do the worst possible thing, under every circumstance—such a nap would have been a godsend at any other time, Adrian asleep being infinitely preferable to awake.

I wonder what would happen if I just kicked him off the bunk. Tempting, but not practical. *The way my luck's been running, he'd break his damned neck—that would be all right—but I'd be lying here like this when Will comes back with the Captain.* There truly were situations worse than death, and they would certainly include being found by one's commanding officer trussed up like the leavings from a Roman orgy. And even though William knew what had been going on, just telling him about it had been humiliating enough. To be seen by him, like this—

A single bell sounded on the quarterdeck above. Well, whatever he was going to do, he'd better do it now. Will would be sitting in the cell, ready to go, counting the minutes. In an hour, he'd expect the deck to be cleared of the guards, and knowing William he would try something even if they were still there. And what Adrian would do to him if this attempt were to fail—

No. It is not going to fail. Not on my account. If he had to crawl, then, damn it, he'd crawl. He could scrub the filth off later. And why worry? There probably wasn't going to be a "later." Not for him.

Into the muck, then. He took a deep breath. "Captain—" He had not used that title before, nor any other respectful address. It had been the only way he could retaliate for the utter absence of respect with which he'd been treated. He nudged Adrian with his knee. "Captain?"

Adrian's eyes opened. Archer could tell by his expression that he'd noted the formality. "Yes, laddie, what is it?"

Archer licked his lips. "Could—could we try something else now, please? My hands have gone numb." It sounded horribly contrived...but that was Adrian's style.

He took the bait, too, with a self-satisfied smirk. "You want more, do you? I expected you would come around. You are very like...someone I once knew. Stubborn, but malleable." He sat up and trailed a hand along Archer's arm to the rope, letting his fingers linger on the knots. "Very well. What would you like? I'll untie this...as soon as you tell me."

Archer's mind went blank for a moment as he tried to find the least objectionable possibility. Or the quickest. "The...the French thing from the second night?"

"Frottage? Rather tame, don't you think? And you were really very dull that evening."

"I'd...never done anything like that before. I really wasn't sure what to do." Archer realized he was speaking in fragments, still dancing around an actual lie, trying to hold out in that last stronghold.

Adrian laughed. "I'll wager you've never done most of what you've done this past week. But since you ask ..." He started to undo the knot, then turned those pale eyes on Archer's, like a hound catching a scent, holding the look with a knowing smile. "If you can ask politely." His other hand stroked up the inside of Archer's thigh. "Is that what you want, laddie? Say it."

You son of a bitch. Averting his eyes, Archer made his face as bland and ingenuous as he could; he couldn't simulate desire to save his life—or even William's. But he could lie. "Yes. Please?"

"That wasn't so difficult, was it? Keep still, now— There." The rope came free, sliding through the eyelets, and Archer let out the breath he'd been holding, relief making him nearly oblivious to Adrian's hand on his body. "I do expect you to be a little more...active...this time."

"Of—of course." He rubbed his wrists, loosening the rope still fastened to the left. "What would you like me to do, sir?" That last was an effort, but he was past pride, now, and even past fear. This was war.

"That's more what I want to hear. What would I like you to do? Let me consider that most excellent question—" He reached lazily for the brandy he'd left on the little bedside table.

As he half-turned something clicked in Archer's mind, like a pistol's hammer being drawn back. He lunged, reacting almost before he consciously recognized his chance. His world narrowed into immediate focus: the scrape of beard against the inside of his elbow, the startling splash of brandy on the side of his face as Adrian flung it backwards—a crash as the glass broke somewhere—the tremendous resistance of shoulder muscles as Adrian struggled to dislodge him.

But he had the angle right, the chin up and back, and a slight advantage of leverage since his adversary was on the wooden edge of the berth. Archer locked his right arm with his left, counting the seconds.

Pain shot up his arm; Adrian was digging his fingers into the muscle, raking with nails, desperate now. Archer closed his eyes and hung on, ignoring his right arm, holding tight with the left. In a little while Adrian was still. Sixty seconds—70—80... It was too easy; it must be a trick.

Archer glanced up, and past Adrian's shoulder he could see a reflection in the mirror bolted to the wall opposite the bed. His own face was a mask of rage, ugly and frightening...and Adrian's lips were blue above the neatly trimmed beard.

No trick.

He let go apprehensively, nonetheless, and was wholly astonished when his erstwhile tormenter slithered to the floor like a loose halyard. He stared in disbelief, but his body was already moving, tugging the end of rope from his own wrist, freeing his feet, heaving Adrian back up, tying the bastard— still breathing—just as he'd been tied himself minutes earlier.

It was not until he had the rope secure, and Adrian gagged with his own silk cravat, that he allowed himself a deep breath and noticed that his foot was wet. Blood? The broken glass on the carpet. Superficial cuts; he hardly felt them. He rolled up the little carpet and put it beneath the chest of drawers.

The mirror caught his eye once more, and he realized why Will had been so appalled the other day. The bruises were several days old now, and turning colors; he looked like Jonah's whale had swallowed him, chewed awhile, and spat him back out. *How could Will have wanted me, looking like this?* It hadn't felt like pity... No, he'd forgotten. It had been dark. William must have forgotten how horrible his body looked. Thank God.

Two bells sounded overhead. William was on his way. Archer surveyed the cabin. Weapons. He needed to find where Adrian kept weapons. Before doing that, though, he took a few seconds to pull on his breeches. He would have dearly loved to don the rest of his uniform, but he had no time—and he could not be fully dressed when he called in the guards.

Weapons. None in the drawers under the berth—though some of the things he recognized there made him glad he was leaving. He went through the chest of drawers, glancing at Adrian every few seconds to be sure he was still unconscious. In the third drawer, under some shirts, was a case containing a brace of pistols, complete with shot and powder. Archer charged the pistols and stuck them into his waistband. Now it looked like foresight—of course he'd had to put his breeches on, where else would he keep the pistols?

He found another pair of guns in one of the sea chests, and he loaded them, too. They weighed down the back of his waistband. Boarding party, indeed. But he could not go to the door arrayed like this—

His eye fell on Adrian's dressing gown, black silk with some sort of China dragons picked out in gold. Yes, that would serve, it would look as though he'd snatched up the first thing that came to hand—but it could wait. He found his shirt and tied it around his waist, in case of a hasty exit. He wanted no part of that bastard's clothing, but he had to cover the damage, hide it from the Captain's eyes, and William's, until he had time to heal.

Time? Adrian's watch said 1:21 a.m. William might be at the rail even now, though he wasn't due for another nine minutes. A furious sound from behind made him jump— Adrian, awake and glaring.

Archer felt a small, spiteful surge of triumph. "What's the matter, Captain? Aren't you *enjoying* yourself?" He pulled out one of the pistols; Adrian's eyes took on a new look.

Fear.

It occurred to Archer that he probably ought to take some pleasure in this moment, but it only disgusted him. He reversed the gun and rapped Adrian sharply on the skull, managing to use just enough force to knock him unconscious. That should keep the bastard out for a little while. He wouldn't need long.

His arm throbbed dully, and he dabbed at the gouges. They were bleeding a bit, but the dressing gown was dark enough that it wouldn't show, and the brightly-lit cabin would dazzle the eyes of men coming in from the night.

He removed Adrian's gag, for appearances, and checked the watch. 1:25. If Will said three bells—1:30—he would be hanging on the shrouds just below the deck by now. The plan was working, so far. Time for the next step.

Archer pulled the dressing gown over his armamentarium, checking in the mirror to see that the pistols weren't making any unnatural bulges. He had to draw the guards in, and anyone else he could get, and hold them while William found the Captain.

At least the indignity of his position would work in his favor. He shouldn't seem much of a threat. He took a deep breath, then crossed to the door, counting down the minutes. Just as the watch rang three bells, he pounded on the door.

"Guard! Guard! Anyone out—"

The door swung open; one of the guards stood scowling, pistol ready. Archer held his hands up, away from his body—that also kept the dressing gown out and away from the hidden pistols. "Don't shoot! Please come in, it's the captain. He's—he's had some kind of fit, I think."

He stood well back as the guard entered. A second man stayed in the doorway. "What the hell's going on here?" the first demanded, seeing Adrian tied.

Archer didn't have to try to look nervous. "He—I know this sounds mad, but he—he wanted me to tie him like that and—and he—started to flop around—" They'd had an epileptic midshipman on the *Calypso,* for a short time; Captain Smith had sent the boy home, but Archer knew what a fit looked like "—and then he went unconscious. He'd had a lot to drink," he added as he realized the smell of brandy was heavy in the air. "I didn't know what to do—" He backed away as far as he could, until he stood just beside the door.

"Oh, bugger," the first guard growled. "The crazy bastard's really done it this time. Get Brown down here."

The prosaic reaction was reassuring. Adrian was clearly not beloved by his crew. The second guard took a couple of steps back and called out to someone up on the quarterdeck. Footsteps thumped across and down the stair, and another man came in, better dressed than the first two, hastily tying a mask over his face. "What am I supposed to—" He went over to Adrian's bunk, followed by the second guard, and gave a variation on the first guard's theme. "What the hell is this all about?"

Archer unshipped two of the pistols and aimed carefully. "It's about time we parted company, gentlemen. If you'd be so good as to put your weapons down—"

He saw the third man gauging the distance. "You're right," he said, feeling in control of himself and the situation for the first time in ages. "I can only shoot two at a time, and there are three of you. That means I'd have to shoot to kill, and take my chances with the survivor. Who would like to be first?"

No one volunteered. "In all honesty," Archer said, "I wouldn't say the man's worth dying for. All we want to do is leave. Put your guns on the deck, if you would, and push them over here."

"You can't get away," the senior man said.

"Perhaps not, but it seems worth a try. Or you could consider the offer Captain Smith made when we first came on board. He might still be willing to negotiate."

Was he imagining it, or did they look thoughtful? "Your guns," Archer reminded.

The two guards turned to the other man, who shrugged, took a pistol out of his waistband, and placed it on the deck. The others followed suit.

"Kick them over here. One at a time. You first." He pointed to the third man. That done, he repeated the process with knives. When they'd all been disarmed, he took a page from the guards who'd stopped them signaling the ship, and had the three men lie down with their hands in sight.

"Now what?" one of them asked.

"Now..." Archer tried to hear what he could from the deck. Nothing but the sea, and the quiet creak of the rigging. He closed the door. "Now, we wait."

Chapter 23

Marshall risked a peek over the railing. Starlight was assisted by a candle-lantern hung on the quarterdeck near the binnacle, and another beside the door of Adrian's quarters. The guards were at their posts—but as three bells sounded, he heard a pounding, and Archer's voice, high and excited. The guards went into Adrian's cabin; someone called out a moment later, and a third man came down from the quarterdeck and went inside, as well. The door closed. *Bless you, Davy.*

The deck was quiet again. Marshall saw no one moving—though there would in all likelihood still be a man at the helm. He eased himself over the rail, still watching the cabin door, and heard a gasp behind him.

Halfway across the deck, a sailor was just coming down off the forecastle. His head snapped around toward Marshall, then he whirled and ran down the nearest stairway into the hold.

Marshall started after him, but heard footsteps on the quarterdeck approaching the stair. He ducked back into the shadow of that stairway, pulling the iron bar out of his waistband.

"Mr. Brown," the helmsman called. "Mr. Brown, do you need any—"

Whatever Brown might have needed was lost forever as Marshall hit him over the head and scooped up his pistol before diving for the stairway after the first man. That should have cleared the deck; if only he could catch that sailor before he woke the ship—no, he must get to the Captain. He hadn't been down this way before, but it had to be similar to the companionway by the cell he'd been in. A short stairway, a turn—and a faint light glimmered ahead.

He stumbled and nearly fell over a warm body.

"Cap'n! Cap'n, get up!"

Smith was on his feet, almost without thinking, at the note of alarm in Bert's voice. "What is it, man?"

The sailor looked worried in the light of a dim lantern. "Your lads 'ave jumped the gun, Cap'n. One of 'em's out on deck, I don't know what 'e's about. I sent Peters off, told 'im I was here to relieve 'im. I hit Alf over the head, but we've only—"

Out of the dark, a pistol barrel pressed against his temple. "Unbar the door," a familiar voice ordered coolly, "and stand clear. I'd rather lock you up than shoot you."

"Put the pistol away, Mr. Marshall," Smith said, pleased at the turn of events. "We have a new recruit. Bert—damn it, you're committed, man, what is your full name?"

"Hubert Parker, sir."

"Very well, Parker, get the door open and go fetch your comrades. Which hatch will you need?"

"Same's I come down, sir. Larboard aft."

"Good. Meet us on deck as quickly as possible." Parker saluted and disappeared as the door swung open.

Marshall held up the lantern the sailor had given him. He looked a little too thin, but seemed in high spirits. "Good morning, Captain. Are you well, sir?"

"Quite well, Mr. Marshall. And you look fit. I presume there is a reason you're out of uniform—" he was pulling on his own jacket and stepping into his shoes as he spoke. "But we can discuss that later. Where is Mr. Archer?"

"Above, sir." A small muscle twitched at the side of his jaw. "Dealing with Adrian. He will be expecting our assistance."

"Then let us not disappoint him. One moment." He retrieved the weapon he had fashioned for himself over the past several days. He was amused by Marshall's expression, but ignored it, only telling him to put out the lantern as they hurried back to the stairway.

"Where did you get a sword, sir?"

"It was originally a table leg, Mr. Marshall. Only good for one thrust, but I had nothing else to do, and it appears more impressive in dim light."

The deck was still quiet when they came up; they found the hatch covers and battened one down, leaving the other open for their allies. As footsteps thumped below Marshall frowned at the wooden sword, and handed the Captain the pistol. "I'll hold this exit," Smith snapped. "Go find Archer."

⚓ ⚓ ⚓

Marshall ran for Adrian's cabin. He knocked as they'd arranged—two raps, a pause, then a third—and the door swung open. "Will—come in, quick!" He looked back first; three men were on deck, helping Smith secure the other hatch. Archer handed him a pistol as he slipped inside. "Did you find the Captain?"

"He's on deck now. And he's recruited three crewmen." It looked like Archer also had things well in hand, with three prisoners on the floor and Adrian tied unconscious in his berth. "I see you've used the time well. Is there any more rope?"

"Use this." Archer pulled loose the belt of the dressing gown he was wearing and stripped it off, revealing an excess of weaponry and a nasty wound. His arm appeared to have been clawed by a wild animal, and the rest of him looked like a battlefield.

Marshall winced in sympathy. "Better put your shirt on, Davy—"

"I know." He pulled it on over his head and took his pistol back, covering Marshall while he bound two of the three men back-to-back. "Check them for knives, Will. I collected two belt-knives, but I couldn't search them."

The third man—the one who'd been on the quarter-deck—started to move. "Hold still, damn you!" Archer ordered. "Will, there should be rope in the left-hand drawer under the bunk."

There was rope, as well as some other things Marshall didn't want to speculate about. He trussed up the third man, tying one of his feet to the left and right of the other two. It would take them awhile to figure that out, much less get free. A search of their pockets turned up two clasp-knives and, from the helmsman, a small telescope.

Marshall went back to the bunk and pulled a blanket out of the rumpled bedclothes to throw over Adrian. This would look peculiar. They didn't have time to stuff the swine back into his clothes, nor could they do it with his crewmen present.

Then he recognized the little heap of clothes on the settle: blue midshipman's coat, waistcoat, the shoes and stockings beneath. That—that was damning. And for some reason, despite having known what the bastard had been doing to David, it woke a deep anger that made him want to kill. He took a breath, suppressed the impulse. The man was bound. He was unconscious. *He's a prisoner, damn it. You can't.*

Archer had been watching, of course, his face set in resignation, his eyes haunted. Marshall removed himself from the sleeping cabin before outrage got the better of his scruples; when he was close enough, David asked in an undertone, "How do you propose we explain his state to the Captain?"

"Sleeps in the nude, stinking drunk," Marshall said shortly. "You were wise to just tie him where he lay." He turned his back so the others could not hear, and lowered his voice. "We may not have to explain, if the Captain stays on the quarterdeck." Nodding toward the prisoners, "I'll play the oblivious ass, can't reach the obvious conclusion. Go get dressed, Davy."

Archer brightened for an instant, then shrugged. "What

difference will it make? There's no time—"

"*Put your clothes on*," Marshall ordered through clenched teeth. "You came down here for dinner, the whole ship knows that. You've been in a fight, it doesn't matter if you're neat, but for God's sake—" Louder, he said, "It will only take a moment to make sure they can't get their hands on any weapons. If there are any in here, we'll need them." He nodded at the sleeping cabin. "You take that side, I'll get the other." The partly-drawn curtain would screen Archer as he dressed.

Searching the room turned out to be a very good idea; Marshall found a musket, five swords—two Navy-issue, one excellent, serviceable blade, and an overly bejeweled but probably usable ornamental weapon—hanging in the clothes-press. There was one more. Marshall frowned at the last sword, which looked familiar—and realized that it was Captain Smith's own weapon, a presentation sword with an inscription. He also confiscated nine sharp knives from the sideboard, bundling them up in a towel. By the time he was finished, Archer was back in uniform and retrieving his pistols.

Marshall checked the bonds on their prisoners once more and saw that Archer had done a commendable job on Adrian. "I wonder you didn't smother the bastard when you had the chance," he said as they left the cabin and bolted it from the outside.

"I thought about it," Archer said. "Then it occurred to me, that was just the sort of thing Adrian might have done himself. I'd sooner let the Captain deal with him."

The deck was secure. Someone had tied the still-unconscious helmsman to the foremast; Captain Smith was up on the quarterdeck, now armed with a real sword and a brace of pistols. He returned Archer's salute. "A pleasure to see you well, Mr. Archer. Our ship's company has been increased by gunner's mate Parker and his friends from the galley, Nearns and Vincent. They have not formally signed on as yet, but they are now members of the *Calypso*'s crew;

we'll sort out the details when we return to Portsmouth."

It took Marshall a moment to realize what looked strange about the men's faces. Then it struck him: they weren't wearing masks. They had perfectly ordinary features, but it was startling to see even ordinary faces after all this time.

"Parker informs me that we are currently on course for Tor Bay, if we keep to this heading," Smith continued. "I trust your confinement has not affected your ability to handle sail?"

"No, sir. Captain—"

"Yes, Mr. Marshall?"

"I suggest we secure the ropes holding open the hatch on our cell. We removed the bar, sir, and if we could climb out—"

"See to it."

Marshall arrived at the side of the rail just in time to bang the hatch closed on a man attempting to follow his example. He tightened the line, pulling the hatch shut, and dogged the small capstan that controlled it. No one would get through the hatch silently. He reminded himself to keep an eye on the starboard mizzen shrouds, all the same.

"We'll stay on this heading until I get a look at the charts," Smith was saying when he returned. "The crew was 40; subtracting our new recruits, that fellow at the mast, and your prisoners—?"

"Adrian and three others, sir," Archer said.

"Excellent. We should have 32 prisoners below. My former quarters will hold nine, and if the hatch in the other is nailed shut, that's another nine. Parker, is there a room where we can conveniently confine the rest?"

"The sailroom, sir, where Mr. Marshall was—"

Smith glanced at Marshall. "Four-foot ceiling, sir," he said. "They won't be comfortable, but neither were we."

Smith nodded. "That should do. We'll be in port soon enough. I intend to deal with Adrian immediately. He appeared to me to be in sole command. Did either of you see any others who might be considered officers?"

Marshall looked to Archer, who shook his head. "Not that we could tell, sir," he said. "He appeared to have a navigator at the helm, but I do not recall anyone else ever giving any orders."

"That simplifies matters." Smith's face was grim. "Well, gentlemen, we have a distasteful task at hand; let us get it over as quickly as possible. Mr. Marshall, Mr. Archer—bring that pirate on deck." To the three others, he said, "Men, find a line and get it over the mainmast yard. I regret the necessity that requires you prove your sincerity by participating in this matter, but you are at present all the crew we have."

"I dinna mind at all, sir," Nearns said, and the other two nodded. The third recruit, Vincent, was probably still in his late teens, and from his expression Marshall guessed he probably had good reason for not minding.

He didn't mind, himself, in principle. In principle—especially on Archer's behalf—he heartily approved. But however much he and David had spoken of this very thing, the reality of executing anyone in cold blood, taking a living, breathing human being and turning him into cold meat, was revolting. He knew he might well have to order such a thing himself someday, if he were ever to win the command he yearned for. Still, he was glad it was not this day.

"Thank God it's on the Captain's head," Archer said under his breath, as they made their way down the few steps from the quarterdeck. "I hate that bastard, I'd kill him in a fair fight, gladly, but—"

"I know." And they would have to get him awake, and dressed, and, dear God, what if his last words were something that would fulfill all Archer's worst fears? Nothing to be done for it. The Captain was back in command, and he had both the experience and the stomach for what had to be done.

Marshall would never know what it was that made him hesitate that split-second after putting his hand on the door handle, but the moment probably saved his life. He turned to tell Archer, "I'll get him into his clothes—" but he had not spoken two words before a bullet punched a hole through the door where his head had been an instant before, and a body crashed against it.

He threw his own weight against the door, and Archer slid the bolt home. "The windows!" Marshall cried, hearing pistol shots and shattering glass behind them.

They hurtled up the steps to the quarterdeck, where Captain Smith was leaning on the railing, hacking with his sword to prevent someone from climbing out the aft windows of the captain's cabin as Nearns bundled a sail over the railing. Parker and Vincent were wrestling part of a spare mast up from the maindeck. "Get the mast down to brace the sail!" Smith directed. "Mr. Marshall, we need spars for a barricade!"

"They're at the cabin door, too, sir," Marshall reported. "Davy, stand at the rail, I'll pass the spars up." The next few minutes were too hectic for conversation, but they managed to get enough spars piled over the canvas to effectively block the exit from the captain's cabin.

"There must be a hidden hatch from the cabin to the hold." Smith scowled. "We have no way of knowing where on the ship he is, now."

A scrape, clunk, and splash floated back to them from the starboard bow. "What the devil—?"

"The entry port?" Marshall guessed, and tore off to the other end of the ship. A shot whined past him as he poked his head over the rail and he ducked back, but not before he recognized Adrian in a small boat with eight crewmen at the oars, pulling rapidly away from the *Elusive*.

"Parker! Man the bow-chaser!" Smith called. "Mr. Marshall, Mr. Archer, assist him, if you please! Fire as you bear!"

The bow-chaser was a swivel gun, mounted not on the bow itself—the wood was probably not strong enough—but on a small cannon carriage, which would give it virtually unlimited aim. Parker must be a gunner of some skill; he had the little gun run out and primed almost before Marshall and

Archer stationed themselves on either side.

The gun spoke; the shot was a little high and a few degrees larboard. They ran the gun back in, Archer swabbing the muzzle out while Parker handled the powder and Marshall dug another round out of the netting.

"Rear starboard gun!" Smith shouted.

Marshall saw that the boat had started to head out around the side of the ship. The 'chaser was reloaded; no point in wasting the shot. "You two go on; I'll fire from here."

The others ran off. It looked as though Parker had loaded that other gun in advance, as well; he and David ran it out and set about aiming it without any other preparation. Marshall aimed by his best reckoning, and touched a match to the hole.

Both guns sounded within seconds of each other, and a sharp crack of impact carried across the water. When the smoke cleared, the ship's boat was in pieces; bodies and debris floated in the dark. Marshall strained to see any movement, but could detect none. He began almost automatically to clean and reload the swivel-gun. "See anything, Davy?"

"No," Archer stood at the rail, staring across the water. "I can't tell—"

A pounding started inside the captain's cabin, then the door crashed open and the rest of the crew came charging out.

A shot from Smith dropped the first man; the second tripped over him and sprawled headlong on the deck, but a few got out past them and took cover, firing with an assortment of weapons.

"Davy, give me a hand up here!"

Archer dropped his empty pistol and ran up to the forecastle. "Let's get this thing turned around!" Marshall said, tugging at the pins that locked the swivel gun's carriage in place.

"Loose cannon?" Archer said.

"We'll only need one shot—stand clear." Even a little swivel gun weighed several hundred pounds; they wrestled it over to the edge of the forecastle and tilted it down to aim below the quarterdeck. Risky; he didn't want to send a shot into the hull. "Put down your weapons!" he shouted, and fired the pistol that had been stuck in his belt.

Someone on deck noticed them and yelped in alarm. The charge out of the captain's cabin changed abruptly into a retreat, and the door slammed again.

In the sudden quiet, Captain Smith leaned over the rail of the quarterdeck. "Good work, gentlemen. Parker, stand a grating against that door and anchor it in place with that gun. We've had enough traffic," he finished irritably. "As the crewmen carried out the order, Marshall and Archer returned to the quarterdeck. "Mr. Marshall, how many were in that boat?"

"Nine, sir, including Adrian. There should be—" He saw only two bodies on deck. "Twenty-three men below or in the cabin."

"Only four to one, now. Quite an improvement." Smith looked up. The stars were hazy now between the smoke and a light fog that had come up in the cool of night. "Ordinarily I would send a boat for survivors, but we've no men to spare. If you hear anyone calling, throw them a rope. Come morning we'll get below and confine the prisoners."

"Aye, sir."

"And, Mr. Marshall, you had better avoid aiming any more artillery at the deck. I applaud your quick thinking, but we are carrying a cargo of gunpowder."

Marshall found himself standing with his mouth open, unable to utter a word. No wonder those men had run so easily. He nodded and finally managed another "Aye, sir."

Smith squinted up at the sail. "It may take all of us, but we must at least reef courses and topsails, and get the anchor down. We were on a heading for Tor Bay, and should be even with Bolt Head by now, but I won't go blundering about in the dark."

Marshall shared a glance with Archer. Bolt Head was nearly home. "Blundering, sir?"

"Some clever fellow cut the tiller rope, Mr. Marshall," Smith said. "We cannot steer this ship, except with sail, and we cannot work the sail with so few men. But His Majesty has other ships in the vicinity. If our luck holds, we may meet one and borrow a few crewmen—or we may persuade some of our prisoners to act in their own best interests and join their more sensible shipmates."

"I see. Thank you, sir. Davy, see if the anchor's catted." Archer checked; it was.

"Let go!" Smith called out. At the bow, Archer and Vincent sent the anchor plunging down. Once the others had finished organizing the deterrent at the cabin door, Marshall collected them all and went up into the rigging with Parker and Vincent. Nearns, the cook, professed a fear of heights, and with his barrel chest and short limbs he would never manage in the top—but he was more than happy to handle the lines on deck, and he was needed there; Archer could not haul the lines single-handed, and Captain Smith himself was apparently going to have to stand watch against any further breakout attempts.

With so few men, a job that should have taken minutes took nearly an hour. At least, since this was a brig, there were only two masts to worry about, but Marshall had not spent so much time in the rigging since his days of learning the ropes as a midshipman. He looked down at one point and saw that Captain Smith had pitched in as well, coiling the ropes; even a small ship like this had miles of lines that had to be kept in their places or risk a tangle that could pull the sails down. Everything had to be done just so, and every time; there was no room at sea for sloppiness.

They got the job done, at last; by the time Marshall climbed down he was hungry and thirsty, his body so over-used that his knees felt like rubber. But they were a long way from finished. The few steps to the quarterdeck seemed a long climb. "Sails reefed, sir."

"Very good, Mr. Marshall. Parker, if you are capable of heaving the lead, take a sounding."

"Aye, sir, I am." Parker touched his forehead and took Nearns along to the bow. They disappeared over the edge of the rail, to the ledge where he would stand to toss the lead-weighted rope marked off in fathoms.

"Get yourself something to eat, Mr. Marshall," Smith said. "Having the ship's cook as a conspirator has its advantages; he stocked the boat with provisions in the event we had to abandon ship."

"Thank you, sir. Captain—I'm sorry I didn't think to get the charts from the cabin when I had the chance—"

"You left four prisoners secured, Mr. Marshall. I had no more idea than you that there was a passage below. Did you not hear my order to get yourself some breakfast?"

"Aye, sir."

The boat was on the other side of the mainmast; Archer was there, sitting on a spare coil of rope with a cup in one hand and a biscuit on his knees. "Good morning, Davy. What's for breakfast?" He leaned over the edge of the boat and spotted a couple of casks with lids ajar.

"Cold tea, boiled eggs and biscuit," Archer said cheerfully. "Sorry, there is no oatmeal."

"Bad luck. I know you must have been hoping for some nice congealed porridge." He located the water barrel, first—he was thirsty more than anything else—then fished out an egg and a piece of biscuit. It was a relief to get back to such ordinary matters, and even more reassuring to find that his need for David's presence had diminished now the danger was gone. He was glad his friend was there, but no more; nothing dangerous. And David seemed equally relaxed.

But he'd only had a few bites, leaning against the ship's boat, when Captain Smith called from the quarterdeck. "Mr. Marshall, we have a problem."

He glanced over—and froze. Smith was at the rail of the quarterdeck, near the starboard stair; standing behind him, a sword in one hand and a pistol in the other, was Adrian. Back from the sea, apparently—even in the dim lantern light it was clear his clothing was hanging on him, soaking wet.

He must have somehow reached the stern ladder, and come up that way. "Oh, my God," Marshall breathed. "Davy, stay down."

"What is it?"

"Adrian," he said without looking down. "He's got the Captain."

Chapter 24

Parker and Nearns were still out of sight; no help there. Marshall moved out and away from the boat, hands in plain sight. There was a pistol tucked at his back; if he could get closer—

"That's quite far enough," Adrian said. "You may not see the point of this sword, but it is against your Captain's spine. I once served with a man who took a sword wound there; he lived, but never walked again."

Such a wound would more likely be fatal. "So here we are," Adrian continued. "But where is my dear friend Mr. Archer?"

Marshall deliberately looked as far away from Davy as he could—up into the mainmast rigging. The youngster, Vincent, was still up there, watching for a sail. He was wearing light-colored clothing, and it was impossible to tell his identity.

"Stay where you are!" Smith shouted. It was, Marshall realized, an order to everyone not in Adrian's line of sight.

The pistol exploded behind Smith, and for one heart-stopping moment Marshall expected to see his captain fall. But the shot had been aimed at Vincent, and the body that dropped was from the rigging. As Marshall watched, horrified, it bounced off the maindeck rail and splashed down into the sea.

"Very bad advice, Captain," Adrian said. "But thank you both for telling me where to find him. Now, Mr. Marshall, if you would kindly step over to my cabin and open the door—"

Marshall ignored the command. Even if he'd been willing to obey, what Adrian wanted was not possible; the deck gun and grating would require two men to move. He couldn't see that, of course. But the hatches on either side would be easy enough to get into, if he wanted the deck overrun with the remainder of Adrian's crew. He eased his weight onto his left foot, shifting slowly to starboard.

"Belay that, order, Mr. Marshall." Smith sounded extremely angry but not particularly intimidated. He turned his head slightly. "Surely you realize that if you kill me, you will effectively lose all bargaining power. Likewise, if you fire at Lt. Marshall, you would give me the chance to disarm you. You may kill one of us, but the other will certainly stop you."

"A standoff? Do you think so? Time is on my side, Captain. This is my ship. I've at least 20 men below decks, and sooner or later they will break out—I said *hold still,* Mr. Marshall, I have a fresh pistol."

Before going up to take in sail, they had put their dozen or so empty guns on the poop deck, and Nearns had recharged them; that must have been how Adrian armed himself. Marshall looked down, as if in defeat, and glanced over without turning his head, to see whether Archer had a pistol as well.

Archer was gone.

There was only one place he could have got to—around the back of the boat, and the neat rack of spars and mast sections on the other side of it. He must be heading for the larboard stair to the quarterdeck. He would only be visible for a space of six or eight feet. It was dark; he might make it.

"I have a suggestion." Marshall took another step to his left, toward the starboard stair, forcing Adrian to turn to follow him. "I'm sure by now your men ashore have collected the ransom for all of us." He caught a flicker of movement out of the corner of his eye, and spread his hands a little wider, moving them as he spoke, to keep Adrian's attention on him. "If you let me lower the boat and set Captain Smith adrift, you can release your men and keep me as a hostage until you have time to make your escape."

"Mr. Marshall, your suggestion is unacceptable." Smith's face was in the light from the lantern hung just above the stair; the Captain's eyes slid to his left, toward a spot Marshall couldn't see. Then he shifted slightly, too, turning just a little to starboard. Between them, they had maneuvered Adrian so he could no longer watch the entire deck. "What neither of you are aware of is the fact that I was able to send a message to the Admiralty along with the ransom letters."

"Impossible! I examined your letters myself—"

"The front of them, no doubt. Did you pass them over a candle to heat the paper?"

"What nonsense is this?"

Marshall wondered the same thing. He was completely lost, but Smith obviously had Adrian's full attention and he was not about to interfere with the Captain's very effective diversion. Adrian was completely focused on him, turned away from the larboard stair.

And Davy was at the stair.

"The reports of modern scientific investigators are of great interest to me," Smith said. "Are you aware that certain inks dry invisibly, then reappear when heated?"

"And I suppose you carry them around with you in the event of an abduction."

"As a matter of fact, I was carrying one—lemon juice. What ship is without it? I was conducting an experiment to see how long the substance would remain usable when kept on one's person," Smith explained. "You allowed me ample time and privacy to use it. You were so confident—I might say overconfident—that the Admiralty now has a description of you, your ship, and some of your men. If you delivered those letters to Lt. Drinkwater, as I suggested, your chance of escape is almost nonexistent. Your 'business' is at an end."

"Then I've nothing to lose by killing you both." Adrian was reciting his set pieces, but his audience was not reacting with the fear he intended to evoke. His manner was becoming a bit strained.

Smith, on the other hand, was as composed as he would be standing on the quarterdeck in the heat of battle. "On the contrary. You may still have a chance of escape. If you were to let Mr. Marshall lower the boat—he might require my assistance—you could take the loaded pistols with you and make for shore. We could not pursue you. There is only the one boat, and your men below have cut the tiller rope."

"You cannot expect me to believe such a wild tale."

"Upon my word, it is truth. I still have the bottle in my pocket, if you would care to examine—" Smith moved as if to reach for an inner pocket and kept moving, turning in place as he brought his left arm up to knock the sword aside.

But Adrian was quick enough to recover and bring the sword back around, slashing down. Smith was in the line of fire; Marshall sprang for the stair, knowing he was not close enough to stop him from shooting.

Archer was. As Smith leapt back out of reach, his left hand bleeding, David launched himself from the opposite stair and caught Adrian's gun arm with both hands. His momentum spun them both tumbling across the quarterdeck, fetching up against the poop deck. Marshall stood staring for a blank second, unable to fire at the tangle for fear of hitting Davy. He dropped his pistol and got hold of Adrian's sword-arm just as the gun went off.

For a very long instant everything stopped. None of them moved. Then Marshall felt Adrian trying to pull away, and realized Davy wasn't moving at all.

Something white-hot and wordless forced a growl out of him. He redoubled his hold on the sword-arm, set his foot on the blade, and heaved Adrian up by main force, intending to throw him against the binnacle.

He threw him onto the point of the Captain's sword.

The Captain had drawn steel, and he might have seen it coming; Marshall had not. It barely registered, anyway; he dropped to his knees beside David, lying just as he'd seen him in his vision, still and quiet, unmoving. Marshall pulled open Archer's jacket, searching in the inadequate light for blood, for a wound, for any hope that the shot had not been fatal. This damned barge probably had no surgeon, and any medical supplies they might have would be below decks— "Davy? *Davy!*" He felt as if his own blood had turned to ice, and any moment it would shatter. No matter how he thought he'd prepared himself for this, it hadn't been enough.

"How is he?" Smith asked, behind him.

"I don't know, I can't see anything—I can't find a wound. Sir," he added, remembering who it was asking. A light appeared over his shoulder; the Captain had brought one of the lanterns. That helped, but all it revealed was a scorch mark on David's waistcoat. He unbuttoned it, worried that the burn might cover an entry wound, but the shirt beneath it was unmarked. He rolled David over. Nothing.

"It appears he trapped the gun between his arm and his body," Smith said. "Sensible move. Is he breathing?"

Under his hand, there was movement, the rise and fall of breath. And a heartbeat? "Yes, sir, he is." And he remembered to breathe, himself, and checked for a pulse at the throat. That was all right, too. Relief flooded through him. "Do you think he might have hit his head?"

"I can think of no other explanation. Give him a few minutes, Mr. Marshall. I believe he will come around."

"Yes, sir." The rest of the world came back into focus, and he saw the blood dripping on the deck. "Captain, your hand!"

"The edge of his blade sliced the thumb. Messy and inconvenient, but superficial. If you would—?" Smith handed him his handkerchief; Marshall had nearly finished binding his hand up as their two recruits returned from the forecastle.

"We 'eard your order to stay put, Cap'n—"

"Yes. He shot your young shipmate before we could stop him. I am very sorry. Mr. Archer was also injured. Please fetch a blanket from the boat and put it over Mr. Archer, then remove my sword from that—" He jerked his head at the gruesome object near the poop deck, "and get it off the quarterdeck."

Parker's eyes widened, but he only said "Aye, sir."

By the time he brought the blanket, David was stirring. His eyes went first to Marshall, then to Smith, who was frowning at something off the starboard rail. "I'm alive." He sounded surprised.

"Yes," Marshall said. "Through no fault of your own."

"Where's—"

"Lie quiet for a moment, Davy," Marshall had put himself between Archer and the corpse, blocking his view. "How do you feel?"

"Like someone shot my head out of a 20-pounder." David grimaced. "I—I was so intent on getting hold of that gun, I didn't think to—to consider my own trajectory. You're all right—and the Captain—it worked?"

"Splendidly. The Captain delivered the coup de grace."

"He's dead?" Archer pushed himself up on an elbow.

"Quite dead." Marshall moved aside so he could see. Parker hadn't yet removed the sword, which had transfixed Adrian just below the heart. There was very little blood; the sword was holding it in. "No doubt this time."

Archer stared for a long moment, then nodded. "Thank God that's over."

"Nearly. We are still afloat with no rudder and a hold full of armed prisoners."

"Well, you wouldn't want life to be too easy, would you?"

"Heaven forbid we should be bored. Rest now, Davy."

"I'm all right." He tapped his temple cautiously. "Head of oak. There's too much to do, I can't just lie here."

He made it to a sitting position, then started to list to larboard. Marshall caught him. "Damn it, Davy—"

"As you were, Mr. Archer," Smith called. "Mr. Marshall, a moment, please."

"Sir?"

Smith had moved the lantern away from the starboard stair. He pointed. "There. Unless I'm mistaken, we are about to have company."

Marshall squinted off into the darkness. After a moment he saw something—not an object so much as an absence of light on the sea, a place where the starlight did not reflect. He remembered, suddenly, the telescope he'd taken from the helmsman, an age ago, and handed it to Smith.

"I don't like the look of this, Mr. Marshall. Go aloft and see what you think."

"Aye, sir." He took the glass and climbed halfway up the mizzen, far enough to get clear of the lights on deck. It was miserably cold for July—he'd not noticed that before, but now he found himself wishing he'd confiscated one of Adrian's shirts when he'd had the chance.

Even up here, he still could not see much. There was definitely a vessel of some sort out there, though, under full sail, beating toward them. The glass brought it closer. Too dark to see any colors, of course, but as she tacked into the wind he could make out a faint silhouette of sails and masts. Three masts. Three masts, of equal height.

Oh, for God's sake. He let out a pent-up breath and dropped his head against the mast, not sure if he was going to laugh or cry. *With all the English ships in the damned channel...and all we have are four six-pounders and two popguns and two crewmen and Davy's hurt and we've no helm at all...*

He stowed the glass, clambered back down to the deck, and returned to Smith. "She's French, sir." The idea of being taken prisoner again, now, after all this... "She's French."

Smith swore. Marshall could seldom read the man's expression, but for an instant the Captain looked just as disgusted and discouraged as he felt himself. Shivering a little in the cold, he pulled himself to attention. "Captain? Sir— when do we attack?"

"Mr. Marshall—" Smith stopped himself, and almost smiled. He frowned off at the approaching ship, then at the deck. After a moment, he narrowed his eyes. "No. We're not going to attack. We are going to give them a boatload of pirates. Mr. Marshall, assemble the crew."

⚓ ⚓ ⚓

Two lights burned on the brig's deck, at either side of the empty quarterdeck. No one moved anywhere, she showed no colors, she appeared to have been left adrift...but for those lights. It was a conundrum that no captain with a grain of curiosity could possibly resist.

The little French trading ship hove to a short way off, and her commander made use of signal lanterns. The brig made no response. After a short interval, the ship lowered a boat—a large boat, for such a small ship, 20 men or more—and it pulled rapidly for the brig.

Marshall watched from his wet vantage point just behind the keel, where the ship's bow met the water. Too caught up in the moment to feel the cold, he gave one tug on the line around his waist that connected him to the *Elusive's* second boat, lying in the brig's lee and invisible to the Frenchman. That would tell the others that the strangers were approaching; with luck, he would overhear enough to tell him whether they were indeed French, or if the French ship was a captured, converted vessel. If the former, they would leave as quickly as possible, and would be out of sight by sunrise. They knew that if they rowed west, they would be on English soil before the sun went down, and whoever remained on the ship would be on their way to France as prisoners.

But there was a fair chance that a ship this close to the English shore might be a captured vessel crewed by Englishmen. Captain Smith had decided it was worth the risk; after going to the trouble to capture and hold the brig, he was loathe to leave it and risk the crew escaping.

The soft splash of the French boat's oars drew closer. They were being extremely quiet for sailors paying a social visit, but of course, any ship that appeared deserted and made no response would be one to approach with caution.

"...not a bloody soul." The whisper carried across the water with astonishing clarity. "God 'elp us, what if she's a plague ship?"

Englishmen! Marshall was so startled that his hand slipped off the keel and he submerged; as soon as he surfaced and caught his breath, he gave three sharp tugs on his lifeline.

He shook the water out of his ears and heard someone's response. "—'ad time to go anywhere she'd pick up plague, O'Reilly, don't go scarin' the men."

O'Reilly? It wasn't possible—Yes, it was. O'Reilly was afraid of no man, but he was frightened as a girl of contagious disease. And that was Barrow admonishing him, as usual. Marshall didn't know how it was possible, but he could find that out later.

"Ahoy!" he shouted. He realized he couldn't hail the boat properly; he didn't know the name of the ship. Then he realized he did know; of course he knew. "Ahoy, *Calypso!*"

The oars stopped. The silence was so thick you could cut it. Then Barrow said, cautiously, "Mr. Marshall?"

They were home.

Chapter 25

Captain's Log, HMS Calypso, in for repair, Portsmouth. 11-8-1799 (Temporary Command: HMS Artemis, Spithead.)

I have resumed command after concluding matters with the Admiralty regarding our abduction; Act. Lt. Archer has recovered from the concussion sustained during our escape. Repairs are proceeding on the Calypso, *and we should be back on active duty in approximately one month.*

⚓ ⚓ ⚓

Captain Sir Paul Andrew Smith returned from the Admiralty on the pleasant warm morning of August 1 with a little information, a bellyful of apologies, a decision to make—a decision he did not have adequate information to make properly—and the onerous task of obtaining that information.

He was piped aboard the *Artemis*; he had been given the ship, temporarily, until *Calypso* was seaworthy again, and the *Calypso's* artificers were keeping themselves busy converting her from a French trader to an English warship. She was serving to berth the *Calypso's* officers and many of the men who had been in on the rescue—she was not large enough to hold them all—and the rest were still berthed on a hulk under Second Lt. Watson's command.

Some of the crew were off on shore leave, but Drinkwater was there to greet him. Marshall and Archer were not, and Smith inquired after them.

"They went to the shipwright, sir," Drinkwater said. "Mr.

Marshall wanted to observe the reconstruction of the quarterdeck gun-mounts, and Mr. Archer also felt it would be instructive."

"Very good. When they return, I would like to see you and Mr. Marshall in my cabin. I received some information of which you both should be aware."

"Not Mr. Archer, sir?"

"I...think not. Some of the information is highly sensitive, and I was instructed to share it only with those commissioned officers directly involved in the matter." With his acting status, Archer could be considered a commissioned officer if the situation warranted it, but in this case... "Mr. Marshall can relay whatever information is appropriate."

"Yes, sir." Drinkwater looked troubled, but said no more. He had assisted Smith in searching Adrian's cabin after the prisoners had been confined, had seen what Adrian kept in the drawer under his bunk. He had been present when Smith found Adrian's private journal. And he had not asked awkward questions when Smith sent him away.

Smith had read the journal. And burned it. And wished, quite vindictively, that he and Marshall had not given that unspeakable creature such a quick, clean death.

But that still left the problem of what to do about Archer. Smith was certain that the individual referred to by that name in the journal was a construct of Adrian's imagination, distorted almost beyond recognition—but the fear that had hovered over Archer since their return was not imagination.

Still, if any of what was in there was true, small wonder. If Archer were inclined to love his fellow man in a physical way, Smith had seen no sign of it—and in his years of service he had known a few men who were, and kept themselves to themselves, and done their duty, and caused no trouble. But he'd seen nothing to suggest Archer was like that.

But if there were the slightest chance...Archer was up for promotion. Once he was made lieutenant, he would be on a track that led to commander, captain, and even, eventually, admiral. Smith had seen damage done before this, by men who misused the power of their rank—not always, or even often, through sex, though that was the worst. Granted they would all have a special place in Hell, but it was what they did on Earth that concerned him. And if he were to promote someone who might misuse his power, he would share the responsibility.

Of course, Archer could be left as a midshipman indefinitely. When the war ended, he would most likely be released from the Service. The easy way out, from a commander's point of view. But Archer was a good officer. He might well be—probably was, in fact—an innocent victim. Who had overpowered and captured his tormentor. And had not killed him.

He could not have known about the journal or he would have destroyed it, but he had let Adrian live, despite the fact that he knew the man's testimony would impugn him, perhaps irreparably. That could be seen as high moral courage—or sentimentality.

On the encouraging side, Archer had shown no regret at Adrian's death. Groggy and concussed, he had hardly been capable of dissimulation. And Archer had come out of a protected position to assist in recapturing the pirate. Judging by his first words after he awoke, Archer had, in fact, saved his captain's life expecting to lose his own. Smith's inclination was to view Archer's misfortunes as he did Marshall's unwarranted beating—something beyond his control—but the nature of the problem was just different enough to raise some ugly questions.

A knock at the door interrupted his inner debate. "Come."

Drinkwater put his head in. "Mr. Marshall has returned, sir. If it's convenient?"

It was not convenient. It was a damned unpleasant prospect; he wished the entire situation would just go away. But a captain never had that option. "Yes, Mr. Drinkwater. Thank you."

They were already at the door. "Come in, Mr. Drinkwater. Mr. Marshall. Please be seated, both of you." The captain's cabin on the *Artemis* was small but comfortable, and the charts were stowed away, leaving the table clear. He began with the facts, which were simple enough.

"Gentlemen, as you know, I spent some time at the Admiralty sorting out the details of our little adventure, and it is my pleasure to convey the First Admiral's appreciation for ending Adrian's criminal activities. Commendations will be noted in the records of every man involved.

"As to the origins of the situation... Our surmise was accurate. The man we knew as 'Adrian' was at one time an officer in His Majesty's Navy."

The question was so clear on Marshall's face he might as well have asked it. And Smith could not give him the answer. When they had finally unmasked the pirate, after the *Calypso's* men had the situation under control, Adrian's face had looked vaguely familiar; it was only at the Admiralty that Smith had realized why. He had met Adrian, in his father's company, at a Royal Levee some years ago. "He was the son of an admiral whose name I cannot reveal, so I will continue to use the name he affected. He was the Admiral's heir, brought up in naval tradition; he was entered on the books from the age of eight, even though he did not actually set foot on a ship until his late teens, after his education.

"No one can say with any certainty when he first began to abuse his authority, but he had a reasonably normal career as a midshipman and then lieutenant. After a few years' service, he was given command of a sloop-of-war. That appears to be when the trouble started. Over the course of three years, his record began to show an abnormally high loss of young midshipmen."

Marshall's expression tightened, then returned to its neutral facade.

"The record shows one desertion. The boy was never found. He may have escaped. Having met Adrian, I doubt that. Another four or five accidents could have been carelessness; three were fatal."

"And no one noticed?" Drinkwater asked incredulously. "I beg your pardon, sir."

"If anyone noticed, they did not comment. It was a small ship; he had only two lieutenants and neither was in a position to enter an unprovable charge against an admiral's son. The matter was brought to a crisis by two suicides within a year's time. One boy left a vague letter, but the other had mailed a farewell to his father, explaining exactly why he felt he had to do away with himself. The man took the note to 'Adrian's' father, who, naturally enough, did not want to believe it, but...he examined the record and, to his credit, was honest enough to be worried. He arranged to have a young officer whom he trusted sent on board to investigate, and within a few months his agent reported back that it was indeed as he had feared. Adrian had thoroughly demoralized his crew and was cannibalizing young men put in his charge.

"The Admiral had his son removed from the Service, but for obvious reasons preferred to conceal the cause. Apparently he was officially released 'for reasons of health'. His father bought him a merchant ship, arranged for a government supply contract, and paid a monthly remittance into his account so long as he never set foot in England."

His officers said nothing, but their expressions were eloquent.

"I agree," Smith said, "Such treatment seems more a reward than a penalty. At that point, however, despite this leniency, Adrian became a rogue. He seems to have decided that he would punish society for rejecting him—to literally make them pay. At first he had a confederate—God knows what the circumstances were—but after Adrian began behaving inappropriately toward those he abducted, his...partner objected vehemently and then vanished."

"Murdered?" Drinkwater asked.

"I doubt anyone but Adrian knew. If the man is alive, we have no idea who he is or where he might be. Due to the Admiral's continuing influence, Adrian will be officially listed as 'killed in action'. I believe a dose of spirits might make this easier to swallow. Gentlemen?"

Drinkwater nodded. Marshall said, "Thank you, sir," but he merely accepted the glass and frowned at it.

"I feel obliged to point out that the important word is 'killed'," Smith said. "We may be grateful he was not captured, since he might well have been turned loose again." He suspected that, at some deep level, he had recognized the renegade, and known he would most likely escape justice if he were only captured. "I can understand the Admiral's desire to protect family honor, but if he had been my son I would have shot him myself."

"So his mask never will come off," Marshall said. "No matter what he did."

Smith shook his head. "I'm afraid not. There is a small consolation, of a financial nature. Since Adrian's ship, the *Morven*, was registered under an alias, and the Admiral wants no traceable connection of any sort, the ship has been condemned as a prize of war. Because of the peculiarity of the circumstances, and as we were already on detached duty, we will all be considerably enriched for our inconvenience. The division is among myself, commissioned officers, midshipmen and warrant officers, and the crew of the rescue ship. As members of the original kidnapping gang, our two new recruits will have to be content with their earlier ill-gotten gains, but they will be pardoned."

He saw the objection on Marshall's face. "If one were to wax philosophical about that decision, it might appear to be something in the nature of buying our silence," Smith agreed. "However, the matter will be handled as I have just described, regardless of what might be said. Since nothing would be gained by causing pain to Adrian's surviving relatives, themselves innocent of wrongdoing, I prefer to look on it as the Admiral's reparation for damage done. As you were the only officer on the scene, and Mr. Archer the only midshipman, you will each be receiving a quarter share of the proceeds. A ship that size should run 20,000 or so, at the very least. If you invest wisely, you should never again need worry about replacing your uniforms."

Marshall had the dazed expression of someone who'd stood too close to a cannon during firing practice. "Thank you, sir."

"Mr. Drinkwater, my thanks again for your handling of this matter. Much as I regret the eventual loss, I have recommended to the Admiralty that you be given command at the earliest opportunity; you have clearly demonstrated your readiness."

Drinkwater flushed with pleasure. "Thank you, sir!" He recognized the hint, and rose to leave. Marshall began to follow.

The Captain cleared his throat. "Mr. Marshall, a moment, please."

Marshall sat back down, serious. "Yes, sir?"

"Mr. Marshall...I am deeply sorry this matter has come up, but the problem is like stale bilgewater—everyone knows it exists, but it's not a subject for discussion. In a way, it may be just as well; you are almost certain to encounter it sooner or later—when you have your own command, if not before."

Smith realized he was doing it himself—edging around the subject. "Part of the problem is that you will never be trained in how to handle it; you will likely never hear anything about it—officially—but you will have to deal with it."

Marshall's puzzled frown deepened. "Sir?"

"I refer to men like Adrian—although I admit he is the worst and most extreme case I have encountered. The conditions of naval service make it difficult to eliminate the problem. Considering how many men are kept at close quarters without women for such long periods of time, that may not be possible. Of course, having women on board would create a different set of problems, and they would be worse, I'm sure..." Damn. He was rambling, and rambling badly, a reflection of his own turmoil.

He started over. "In any event, the important principle is that youngsters coming aboard a ship have enough to contend with; they should not have to fear being preyed on by those responsible for their safety, don't you agree?"

"Of course, sir."

Marshall was not making this easy. "I'm afraid I must be blunt, Mr. Marshall. Did Adrian...force himself...upon you or Mr. Archer?"

He did not seem as startled as Smith would have expected him to be. "I...was never alone with him, Captain. The only damage he did me was what you saw, that night on deck."

"And Mr. Archer?"

Marshall brought his fingertips together on the tabletop and studied them. "I would rather not speculate, sir."

"Mr. Marshall, I already know that Mr. Archer was alone with Adrian in his cabin for extended periods of time. As you well know, I do not rely upon hearsay, but under these circumstances I have only my assessment of Adrian and my knowledge of Mr. Archer. You were in a much better position to observe what occurred. Please report."

Marshall did not look up. "Nothing was done to Mr. Archer in my presence, sir."

Smith's own discomfort was turning to irritation at Marshall's careful discretion. "Of course not, man. I appreciate that you might feel a conflict of loyalties if Mr. Archer has told you something in confidence..." Marshall opened his mouth as if to speak, then shut it again, looking wretched. Naturally, he could not say even yes or no without breaking the confidence.

Smith had to press the matter, but he tried to soften his tone. "Mr. Marshall, we are having this conversation because I believe that Mr. Archer has endured enough. I would prefer not to put him through an interview that would, if my estimation of him is correct, be an unnecessary and painful intrusion. I assure you, I have no intention of punishing one of my officers for something that was inflicted upon him without his consent."

"Thank you, sir."

"But as an officer in His Majesty's Navy, my primary concern—and yours—must be the safety and security of all the men under my command, as well as those who will someday be under his. I need to know whether you believe Mr. Archer was a willing participant in whatever may have passed between him and our late host."

Marshall's jaw dropped. "Absolutely *not,* sir."

He hadn't the guile to feign that conviction. Smith was enormously relieved by his vehemence. "You sound quite sure."

"I am, sir. Captain—" He met Smith's eyes. "I mean no disrespect, sir, but may I ask that what I say be kept in confidence between us?"

Thank God he realized where his duty lay. "So long as it does not jeopardize the safety of our men, you have my word."

Chapter 26

A rcher sat waiting in the officer's wardroom. Between the small crew on *Artemis* and the number of men on shore leave, he had the place to himself; the solitary vigil had gone on until he knew he might as well accept the worst. *What can be taking them so long? Why not just throw me overboard and be done with it?* He hoped Marshall wasn't trying to plead his case and discrediting himself in the process. *And, please God, don't let Will's overactive sense of responsibility ruin him, let him have enough sense of self-preservation to leave—us—out of it.*

Apart from a day or two under the surgeon's care for concussion—he'd managed to keep his shirt on—Archer had spent the last couple of weeks in limbo. He'd been returned to duty, but with the *Calypso* in for repair, duty for everyone aboard the *Artemis* was light. A few days after their triumphant return to Portsmouth, Captain Smith had departed for London, to report directly to the Admiralty and get his recovered ransom money back into the bank. No one had mentioned the situation with Adrian; Archer had begun to hope that William was right, and the Captain had never caught wind of it.

But now—what else could that meeting be about? Will had been included; why exclude him, unless a decision had already been made, at a level that would brook no appeal? He had no illusions left on that score, and no hope. Drinkwater's look of concerned sympathy, when they'd returned from the shipyard, had told him all he really needed to know.

Well, if he couldn't have their respect, he'd be damned if he wanted their pity. He hadn't survived that bastard Adrian to be broken by this. He would survive. Once he had word, he could clear out his dunnage in an hour. Less, really. Fifteen or 20 minutes, shipboard life didn't encourage accumulation.

And then what?

Archer had no idea what he was going to do, now. He would have a few months' salary coming, and the money from those last prizes. That would last for awhile, but a midshipman released from service, even on good terms, wasn't entitled to half-pay. He did not want to go home to face his father's interrogation. He could not possibly explain the situation—especially not to his mother, or sisters—and he would not accept the inevitable offer of Army enlistment.

Hunt a job on a merchant ship, without being able to explain why he'd left the Service? Even if he found one, that would mean every time they met a Navy vessel, he would chance meeting someone who'd known he had been an officer who left under unnamed and therefore suspicious circumstances. No.

Survival was all very well, but one did eventually need a reason for it, and finding a reason was rather difficult at the moment. He wouldn't even have Marshall's friendship—for William's protection, the break would have to be complete. *The bastard's won after all, hasn't he? He's taken everything.*

He was now effectively cut off from everyone and everything he'd ever known—except, perhaps, Drury Lane. But if he found work there—doing what, painting scenery?—it would last exactly as long as it took for someone to recognize him and get word to his father. The Earl was entirely capable of pulling strings to save himself the embarrassment of a son following such a disreputable calling.

Perhaps he might change his name and ship out to North America. He could disappear into that vast wilderness, start over somewhere. Others had, with much less cause. But it would be a long, bleak, lonely way to go, and hardly seemed worth the effort. Maybe he would be lucky, and the ship would sink. *No. The way my life's been going, the ship would sink, but I'd float, and I'd be rescued by a shipload of French sodomites.*

It would be funny, if it didn't hurt so much.

⚓ ⚓ ⚓

Dear God, Davy, you were right. How am I ever going to get us out of this?

Captain Smith's questions were like a broadside out of thin air. Never mind how he found out; it was no secret anymore. Marshall was both honored and chagrined that Smith would put such weight on his observations; he felt caught between two points of honor. True, David had told him to go ahead and tell the Captain about Adrian, but he hadn't told him about the matter in confidence; it had come out through Marshall's own clumsiness. And he could hardly explain what else had happened after that.

But if he wouldn't or couldn't provide sufficient answers, the Captain would no doubt call Davy in. To make him suffer that again, in an official inquiry...and what if Davy blurted out something that would incriminate them both?

No, Davy would never do that; he would sacrifice himself first. As he had all along.

The Captain was waiting.

"Thank you, sir." Marshall looked at his hands, and forced his voice to a formal, detached tone. "Shortly after Mr. Archer was first taken to Adrian's cabin he began having nightmares that woke us both." That was literally true, at least. "Eventually I realized that something was amiss and—and confronted him. Based on what he said, as well as injuries to his person, it was clear that he was...extremely distressed at what was happening."

"Injuries?"

Marshall closed his eyes briefly. "He had been bound, sir, tightly enough to leave lasting marks. And... mishandled... in a way that caused severe bruising over the greater part of his body." Never mind how he happened to see that damage. "Further than that, I did not inquire in detail, though I assume that whatever else may have been done to him was in keeping with Adrian's habits. Mr. Archer also told me that Adrian had threatened to injure you and myself to coerce his participation and his silence. That beating I received occurred immediately after Mr. Archer had first rejected his advances."

"I see," Smith said. "Not that I would have wished to see you mistreated, but surely Mr. Archer realized that Adrian needed us alive?"

"Yes, sir. But not..." Marshall struggled to find the right word; he felt like he was walking on broken glass. "Not *intact,* sir. And I believe Mr. Archer was correct in assuming that Adrian was ruthless enough to follow through on the threat. He would only have had to...demonstrate...upon one of us. Sir."

"I see." And he clearly did; Marshall had never seen so black a scowl. "Not much of a choice for Mr. Archer, was it? Calling that filthy pirate a whoreson would be an insult to any whore."

He rose and paced the short strip of deck behind the table. "Well, I have one more question, Mr. Marshall, and I ask you to bear in mind that it is not only the well-being of your friend you must consider, but your duty to all the men—and boys—who will one day be under his command. Do you believe there is any likelihood that, given his own command, Mr. Archer might..." It was the Captain's turn to search for words; the question was no doubt difficult to phrase neutrally. "...be tempted to abuse his authority?"

That was easy enough to answer, for himself and David, with no prevarication. "Sir, I believe that Mr. Archer would sooner be roasted alive—as would I. His comment to me on the subject was—" *'I know too well how it feels to be on the receiving end.' No, I can't tell him that...* "I believe his exact words were that we could do our best to keep such predators out of the Service, since we would recognize them in future."

"I see." Smith held his gaze for a long moment; Marshall felt almost as if the Captain could see right into his mind. "And you are convinced of his sincerity?"

"I am, sir. Mr. Archer also told me, specifically, that he did not want me to risk compromising myself by trying to conceal what I knew, lest I jeopardize my career. He feels that his own..."

Marshall looked at the brandy before him, forgotten until now, and swallowed it like a dose of tonic. It burned going down, but didn't help at all; he could still hear the despair in Davy's voice. *"I'm tainted now. He won't want me anywhere near his ship."*

And here Marshall sat, above suspicion, almost sitting in judgment, when his own behavior had been much more reprehensible. Wrong? No. Not by his own inner compass. But certainly contrary to both regulations and English law.

"Captain," he said, "Mr. Archer is convinced that—that what was done to him will result in his expulsion from the Service. I thought he was worrying unnecessarily; he obviously saw the potential difficulties more clearly than I. But I believe..."

He believed he would rather not be any part of a Navy that would be stupid enough to discard a treasure for so little reason. But to say so would sound like an ultimatum, and Smith would not—could not—accept what amounted to a threat. If Marshall said what he felt, he would almost guarantee that Davy would be dismissed, and he would have to leave, as well; and despite all its difficulties, he loved this life, could not imagine himself out of the Service.

But he knew where his loyalty lay. *If they throw Davy away, I'll resign, too. It's only fair. He was forced. I wasn't.* But he would hate to do it. There had to be a way...

He took a deep breath and chose his words with care. "Sir, Mr. Archer gave himself as ransom for our safety. I cannot conceive of him ever behaving as Adrian did. I further believe that to dismiss him would not only be a monstrous injustice in return for his loyalty and sacrifice, but a serious loss to the Service. If—if I were ever to have a son, I would place him under Mr. Archer's command without hesitation."

"I see." Smith sounded almost surprised. "Since you put it that way, Mr. Marshall, I must admit that my concern is that of a father as well as an officer. I have two young sons myself, and the eldest clearly intends to follow me into His Majesty's Service. Either he or his brother may one day serve under Mr. Archer—or yourself."

Marshall had never thought of that; it went a long way toward explaining Smith's vehement insistence on executing Adrian on the spot. The sort of creature that would force himself on anyone, let alone youngsters, had no place in the Service. "They would be safe in either case, sir," he said honestly. "And not only because they are your sons."

"As safe as one can be on a fighting ship going in harm's way," Smith amended. "Very good, Mr. Marshall. Thank you very much for your candor." The Captain let out a deep breath, and his shoulders relaxed. "That being the case, there is one other thing I wish to tell you. You are aware that Mr. Archer missed his examination for Lieutenant due to our...hiatus."

"Yes, sir. He—he has not mentioned it since our return."

"Another examination is scheduled in five days' time at the Admiralty in London. As the *Calypso* will be in for repairs for another three to four weeks, I am sending Mr. Archer to London to take his examination there."

Marshall heard the words through a haze of disbelief. *It's over? So quickly?* His heart leapt. "Thank you, sir!"

"And I'm sending you with him. You both deserve shore leave, and I don't want you wandering off alone and getting into trouble. Again."

"Yes, sir." He realized that Smith must have put David's name in for the examination before he left the Admiralty, and the relief left him tongue-tied. "I mean, no, sir. We won't."

"See that you're issued pistols before you go, just in case. And Mr. Marshall, I realize this is a matter of extreme delicacy, and you may not have the opportunity to discuss it, but—" He extracted a slip of paper from his waistcoat. "This is the name of my own physician in London. Please assure Mr. Archer that if he feels the need for medical attention, the doctor can be relied upon for discretion."

"I think he's recovered, sir, but I'll...find a way to let him know. Thank you, sir."

"A captain is responsible for the health and safety of his crew," Smith said noncommittally.

"Yes, sir." Marshall took a step toward the door. "Sir—I hope one day I can live up to your example of what a captain is."

"Thank you, Mr. Marshall. I believe you've made a good start. The job is never an easy one, and it can sometimes be an ordeal. But every once in a long while, it has its compensations." He cleared his throat. "Now—stop dallying. It's a long way to London; go find Mr. Archer and make your preparations. That's five days from now—not as much time as you seem to think. I'll see you back here two weeks from today."

"Yes, sir!" He wasn't sure where David was, but there were only a couple of places to look. So much to tell him: his lieutenant's examination, the trip to London and the *Morven* as a prize, simply unbelievable. But how exactly did one go about finding the quickest way to London?

Davy was waiting for him in the officer's wardroom. Apparently he'd spent the whole time working his nerves to shreds; he looked like he expected to be taken out and shot. Well, what else could he have expected, being excluded from the meeting? Not that it would have been any kinder to make him sit through that last bit...

"Will!"

"You'll never believe me—" Marshall began.

"Oh. So they've given you the dirty work." David blinked rapidly, then his expression closed down. "One way of making sure I won't shoot the messenger, I suppose." His attempt at a smile failed dismally. "Don't worry, Will, I'll go quietly. I—I can be packed and gone in an hour. There are a few things I'd like you to have—"

"Davy, no. It's all right." Anxious to reassure him, Marshall got it all wrong. "You're not going anywhere. No, I'm sorry, you are, but—"

"Will—" David's composure cracked. "For God's sake, get it over with!"

"Davy, you were only half-right. The Captain is sending us both—"

"He can't!" Archer lost all his apprehension in a burst of indignation. "No—you don't deserve—"

"No less than you." Marshall seized his shoulders and pushed him back down to his seat. "Listen to me, Davy. It's only good news, I'm just making a mess of it." He sat down himself. "First: you are *not* in disgrace, nor out of the service. Second: the Captain has arranged for you to take your lieutenant's examination in London, and since he thinks you might get into trouble alone, he's sending me along to look after you."

Archer frowned and shook his head. He looked afraid to hope. "Say that again?"

"I know it's a terrible blow, Mr. Archer, but we have been ordered to take shore leave in London so you can have a chance at a new uniform before we sail. God knows your old one is in worse shape than mine."

"Didn't he ask—"

"Yes." Marshall said. "I'm afraid you were right about that, Davy. He did ask. He asked if I knew whether anything happened between you and Adrian, and how I thought it would affect you in future, when you had your own command. *When,* Davy. Not *if.*"

"And?" Archer asked doubtfully.

"And I told him the truth: that you were trying to protect both of us, besides being physically overpowered. I told him that whatever might have happened, you would probably

have the safest youngsters in the Fleet. And he accepted
that—I think because it only confirmed what he already
knew." Should he tell him the rest? Yes. Better that he know.
"I wouldn't have brought it up at all, Davy, but somehow the
Captain learned that Adrian had gotten at you."

"Oh, God."

"Parker or Nearns, I imagine. I can't believe the rest of
the crew would have incriminated themselves as accom-
plices. I don't think you'll hear any more about it from any
of them, especially the Captain."

"But he knows—"

"That's *all* he knows. What Adrian did to you. He already knew. And now he knows how it happened, and why."

There wasn't likely to be anyone in earshot, but there
was no counting on privacy aboard a ship. He held Archer's
eyes and said, very quietly, "That's all, Davy. Only Adrian.
No unlikely, improbable...wonderful dreams." And, louder,
"Bear in mind that even before he knew why, he nominated
you for the examination. The Captain did that before he left
London. He didn't doubt you any more than I did."

"But if he knew—"

"As you once said, it wasn't the first time and won't be
the last. The Captain just wanted to be sure of you. But it's
over now, Davy. It's over," he repeated, aware that Archer
was having trouble absorbing the fact. "And that damned
brig has been declared a prize ship, and if I understand correctly—I can't have understood correctly—we each get a full
share of the thing—thousands of pounds. We are both almost
rich."

Archer looked like someone had smacked him with an
oar; Marshall gave him no more time to think. "That's all the
important bits. I can tell you the rest of it later. Go pack your
things, Mr. Archer. Now. The Captain has ordered you to go
take that test, and if we aren't away with all due speed, we
could find ourselves becalmed."

"You aren't joking," Archer said, the color finally coming back into his face.

"Do you think I could joke about this?" Trying to get through to David was finally making it real for Marshall. Two weeks in London! "I can hardly believe it myself, Davy. We will go to London. You will take your examination. Considering the circumstances of our return, and that the Admiralty is very pleased with us for stopping Adrian, I think you would have to exert yourself to fail. We will find ourselves a good tailor, and while he's working on our uniforms, we can see the sights. We will do anything else you want to do so long as it doesn't get us arrested. If you want to visit your family, I'll even go along and meet your sisters, God help them. Just get your things together, I'm going to see if Mr. Drinkwater can tell me how to arrange transportation."

Archer nodded, a smile tugging at the corners of his mouth. "If speed is important, I suppose we could send our things ahead, and hire horses," he suggested.

"Horses?" Marshall asked uneasily.

"Four legs, ears, tail...riding hacks. Faster than a coach. Riding can be fun, Will."

There spoke a son of the landed gentry. But Archer's expression had gone unnaturally bland, and as Marshall stared in disbelief he realized his friend was doing his best not to laugh. Well, if Davy was feeling good enough to indulge in a bit of teasing, all the better. "I would rather go to sea in a jollyboat than trust my neck to one of those oat-burning brutes. If we take a coach, we can review your navigation."

Archer just nodded. His mouth twitched.

Wishing they were alone so he could kiss that mouth, Marshall conceded. "I suppose we can ride back, if you must."

He did laugh, then. "Fair enough. Will—thank you."

"Thank the Captain. But first pack your things, Acting-soon-to-be-Lieutenant Archer. It's time to weigh anchor."

Chapter 27

"If you are making eight knots on a strong wind out of the south-southwest with a following sea, and your latitude—"

"Will—"

"Mm?" Marshall looked up from the chapter of navigational problems, his own mind racing along the path of the question.

"Enough, please. My brain feels like a roast duck stuffed with breadcrumbs." David smiled apologetically. "We should be stopping soon; can we resume this torture after we've eaten?"

"I suppose so." Davy couldn't possibly mean it was torture, of course, but he was not fascinated as Marshall was by the clean beauty of the mathematics of position. To Davy, navigation was just part of the job of a naval officer, and not his favorite part. "We could review—"

"Yes, we could. But I'd rather not, for a little while. There is so much more to think about. London, Will! London!"

"Yes, but—" Smiling at his friend's enthusiasm, Marshall gave up and tucked the book back into his bag. They had been on the road since just after daybreak, and their coach would not reach London until dark, including at least three more stops to change horses. They did have time. Even after they arrived, they would have a few days before Acting Lt. Archer was obliged to present himself at the Admiralty to take his examination for the rank of Lieutenant.

If Captain Smith's hints had been anywhere near the truth, Archer would be facing an examining board that very much wanted to promote the young officer who had saved his captain's life in the midst of heroic action against insurmountable odds. And if anyone deserved the promotion, Davy did. The Admiralty would never know just how much he had endured, those weeks that they were prisoner on that damned pirate's ship.

And even the Captain would never know what had passed between his two junior officers, when Archer found a safe harbor from his nightmares in Marshall's arms. Twice, they had been lovers—the first time a confused grappling that followed a bad dream, both of them half-asleep, hardly anyone's fault. But that second time...

Marshall shook his head. This was a thing he must not dwell upon, should not even think about. "Davy, we'll have a whole week of London once you've passed. First things first."

"Of course," Archer agreed. "But once that's done, even if I don't pass—"

"You will."

"I think I might." He said it cautiously, as though expecting contradiction. "After Adrian, no Admiralty gargoyle will ever be quite as frightening again."

"Just so long as you don't admit that to their faces," Marshall warned.

Archer raised an eyebrow. "Do I look that witless?"

"Not at all." He looked anything but. His blue eyes sparked with the excitement of the trip: the chance at promotion, a visit to his beloved theatres, and the beginnings of something—confidence?—that made his shoulders seem a little squarer, gave a challenging tilt to that blond head. "You look like you should be wearing a new uniform before the week is out."

He had to tear his eyes away from the brightness of David's smile, and the road gave him an excuse. "It seems we're almost there." The horses slowed, and their coach rolled to a stop before an inn, not as big as some they'd seen back in Portsmouth, but bustling with activity.

"Take your ease, gentlemen," the coachman called down. "Be the best part of an hour whilst I tend the beasts."

"Thank you." They climbed down from the coach, stretching their legs from the unaccustomed inactivity. The inn's little courtyard was crowded, travelers, horses, and vehicles of various description all trying to occupy too small a space. They found the necessary facilities without looking too much like fish out of water; Marshall found it a relief to clear the dust of the road from his face. Strange, how one could forget the little discomforts of land travel.

And the little comforts. Their midday meal was a tasty rabbit pie, with a rough but refreshing house ale, followed by apples and cheese. By the time they were called back to their coach, both were replete and slightly drowsy. They would reach London sometime late at night, and had a short list of decent inns at which they might find a room. In the meantime, there would be one or two more stops where they could stretch their legs while the postillion changed horses. Even though he no longer had to, Marshall worried about the price of a room in London, consoling himself with the fact that they had to sleep somewhere and at least he and Davy would be sharing the room.

As though he shared the thought of that too-distant bed, David yawned as he settled into the opposite seat, facing the rear of the coach. "Will, would you mind very much if we wait a little while?"

"No, not at all. You might as well rest now. I'm not sure I could stay awake to read the questions, myself."

"Oh, good." He took off his jacket and rolled it into a pillow. "The all-purpose naval uniform," he joked. "Garment, cushion, and occasional blanket."

"Just so long as you have it brushed and pressed for the big day," Marshall said.

"Oh, there'll be time, Will. We have prize money enough, I'm sure we can find some helpful person."

"I suppose so." The idea of having enough money was going to require some time and use to settle in. He and Archer had been rewarded for their part in Adrian's downfall by an enormous beneficence—a quarter-share each of the captured ship, an astonishing £6,000 apiece. Captain Smith had suggested they entrust their bounty to the prize agent he himself employed, and they would have been fools to do otherwise.

But, being young, they had each kept out £50—not that either expected to spend such an enormous sum. It was more than twice a midshipman's annual pay, and six months' pay for a lieutenant. Such wealth folded in his pocketbook Marshall could accept, even though he had no idea what he was going to do with it. The balance of it was more than his mind could accept.

He tried to doze as the coach settled into a regular pattern of movement. David looked sinfully comfortable, his waistcoat buttons undone, his face relaxed, hair spilling over his forehead. He had been working hard, the long hours they'd been on the road. And his body might still be mending from the concussion he'd suffered in their last fight aboard Adrian's ship; he likely needed the rest.

Sleep eluded Marshall, though he loosened his stock and unbuttoned his own waistcoat. Finally he gave up and fished out one of his books instead, paging idly through it. Nothing caught his attention; he had pored through it so often he could probably recite parts from memory. The quiet wooded lane they drove through was peaceful and lovely, the afternoon sun flickering dapple-green, hypnotic with the vehicle's movement and the steady thudding of 16 hooves.

And then the coach hit a rut. Marshall took the jolt in stride with a mariner's unthinking balance, but David's head banged back against the coach wall and he pitched forward. Marshall caught his friend as he was flung half across his lap. "Steady there, Davy!"

He could read Davy's reactions in his face: the first split-second of total surprise as he clutched instinctively at Marshall's arms, a blink of puzzlement followed by recognition—and then a brief glorious moment of contact as Davy relaxed completely, melting against him. *Oh, yes.*

Reason asserted itself. *Oh, no.*

But he didn't have to say anything; before he could object, Davy tightened up, pulling back and resuming his seat. "Sorry, Will. Should've lashed myself to the thwarts, I suppose."

"Except there are no thwarts."

"There is that." David bit his lip, looking down at his feet, at his hands, out the window. "Will, I am sorry, I didn't intend—"

"Oh, for pity's sake, Davy, you were asleep. It's all right."

But it wasn't, not really. He was aware of David now, achingly, physically aware. He knew how it would have felt if David had stayed there upon his knees, with their arms around each other, how easy it would have been to incline his head just a little, so their lips might meet. How sweet those lips would taste.

"What are we going to do about this?" David asked. His face was strained and slightly flushed, and Marshall realized that he was not alone in feeling that intense physical reaction.

"I don't know," he admitted. "What I'd like to do— Davy, we can't. Not now, not when things are getting back to normal on the *Calypso*—"

"The *Calypso* won't be ready for the better part of a month," Archer said. "And we are on our own for two weeks. But you're right. On board, I know it wouldn't be possible. I haven't even thought of it these past weeks, under the Captain's eye. But being so close, alone like this..." he shrugged helplessly. "Will, I've been wanting you ever since we climbed into this damn rig back in Portsmouth. I'm sorry."

Marshall closed his eyes. He hadn't wanted to hear this. His mind reviewed the Articles of War. His body refused to listen.

"I'm sorry," David repeated woodenly as the silence spun out. "I... Will, after I take the examination, I can ask the Captain to—to allow me to transfer to another ship. I would not wish to jeopardize your safety—"

Christ, he was blaming himself again. "Davy, stop. It isn't you."

"Oh, yes it is," Archer said quickly.

"It's both of us, then. I feel the same way. All I want to do—" He was wholly unable to articulate his wishes; he still felt that strange schism between what his body and heart said, and what the rest of the world expected of him, and what it forbade.

He shook his head in frustration, glanced up to meet the anguished blue eyes, and the decision was made. He reached to undo the dust-curtain above one of the coach's tiny windows. If he let himself think about what he was doing, he would not; he knew that. But he was not going to court death or disgrace from sheer carelessness.

Once the curtains were tied closed, shutting out the world, he reached across the dim space and caught Davy's sweet face between his hands. "I want to do this," he breathed, and covered Davy's mouth with his own. David let out a small muffled sound and slid forward into the embrace, going to his knees in the cramped space between the padded benches. Marshall felt his lover's arms wrap around his back, beneath the unbuttoned jacket; he spread his knees and pulled David tight against him.

They stayed like that for a long time, greedy for the contact. It felt like drinking fresh spring water after weeks on stale short rations. He felt near to weeping with relief. Then Davy's hands were tugging at his shirt, pulling it out of his breeches. "What—?"

"Want to touch you," David murmured against his cheek. His mouth moved down, and William let his head drop back to receive the delightful attentions upon his throat. David's hands slid up his spine, skin to skin, and he arched back even further. The thinking part of his mind simply gave up under the onslaught of sensation; he knew he should be returning the caresses, but blind pleasure held him in thrall. It was all he could do to run his hands along David's back with the rhythm of the rocking coach. The rhythm was so comfortable, so regular—

He caught himself as he began to rub against the belly pressed so wonderfully close. Too soon. "Davy, wait—"

He put his hands on Archer's shoulders, intending to hold him off, but David pushed his shirt up and captured a nipple with his mouth. A current of pleasure shot right through him. Somehow, another hand was on his fly buttons, the intermittent pressure completing his distraction. With the little wit he had left, he wondered at the way that Davy, so respectfully subordinate on the quarterdeck, could take command so easily when they were together this way.

And then Davy had Will's breeches open and his cock out, holding it tight, polishing the tip with his thumb while he cradled the balls in his other hand. Davy didn't move his hand. He didn't need to; the jolting of the coach was movement enough. Reason fled, replaced by need. It felt so good... Davy had done this once before, but it seemed magnified now. Or perhaps Davy was bolder, laving the shaft with his tongue, sucking gently on the balls.

"Shhh," Davy whispered suddenly. The cool stream of breath against sensitive flesh was maddening, but Will realized he was making a low moaning sound. He muffled his own mouth with one hand, digging the fingers of the other into that golden hair, squeezing his eyes shut and gulping back a cry as his world contracted into the narrow focus of that mouth as it drew him into a perfect caress and released and pulled again...

He held his breath. Had to keep silent. Had to. Must be careful of Davy, too, mustn't confine him, never hurt him, make him feel forced. He ordered himself to open his hand, letting it rest without pressure on his lover's head as his hips jerked forward almost with a will of their own, and then he had to breathe as his body released itself into Davy's throat, over and over until it seemed as though his soul was somehow flying out of his body.

Then he was utterly limp, drenched in sweat, with a tousled Davy there between his legs, grinning like a debauched angel. "Davy..."

"Mmm?" He swarmed up William's body and reclaimed his mouth, tongue darting inside like a diver after pearls. Marshall's needs might be satisfied, but he could taste Davy's still-urgent desire.

He reached down, tipping Davy back and getting an arm behind his knees. With one effort, he swung him up onto the seat, legs across his lap.

"What—?" Davy's eyes were unfocused.

"We must attend to you, now."

"Oh. Yes. Lovely." He leaned back into the arm Will had around him, and slipped a hand under the rucked-up shirt. William's breath hissed in as the searching fingers found a nipple and pinched it lightly. His jacket was suddenly too confining; Davy helped him pull it off. Kissing and laughing softly, they peeled each other out of their waistcoats and tossed the clothing on the seat opposite.

"We'll need to keep the rest on," Marshall decided. "What if the coach were to stop?"

"I'd no idea you were such a bedchamber strategist," Davy said, fumbling with the buttons of his own breeches. "We'll have to undo these, at least a little..."

Will pushed his hands away. "Let me." He let his hand rest there a moment, marveling at the way Davy's body followed his slight movements like a compass finding true north. "What shall I do?" he asked, opening the first button and letting his fingers slide between the others. "Is this—oh, Lord, you have drawers on, don't you?" he said, as he found another row of buttons inside. "No matter, I shall overcome all obstacles." He wiggled his fingers, teasing.

"Will—ohhh..." Davy drew out the last syllable, writhing against his hand, and Marshall had to kiss him again as
his lips rounded into a shape perfect for it. He took the opportunity to finish opening the fly buttons as he did so, rubbing Davy's cock through the drawers and giving it a small
promissory squeeze before starting on the smaller buttons of
the underclothes.

Davy's hips moved upward in response. Eyes half
closed, he seized Marshall's wrist, pushing the hand against
his body. "Yes. Now." His free hand caught the back of
Marshall's neck and pulled him close for another kiss. *"Now,*
Will. *Please."*

He had intended to take his time, prolong the pleasure as
Davy had done for him, but the urgency of that entreaty
changed his mind. He pushed the drawers down, got hold of
Davy's cock, smooth and hot, alive in his hand—and was
suddenly at a loss. It felt so different from when he did this
for himself. Not that they were that different, physically;
Davy was not quite identical, perhaps a bit shorter, a little
bigger around—but for all that they'd tried before, he hadn't
done this for more than a few seconds.

Well, when in doubt, improvise. He squeezed carefully,
and Davy shuddered in his arms and bit the side of his neck.
Good enough. He moved his hand slowly up and down, falling into a rhythm as Davy thrust into his grasp. A little
longer, and he felt confident enough to try another kiss.
Davy sucked at his tongue as though he'd been starved, both
arms wrapped around Marshall's neck now. He felt so warm,
so good, and he was so close to spending... "Davy, you'll
have to let go so I can—"

"No!" Sweat beaded his upper lip, he slurred a bit. "No,
just keep on—"

Marshall was keeping on; his body seemed to have more
sense than his brain did. "But it'll go all over—where—?"

"Here—" Davy freed one hand, fumbled in a pocket,
shoved a handkerchief over Marshall's fist. "Oh, God—" He
stiffened, and shivered, and stiffened again as his cock leapt

and spurted. He pressed his face into Marshall's shirt so barely a sound escaped, nothing that would be heard above the creaking of the coach's leather and wood. And then he relaxed profoundly, a dead weight.

The handkerchief had done the trick; Will let it drop for the moment and gathered David against him, a curious tenderness stirring in his chest. "Are you all right?"

"Yes," came the muffled reply. He held Marshall very tightly for a moment, then sat up, his eyes wet. "Will, you have no idea how good this is with you...how different."

Considering his other experience with men had been rape, Marshall was touched but hardly surprised. He smiled, uncertain how to reply. "Well," he finally said, trying for humor, "I would say you were my best ever, but that would not be saying much."

David chuckled. "You could say 'worst ever', I suppose. I do appreciate the distinction. Thank you—"

"No need." He felt a little embarrassed at David's openness, his vulnerability. And he realized, suddenly, how different it had been this time, being able to see his lover, even in the dimness of the closed coach. In their cell, it had been pitch-black.

David touched his face tentatively, even shyly. "You looked so...so beautiful, a little while ago," he said, as though his thoughts had been traveling the same path. "So intent. I love being able to see you."

"You will need to see a doctor about getting your eyes examined," Marshall said, thoroughly self-conscious now. "You are hallucinating."

"No, I'm not." David leaned in close, his breath warm just below his ear. "The line of your jaw, the way your lips part—" He licked at the edge of the ear, sending shivers down William's spine, making him gasp. "Yes, like that. I cannot imagine anything more perfect."

Marshall studied the face turned up to his, the blue eyes dark with emotion, and the tenderness within bloomed into passion once again. "I can."

He pulled Davy to him, kissing him desperately, wondering whether he could ever get enough. It frightened him a little, this wanting. To give another so much power...yes, Davy was just as passionate, seemed to want him every bit as much in return, but—what if he did not? What if he were to change his mind? Or, God forbid, be transferred away, or killed in battle?

The fear that engulfed him was nearly suffocating, and the sweet warm body in his arms life-giving air. David held him just as close, just as tightly. For an immeasurable time they simply kissed, and held one another, and gradually the intensity of emotion lessened, the storm inside calmed a bit.

Finally Marshall was able to sit back and take a deep breath of ordinary air. "Does this ever …" He didn't know how to ask.

"What?" Davy studied him anxiously. "What, Will?"

"I—Davy, I feel as though I could spend the rest of my life here—with you—and never miss the rest of the world. How does one live with such a feeling?"

David regarded him bemusedly. "From my not-so extensive experience," he said, "if we give this horse its head I believe it will eventually gallop itself down to a walk. What are you so worried about, Will? We've been back to normal—more or less—since our escape, and not once have we ripped each other's uniforms off. Not that I wouldn't have liked to." He punctuated his words with light kisses to William's face. "But I have no intention of hanging. I wish to live a long, happy life."

"An excellent plan." But that hunger was still there, humming in him at the touch of Davy's face against his, his body so close. "What shall we do next, then?"

Davy frowned, and leaned over to lift one side of the window-curtain. "Pull ourselves together, I think. Unless I'm very much mistaken, we'll be at our stop in a few minutes."

He was not mistaken. They had barely made themselves presentable, with David's balled-up handkerchief stowed in a pocket, when the coach wheels bumped onto a cobbled roadway. Another inn, this one three storeys high, another bustling courtyard, the scent of food wafting over the other odors of man and beast. And above even that was the smell of a change in the weather—sure enough, off in the distance they could see heavy clouds with a towering thunderhead, approaching like a French line of battle. The final part of their trip promised to be messy, as well as slower due to the rain and a muddy road.

They wasted no time in the courtyard. The ale at the nearest inn had been recommended by Mr. Drinkwater, who'd also warned them to act as penniless as possible to avoid attracting unwanted attention. There was nothing about them that would catch the eye of a casual observer—a couple of very junior officers taking advantage of a break in their journey to sample the local brew was nothing out of the ordinary.

They were halfway through their drinks when their coachman appeared at the door. He squinted into the darkness of the common room until he located them, and approached with an oddly reluctant air. "Was you gentlemen in a hurry to get to London tonight?" he asked.

"We had expected to arrive this evening," Marshall said warily. "But no, our business is not urgent. Is there a problem?"

The coachman spread his hands. "It'll not stop us for long, if the smith can make time for me. One of the fells is cracked clear through, and I don't like the looks of another."

Marshall had no idea what the fells might be, and would not betray his ignorance by asking. "Is that serious?"

"Na, but we best fix it before we go on, with that storm movin' in. Dougie Smith's good at his job, once I find him. Might take an hour or two. I was just wondering if you'd want to press on when the job's done, or stop over 'til mornin.'"

The comfortably padded fellow presiding at the nearby bar called over, "You'll not find him tonight, Freddie. An' if you do, you'll be sorry you did."

"Oh, aye? Why's that?"

"'Cause he just got back to town an hour ago, from 'is daughter gettin' married yesterday, over to Ashford, an' he's got a ragin' head on 'im. Wouldn't go near the smithy if King George himself asked, told his boy what brought him home if he heard anybody even breathe on the anvil it'd be the last breath he took." He shook his own head, obviously unafflicted by hangovers. "He'll be right as rain tomorrow, you'll see. Poor Dougie—three daughters, you know, all married since Christmas."

"And he'll be three times a grandfather by Christmas, I'll wager," said Freddie and grinned at the laughter from the locals within earshot. "Thanks for the warning. Eh, Lieutenant, I'm sorry. If you want to roust Dougie out, it's on your heads. I'm not so brave as you Navy men."

"Now, don't you get the King's men murdered," the landlord scolded. "I can find you gents a room with a clean bed, if you don't mind sharin' it."

Marshall exchanged a look with his friend. He was both excited and alarmed by the sudden gleam in Davy's eye. "Sharing's not a problem. I'm sure it's more space than we have aboard ship."

"Cost you less than a room in London," the landlord added by way of enticement. "And better food, too, I'll reckon. My wife's the best plain cook on the Portsmouth run." The locals within earshot agreed enthusiastically.

Davy shrugged, his expression guileless. "Why not, Will? We have to sleep somewhere. Better for us all to be under a roof when that storm blows in."

Marshall shrugged as well, knowing there was deviltry lurking under that blue-eyed innocence. They wouldn't just be *sleeping*, he was certain. Still... "Why not?"

Chapter 28

They settled on a price for a room and supper, and the coachman departed with a promise to bring their bags round before taking the coach to the smithy. They finished their drinks as they waited, while the landlord bustled off to see that the room was prepared.

Their bags arrived at the same time he returned. "It's all ready for you, gents, I've got the boy settin' out a fire in case you wants a bath before supper. Pretty warm up there, I told him not to light it 'til you said."

"A bath! Yes, thank you, that would be fine," Marshall said.

"I'll send up plenty 'o hot water. First thing a sailor asks for." He grinned broadly. "Well, almost the first thing!"

"We've been a few days in Portsmouth already," Archer put in, covering Marshall's embarrassment. "We've had all the 'first thing' we could afford. At this point, it's a choice between company and supper."

"Definitely supper," William thought he should contribute his bit. "But I'd rather have a wash first. Top floor, you said?"

"Top floor, toward the back. Pull the curtain if the sun's too bright for you."

"We'll do that, thanks." They hefted their bags and made their way through the crowd to the stairs at the back of the public room. As David bounded up ahead of him, Marshall found himself hanging back. It was absurd to feel shy now. After all they'd been through together—Christ, after that coach ride!—but for some reason he was just a little frightened of the night ahead. This was no chance occurrence, no last grab at happiness because they were both likely to die; this was an assignation, plain and simple. A very risky assignation, in this inn full of strangers.

But then they were up in their room, and the door closed, locked and bolted. David was hanging his jacket from the doorknob to block the keyhole, and then Marshall's arms were full of his lover, his body responding as though his mind had no say at all in the matter. Their lips met, and Davy pulled Marshall against him, easing back to lean on the wall. It hadn't been an hour since they'd let go of one another in the coach, but here he was again, hard as iron, hot all over, the one thought in his mind that he must get closer. Impossible to do that; they were mashed together. But he could get the clothing out of the way…

He forced himself to draw back, locate the bed. Not difficult; there wasn't room to swing a cat. A sleeping room, with a tiny fireplace, a small table under the window, a bed big enough for two, with a smaller window above. What more did they need? He giggled at how serious Davy looked, reaching up to untie his neckcloth, as though he couldn't manage that himself. Perhaps it was the ale making him giddy. Perhaps not.

He did the same service, fussing with the fastenings of Davy's waistcoat, popping one button off in his hurry so that they both had to chase it under the bed. Davy found it and backed out, mischievously pulling loose the lacing from the back of Marshall's breeches as he got to his knees.

"Hey—" Belatedly, Marshall realized that the knees of his breeches were now smudged, and he swatted at David's behind. But Davy danced out of reach and Marshall's breeches dropped, and that was the end of it.

They both wound up on the bed, struggling out of the rest of their clothing as the tantalizing touch of bare flesh overwhelmed them. Before he had time to consider whether this was wisdom or folly, he was flat atop his lover, driving against him, while Davy gasped in his ear and dug his fingers into the back of Marshall's thighs, pulling them tight together as he bucked upward. "Will—oh, God—!"

Whether it was the hot spurt of Davy's seed against his belly or his soft, restrained cry, Marshall didn't know. He buried his own face in the hollow of Davy's shoulder to muffle his voice, but just as he was about to come—

Someone pounded on the door. "Hot water, gents!"

Marshall froze, shriveling. "That's a *woman*!" he whispered in horror.

"I do believe you're right," David said. Easy enough for him to find this funny! "Just leave it by the door, dear," he called out. "Wouldn't want to provoke any maidenly blushes!"

"Like you've got somethin' I ain't seen before!" the unseen woman scoffed. She sounded old enough to be their mother, but probably *not* old enough to have forgotten how to become one. "Suit yourselves, boys! I'll be back with your supper in an hour." Something clanked in the hallway, and her laugh grew fainter as she walked away.

Marshall envied Davy's ease in talking to women, even though he was appalled at what his friend had said. "Davy—she'll think—"

David shrugged. "She'll think we took our clothes off so we can have a wash. Which we did. We can give her tuppence when she brings the food." He wriggled a bit. "Do you want to fetch the water, or let me up so I can do it?"

Marshall resisted the temptation to respond to that wriggle, pushing himself away from David and off the bed. He opened the door warily, but found himself faced only with a brace of water cans and a small washtub. It wasn't big, perhaps two feet in diameter. They'd have to stand, but he could not remember when he'd last had a real bath; the idea of sitting in water seemed almost unnatural. When he pulled it in he found it contained a lump of soap and a couple of towels. He hauled the cans into the room and set them alongside the tub in the only clear floor space. "They're generous with the washwater," he said, "and it is hot." Hot water, and fresh, not briny. They could be really clean for the first time in months. "Would you like to go first, or shall I?"

But Davy was frowning at the tub. The westering sun cast its light at an angle through the small window, glowing in his hair but slanting a shadow that gave an odd, distant look to his face.

"Davy? Something wrong?"

He shook him head. "No, of course not. Do you want to go first, or shall I?"

The echo of his own words jangled even Marshall's unsubtle ear. "Davy, what is it?"

"Just...just thinking. Sorry." He slid off the bed and lifted the pitcher from the wash-basin that sat on a little table under the window. "You go ahead, I'll pour." He tipped a watercan enough to fill the pitcher and motioned for Marshall to get into the tub. Eyes down, jaw set, David looked as though he'd just been assigned to a punishment detail. What the hell—?

Totally bewildered, Marshall took the pitcher from him and placed it on the floor. He was uncomfortably conscious of his nakedness, standing so close but feeling such a distance. "Davy. What have I done?"

"What?"

"A moment ago you were—you seemed to be—quite merry. Now...." He didn't know what to say. He had never had a lover before and had no idea what to do when one went all silent like this. "There's no one else here, is there? I must've done something to distress you. Can't you at least tell me—"

"No!" Davy looked up, finally. "No—for god's sake, Will, it isn't you. Just that tub."

Marshall blinked. It seemed a perfectly ordinary utensil.

"And memories." David straightened, moving to the window again as a chill wind suddenly blew up, and clouds blotted out the sun. With the unpredictability of August weather, rain began to spatter in.

Uncertain, Marshall waited, torn between concern and an intense desire to run his hands down that smooth bare back. The bruises Adrian had left on David's body were gone now. But on his spirit—? Davy had never said much about what had been done to him, and Marshall had not asked. What he did know was bad enough.

"He'd make me strip and wash first," David said abruptly. "As though I wasn't clean enough for his filthy games!" He brought the sash down with a bang that rattled the glass. "Not afterward, when I'd have given anything to wash him off me." He leaned against the sill a moment longer, his whole body tight and angry. Then, amazingly, he gave a short bark of a laugh. "Well, I'm damned if I'll let that bastard frighten me out of a hot bath!"

"Come here, Davy," Marshall said. "Please."

Davy turned and met his eyes. Through the cloud of his own turmoil, he seemed to recognize Marshall's distress. "I'm sorry, Will."

He held out his arms; David crossed the room—two strides, the room was not much bigger than the cell they'd shared—and as soon as they touched things were somehow all right again.

"I'm sorry," David repeated, against his neck as the storm rumbled outside.

"Nothing to be sorry for. Nothing."

David let out a breath, finally. "Unless I let the water get cold, eh?" He stepped in, scooping up the soap. "Wash my back?"

Grinning, Marshall picked up the pitcher, reached for the soap—and a thought stopped him. He nearly asked if Adrian had done this, too, but caught himself just in time. If that had been the case, a reminder was probably the last thing Davy would want. "You will tell me," he said carefully, "if I should do anything against your wishes?"

"We shall both be very old before that happens, Will."

Whether David's spirits had really lifted, or he was just making an effort to lighten the mood, Marshall was not sure.

He felt Davy shiver a bit as he poured the warm water across his shoulders, but when he lathered his hands and began to scrub, Davy relaxed into his touch.

It felt so good to touch him like this. He had bathed Davy before, to be sure—half the ship came down with a fever once, and David was so sick and weak he could not even wash himself. Then it had been only a matter of common decency, something to be done as quickly and impersonally as possible to minimize the embarrassment to them both.

Marshall could never have guessed how different it would feel to perform essentially the same act with this new intimacy between them, to let a lover's hands slide over David's body, the slippery wetness magnifying his perceptions. He had never really considered male beauty before; he had known his own physical shortcomings, knew Davy was much better-looking by comparison, but he had never been so aware of it, so attracted. Broad shoulders, trim waist...and such beautiful, rounded buttocks. Why did that physical perfection not show more clearly when Davy was in uniform?

He smiled to himself. Just as well it didn't. It would be worse than embarrassing to have his cock come to attention every time David walked past on the quarterdeck! And he'd better stop thinking about that happening or it would, and that damned woman could be back at any time.

He rinsed off where he'd washed—back and shoulders only. He was tempted to do more but uncertainty prevented him.

"What's wrong?" David twisted around. "Why did you stop?"

Marshall suddenly realized that the wonderful thing about David Archer was his ability to speak up. Unlike his own tongue-tied condition. "I—I wasn't sure if it was all right..."

"Will—" David sighed, turning to face him. "I told you some time back, nothing you do is unwelcome. Nothing. Quite the opposite." He laid a hand on Marshall's chest, above his heart, which leapt at the contact. "When you touch

me, it seems as though you're washing away all the
old...memories, the old troubles. You can touch me anywhere. Everywhere. I want you to. In fact—" He stopped.
"Never mind. But please, don't stop. Unless you would
rather not?"

There was no answer for that but a kiss, and Marshall
wondered absently if the film of water between them was
going to evaporate as steam. "I'd better finish, then," he said
eventually. "Before your lady-friend returns with dinner."

He refilled the pitcher and resumed his pleasant task.
Since David was now facing him, it seemed only logical to
wash his face, smiling at his friend's sputtering. "Anywhere,
you said," he reminded.

"I was hoping for something a bit lower," Davy complained.

"Yes, your neck *is* in need of a wash." He was playing.
Playing, by God—and not a game that required a winner or a
loser, but a gentle, happy amusement in which they both
won. It was very strange. Some magic of Davy's, without a
doubt; none of his own doing.

Neck led to shoulders, chest...the springy golden hair
there was stuck down now with lather. Arms...and on the
right arm, a bumpy irregularity—the ragged criss-cross of
pink scars, still bright and visible on either side of his elbow.

"Those are healing well," Marshall said, remembering
the vicious wounds Adrian had inflicted in trying to fight
free of David's stranglehold.

"I expect there'll always be some trace of them, though."
David's lips pulled tight in what was not quite a smile.
"Truly, Will, I am almost glad of that. They're a reminder
that I *did* beat him."

"True indeed. Do you want your hair washed?"

"Mmm." David pulled loose his ribbon and tipped his
head back. "You're going to spoil me, Will."

"Not at all. I expect the same service in return."

"A clever ploy." His eyes suddenly opened wide.
"Will—did you lock the door?"

"No!" Water splattered as Marshall lunged across the room and slid the latch shut.

"Just thought of it," Davy said apologetically, blinking as water from his hair ran down his face. "She'd likely knock first, at any rate."

"I should hope so!" He covered his receding panic by considering the task at hand: he'd cleaned everything from the waist up; should he proceed back or front?

Or both?

David caught his breath as Marshall's right hand slid down his belly. His hips tilted forward a tiny bit, in anticipation...and Marshall slipped his other soapy hand right down David's arse.

"Hey!"

His finger slipped between the cheeks, into a warm cleft. Necessary, was it not? The object of the exercise was, after all, a bath. No part of this fine supple body should be left unwashed! Besides, Davy was not trying to avoid his touch, or even objecting..."You said anywhere."

"And *you* said you expect the same in return." David said nothing more, but a wicked smile crept across his face as he rocked back and forth between Marshall's hands.

"Oh, dear." Perversely, his cock twitched and began to grow, whether from Davy's movement or the notion of receiving such attentions, he could not say. Somehow or other, Davy had maneuvered his own cock into Marshall's hand. It was not hard, exactly, but it seemed...interested. And was Davy really pushing back against his finger?

"But I fear we will not have the time for a proper exchange. Unless you want to give the serving-maid an education in naval maneuvers. You're doing a fine job of sounding the bottom!"

It felt more like running out the long guns with no powder for firing. Marshall hated to admit it, but Davy was correct; after all those years at sea, with the watch rung every half-hour, he had a sort of internal clock that anticipated those bells, and he knew their hour was at least half-gone.

"Very well, then..." What was he supposed to do now? "Davy? Do you...um...Shall I—" How awkward it was!

David didn't make it any easier by chuckling. "Just get all the soap out, Will, I don't need a rash down there!"

By the time David was thoroughly rinsed, he was giggling so hard that Marshall was tempted to smack his wet bottom, and annoyed at the hilarity that had subdued his libido once more. He consoled himself with the thought that if a little frustration was all it cost to chase away some of his friend's old demons, it was cheap at the price.

And besides—if Davy was finished, it was his turn next.

"If you can get hold of yourself—" he began, proffering a towel. And, "oh, hell!" as the phrase sent David into another spasm of laughter. *"Mister* Archer—"

David caught him around the waist and kissed him, his mirth finally subsiding. The feel of his slick warm flesh chased away any lingering aggravation. "Sorry, Will. Here, let me do the honors. Step in, if you please, milord." He studied William in the tub as though he were a project to be undertaken. "Hair first, I think—start at the top."

It was sheer luxury to simply stand there and let the warm water trickle down his back. Deft fingers scrubbing through his hair, massaging his scalp—no wonder the Romans were so devoted to their baths, if they had this sort of attention! "We should do this every day," he said dreamily.

"If we have—head *back,* Will!" A cascade of warm water ran down his face and, as he tilted his head obediently, up his nose.

His turn to sputter, though not with laughter, and by some lucky chance Davy didn't find it funny either. He simply passed Marshall the towel to mop his face and waited until his head was at the proper angle to finish rinsing his hair.

"Sorry, you moved just as I began to pour. There, that should do it." David flipped the wet tail of hair to the front of Marshall's shoulder, then commenced scrubbing his back.

It was heaven. The room was cooling with the sun's

warmth gone, but the hot water kept him comfortable enough. That, and Davy's hands defining the boundaries of his body with affection unspoken but apparent. Marshall could not recall ever having felt so cherished; perhaps his mother had bathed him with such care, when he was very young, but if so there was nothing of that left in his memory.

Davy was washing him everywhere. Even his genitals; his cock was rather long—he was both proud of and embarrassed by the fact—but it got the same sort of careful attention as the rest of him. David made no remarks, only squeezed it gently as he finished, and sighed. "We just don't have time," he said, very close to Marshall's ear. His grip suggested otherwise, and he was standing so near the tub that Marshall could feel a nudge from behind.

The situation required a command decision. "We'd better dry off and get dressed. That feels very good, but I am not certain much would come of it." A bald-faced lie; if Davy kept on with what he was doing they'd both be flat on the bed again in no time.

He had made the right choice, though. They'd pulled on shirts and breeches, unlocked the door, and were wondering how long they'd have to wait for someone to remove the bathwater. The tub made it nearly impossible to move in the room, but would block the narrow hallway if they set it outside. They were relieved of the decision when—as Davy had predicted—the maid knocked upon the door.

"Do you have anyone to help you with that?" David asked her, gesturing at the thing. "It's a hazard to navigation in here."

"Na, Toby can just pitch it out the window. Garden down below."

Marshall glanced at the boy who'd helped bring up the meal. He hardly seemed large enough for the task. It would take him a long time bailing with a bucket, time that they could otherwise spend alone together. Marshall raised an eyebrow in David's direction. "Not that it's likely to make much difference this afternoon..."

David grinned. "We'll be heaving to windward, I'm afraid. Here, mate—" to the boy, "When I give you the nod, open the window, right?"

Toby nodded and stationed himself. Marshall seized one of the tub's handles, David the other, and as they swung for the third time Davy said "Now!" to the boy. He opened the window and they flung the water out. Marshall automatically yelled "HEADS!" A gust of wind blew in a spray of water back at them, but the youngster got the window down fast enough that nothing was seriously doused. Still, they sat down to eat a little damp for their efforts as the highly amused servants took their leave.

In the entertainment of having their guests take on his chore, the boy had forgotten to light the fire, but the meal was a distraction from that. The innkeeper's wife had made good his boast. Roasted chops, soft rolls, a hearty dish of mashed potatoes with butter, fresh green beans... Marshall forgot his wet clothes as he happily tucked it away. He had been on short commons during their weeks as prisoners; might as well make up for it while he had the chance. He could not remember when he'd last finished a meal with apple pie, and he didn't think he'd ever had one as good as this. After a few minutes, though, he realized that his companion was uncharacteristically quiet.

"Something wrong, Davy?"

"No." He poured himself more ale from the pitcher that had arrived with their meal, peering down into the mug as though there were something fascinating in there.

"It will be nice to have a fire. I'd not have thought we'd want one, a few hours ago."

David shivered. "Yes. Very pleasant."

Marshall very nearly asked him once again if he'd done anything distressing, but guessed that Davy would say no even if it were not true. They finished the meal quietly, put the empty dishes outside on the tray, and made certain the door was locked once again. The remains of dinner—the ale pitcher, a couple of rolls and butter—stayed behind.

A fire would be pleasant, with their damp hair, but it was not as enticing as his companion. Marshall smiled. "A good meal...and now to bed?"

David nodded, and moved into his arms, still shivering. His kiss was hardly reluctant, but there was some unspoken reservation in the contact. Marshall drew back just a bit. "I know something is wrong, Davy. Will you please tell me what it is?"

"It is nothing..." He sighed. "Very well. Will...if I were to ask you to do something...something you did not wish to do...would you tell me so?"

He shook his head—not in refusal, but in puzzlement. "I don't understand. You've asked nothing against my wishes..."

"Not yet. Not today. But do you remember...back on that ship...I asked if you would like to be inside me? To—to take me, as a man would a woman?"

He was shivering harder, now, and although Marshall now realized it was not from cold, he left David standing beside the bed. "Just a moment, let me start the fire." They might want it later, if the night was chill, and tending it gave him something to do with his hands; it also let him hide the physical effect of Davy's hesitant question.

He had not thought of doing any such thing before today, but the memory of that bath—of Davy pushing against his fingers in what felt like open invitation, that hot channel between the cool, slippery curves—he was hard again already, from just the thought of letting his cock ride in the crevice of Davy's lovely arse.

"Do you remember, Will?"

"I remember," he said hoarsely. He moved the logs in the firedog apart a little, giving them room to let the air flow, threw in a handful of tinder and blew on it to raise a spark. "Why do you ask?" *Why do you ask, if you're shaking with fright?*

"I would be—" Davy stopped, and swallowed. "I would be obliged if you would do me that service."

He could not say, "Are you mad?" But he thought it. The tinder caught, flared, sent flames licking greedily into the kindling. "Are you certain?" he managed finally.

"Yes," David whispered.

"Why?" He turned, looking up at his lover, who was staring into the flames. "You don't need to do that for me."

David smiled wryly, without raising his eyes. "I know." He shifted a few things around on the table, then left them to sit on the edge of the bed. "It is something I would like to do for myself. With you. If—if it does not repel you."

Of all the words he might have chosen! "No. Not at all." He rose and sat beside Davy in a single movement, wanting very much to touch him. "But I would not cause you pain. On my life, I would not."

"As I said before," David said cautiously. "When we are together, the things you do seem to—to clear away the wreckage. I want your touch on me, Will. Everywhere his was." He ran his tongue over his lips, nervously, not seductively. "On me... *In* me."

Marshall did touch him then; he had to. Just a hand on his arm. "Davy, you're shaking. Are you cold?"

"No, no… Well, just a little."

So far, so good. But that had not been the real question. "Are—are you afraid of me?"

"*No!*" He pitched into Marshall's arms so abruptly it knocked them both back onto the mattress, holding on as if he had fallen into deep water. After a moment he let out a long, ragged sigh, and Marshall realized he was weeping softly, almost noiselessly.

"Davy! Davy, what is it?" He had, now and then, seen youngsters react with tears, when they were first wounded or lost a friend in battle, when the grand adventure suddenly changed into bloody, ugly reality. The other men usually distracted them with rude jokes or religious consolation. Marshall had neither to offer, and he had never seen David this way. It had to be connected with Adrian; it had to be. But why now?

On second thought—when, ever, could an officer in His Majesty's Navy behave this way? There would never have been a good time. If Davy could release whatever he had been holding inside himself and let it go, surely that was better than putting on a brave face and tearing himself apart inside. Marshall only wished that his own desires would be more respectful of his lover's distress; the warm damp body plastered against him should have evoked sympathy, not lust. If only that woman had brought the tub two minutes later—!

After a little while the weeping stopped; David cleared his throat. "I'm sorry," he mumbled into Marshall's shoulder. "I had not meant to— The—the ale must've been stronger than I thought."

"Will you please tell me—"

"You..." He would not look up. "You are not repelled?"

It would be stupid to claim he was; his cock was hard and hot, pressed against Davy's through the two thin layers of fabric. "I am not. I am afraid, though. For you."

"Will... You will *not* hurt me. Please. I want you. I want—for once in my life, I want to be fucked by someone I love."

The words sent a rush of heat through Marshall's body. He held Davy tighter, at an utter loss for words.

David sighed suddenly. "You don't want to," he said. "Damn me, you simply don't *want* to. My apologies, Will. I am a stupid, oblivious, witless—whuf!"

The rest of the litany went unfinished as Marshall rolled atop him, driven past reason. "Does this feel as though I don't want to?" he demanded, grinding downward. He seized Davy's hair, pulling his face up so he could ravage his mouth. He knew he was clumsy at it, but there weren't any words left and in another moment he was going to explode.

Davy grabbed him just as fiercely and gave as good as he got. When he ran out of air, Marshall rolled to one side and fumbled Davy's breeches-buttons open, dragging them off with reckless haste. He shed his own clothes nearly as quickly, tossed them toward a chair. Davy had his shirt half-off, so he grabbed that and it flew off to join the rest of the heap.

Decks cleared for action, he dropped back onto the bed and grabbed his lover again, this time rolling over so that Davy was on top of him. "Listen carefully," he said, brushing his lips against Davy's mouth, sucking on his lower lip, dizzy from the ale and intoxicated by the heat and pressure against his cock. "I want to." He caught Davy's arse, one cheek in either hand, and let his fingertips slide between. He squeezed. "I want *you*. Are you listening, Mr. Archer?"

"Yes," Davy breathed, undulating against him. His eyes were big and dark in the dim light, and, brave words or no, he did seem apprehensive.

"But you must show me what to do. Davy, I don't *know!*" That seemed stupid, it was so obvious: turn him over and put it in...but... "If I were to hurt you—"

"It will be all right, Will. I promise. Here, let me—" Looking more than a little dazed himself, Davy moved back to sit on Marshall's thighs. "See, it's a bit wet already... so's mine..." He ran a fingertip over the head of Marshall's cock, spreading the fluid seeping out. Marshall shivered at the touch, and gasped when it ceased. "No..."

"Wait," Davy said. He took his own cock in hand, leaning forward, and rubbed its wet tip against Marshall's shaft.

The sensation was indescribable. Davy was concentrating, biting his lip. How beautiful he was...how good it felt...Will's cock felt like it was growing harder with every touch. "You're going to kill me!"

"I don't think so. There." He moved around again, hovering over Marshall, his cock making small damp kisses on Marshall's stomach. "There. Now you hold it—no, hold *yours,* Will, hold it up, that's it—'steady, boy, steady...'"

"You aren't singing...are you singing? That's— *OH!*" Davy had lowered himself, just a bit, and Marshall nearly fainted at the intensity of feeling as the very tip of his cock slipped inside his lover. His body surged up, and Davy gasped, and Marshall froze. He felt the blood rush to his face, as it seemed to be rushing everywhere in his body.

"Are you—?"

"I'm fine," Davy said breathlessly. "Fine. Let me just...relax... It's been a little while," he said, sounding more normal. "You're big... It's fine...there."

The enveloping tightness eased a fraction, and then shifted as Davy slowly slid on down, his hands on Marshall's shoulders, golden hair falling forward to veil his face. Marshall instinctively reached up to support him, but he couldn't think beyond that. He couldn't think at all. It was as though that small part of himself now surrounded by Davy was the only thing that really mattered. Brain, body, will—all of that was only there to transport the important bit to its present location, where it was nearly ready to die of bliss.

"There." David said again. "You can move now, Will. Remember that horse you tried to ride, last summer? You know how you sort of rock forward..."

He did just that and Marshall's body followed automatically. One utterly idiotic thought crossed his mind: *if this be sodomy, let's make the most of it.* He thought it somehow connected to the American rebellion, but he couldn't hold a thought in a bucket, he was hot and cold and Davy was touching him everywhere, hands on his belly, his chest, nipples *dear God in heaven*—! His whole world exploded.

"I'm sorry," he said when he could talk again. Davy was still astride him, and clearly still unsatisfied, even though Marshall could feel himself shrinking.

David only smiled. "That may make things easier," he said.

"What?"

"Your spend. It should help. There wasn't much butter left."

"Davy, you didn't!"

"I had to, Will, mashed potatoes are too sticky." Smooth muscles tightened around Marshall's cock, and he was amazed to find it responding already. "The last time," Davy said, "the last time we had a night to ourselves, at any rate—

you reloaded thrice to my twice. I believe if I just sit here and wait ..." he wiggled a bit.

Marshall groaned. He had never imagined anything could feel so good. Slick, tight...he could not find words to describe the feeling. "Pleasure" was a pale ghost of the truth...it was like the excitement of battle a hundredfold, without the pain or danger.

David cocked his head quizzically at Marshall's inarticulate response. "Unless you'd rather not?" He leaned forward, smiling, and their lips met, just touching.

Marshall felt the flame of desire increasing as Davy lapped delicately at his mouth. "You are enjoying this far too much."

Davy sighed happily. "Impossible."

He had been holding tight to Davy's thighs; now he shifted one hand to circle his lover's cock, and tried to match the rhythm Davy was setting. How long they moved together like that he could not tell and did not care. There was the faint creak of the bedstead, the crash and rumble outside, the rain slapping against the window, the familiar wind and water that made this feel almost like home. He let his eyes slide shut, and that somehow intensified the feeling, and that was wonderful. His first climax had taken the edge off, and now he felt he could go on like this forever.

For a time it seemed Davy felt the same, but eventually he slowed, then stopped. "Will..."

He had to open his eyes, but that was all right too, he could look at Davy sitting atop him naked and sweating, his damp hair ruffled around his face. "Yes?"

"Would you...would you mind if we did this in a different way?"

He felt a twinge of anxiety. "What do you mean?" If Davy wanted him like this...well, he'd do it, of course, it would only be fair, but his gut tightened at the very idea.

"There's a place inside...it feels good, Will, I can't explain it, but—I think you have to come in from behind me to reach it."

"Um..." Marshall tried to make sense of that and finally gave up. "How do—hell, Davy, what do you want me to do?"

"Hold still a moment, I think—" Without breaking their connection, Davy pivoted around until his back was to Marshall.

It was a very exciting view, but Marshall didn't much like being bent at that angle, and he had serious reservations as to how well it would work. He had a feeling that if he were to heave upward, Davy would go flying. "I—Davy, are you comfortable in that position?"

"I—Well... No."

A moment of strained silence, and they both began to giggle. When that settled down, David said, "But really, I think it will work best from behind. The one time—" He broke off, hunching slightly.

"Davy?"

No response. Staring at Davy's unresponsive back, Marshall wondered whether everyone had such awkwardness in romantic encounters, or his stupid inexperience was making everything more difficult. "Davy, we cannot make love or carry on a conversation in this position. Could you at least lie down beside me?"

"All right." Suddenly, David sounded very subdued.

They shifted around awkwardly until they were lying like spoons, still joined. Marshall had one arm under Davy's neck, but the body in his arms was stiff with tension. "What is it?"

"I'm sorry, Will."

"For what?"

"I—Will, please believe me, I was only trying to make it a little easier—"

"Of course I'll believe you, Davy. But would you please tell me—?"

"I—forgive me—I imagined it was you. When he took me." David was lying dead-still, breathing rapidly. "I only meant...it was easier, a little. There was one time—some potion, he made it feel good, I could not prevent it, I could not bear it feeling good with that bastard, so I pretended it was you. I'm sorry...."

"I'm not." Was it pity that wrung his heart, or Davy's tight arse squeezing his cock? Either way, the notion of Adrian claiming Davy like this, forcing him, sent a surge through him that was not at all loving. He kissed the back of David's neck, hoping the trembling that resulted was from pleasure. "I do see, Davy. It's all right. I'm glad you did."

"I—you are?"

"That you wanted me? Thought of me, instead of that swine? Of course." Of course? At the time, it would have horrified him. What a sea-change he had been through, these past weeks! He was still uncertain what they would do in the future, could not even guess what they would do tomorrow. But at this moment Davy was somehow inside his own heart as surely he was inside Davy's body, and he had no thought to spare for anything else. Every shiver that went through his lover shot sparks through him, and if he did not move soon—

"What would you like me to do, Davy?" He thrust as gently as he could, stroking Davy's chest and belly, finally understanding why things were so bloody complicated. That damned bastard's ghost was in bed with them even now, between them—uninvited, unwelcome—and Marshall had no idea how to exorcise it. "What do you need?"

"You." Davy held Marshall's arm tightly, reached around with the other hand to clutch at his thigh. Freed now, the words tumbled out. "I want you, Will. On top of me. Hard. So I can't even think of anyone else."

His cock leapt at the words. He'd nearly been ready to stand down, Davy's anxiety draining his passion. He would not have imagined any words could have such an effect on his vigor, but the raw desire in Davy's voice combined with his own urge to pound Adrian to a paste, and he suddenly felt like a stallion.

"All right, love," he said, amazed at his own confidence.

"All right." He held Davy close, thrusting more firmly. "Just...just move however you need to." He kissed Davy's neck, licked, nibbled, and was delighted at the little cries that elicited.

Davy rolled over, and then shifted to hands and knees. Marshall followed his lead, finding the final position nearly perfect. The sight of his cock disappearing into Davy's arse, the feel of their bodies moving together...to hell with George Correy, to hell with Adrian, with whoever and whatever had ever hurt him before. That was over now, over and done with. He could not see why Davy would have chosen him, but by God he was going to be worthy of that trust.

He pulled Davy closer, reached beneath to bring him along. Davy sobbed once as he touched him. "He's gone," Marshall whispered. "They're all gone, Davy, it's just me... come with me, love, come on..." Some inner wisdom he didn't know he had was guiding his actions, endearments he hadn't thought he'd known coming out of his mouth. And that overwhelming sense of the rightness of this all pounded through him and into Davy with the force of a 30-foot wave, carrying them both along as it surged and crested and threw them both up onto the beach. Davy's arms and knees buckled, and they both fell haphazardly onto the bed. Limp with release, Marshall wrapped his arms and legs around Davy, who lay relaxed and panting in his embrace. "Are you all right?"

"Oh yes," Davy murmured, snuggling close. "Better than...what a fool I was...better than I could have dreamed, I...I am falling asleep, Will. Jus' for a moment..."

"Mmm." Marshall let his face sink forward onto Davy's hair, overcome by lassitude and contentment.

⚓ ⚓ ⚓

He awakened some time later with one arm half-numb and golden light filling the room. Clouds were still visible from the window over the bed, but away westward the setting sun had peeked out from below the storm.

He shifted, and Davy rolled over. His eyes opened, and focused, and a slow smile started in them that spread across his face. "Will."

Thank God he was smiling. "Was it—was it all right?"

The smile bloomed, brighter than the sunshine. "Will, it was not 'all right'. It was splendid. If you could be promoted for your performance, you would be an admiral." He chuckled. "Rear admiral, no doubt."

Even the excruciating pun could not annoy him. He had never seen Davy so unreservedly happy. "How do you feel?"

"I'm not sure, Will. Different." David frowned thoughtfully, shook his head. Then he sat up, swung a leg over and leaned down for a kiss. One thing led to another; before Marshall knew what happened his body was responding to the enticement, and Davy was riding him once again.

From time to time, aboard ship, some angle of light would make a picture of extraordinary beauty. The pictures never lasted very long, and Marshall had no talent for art, no way to capture the moment. But this image, he knew, would live in his memory as long as he drew breath: David astride him, lips parted, hair ablaze in the red-gold sunset, his strong young body limned in liquid light. He looked more than human, some legend come to life. Apollo in his chariot.

He smiled down at Marshall, and said, "I feel free."

⚓ ⚓ ⚓

The transcendence had dimmed when they awoke the following morning, startled from sleep by someone knocking on the door with hot water for shaving. They would have time for breakfast, the boy informed them, but the smith was already working on the repairs and they'd be on the road within an hour.

David bounced out of bed, whistling merrily. Marshall left the covers reluctantly, aching in a few odd places but feeling incredibly content with life. He appeased his barely repentant conscience by using some of the shaving water to clean up a telltale spot on the bedsheet.

"Just pull the sheets off the bed," David suggested with the ease of a gentleman born to household servants. "They'll have to change them anyway—the washerwoman won't know who left the spots, and I'm sure she won't care."

He realized with some relief that Davy was correct, and stripped the bed in a trice. "Davy—are you certain I did not hurt you?"

David laughed. "I'm tough, Will. You did no damage. No one's ever been as gentle as you were." He made a mock-grimace and rubbed his backside. "You're a little bigger than any natural object I've had to accommodate, but I don't need to ride into London with a bandage round my rump."

Marshall shook his head in wondering affection. "You are—you are like an onion."

David stared at him, brows drawn together, then a grin tugged at the corner of his mouth. "I see. I stink and I make your eyes water. Thank you so much, Mr. Marshall."

Marshall sighed. "That is not what I meant, Davy. You seem to be to be made of more layers than I can ever penetrate."

Davy wiggled suggestively.

"*That* is not what I mean, either. To most, you seem bright and carefree, as though you had not a worry in the world, but I know you better than that. I look more closely and see a trace of old pain—then beneath that, a deeper strength. Layers. The more I look upon you, the more I wonder what I have not seen."

He was instantly embarrassed at speaking so plainly; David's smile was warm, but his reply was lighthearted. "I shall be pleased to give you every opportunity to continue your observations, sir. The onion does not quite suit my aspirations. I hope you find something more poetic."

He smiled back, relieved. "What does a simple sailor like me know of poetry?" He made sure his bag was buckled securely, buttoned his uniform, and grimaced when he found Davy's petrified handkerchief in his pocket. He'd have to wash that out in London, without fail.

298 *Lee Rowan*

One last kiss, a close embrace, and they swung the door wide to leave this unexpected haven.

It felt as though they had spent much more than one night in this room, and Marshall was only beginning to realize how much had changed in a dozen hours. On the surface, all was as it had been: they were on leave, Davy was still facing his examination, they had not yet even arrived in London. But in a deeper sense Marshall realized he had at last reached the destination he had been seeking all his life.

And he had not arrived alone.

The End

Coming soon from
Cheyenne Publishing

Book Four of the Royal Navy Series:

Home is the Sailor

by Lee Rowan

LaVergne, TN USA
08 November 2010
204044LV00003B/72/P